The Log of a Sea-Waif / Being Recol of My Sea Life

Frank T. Bullen

PREFACE.

Notwithstanding the oft-reiterated statement that the days of sea romance are over, it may well be doubted whether any period of our literary history has been more prolific in books dealing with that subject than the last twenty-five years. Nor does the output show any signs of lessening, while the quality of the work done is certainly not deteriorating. Writers like Kipling, Cutcliffe Hyne, Joseph Conrad, and Clark Russell, each in his own style, have presented us with a series of sea-pictures that need not fear comparison with any nautical writers' work of any day, although they deal almost exclusively with the generally considered unromantic merchant service. Having admitted this, the question perforce follows, "Who, then, are you, that presumes to compete with these master magicians?"

To that inevitable question I would modestly answer that the present book is in no sense a competitor with the works of any writers of nautical romance. But having been for fifteen years a seafarer in almost every capacity except that of a master, and now, by the greatest kindness and indulgence on the part of men holding high positions in the literary world, being permitted to cater for the reading public in sterling periodicals, it has often occurred to me how little landsmen really know of the seaman's actual life. "Two Years before the Mast," although written by an American, and of life on board an American merchantman, has long held undisputed sway as a classic upon the subject. And for the only reason, as it seems, that no serious attempt has been made by a Britisher to do the same thing for life in British ships.

Still, conscious as I certainly am of small literary equipment for such a task, I should hardly have dared to try my hand but for the encouragement most generously and persistently given me by Mr. J. St. Löe Strachey, who, with that large faith in another's abilities that breeds confidence in its object, however diffident, urged me strongly to tell the public some of my experiences of sea life. And his advice to me was to set them down, just as they occurred, as nearly as memory would permit. Of course, it was not possible to cover the whole field of my experiences at once, except in the most scrappy and unsatisfactory way, and therefore I decided to take the first four years—from the age of twelve to sixteen. Following my friend's advice, I have written nothing but the truth, and, in most cases, I have given the real names of ships and individuals. If the book, then, does not please, it will be owing to my lack of discrimination between interesting and commonplace details, and not because the pictures given of life at sea in the forecastle are not faithful.

And now, as I know that there are a great many people who do not read prefaces, I will close mine by humbly commending this "autobiography of a nobody" to that tremendous tribunal, with whom lies the verdict of success or failure, and from whose fiat there is no appeal—the Public.

Frank T. Bullen.

Camberwell, *September, 1899.*

CHAPTER I.

MY FIRST SHIP.

Many boys clamour for a sea life, will not settle down to anything ashore, in spite of the pleading of parents, the warnings of wisdom, or the doleful experiences of friends. Occasionally at schools there breaks out a sort of epidemic of "going to sea," for which there is apparently no proximate cause, but which rages fiercely for a time, carrying off such high-spirited youths as can prevail upon those responsible for them to agree to their making a trial of a seafaring life. All this is quite as it should be, of course, in order that Britain may continue to rule the waves; but many a parent, whose affectionate projects for the future of his offspring are thus rudely shattered, bitterly resents what he naturally considers to be unaccountable folly.

In my own case matters were quite otherwise. I belonged to the ignoble company of the unwanted. In spite of hard usage, scanty food, and overwork, I ridiculously persisted in living, until, at the approach of my twelfth year, an eligible opening presented itself for me to go to sea. Being under no delusions whatever as to the prospect that awaited me, since I had known intimately those who had experienced all the vicissitudes of a sailor's life, I was not unduly elated at the idea. Nevertheless, food and shelter were objects peculiarly hard of attainment ashore, while I felt satisfied that at sea these necessaries would be always provided, even if their quality was none of the best.

The vessel in which I obtained a berth as cabin-boy was commanded by my uncle: a stubborn, surly, but thoroughly capable old seaman. Soured by misfortune and cross-grained by nature, it was small wonder that he had no friends, not even the sterling honesty of his character, or his high ability, being sufficient to counterbalance the drawback of his atrocious temper. His latest command was not calculated to improve him, for she was a survival of a bygone day, clumsy as a Dutch galliot, impoverished by her owner, who was heartily sick of seeing her afloat, and would have rejoiced to hear that she was missing; and withal leaky as a basket. When I first saw her huddled into a more than usually dirty corner of the West India Docks, I was filled with wonder to see that her cutwater was sunken between two swelling bows like the cheeks of a conventional cherub. Though I could be no critic of marine construction, this seemed an anomaly for which there appeared to be no excuse. Her bowsprit and jibboom soared into the air exactly like those of the galleons of old, and her three skimpy masts stood like broomsticks at different angles—the foremast especially, which looked over the bows.

It was a bleak, gloomy day in January when I first beheld her. The snow, which had fallen heavily for some days previously, was, wherever it could be, churned into filthy slush, and where undisturbed, was begrimed more into the similitude of soot-heaps than anything else. Everything wore a pinched, miserable appearance. So forbidding and hopeless was the outlook that, had it been practicable, I should certainly have retreated. But there was no choice; I had burned my bridges.

Climbing on deck, I found such a state of confusion and dirt reigning as I could hardly have believed possible. Owing to the parsimony of the owner, not even a watchman had been kept on board, and, in consequence, the decks had not smelt a broom for a month. The cargo and stores were littered about so that progress was gymnastic, while in every corner and hollow lay the dirty snow. Several discontented-looking men were engaged aloft bending sails, others were gradually coaxing the cargo on deck into the hold, but no one seemed to have any energy left. Seated upon an up-ended beef-cask was a truculent-looking individual whom I instinctively regarded as the boss. Him, therefore, I timidly approached. Upon hearing my message, he rolled off his throne and led the way aft, uttering all the time some, to me, perfectly unintelligible sounds. I made no pretence of answering, so I suppose he took me for a poor idiot hardly worthy of his attention. When, after some effort, he disappeared down the cabin companion, I was close behind him, and, understanding his gestures better than his speech, made out that here was to be the scene of my future labours. The place was so gloomy that I could distinguish none of its features by sight; but the atmosphere, a rank compound of the reek of bilge-water, mouldering stores, and unventilated sleeping-places, caught me by the throat, making my head swim and a lump rise in my chest. A small locker by the ladder's foot, reminding me curiously of a rabbit-hutch, was pointed out to me as my berth, but I naturally supposed it to be a place for my bag. How could I have dreamed that it was also to be my chamber? But everything began to reel with me, so, blindly clutching the ladder, I struggled on deck again, where the bitter wind soon revived me.

Henceforth no one noticed me, so I roamed about the deck, prying into holes and corners, until the stevedores knocked off for dinner. Presently the mate came towards where I sat, shivering and solitary, on the windlass end, and made me understand that I was to come ashore with him. He conducted me through a labyrinth of mean streets to a spacious building in a wide thoroughfare, around which were congregated many little groups of seamen of all nations. We entered the place at once, and soon reached a large bare room crowded with seamen. Here I was told to wait while Mr. Svensen went to seek the captain. While I stood bewildered by the bustle of the crowded place, I heard occasional hoarse demands for "Three A.B.'s an' one ordinary for Pernambuck!" "Cook an' stooard for Kingston, Jamaica!" "All the croo of the *Star o' Peace*!" and similar calls, each followed by a general rush towards the speaker, accompanied by a rustling of discharges in the air as their owners sought to attract attention.

After about an hour's wait I heard the cry of "Croo of the *Arabella* here!" which was followed by the usual rush; but, to the disappointment of the watchers, the whole of the crew had been already selected. One by one they squeezed through the crowd into an office beyond, whither I managed to follow. I was too much amazed at the hurly-burly to notice who were to be my future shipmates, but I paid a sort of awe-struck attention to the reading of the "articles." Doubtless much excuse must be made for the officials, who have to gabble the same rigmarole over so many times each working day; but I certainly think some attempt might always be made that the essential parts of the agreement should be clear to men who are about to bind themselves for a long period to abide by it. In our case, the only words clearly accented, heard, and understood by all, were the last three, "no spirits allowed." Each man then signed the articles, or made his mark, ending with myself, when I found I was entitled to receive five shillings per month, without any half-pay or advance. Each of the men received a month's advance, in the form of a promissory-note, payable three days after the ship left the Downs, "providing the said seaman sails in the said ship." None of them lost any time in getting away to seek some accommodating (?) shark to cash their notes at an average discount of about forty per cent., most of the proceeds being payable in kind.

This important preliminary over, I was free till next morning, when all hands were ordered on board by ten o'clock. Not feeling at all desirous of returning to the ship, yet being penniless, and in a strange part of London, I made my way westward to the Strand, where I soon managed to pick up enough for a meal. I spent the night in Hyde Park in a snug corner, unknown to the police, that had often served me as a refuge before. At daybreak I started East, arriving on board at about half-past nine very tired and hungry. The mate eyed me suspiciously, saying something which I guessed to be uncomplimentary, although I was still unable to understand a word. But, as before, he did not interfere with me, or set me any task.

The litter of cases, bales, etc., about the deck was fast disappearing under the strenuous exertions of the stevedores and dock-wallopers, while the raffle of gear aloft was reduced to as near an approach to orderly arrangement as it could ever be expected to assume. Presently a grimy little paddle-steamer came alongside, through the clustering swarm of barges, and was made fast ahead and astern. An individual with a stentorian voice, a pilot suit, mangy fur cap, and brick-red face mounted the forecastle, bellowing out orders apparently addressed to no one in particular. Their effect was at once evident, however, for we began to move deliberately away from the wharf, splitting the crowd of barges asunder amid the sulphurous remarks of their attendants. Once out into the comparatively clear centre of the dock, we made good progress until the last lock was reached; but there we came to a full stop. As yet none of the crew had arrived, the vessel being handled by a shore-gang so far. After about a quarter of an hour's delay, during which the captain and pilot exhausted their vocabulary in abuse of the laggards, the latter hove in sight, convoyed by a motley crowd of tailor's "runners," boarding-masters, and frowsy looking women.

They made a funny little group. The sailors were in that happy state when nothing matters—least of all the discounter of an advance-note; hence the bodyguard of interested watchers, who would leave no stone unturned to see that their debtors went in the ship, although being under the vigilant eyes of the police, they dared not resort to violent means. The ladies, possessing but a fast-fading interest in outward bounders, were probably in evidence more from slackness of business than any more sentimental cause. But having cajoled or coerced Jack to the pierhead, he seemed unpersuadable to the final step of getting aboard. Again and again a sailor would break loose and canter waveringly shoreward, only to be at once surrounded by his escort and hurriedly hauled back again. At last, exasperated beyond endurance by the repetition of these aimless antics, the skipper sprang ashore followed by the pilot. Bursting in upon the squabbling crowd, they seized upon a couple of the maudlin mariners, hurling them on board as if they had been made of rubber. With like vigour the rest were embarked, their "dunnage" flung after them; the warps were immediately let go, and the ship began to move ahead.

Outside the dock-gate a larger tug was waiting in readiness to hook on as soon as we emerged, and tow us down the river. With a final shove, accompanied by a stifling belch of greasy smoke, our sooty satellite shook herself free of us, retreating hastily within the basin again, while, obedient to the increasing strain on our hawser ahead, we passed rapidly out into the crowded stream.

During the uneventful trip the shore-gang, under the direction of Mr. Svensen and the second mate (who, being also the carpenter, was always known as "Chips"), worked indefatigably to get the decks clear for sea—lashing spars, water-casks, boats, etc. But their efforts were greatly hindered by the crew, who, not being sufficiently drunk to lie still in the forecastle, persisted in tumbling continually about the decks, offering assistance while getting in everybody's way. In vain were they repeatedly conducted to their doghole; no sooner were they left than they were out again, until the hard-working "lumpers" were ready to jump on them with rage.

Meanwhile I grew so weary of standing about that I was quite grateful when Chips ordered me to fetch him a marlinespike. What he wanted I had not the slightest idea; but, unwilling to confess such ignorance, I ran forward and asked a labourer who was stowing the cable. He told me that it was a pointed bar of iron with a hole at one end for a lanyard to hang it round the neck by, adding that I should find some in the fo'lk'sle, "right forrard in the eyes of her." Away I went into the thick darkness of the men's dirty cave, groping my way into its innermost recesses among the bags, chests, and beds with which the deck was bestrewn. Reaching the farthest corner, I felt a great bundle of something upon what I took for a shelf, which barred my further search. Tugging heartily at it to get it out of my way, I suddenly felt it move! I did not wait to investigate, but floundered back on deck again almost witless from fright. Breathlessly I reported to Chips my discovery, which brought him quickly to the spot with a light. Sure enough there was a sea-bag, about six feet long, stuffed full—the draw-string tightly closing the mouth. As soon as it was touched, there was a movement within. Its contents were evidently alive. Chips and his assistant promptly muzzled the bag, dragging it out on deck, and, casting the cord adrift, turned it bottom upwards. Out there tumbled, head foremost, a lanky nigger-lad, who had been missing since the previous morning and given up as having deserted. On being questioned as to the meaning of this freak, he humbly explained that, despairing of ever getting warm again, he had put on his entire wardrobe, lain down in his bunk, and crept into his bag, managing somehow to draw the string tight over his head; that he had been there ever since, and was likely to have died there, since he could not get his arms up again to let himself out. He was dismissed to work with a grim promise of being warmed in an altogether different fashion if he was again guilty of skulking.

Upon arrival at Gravesend we anchored; the tremendous racket made by the cable rushing over the windlass giving me a great fright. I thought the bottom of the ship had fallen out. The tug departed for a berth close at hand, the pilot and shore-gang leaving us in a wherry. I looked longingly after them as they went, for I felt strangely that the last link connecting me with England was now broken, and, although I had not a single soul ashore to regret me, or one corner that I could think of as home, there was sufficient sadness in the thought of leaving the land of my birth to bring to my eyes a few unaccustomed tears.

Fortunately the cook, a worn-out seaman, whom, in common with most vessels of that class, we carried for the double duty of cook and steward, was now sober enough to get supper ready. In the emphatic sea-phrase, he "Couldn't boil salt water without burning it;" but, as nobody expected anything different, that passed without comment. My regular duties now began: my uncle, the captain, giving me my first lesson in laying the table sea-fashion, showing me where to find the gear, and so on. The curious atmospheric compound below was appreciably improved, but still there was a prismatic halo round the swinging lamp. The skipper and his two officers took no notice of it, seeming quite at their ease as they silently ate their humble meal, though I got a racking headache. Supper over, I was ordered to "Clear away the wreck," and get my own meal in the pantry: a sort of little-ease in a corner of the cuddy, wherein a man might successfully block all the crockery from falling out by inserting his body in its midst. Hungry as I was, I could not eat there, but stealthily seized the opportunity, as soon as the skipper had retired to his state-room, to flee forrard to the galley with the cook. His domain consisted of an erection about six feet square, with sliding doors on either side, which was lashed firmly down to ring-bolts in the deck. A coal-locker ran across it at the back, its lid forming a seat. Between it and the stove there was just room to turn, while most of the cooking utensils—no great store—had permanent positions on the range.

Here, by the dim flicker of an antique contrivance of a lamp like a handleless teapot—the wick sticking out of the spout and giving almost as much smoke as flame,—I spent quite a pleasant hour with the ancient mariner who ruled there, eating a hearty supper of biscuit and tea. He was not in the best of spirits, for the drink was dying out of him; but his garrulous, inconsequent talk amused me mightily. At last, feeling that I might be wanted, I returned to the cabin, where I found the captain and Chips making melody with their snores; Mr. Svensen being on deck keeping watch, for which none of the crew were yet available. And, finding no other corner wherein I might creep, I made just such a lair as a dog might, in the hutch that held my scanty stock of clothing, and, crawling into it, was soon in the land of perfect peace.

CHAPTER II.

OUTWARD-BOUND.

Something banging at the bulkhead close to my ear aroused me from a deep sleep in great alarm. The hole in which I lay was so pitchy dark that, even when I realised where I was, which took some little time, I fumbled fruitlessly about for several minutes before I finally extricated myself. When at last I stood upright on the cuddy-deck, I saw the captain seated at the table writing. He looked up and growled, "Now then, look lively! Didn't you hear, 'Man the windlass'?" Alas! I knew no more what he meant than as if he had spoken in Hebrew; but I gathered somehow that I ought to be on deck. Up I scrambled into a bitter, snow-laden north-east wind and darkness that, but for the strange sheen of the falling flakes, was almost Egyptian. Shivering as much with queer apprehensions as with cold, I hurried forrard, where I found the mate and Chips hard at work getting the hands out of the fo'lk'sle, and up on top of it, to where the two gaunt levers of the windlass made a blacker streak in the prevailing darkness. Tumbling up against Jem, the darky, he said, as well as his chattering teeth would allow, "Specs yo gotter haul back chain longer me, boy; yars a hook fer yer,"—putting into my hand, as he spoke, a long iron hook with a cross-handle. Then, when at last the half-dead sailors began to work the levers, and the great clumsy windlass revolved, Jem and I hooked on to the massive links of the cable, dragging it away from the barrel and ranging it in long flakes beside the fore-hatch. Every few fathoms, when the chain had worked its way right across the barrel, and the turns were beginning to jam one another up against the bitt, Jem called out, "Fleet, oh!" Then a couple of men descended from Mount Misery and hooked a mighty iron claw, which was secured by a stout chain to the bitt, on to the cable before the windlass. This held the whole weight while the turns of chain were loosed and laboriously lifted back to the other end of the windlass-barrel again. When thick with mud, so that each link was more like a badly made raw brick than aught else, this primitive performance was an uncouth job, and I could imagine many pleasanter occupations.

Two o'clock on a winter's morning, struggling with mud-besmeared masses of iron, upon a footing so greasy that standing was a feat, hungry and sleepy withal, there was little romance about this business. At last the mate bawled, "She's short, sir!" and told the men to "'Vast heavin'." Out of the gloom around the tug-boat emerged, coming close alongside to receive her end of the big rope by which she was to drag us out to sea. No sooner was it fast than a strange voice aft—the Channel pilot's—roared out, "Heave right up, sir!" "Aye, aye, sir!" answered the mate. "Heave 'way, boys!" The clatter of the pawls recommenced, continuing until the anchor was as high as it would come. The subsequent "catting" and "fishing" of the big "mud-hook" was all a confused dream to me. All I knew was that I had to sit down and pull at a rope which was wound round a capstan by the steady tramp of the crew, of whom one would occasionally growl at me to mind my "surge," and I would feel a jerk at my rope that shook me up dreadfully. It seemed an interminable job; but, like everything else, came to an end at last. The mate now walked aft, ordering Jem and my small self to coil ropes up and clear away generally. But he called out almost immediately, "All hands lay aft to muster!" The whole crowd slouched aft, grouping themselves at the break of the poop, where a sort of elevated deck began just before the mizzenmast. Each individual's name was now read out and answered to as announced. I found that there were six able seamen, and the nigger-boy, Jem, "foremast hands." The captain, mate, Chips, cook, and myself formed the "afterguard."

The "crowd" were now divided into watches, the mate having first pick for the port watch, and getting Jem over. This ceremony concluded, the word was passed to "Pump ship." Several grumbling comments were made on the "one-arm sailor" pumps: a mean, clumsy contrivance, only fit for the smallest vessels, requiring twice the exertion for half the result obtainable from any of the late patents. But the amazement and disgust of the fellows can hardly be imagined when, after half an hour's vigorous "Clankety, clankety, clankety, bang!"—three strokes and a pause as the fashion is—there was no sign of a "suck." A burly Yorkshireman, leaning up against the brake to mop his brow, said, "Well, boys, if this —— old scow ain't just sprung a leak, or bin left fur 'bout a month thout pumpin', we're in for a —— fine thing ov it." There was hardly any intelligible response, they all seemed choking with rage and curses. However, they sucked her out, and then the big man asked Chips quietly whether that "spell" was usual. Chips assured him that she had not been baled out for a long time, and that she would certainly "take up" in a day or two. Oil on the troubled waters, but very risky, for he had only just joined himself; nor did he know anything of the old tub's previous record.

Meanwhile the cook, or "doctor," as his sea-sobriquet is, had been busy making coffee. Unlike any beverage called by that name ashore, even the funny mixture sold at a halfpenny a cup at street corners being quite luxurious in comparison with it, yet it was a godsend—boiling hot, with plenty of sugar in it—to those poor wretches with the quenchless thirst of many day's indulgence in the vilest liquor making their throats like furred old drain-pipes. It calmed the rising storm, besides doing them a vast amount of physical good. I was at once busy supplying the wants of the officers, to whom the refreshment was heartily welcome. All the time, we were ploughing steadily along behind the strenuous tug at a greater rate than ever I saw the old barky go afterwards. (I have omitted to mention that we were bound for Demerara with a general cargo, but our subsequent destination was not settled yet.) All hands were allowed a pretty long spell of rest, with the exception of the man at the wheel, and one on the look-out, because, until we were well out, sail would have been more hindrance than help. The wind increased as we got farther down, until, as we passed out of the river, quite a sea was rising, to which the old hooker began to bob and curtsey like a country girl looking for a situation. The relentless tug, however, tore her through the fast-rising waves, making them break over the bows in heavy spray. This was uncomfortable, but the motion was far worse. All the horrors of sea-sickness came suddenly upon me, and, like an ailing animal, I crept into a corner on the main-hatch under the long-boat, wishing for oblivion. Sea-sickness is a theme for jesting, no doubt, but those who have suffered from it much, know how little room there is for laughter at such suffering—suffering too for which, at the time, there seems no hope of alleviation except the impossible one of the motion ceasing.

From that morning for several days I remained in this miserable condition, not caring a pin's point whether I lived or died, nor, with the sole exception of the negro, Jem, did any one else on board seem to give me one moment's thought. Not that I would lightly accuse them of cruelty or callous indifference to suffering; but, being all fully occupied with their work, they had little leisure to attend to a sea-sick urchin that was of small use at his best. However, poor black Jem never forgot me, and, although he had nothing likely to tempt my appetite, he always brought his scanty meals to where I lay helpless under the long-boat, trying in various quaint ways to coax me into a returning interest in life. Fortunately for me, the wind held in a quarter that enabled the ship to get out of the Channel fairly soon, considering her limitations, and, once across the dreaded stretch of the Bay of Biscay, she speedily ran into fine weather and smoother seas.

When I did eventually find my sea-legs, and resumed my duties in the cabin, I was received with no good grace by my uncle or the doctor. The latter had, indeed, special cause to feel himself aggrieved, since he had borne the burden of double duty during my illness: a hardship which he was a long time in forgetting. But she was an unhappy ship. The skipper held aloof from everybody, hardly holding converse with the mate. He even kept the ship's reckoning alone, not accepting the mate's assistance in taking the sun for the longitude in the morning, but doing it all himself after a fashion of his own, so that the chief officer was as ignorant of the vessel's true position as I was. Then the food, both forrard and aft, was, in addition to being strictly on the abominable official scale which is a disgrace to a civilised country, of so unspeakably vile a quality that it was hardly fit to give to well-reared pigs. I have often seen the men break up a couple of biscuits into a pot of coffee for their breakfast, and, after letting it stand a minute or two, skim off the accumulated scum of vermin from the top—maggots, weevils, etc.—to the extent of a couple of table-spoonfuls, before they could shovel the mess into their craving stomachs. Enough, however, for the present on the food-question, which, being one of the prime factors in a sailor's life, must continually be cropping up.

The bleak, biting edge of the winter weather was now gone, the steady north-easterly breeze blew mild and kindly, while from an almost cloudless heaven the great sun beamed benignantly—his rays not yet so fierce as to cause any discomfort. My sensations on first discovering that no land was visible, that we seemed the solitary centre of an immense blue circle, whose sharply defined circumference was exactly joined to the vast azure dome overhead, were those of utter loneliness and terror. For I knew nothing of the ways of navigators across this pathless plain, nor realized any of the verities of the subject set forth in the few books I had read. School learning I had none. Had there been any one to whom I could have gone for information, without fearing a brutal repulse, I should doubtless have felt less miserable; but, as it was, use alone gradually reconciled me to the solemn silence of the illimitable desert around. At rare intervals vessels appeared, tiny flecks of white upon the mighty waste, which only served to emphasize its immensity as the solitary light of a taper does the darkness of some huge hall.

But the sea itself was full of interest. Of course I had little leisure; but what I had was spent mostly in hanging spell-bound over the side, gazing with ever-growing wonder and delight upon this marvellous world of abounding life. This early acquired habit never left me, for, many years afterwards, when second mate of one of our finest passenger clippers, I enjoyed nothing so much as to pass an hour of my watch below, seated far out ahead of the ship by the martingale, gazing down into the same beautiful sea.

There were no books on board or reading matter of any kind, except the necessary works on navigation on the captain's shelf; so it was just as well that I could take some interest in our surroundings, if I was not to die mentally as most of the sailors seemed to have done. As I got better acquainted with them, even daring to pay stolen visits to their darksome home in timorous defiance of the stern orders of my uncle, I found to my amazement, that they could tell me nothing of what I wanted to know. Their kindness often went the length of inventing fabulous replies to my eager questions, but they seemed totally ignorant of anything connected with the wonders of the ocean.

The days slipped rapidly away, until we entered the Sargasso Sea, that strange vortex in the middle of the Atlantic. It was on a Sunday morning, when, according to custom, no work was a-doing, except for the doctor and me. Even our duties were less exacting than usual; so that I was able to snatch many a short spell of gazing overside at the constantly increasing masses of Gulf-weed that, in all its delicate beauty of branch and bud, came brushing past our sides. That afternoon the sea, as far as eye could reach, bore no bad resemblance to a ripe hayfield, the weed covering the water in every direction, with hardly a patch of blue amid the prevailing yellow. Before the light trade-wind we were hardly able to make any headway through the investing vegetation, which overlaid the waves so heavily that the surface was smooth as a millpond. Through the bewildering mazes of that aquatic forest roved an innumerable multitude of fish of every shape, size, and hue, while the branches themselves swarmed with crustacea, so that a draw-bucket full of weed would have furnished quite a large-sized aquarium with a sufficiently varied population. I could have wished the day forty-eight hours long; but I was the only one on board that derived any pleasure from the snail-like progress we made. The captain's vexation showed itself in many ways, but mostly in inciting Chips to order various quite uncalled-for jobs of pulling and hauling, which provoked the watch so much that there was a continual rumble of bad language and growling. Even the twenty minutes' spell at the pumps, which, from its regularity every two hours, now passed almost unnoticed, was this afternoon the signal for a great deal of outspoken and unfavourable comment upon the characters of ship, owner, and captain. The latter gentleman paced his small domain with uncertain tread, as usual; but the glitter in his eye, and the set of his heavily bearded lips, showed how sorely he was tempted to retaliate. But he prudently forebore, well aware of his helplessness in case of an outbreak, as well as being forced to admit full justification for the bitter remarks that were so freely indulged in.

Indeed, it was a serious question how long the present peace would last. The rigging was dropping to pieces; so that a man never knew, when he went aloft, whether he would not come crashing down by the run, from the parting of a rotten footrope or a perished seizing. The sails were but rags, worn almost to the thinness of muslin, every flap threatening to strip them from the yards. There was no material for repairs, no new rope, canvas, or "seizing-stuff;" half a barrel of Stockholm tar, and a few pieces of old "junk" for sennit and spunyarn, representing all the boatswain's stores on board. In fact, the absence of all those necessaries, which are to be found on board the most poverty-stricken of ships, for their bare preservation in serviceable condition, was a never-failing theme of discussion in the fo'lk'sle. And one conclusion was invariably arrived at, albeit the avenues of talk by which it was reached were as tortuous and inconsequent as could well be. It was the grim one that the *Arabella* was never intended to return. This thought tinctured all the men's ideas, embittered their lives, and made the most ordinary everyday tasks seem a burden almost too grievous to be borne.

Had it not been for the overwhelming evidence that the condition of the afterguard was almost as miserable as their own, the abject humility of the mate, in spite of his really good seamanship, and the hail-fellow-well-met way in which Chips confessed his utter ignorance of all sailorizing whatever, I very much doubt whether there would not have been a mutiny before we were a fortnight out. But as the villainous food and incessant pumping were not aggravated by bullying and "working up," matters jolted along without any outbreak. Born as I was under an unlucky star, my insignificance nearly overthrew the peace that was so precariously kept. The deadly dulness of the cabin was so stifling, that I felt as if I should die there in the long, dreary evenings between supper and bunk. Nothing to read, nobody to speak to, nothing to do, and forbidden with threats to go forrard among the men—that I should transgress sooner or later was a certainty. I took to creeping forrard oftener and more openly, because no detection followed, until a sharp rope's-ending from my uncle brought me up "with a round turn," as the sailor says. By this time I had become rather a favourite forrard, as well as something of a toy, being very small for my age and precocious as might be expected from my antecedents. One man especially—Joe, the big Yorkshireman—became strongly attached to me, endeavouring to teach me thoroughly the rudiments of sailorizing. This was at considerable sacrifice of his own time, which, as he was an ardent model-maker, was sufficient proof of his liking for me.

Now I was almost destitute of clothing, and what little I did possess I was rapidly growing out of. So the next day after my disciplinary castigation, Joe walked aft in his watch below demanding audience of the skipper. There was an unpleasant scowl on the old man's face, as he came on deck to see the audacious man, that boded ill for the applicant in any case. But when Joe boldly tackled him for a bit of light canvas whereof he might make me a "Cunarder" (a sort of habergeon) and a pair of trousers, the skipper's face grew black with rage. The insult, all the grosser for its truth, was too obvious. When he found his tongue, he burst into furious abuse of Joe for daring to come aft on such an errand. Joe, being no lamb, replied with interest, to the delight of his fellows, who strolled aft as far as the mainmast to hear the fun. This unseemly wrangle, so subversive of all order or discipline, lasted for about ten minutes, during which time I stood shivering at the foot of the cabin ladder in dread of the sequel. Finally the old man, unable to endure any more, roared, "Get forrard or I'll shoot ye, ye d—d ugly thief of a sea-lawyer! I'll have ye by the heels yet, an' w'en I do ye'll think Jemmy Smallback's gruppin' ye!" With this parting shot he turned on his heel without waiting the retort discourteous that promptly followed, descending abruptly into the cabin with the ironical cheers of the delighted crew ringing unmelodiously in his ears.

Under such provocation it was little wonder that I paid for all. It must have been balm to my relative's wounded pride to rope's-end me; at any rate, he did so with a completeness that left nothing to be desired. And, in order to avenge himself fully, he closed our interview by kicking me forrard, daring me, at the same time, ever to defile his cabin again with my mischief-making presence under pain of neck-twisting.

Of course I was received in the fo'lk'sle with open arms. My reception went far to mollify my sore back, for the seclusion of the cabin had grown so hateful, that I would willingly have purchased my freedom from it with several such coltings as I had endured, not to speak of the honour of being welcomed as a sort of martyr. Before long I owned quite a respectable rig-out, made up, by the dexterity of Joe, from all sorts of odds and ends contributed by all hands at a tarpaulin muster. Now each man vied with the other in teaching me all they knew of their business, and I was such an apt pupil that, in a short time, they were able to boast that there was no knot or splice known to seafarers, that I was not capable of making in sailor fashion. Being no climbist, as might be expected from an urchin born and bred in London streets, getting used to the rigging was unpleasant at first; but that was mastered in its turn, until nothing remained unlearned but the helm. The one aim, apparently, of every man forrard was to so fit me for the work I might be called upon to do, as that no excuse might be found for cruelty of any sort. Whether I had the ability to meet his demands or not, it did not seem prudent for the old man to try his hand on me again in the colting line, and I went gaily enough on my progressive way.

CHAPTER III.

ARRIVAL AT DEMERARA.

If all sea-voyages were like the usual passage to the West Indies, except for an occasional nasty spell of weather in the English Channel, the sailor's life would be a very easy one. Day succeeds day under the same limpid blue sky fringed at the horizon with a few tufts of woolly cumuli. Placid as a sheltered lake, every wavelet melting into its fellow like a caress, the sapphire sea greets the gazer every morning like a glad smile of unfathomable love. Beautiful beyond description is the tender tropical sea, and hard indeed it is to realize that this same delightsome expanse of inexpressible loveliness can ever become the unappeasable destroyer, before whose wrath even the deep-rooted islands seem to shake.

The nights rival the days. During the absence of the moon the blue-black vault appears like a robe of imperial purple, besprent with innumerable diamonds of a lustre unknown to earth's feeble gems. So brilliant is the radiance of the heavenly host that even the unassisted eye can detect the disc of Venus or Jupiter, while the twin streams of the Galaxy literally glow with diffused light, suggesting unutterable glories in their unthinkable depths. And up from the horizon towards the zenith, with clear yet indefinite outline, as of the uplifted finger of God, rises the mysterious conical flame-shadow of the Zodiacal Light. Under such a sky the sea seems to emulate the starry vault above, for in its darkling depths there is a marvellous display of gleaming coruscations. In the foam churned up by the vessel's bows they sparkle and glitter incessantly, while in her wake, where the liquid furrow still eddies and whirls from the passing of the keel, there are a myriad dancing lights of every size and degree of brilliancy. Like a bevy of will-o'-the-wisps they sport and whirl, glow and fade—never still, never alike, yet always lovely.

But when the full-orbed moon in a molten glow of purest silver, before which the eye shrinks almost with pain, traverses the purple concave as a conquering queen escorted by her adoring subjects, the night becomes a sweeter, softer day, in which men may sit at ease reading or working as fancy dictates. They dare not sleep in that white glare, lest with distorted features and sightless eyeballs, they vainly regret their careless disregard of the pale beam's power. And as the stately satellite settles slowly horizonwards, or ascends majestically towards the zenith, how dazzling the mile-wide pathway of shimmering radiance she sheds along the face of the deep! The whalers, with more poetic feeling than one would expect, call it the "moon-glade," as though she must needs spread a savannah of splendour for her solemn progress over the waste of ocean.

Here, perhaps, I should pause to disarm criticism, if possible. Such thoughts as I have feebly tried to express were undoubtedly mine in those youthful days, in spite of squalid surroundings and brutal upbringings. And if I could fairly reproduce the multitude of fancies which throng my memory as being the daily attendants of my boyish daydreams, I should fear no unfavourable reception of such a book as they would make.

But to our voyage. Coming on deck one morning soon after daylight, I was startled to notice that the bright blue of the sea was gone. In its place a turbid leaden flood without a sparkling wavelet extended all around. I asked the doctor what this strange change meant. "Gettin' near land, I s'pose!" was his gruff reply. Nor did I get any other explanation from the men, for none of them knew that we were in fresh water, which, rushing down to the sea from many mighty rivers, overlaid the heavier salt flood for a great distance from land. We did not sight the lightship *Demerara* until next day at noon, although we were going at fully five knots an hour. Behind it the low palm-fringed coast lay like a sullen black cloud-bank just appearing above the horizon, for in truth it was almost level with the sea. Thicker and dirtier grew the water, until, as we passed the light-vessel, we seemed to be sailing in a sea of mud. Between her and the shore we anchored for the night and to await the coming of the pilot; thus closing our outward passage, which might have been as successfully performed in an open boat, so steadily fine had we found the weather.

What a strange sensation is that of first inhaling the breeze from a foreign shore! I stood on the forecastle that evening, hardly able to realize that we had crossed the Atlantic, full of queer feelings as the heavy sweet scent of the tropical forest came floating languidly off from that dim, dark line of land. There was a continual chorus of insects, like a myriad crickets chirping, the sharp, crisp notes curiously undertoned by the deep bass of the sleepy line of surf upon the beach. But this persistent music, by its unvarying monotony, soon became inaudible, or acted as a lullaby to which we all succumbed except the anchor-watch.

Shortly after daylight a large canoe came alongside, manned by negroes, bearing a pompous-looking negro pilot in what he, no doubt, took to be a very swell costume of faded serge, surmounted by a huge straw hat. He mounted the side by the man-ropes, with the air of a conqueror. As he stepped over the rail with a ludicrous assumption of importance, he said, patronizingly, "Good mawnin', cap'n, hope you'se berry well, sah?" "Mornin', pilot, same t' you," curtly answered the old man; and, in almost the same breath, "Dy'e think there's water 'nough on the bar frus? We're drawin' fourteen feet aft." "Neb' mine 'bout dat, cap'n; dat'll be all right. I'se bettin' big money dis yah packet gwine beat 'nuff watah 'head ob her ter float in er linerbattle ship. Gorbress my sole, ef I ebber see sich er front eend on er craf' in my days. Wasser name? de *Ark* doan' it? ha! ha! ha!"—— and he threw back his head, laughing so capaciously that the broad, glistening range of his teeth illuminated his coal-black visage like a shutter flung suddenly open to the sun. But the old man looked sour. Such jeering at his command by a nigger was in some sort a reflection on himself, and, thenceforward, he held no more converse with our sable guide than was necessary for the working of the ship.

We were soon under way, though poor Jem and myself got in a disgusting condition of mud by the time the anchor was up. The fo'lk'sle, too, from the fact of the cable running through it, was like a neglected sewer, the blocks of foul-smelling mud dropping continually from the links as they came in through the hawsepipes. All sail was loosed previously, but only the jib was set until the anchor was out of the ground, when, humoured by the helm, she turned kindly off the wind, gathering way from its pressure on her broad stern, while the "mudhook" was hove right up. Then everything was set that would draw, the wind being fair and strong; but, in spite of the favourable conditions, our progress against the turbulent ebb of the great river was so slow that we were the best part of the day going the few miles that lay between the roadstead and the moorings.

But at last we reached the group of vessels which lay off the business part of the town. With great skill our pilot tried a "flying moor," letting our anchor go while we were forging ahead at a good rate, then immediately clewing up all sail. By the time our way was exhausted, about ninety fathoms had been paid out on the first anchor. The second was then let go, its cable being veered away as the first one was hove in, until an equal amount was out on each; both were then hove in till the moorings were taut, and the vessel swung almost on a pivot. This is a ticklish evolution to perform successfully in a crowded anchorage; but, in our case, the result was entirely satisfactory, saving much labour.

The sails being furled and decks cleared up, work ceased for the day. The curious appearance of the wide verandahed houses embowered in strange-looking trees, the assortment of vessels of all rigs—from the smart Yankee schooner to the stately iron coolie-ship from Calcutta—the muddy rushing river, all claimed attention, but for one attraction that outweighed them all. Waiting alongside were two or three bumboats well stocked with fruit, soft-tack, eggs, and such curios as a sailor might be supposed to covet. I had seen such fruit before, on the other side of plate-glass windows in the West End of London, or in the avenue at Covent Garden, but never in such generous profusion as now. One boat especially was laden to the gunwale with giant bunches of crimson bananas, each fruit treble the size of ordinary ones; baskets of golden mangoes, green limes, luscious-looking oranges flecked with green, and clusters of immature cocoa-nuts: the kind that only contain sweet juice and delicate jelly within a soft shell covered by husk as easy to cut as a turnip. People accustomed to regular meals of decent food cannot imagine how the sight of these dainties affected our ill-used stomachs. Happily there was little delay in choosing our purveyor, who promptly hoisted great part of his stock on deck for us to choose from. In virtue of being the only person in the fo'lk'sle who could write, I was appointed book-keeper, my remuneration being a fair proportion of the good things without payment. In reply to eager inquiries, the bumboatman declared that he had no rum, saying that he very well understood the unwritten law prohibiting the supply of intoxicants by the bumboats, and assuring the men that if he were detected breaking it, he would forfeit his license as well as all payment for goods he had supplied on credit.

We were a happy company that evening. A plentiful meal after such long abstinence put every one in good spirits, although there was much wishing for the cup that both cheers and inebriates. In spite of this want, joviality was the order of the night. Song and dance went merrily round, at which the two darkey boat-boys, hired by the skipper to take him backwards and forwards to the shore, assisted with great glee. Their fun was spontaneous and side-splitting, seeming superior to all external influences—a well of continual merriment bubbling up. Song, quip, and practical joke followed one another incessantly, with all the thoughtless *abandon* of happy children, and mirthful enjoyment that might have thawed an anchorite. All the pent-up laughter of the passage burst out that evening, the first really jolly one I had ever spent.

At daylight all hands were busy rigging cargogear, for our lading was long overdue. The discharging-gang of negroes were early on board, awaiting only our preparations to begin their work. They were akin to the boat-boys in their behaviour. Poor, even to the most utter raggedness of the sacking most of them were covered with—hunger-bitten, for all the provision brought by the majority was a tiny loaf, and about two ounces of sugar each—they were yet full to the lips with sheer animal delight of living. Some, the haughty aristocrats of the party, proudly displayed fragments of salt fish or rusty-looking salt pork, flanked by a green plantain, a coco, or chunk of wooden-looking yam; but though these favoured ones were evidently stuck up, their poorer brethren showed no envy. Their pay was the equivalent of one shilling per day, which, as the price of food was high, except for a very few local products, must have been all too little to keep hunger at bay. Yet, when they got to work, how they did go at it! They seemed to revel in the labour, although the incessant singing they kept up ought to have taken most of their breath. Streaming with sweat, throwing their bodies about in sheer wantonness of exuberant strength as they hoisted the stuff out of the hold, they sometimes grew so excited by the improvisations of the "chantey man," who sat on the corner of the hatch solely employed in leading the singing, that often, while for a minute awaiting the next hoist, they would fling themselves into fantastic contortions, keeping time to the music. There was doubtless great waste of energy; but there was no slackness of work or need of a driver. Here is just one specimen of their songs; but no pen could do justice to the vigour, the intonation and the *abandon* of the delivery thereof.

051

Sis-ter Seusan, my Aunt Sal, Gwineter git a home bime-by-high!
All gwineter lib down shin bone al, Gwineter git a home bime-by.
Gwineter git a home bime-by-e-high, Gwineter git a home bime-by.

The rushing, muddy stream literally swarmed with ground-sharks, who sometimes came to the surface with a rush, looking terribly dangerous. Yet the negroes took but little heed of them, merely splashing a bit before diving if they had occasion to go down and clear some vessel's moorings. Sharks and cat-fish were the only fish to be seen: neither of them available for eating. Strange to say, the great heat troubled me very little. Perhaps because, having for so long regarded cold as one of the chief miseries of my life, the steady searching warmth by night and day was grateful to my puny body. At any rate, but that the bloodthirsty mosquitoes and sandflies tormented me cruelly, as they did all hands, the tropical climate suited me very well. It may have been the healthy season too, for, as far as I know, there was no illness on board any of the ships. All our crew were in robust health, and putting on flesh daily in consequence of the liberal diet.

I wanted much to go ashore, but dared not ask leave; but, to my astonishment, on Sunday afternoon the mate told me to get ready and come ashore with him. Glad as I was of the chance to see a little of this strange land, I felt small gratification at the prospect of being his companion; I would rather a thousand times have gone with Joe. However, it being Hobson's choice as well as dangerous to refuse, I rigged myself up as best I could (a queer figure I made too), got into the boat with my inviter, and away we went. Landing at one of the "sterlings," as the wharves are locally named, we strolled up into the main street in silence. It was a wide avenue with quite a river running down the centre, and doubtless on week-days would have been very lively. But at this time it was deserted, except by a few stray dogs and sleeping negroes. We trudged along without a word, till suddenly Mr. Svensen hauled up at a grog-shop, the bar of which was crowded with sea-farers. Pressing through the throng to the bar he called for some drink, and, meeting a couple of his countrymen, entered at once into an animated conversation with them in Norwegian. For over an hour I waited impatiently, the air of the place being stifling and the babel of tongues deafening. At last, in desperation, I crept in behind him and attracted his attention. He turned sharply upon me, saying, "Vell, 'n vat *jou* vant?" "Please, sir," I humbly replied, "may I go an' have a look round?" "Oh, co to hell ef jou lige, I ton'd care. Only jou ked bag to der poad pefoar sigs o'clog, or I be tamt ef I tond trown jou coin' off—see!" "Thank you, sir," I said gratefully, disappearing promptly before he had time to change his mind.

What an afternoon I had, to be sure. I wandered right out of the town through tangled paths crowded on either side by the loveliest flowers growing wild I had ever dreamed of. I was like a boy in a dream now, except for that haunting reality "sigs o'clog." And, to crown my pleasures, when I had strayed as far as I dared, I came suddenly upon a pretty villa in an open glade, the house itself being embowered in the most gorgeous blossoms. I went up to the back of the premises to beg a drink of water, which an amiable negress gave me with a beaming smile, squeezing into it a fresh-fallen lime with a large spoonful of white sugar. While I drank, a dear little white boy about five years old came running round the corner. When he saw me he stood for a moment as if petrified with astonishment; then, recovering his wits, darted back again. A kindly-faced man in white, with a big brown beard, then appeared, leading the little one. After a few inquiries he invited me into the house to tea, treating me with so much kindness that, between his attentions and those of his beautiful, weary-looking wife, I was several times upon the point of bursting into tears. She plied me with questions, soon getting all my sorrowful little life-story out of me; and more than once I saw her furtively wipe away a tear. The little son sat on my knee, great friends with me at once; and what with the good fare, the pleasant talk, and the comfort of it all, I forgot everything else in the world for a time. Suddenly I caught sight of the clock. It was a quarter to six. I must have looked terrified, for my host, Mr. Mackenzie, asked me with much solicitude whether I felt suddenly ill. As soon as he heard the cause of my alarm he left the house, returning to the front in a minute or two with a beautiful mule and a smart trap. I took a hurried leave of my kind hostess and her child, promising to come again if I could; and presently found myself bowling along a level road at a great rate behind the swift hybrid, who seemed to glide rather than trot. Arriving at the boat, nearly half an hour late, we found the mate not yet there, one of the boat-boys volunteering the information that he was well drunk up at the rum-mill. "That being so," said Mr. Mackenzie, "I will see you on board." So we shoved off for the ship. During our short transit I told my new friend how matters stood between my uncle and myself, begging him not to inadvertently make matters worse for me. He promised to be discreet. We reached the ship and climbed on board. I fled forrard on the instant, while he interviewed the old man. Whatever passed between them in their few minutes' talk, I don't know; I heard no more of the affair. But I was never again allowed on shore while I belonged to the *Arabella.* The mate came on board quietly and turned in, no word reaching us forrard of any trouble about his little flutter.

CHAPTER IV.

THE MUTINY AND AFTER.

It must be confessed that during our stay in Demerara the fellows had a pretty good time of it. Since there were no stores on board of rope, paint, or canvas, the work was mainly confined to washing decks or scrubbing paintwork, a good deal of time also being wasted making sennit, *i.e.* plaiting rope-yarns for chafing-gear. What sailorizing was undertaken was in the nature of kill-time, and well understood as such by the men. Nevertheless they were by no means pleased with their easy times, for they had not yet been able to get any drink; their displeasure being heightened by the knowledge that the mate had been ashore and got a skinful. Any one versed in the ways of seamen should have known that mischief was brewing, even though no definite plan of action had yet been discussed. It only wanted a bottle or two of rum to fire the magazine.

At last liberty day drew nigh. The cargo was all out, the ballast all in, no cargo being obtainable for the crazy old *Arabella* in Demerara. I do not now even know whether it be a legal enactment that seamen shall be allowed twenty-four hours' freedom in foreign ports, with some portion of the wages due to them to spend, but if not, the custom is so well established that it has all the force of law. The men were like schoolboys at breaking-up time, half crazy with delight at the thought of the joys (?) that awaited them ashore. They received but a few shillings each, much to their disgust, because there was as yet little wages due to them, and no amount of begging or bullying could avail to get them any more. The mate's watch went first, among them my stout friend Joe, whom I tearfully begged not to get drunk and kick up a row, for my sake. Looking back I wonder at my temerity, for it must have been like getting between a tiger and a shin-bone; but he took it very meekly, and actually promised that he would come aboard sober. During their absence the ship was strangely quiet, very little work of any kind was done, and the waiting watch were as sulky as bears. Next morning about eight o'clock the revellers returned, all except Joe in a bedraggled, maudlin condition that told eloquently of their enjoyment. Had it not been for Joe they would have all been in the lock-up, or "chokey" as sailors invariably call it; but he had worked like a Trojan to keep them together and out of harm as much as possible. He had quite a triumphant air of unwonted virtue as I whispered my delight at seeing him again, and *sober.*

Then the starboard watch, with the doctor, took their innings, with strict injunctions not to be late the next morning, as we were going to unmoor and drop down stream a little in readiness for sailing. The day passed like the previous one, black Jem doing the doctor's work as well as he could with such assistance as I could give. The next morning at daylight preparations were made for unmooring, and at eight o'clock a pilot came on board, a smart-looking, sharp-featured Yankee who looked around the old hooker with undisguised contempt. Nine, ten o'clock, and no sign of the liberty men. The old man went ashore on business, leaving full instructions with the mate about unmooring, which he expected to be carried on in his absence. He had barely been gone half an hour when the starboard watch returned; but it was evident at once that they had their own views upon the unmooring question, which by no means coincided with the skipper's. They were all half-drunk and quarrelsome, especially the doctor, who strutted about more like a bloodthirsty pirate than an elderly spoiler of ships' provisions. Unfortunately, too, each man had brought with him a plentiful supply of rum, which they at once began to share with the port watch, all except Joe, who would have none of it. They even invited Mr. Svensen and Chips to partake, meeting their courteous refusal with quite gratuitous displays of bad language and ill-temper.

At last the mate, mindful of the wigging he might certainly expect on the skipper's return if no work was afoot, ventured to give the order, "Man the windlass!" the pilot taking up his post on the forecastle. For all answer there came a howl of derisive laughter from the den, where all hands, with one exception, were busy "freshening the nip." Mr. Svensen wisely took no notice; but, in a cajoling tone, said, "Now den poys, gum along, mage a sdart; ids kedding lade, ju dond vant ter ked me indo a row, do jer?" Forth strode the truculent doctor, an uncanny figure, all asway with drunken rage. "Looky hear, yew square-headed son of a gun, yew ain't agoin' ter horder me about any more, so I tell yer! I ain't a goin' ter do another stroke abord the rotten barge-built old bathin' masheen, so there!" (I suppress the every-other-word profanity throughout). During the delivery of this speech he was wildly gesticulating and spluttering right up against the mate's breast, shaking his withered fists in the big man's face, and otherwise behaving like a very maniac. The rest of them gathered around, adding to the clamour; but the burden of all was the same, "No more work, not another hand's-turn aboard this" (collection of all the abusive sea-epithets known) "old lobster-pot." Joe, meanwhile, was calmly doing some trifling job aft, by the break of the poop on the starboard side. To him sauntered an Irishman, hitherto one of his best friends, now laboriously polite and anxious to know whether he intended being a sneak, a white-livered et-cetera and so forth. For all reply, Joe turned his back on him. I was cleaning knives on the same side forrard by the galley door, but not making much progress on account of so many distracting episodes taking place. The babel of abuse around the unfortunate mate was going strong all the time. A thrill of terror went through me as I saw the Irishman suddenly lift his hand and strike Joe on the back of the neck. He turned like a flash, shooting his right fist into Patsy's face, with a crash that laid him out, sounding horrible to me. Without a word Joe turned again to resume his work. Patsy gathered himself slowly up and staggered forward, bleeding profusely, and muttering disjointed blasphemy as he came. He passed me, going into the fo'lk'sle; but my attention was suddenly attracted by a yell of laughter from the other side of the deck. Peeping round the galley, I saw with amazement that the drunken devils had actually triced the poor mate up spread-eagle fashion in the main rigging, and were jeering him to their hearts' content. Then they made a rush for the cabin. Chips was nowhere to be seen. Presently they returned, bringing the ensign, which they proceeded to hoist in the rigging, Union down, a sea signal of the most urgent importance, denoting anything dreadful from fire to mutiny.

A step beside me made me turn, startled, to see who it was, and I just caught sight of the grim blood-besmeared visage of Patsy, who was stowing the long cabin carving-knife in the waistband of his pants. While I stared at him, breathlessly wondering what his little game might be, he broke suddenly into a run aft to where Joe still pursued his peaceful task, all undisturbed by the riot around. "Look out, Joe," I screamed, "he's got the carving-knife!" The warning came only just in time; for as Joe turned sharply he met the raging Patsy at close quarters, aiming a savage stab at him. Naturally lifting his arm, he received the descending blade through the fleshy fore-part of it; but, with the other, he caught the Irishman by the throat, and jammed him back against the rail. Kicking the knife, which had dropped from the wound, far forward as he sprang, he plucked an iron belaying pin from its socket, and brought it down with a sickening thud upon Patsy's already battered face. Again he fell, this time to remain until dragged forward, a limp, disfigured lump.

By this time the inverted ensign had told its tale ashore, and a large canoe well-manned with negro policemen, under a white sergeant, was coming off to us at a spanking pace. This sight drew all the mutineers to the side, whence they could watch her approach, which they hailed with the liveliest expressions of joy. Chips now put in an appearance, looking very sheepish, and, assisted by Joe, released the mate from his undignified suspension in the rigging. He tottered aft, looking very unwell, and muttering bitter reproaches on the carpenter for having abandoned him to such a fate. The police-canoe bumped against the side, her stalwart crew clambering on board like cats. While the officer hastened aft to hear the news from the mate, his myrmidons were amazed to find themselves hailed with delight by the excited crew, who fraternized with them as if they had come to convoy them to a picnic. The mate's tale being soon told, the sergeant of police gave orders to his men to arrest the mutineers, and, with joyful outcry, all hands hurried forward to prepare for their departure.

During the preparations, the pilot, the mate, and the police-officer foregathered on the poop to indulge in a smoke, and discuss the ways of seamen in general. But though their palaver lasted a long time, there was no sign from forrard. At last, his patience exhausted, the sergeant strode forward to the fo'lk'sle, demanding, with many objurgations, the reason of this delay. To his rage and dismay he found that the supply of rum had been so plentiful, and had circulated so freely, that policemen and sailors were involved in one common debauch. Indeed it was hard to say which was the most drunken of the two gangs. Uproarious was the din, nearly every man shouting some fragment of song at the pitch of his lungs, or laughing insanely at the gorgeous fun of the whole affair. Back came the sergeant, almost speechless with anger and apprehension, for this no doubt meant dire disgrace to him. He was made worse, if anything, by the unstinted laughter with which the mate and pilot received the news. Small blame to them, the thing was so ludicrous.

Up went the police-flag again—to the main truck this time. In addition to this the sergeant hoisted a small weft at the peak, explaining sulkily that this was an urgent private signal for reinforcements. He added, "An' all *I* hope is that the infernal scoundrels 'll fall out an' kill one another before my boss comes, or else I'm booked for a reduction in grade that'll dock me of a quarter of pay—none too much as it is." Before many minutes had passed a large launch was seen approaching, rowed by fourteen men, who, unlike the first lot, were all white. With them came our old man, whose face was a study. I just caught one glimpse of it, and its fury scared me so that I dared not go near him. There was now no more fooling; in double quick time all the roysterers, policemen as well as sailors, were collected from the fo'lk'sle, handcuffs put on them, their effects flung into the launch, and themselves bundled after with scant ceremony. So rapid was the work that in less than ten minutes they were all on their way ashore, making the air resound with their discordant yells.

A painful quiet ensued. Joe and I, sole representatives of the foremast hands, leisurely cleared up the decks, after which he busied himself preparing a meal which should do duty for dinner and supper. The captain went ashore again, much to my relief, for while he was on board I couldn't get quit of the idea that in some way or other he would bring me in responsible for his disappointment, and take his consolation out of my poor little carcass. I had been so used to this vicarious sort of payment of old, that the idea was a fixed one with me whenever there was a row. In fact, I often feel the old sensation now. But to-day he seemed unable to give vent to his feelings, so nothing disturbed the calm of the afternoon. Joe informed me that he had gone ashore to ship a fresh crew, and that we should certainly sail in the morning, he having heard the old man tell the pilot as much when he took the dinner aft.

Sure enough, just before sunset the skipper returned, bringing with him a fresh crowd in place of the old hands, who had each, we were told, received summary sentence of two months' hard labour. Quick work, truly. The new crew were a mixed lot. There was a Newfoundland Irishman named

Flynn, a fat-faced blubber-bodied fellow, who was for ever eating tobacco; a stalwart fiery-headed ex-man-o'-war's man who could only be called Ginger; a long, melancholy-looking Englishman, who signed as George Harris; a Eurasian of gentlemanly appearance, but most foul and filthy behaviour; a delicate, pretty-faced Liverpool Irishman, with a fair silky beard, for cook; a broad-shouldered Greek, who had not a word of English; and, lastly, a precious piece of ornament in the shape of a Chinaman, pigtail and all, as if he had just come out of Foochow, whom the captain had shipped as steward for nothing a month. Gloomy Jem, the unfortunate negro youth, of course, remained of the old crew. In some misty fashion he went on his melancholy way, the butt of everybody but myself, his only relaxation an occasional incoherent chatter with me in some dark corner, when there was no work afoot.

Next morning at daybreak we unmoored, and proceeded down the muddy river, without hitch of any kind. The new crew worked well, glad enough, no doubt, to leave such miserable quarters as they had lately been enduring. You Sing, the Celestial, was a great acquisition. He was made to understand at once, that whatever work was to be done, he must take a hand in it, and he certainly toiled like a beaver. Beautiful weather still favoured us, and with an occasional glimpse of what looked to my exuberant fancy like fairyland rising out of the sparkling blue sea, we crept steadily westwards into the great gulf of Mexico. In spite of the miserable food and swinish forecastle, the fresh crew worked well and peaceably. What growling they did was indulged in out of hearing, and, after late experiences, I hardly knew the old ship. Without a single incident worth recording, we rolled along until we sighted the Mexican coast, which, as the position of our first calling-place was somewhat vague, the captain proposed to skirt until he came to it. The weather now became less settled, squalls of considerable violence being frequent, making a great deal of sail-handling necessary. One night, when we were suddenly called upon to shorten sail in a deluge of rain, it happened that the long Englishman, George Harris, and Ginger, the quondam man-o'-war's man, found themselves together furling the main to'-gallant sail. Now, Ginger, though a big fellow, was, as usual with his class, of very little use at furling sail under merchant-ship conditions. Where one man is employed in the merchantman, six or seven crowd in on board of *Andrew*; and the "bluejacket" is consequently handicapped when he finds himself thus lonely. The sail was stiff with wet, the wind was high, and George, in trying to make up for Ginger's deficiency, ruptured himself badly. He got down from aloft somehow, and took to his bunk, a very sick man. The treatment he received only aggravated his mishap, while he grew rapidly weaker from his inability to eat the muck, which even in his case was unchanged. Although never very friendly with me, I was filled with pity for him, and actually so far forgot my dread of the terrible "old man," as to creep below and steal a few cabin biscuits, which were less coarse and whiter than ours. It was comparatively easy to evade the officers, and I chuckled greatly over my smartness, being richly rewarded by the gratitude of the invalid, who made quite a hearty meal of my plunder soaked with some sugar. But I reckoned without You Sing. That slit-eyed pagan in some unholy fashion found me out, and at once betrayed me to the skipper, of whom he stood in such awe, that he was ready to jump overboard at a nod from him. I was called aft, questioned, and found guilty. There and then, with a bight of the gaff-topsail halliards, he gave me such a dressing down as I have never forgotten, You Sing standing by with a face like a door-knocker for expressionless calm. Even amid my sharpest pangs I rejoice to think I didn't howl. Perhaps I gained little by that. At last the skipper flung me from him, saying grimly, "Now ye can go an' thank George Harris for that." And when, twenty years after, I saw that stern old man, reduced to earning a precarious living as a ship-keeper, fall from a ship's side in the Millwall Dock, injuring himself so frightfully that death would have been refreshment, I could not help thinking of the grist which is ground by the Mills of the Gods. Joe, my faithful ally, was furious when I went forward quivering with pain. He was for vengeance, first on the old man, then on the placid pig who had betrayed me; but I begged so hard that he wouldn't make matters worse by interfering that at last he yielded. But he never settled down again satisfactorily.

Just a week afterwards we came to a slight indentation in the coast, where a Norwegian barque lay at anchor. From her we got the information that the place was called Tupilco, upon which we anchored, it being our port of call for orders. The anchor was no sooner down than Harris crawled aft and implored the captain to take him ashore so that he might get some medical aid. Desire of life made the poor fellow quite eloquent, but he might as well have appealed to a bronze joss. When, exhausted, he paused for breath, the old man said, with bitter emphasis, "Ef I'd ben a loafin' on my shipmets s'long's *you* hev', I'd take 'n heave me useless carcass overboard, ye wuthless sojer. Git forrard 'n die. It's 'bout the bes' thing you ken do." George crept forrard again without a word.

We lay at this forsaken-looking spot for four days, holding no communication with the shore except twice, when a launch came off, manned by a truculent-looking crew of "dagoes," *i. e.* Greeks, Italians, Spaniards, and half-bred Mexicans. Soon after their second visit we weighed again, having received instructions to commence loading at Sant' Ana, some distance along the same coast. We had an easy run thither, with a fair wind all the way, and were pleasantly surprised to find that, although an open roadstead like Tupilco, there was quite a fleet of ships at anchor there. They were of all sizes and rigs, from rakish-looking Yankee schooners to huge fullrigged ships, and of several nationalities—British, American, and Norwegian predominating. There was a heavy landward swell on when we passed through them to our anchorage, and it was anything but cheering to see how they rolled and tumbled about in far more unpleasant fashion than as though they had been under way. In fact, some of the fore and afters had actually got staysails set, with the sheets hauled flat aft, so as to counteract in some measure the dangerous wallowing they were carrying on. I watched one Baltimore schooner, with tremendously taunt spars, roll until she scooped up the sea on either side with her bulwarks, the decks being all in a lather with the foaming seas tearing across them, and I couldn't help thinking what a heavenly time those Yanks must have been having down below, for there were none visible on deck.

CHAPTER V.

THE LAND OF LIBERTY.

We came to an anchor near the middle of the roadstead in seamanlike fashion, every sail being furled before the anchor was dropped, and the old tub brought-to as if going into dock. Then, as it was understood that our cargo was ready for us, preparations were immediately made for its reception. A stout spar was rigged across the forecastle, protruding twenty-five feet on the starboard side, with a big block lashed to its end through which ran a five-inch rope. A derrick was rigged over the main-hatch with a double chain purchase attached, and a powerful winch bolted to the deck, round which the chain revolved. Numbers of iron spikes (dogs), with rings in them, were fitted with tails of rope about three feet long, and lengths of hawser cut for "mother-ropes." The rafts of mahogany and cedar logs are made by driving a tailed "dog" firmly into the side of each log a foot or so from the end. As each one is thus spiked it is secured by a "rolling-hitch" of the tail to the "mother-rope" (*cabo madre* of the Spaniards), until as many are collected as required. This operation is always performed in the river just inside the bar, where the logs are sorted after their long drift from the interior. Then the raftsmen, who are equipped with capacious boats pulling six oars, and carrying about three hundred fathoms of grass rope, secure one end of their tow-line to the mother-rope, and pull away seaward in the direction of the ship, the steersman casting out line as they go. Arriving at the end of their tether they anchor, and all hands turn-to with a will to haul the raft up to the boat. This operation is repeated as often as is necessary to cover the three or four miles between ship and shore, until at last the long line of tumbling logs are brought alongside their destined vessel, and secured to the big spar on the forecastle. At whatever time they arrive all hands must turn out to receive them, and on board the American ships the uproar used to be fearful; oaths, yells, and showers of belaying pins rattling against the bulwarks, bearing eloquent testimony to the persuasive methods of discipline in vogue on board of them. The stevedores, or stowers of the timber, arrived on board shortly after we anchored; like the rest of the population, they were a mixed crowd of Latins and Greeks, but all speaking Spanish. Owing to their presence we fared much better than we should otherwise have done, for they were fed by the ship, and by no means to be offered any such carrion as usually fell to our lot. Their pay was high, five dollars a day; but they certainly worked well, besides being very skilful. With our first raft there was trouble. Flynn, the "blue-nose" Irishman, was sent upon the uncertain row of logs alongside to sling them; but after several narrow escapes from drowning or getting crushed between the rolling ponderous masses, some of them over five tons in weight, he clambered on deck again, and flatly refused to risk his bones any longer. Nor, in spite of the skipper's fury, could any other man be persuaded to attempt so dangerous a task. Finally, the old man turned to one of the Greeks of the stevedore gang, and ordered him to act as slingsman. "Oah yez, capane," said Antonio, "sposa you giva me eight dolla day." After a little more language the old man said, "All right, 'Tonio, I'll give you eight dollars. An' I'll stop it out of your pay, you skulking sojer you" (to Flynn). Which was mirthful, seeing that eight dollars represented a fortnight's pay for our shipmate.

However, Antonio proved a most expert raftsman, being almost amphibious and smart as any eel. But the work was exceedingly severe. Lifting such great masses of timber tried the old sticks terribly, and when she rolled suddenly to windward, tearing the log out of water with a jerk, you almost expected her to fall apart. When, at last, the log showed above the rail, if she started her antics, all hands near stood by for a run, for the log would suddenly slue inboard, and come across the deck like a gigantic battering ram. The whole process was a series of hairbreadth escapes. Down in the hold, where the stevedores toiled with tackles, rousing the logs about, there were many casualties; but these dagoes never seemed to care. For every hurt they had one remedy: plenty of "caña," a fiery white spirit, fresh from the still. Poured into a gash, or rubbed on a bruise, with half a pint to drink, this vitriolic stuff seemed to meet every emergency.

The enormous rate of pay prevailing here during the height of the season, had the inevitable effect of causing frequent desertions; so that as much as three hundred dollars was freely offered for the run to New York or Europe for seamen. Consequently a vigilant watch was kept by the officers of ships, lest any of the crew should take French leave, although getting ashore was difficult. We, however, had a very large long-boat, for which there was no room on deck, and, contrary to the usual practice it was put overboard, and kept astern at the end of a small hawser. The temptation was too much for my friend Joe, who, accompanied by the Eurasian, slipped over the bows one dark night, and swam aft to the unwieldly ark, unheard by the officer on watch. Poor fellow! he couldn't keep awake night and day. At daybreak, when the skipper came on deck, and looked over the taffrail, always his first move, the idle rope hung down disconsolately—the long-boat was gone! Seizing his glass he mounted to the cross-trees, and scanned the horizon, discovering the derelict far out at sea. The gig was lowered and manned by Flynn and Jem, the skipper himself taking the tiller, and off they went in pursuit. It was nearly noon when they returned, towing the runaway, and half dead with thirst and fatigue. Then only did the skipper learn that two of his best men were gone. In his hurry he had not stayed to inquire, and now his rage knew no bounds. Judge, then, how he felt when he discovered, by the aid of his glass, that the deserters were no further away than our nearest neighbour, an American brig that lay less than half a mile away. Anger overcame his prudence, and he actually went alongside the Yank, intending to go on board and claim his men. He was received with contumely, the American skipper refusing to allow him over the rail. His state of mind on his return must have been pitiable; but he sought his cabin without a word, and remained there all the rest of the day.

In some way the news spread round the fleet, and that evening we were boarded by the captain of the *Panuca*, a Liverpool barque, who came to condole and relate his woeful experiences. He said that his men had refused duty altogether, upon which he was advised to take them ashore to the "Commandant," who would deal with them in summary fashion. Accordingly he took them, finding the *soi-disant* official to be a stalwart Greek, who held the position by virtue of his election by his fellow rascals, for law there was none. El Señor Commandante, however, told him to leave his men with him, and he would soon bring them to their bearings. Very reluctantly he followed this advice, since he had no choice, and returned on board, cursing his stupidity for ever taking them there. To his joyful surprise they returned on board, next morning, as meek in their demeanour as if they had, indeed, been taught a lesson. But two nights afterwards there was a desperate hubbub raised, during which the rascals looted the cabin, and, getting into the whale-boat hanging at the davits, went ashore with their plunder. They had strictly followed the instructions given them by the commandant, who made them a handsome present in return for the fine boat they brought him. When the half-frantic captain arrived on shore, and learned the truth, he was so enraged that he actually tried to take his boat off the beach where she lay, narrowly escaping being shot for his pains. This tale, poured into our skipper's sympathetic ears, somewhat reconciled him to his loss, since he still retained his boat.

But one disaster succeeded another. A curious malady of the feet attacked every one of the crew. It caused the legs and feet to swell enormously, and culminated in a suppurating wound horribly painful and slow to heal. Then a deadly encounter took place between the cook and You Sing, which was only settled by sending the Chinaman ashore, since the two seemed bent upon murdering one another. Worst of all, when the ship was half-full, the timber ceased to arrive. Ship after ship sailed away, until there were only three of us left; and the season of the "Northers" being close upon us, when those destructive gales blow right home all along the coast, every one began to look very glum. The unfortunate invalid, George Harris, after lingering longer than any one could have believed possible, was set free from his misery at last, to the manifest relief of his shipmates, who were heartily tired of his taking so long to die. Sounds horrible, doesn't it? But it is the naked truth. Under such circumstances as ours were, the better part of humanity generally disappears, or only shines in individuals who are often, almost always, powerless to help.

Miserable as the time had been, it was not all lost upon me. As far as the hardship went it was no worse, if as bad, as I had endured in the London streets; and here, at any rate, it was always warm. I had learned to chatter Spanish fluently, although much of it I would gladly unlearn if it were possible, for I have always noticed that, in picking up a language colloquially, one learns easiest and remembers longest the vilenesses. And how vile the Latin tongues can be, few Englishmen can realize. I did not grow much, not being well-enough nourished; but I was wiry, hard as nails, and almost as brown as an Indian, being half naked from want of clothes. At last, one morning, my uncle sent for me. Although unconscious of any offence I was terribly frightened, but went, shaking with dread, to meet him. To my utter amazement he spoke kindly, saying that the ship was so old, and the season so late, that he feared there was great danger of her never reaching home. Therefore he had decided to send me on board the barque *Discoverer*, commanded by a friend of his, in which, as she was a splendid vessel, I should be far safer. She was to sail the next day, so I must go on board that night. I only said, "Thank you, sir," but volumes could not have expressed my gratitude. To leave this awful den, to be once more treated to a kind word occasionally—for, since Joe was gone and Jem had been driven ashore (which I have forgotten to mention), I had no friends at all on board; the prospect was too delightful for contemplation.

My wardrobe being on my back I was spared the labour of packing up. Farewells there were none to say, although, being naturally a tenderhearted little chap, I should have been glad of a parting God-speed. But no one said anything to me as I bundled into the boat and was rowed alongside my new home. As soon as I climbed on board I was met with a very chorus of welcome. The warmth of my reception amazed me, accustomed as I had been for so long to the miserable state of affairs on board my old ship. But I soon overcame a strong temptation to cry for joy, and, steadily choking down the lump in my throat, set about taking stock of my new vessel. To my inexperience she seemed a most noble ship. Everything was on a much finer scale than anything I had yet seen in my brief travels. She had been built for the purpose of Arctic exploration, and consequently presented a somewhat clumsy appearance outside from the doubling of the bow planks and stern bends, and the diagonal oaken sheathing with which she was protected. Inboard, though, she was roomy, clear, and comfortable as could be imagined, while her rigging and spars were all of the very best, and in tip-top condition.

Quarters were assigned to me in the comfortable cabin of the steward, whose helper I was supposed to be, although, from the first, I had the free run of the ship fore and aft. Next morning we weighed with a gentle favouring breeze, homeward bound. But I soon discovered that there was one drawback to all this comfort—the captain was a confirmed drunkard. While the process of getting under weigh was going on, he was mooning about the deck with a fishy eye and an aimless amble, getting in everybody's way, and causing much confusion by giving ridiculous orders. Had he confined himself to that all would have been well, for the men humoured him good-temperedly, and took no notice of his rubbish. But when they had "catted" the anchor, they were obliged to leave it hanging while they got some sail on her, the fall of the cat-tackle being stretched across the deck and belayed to the opposite rail, as there was no fo'lk'sle-head, and consequently no capstan. All hands being aft, the skipper maundered forrard, to find his further progress stopped by this rope. Muttering unintelligibly, he cast it off the pin to which it was belayed. The result staggered even himself, for there was a rush and a roar, a perfect blaze of sparks, a cloud of dust, and, with a jerk that almost threw everybody flat, the last link of one hundred and twenty fathoms of cable brought the ship up all standing. All hands had flown forrard at the first bang, but they were powerless to do anything except pray that the cable might part. It was too good for that, bearing the terrible strain to which it was subjected of bringing a ship up, in twenty fathoms of water, that was going nearly four knots an hour.

The mate got the old man aft into his cabin while the fellows clewed up the canvas again, and then issued the order to man the windlass once more. But this the men flatly refused to do, alleging that after their forenoon's work, it was unreasonable to expect such a thing. The mate was powerless to insist, so nothing further was done till next day but give the sails the loosest kind of a furl. At daybreak next morning the heavy task of getting the anchor was begun, the skipper keeping out of sight. There was a great deal of growling and bad language; but the mate managed to get hold of a demijohn of the old man's whisky. This he dispensed with no niggard hand, and so the peace was kept; but it was late in the day when she was again fairly under way for home.

After that, everything went on smoothly enough. Although, as usual, the crew were of several nationalities, they all pulled together very well, nor did they take the advantage they might have done of the utter absence of any shadow of discipline on board. The whole working of the ship devolved upon the mate, for the skipper was always more or less drunk, and the second mate was helpless, having had his right foot smashed by a log of mahogany in loading. What work was necessary during the daytime was done cheerfully enough, and a general air of peace and contentment pervaded the ship. For one thing the food was really good and plentiful, and none of the men were of that blackguardly kind that glory in taking every advantage of any weakness aft. Of course the watch-keeping at night was bad. A big London boy, who was much disliked for his lazy, dirty habits, was made to keep the look-out always in his watch—a duty which he usually performed with his head between his knees. The rest of the men slept the night through, seldom knowing whose watch on deck it was; so that if sail required trimming all hands generally turned out to it after a good deal of inviting. The captain was supposed to keep the second mate's watch, but he set a shining example to his crew, by sleeping it out wherever he happened to drop when he came on deck.

I was very happy. Never since the time my troubles began, that is, at about eight years old, had I been treated so well. Being very small, and fairly knowing, besides having a rather sweet treble voice, I was made a sort of plaything—an universal pet. And in the dog-watches, when seated upon the main hatch surrounded by the crew I warbled the songs I knew, while not another sound disturbed the balmy evening but the murmur of the caressing waters alongside and the gentle rustle of a half-drawing sail overhead, I felt as if my halcyon days had dawned at last. That fortnight is one of the pleasantest recollections of my life. The weather was delightfully fine, and by day the ship was like a huge aviary, a multitude of brilliant-hued little birds being continually about her, although we were out of sight of land. They were of many kinds, but all so tame that they freely came and went through cabin and forecastle, hunting for the cockroaches with which she was infested. On the upper yards a small colony of kestrels kept vigilant watch, descending like a flash upon any unwary birdling that dared to venture far into the open. The men made many nocturnal excursions aloft after the "pirates," as they called them, giving them short shrift when they caught them. So the days drowsed on quietly and peacefully, seeming, to my youthful ignorance, as nearly perfection as they could possibly be. Not but what I felt an occasional twinge of sorrow at the continual drunkenness of the captain. Mixing with the men forrard freely as I did, their rough but half-pitying comments upon him and his behaviour could not fail to impress me, although I often wondered how it was that, being so well aware of the danger they ran by reason of such general neglect, they were not themselves more watchful, instead of taking such advantage as they did of the captain's fault, to sleep all night.

At last, on the fifteenth day from leaving port, on a clear starlit night with a gentle, fair wind blowing, and all hands, including the captain—whose watch it was—asleep, the vessel ran upon a coral reef and became a total wreck. Having told the story in another place, I cannot enlarge upon the circumstances attendant upon her loss here; it must suffice to say that, after many perils, all hands escaped safely to land upon the "cay" or sandy islet which crowned the highest point of the reef. A fairly large quantity of food and water was saved; so that we ran no risk of privation, even had the islet failed to furnish us with fish, fowl, and eggs in plenty as it did. One circumstance I must record in passing as being well worthy of notice. As soon as it was evident that the vessel was hopelessly lost, the seamen forrard, though perfectly well behaved, insisted that every drop of intoxicating liquor should be thrown overboard, and, in order that it should be done thoroughly, themselves carried it out. As the giant breakers destroyed the upper works of the ship, much useful wreckage came ashore, and one calm day a visit was paid to her, which was rewarded by the salvage of several sails and a quantity of cordage. With these, comfortable tents were rigged, and I have no doubt that, had it been necessary, we could have put in several months on that barren patch of sand quite happily. Huge turtle came ashore to deposit their eggs, and were easily caught. Sea-fowl of many kinds, principally boobies and frigate-birds, swarmed in thousands, whose eggs, especially those of the frigate-birds, were delicious eating, although, never being pressed by hunger, we left their rank, fishy flesh severely alone. Fish of course abounded, while the crevices of the rocks concealed great numbers of clams and oysters, and at night the lighting of our beacon fire attracted quite a host of crabs from the sea, who fell victims in great numbers to their curiosity. Hardships there were none, and I would far rather have lived there for six months than for one week on board the old *Arabella.*

Ten days passed gaily away, during which the sail-maker and carpenter had made a fine seaworthy craft of the pinnace in which most of us reached the shore. Fitted with new sails and rigging and half-decked, she was fit for a much longer voyage than was necessary to reach the mainland of Campèche, the nearest town of which, Sisal, was barely a hundred miles distant. But one morning as the look-out man was ascending the rocky promontory, where a flag-staff was erected to hoist the signal of distress we always kept flying by day, he saw a handsome barque lying-to only about two or three miles away. The French ensign was flying at her peak, and a boat had left her side which was being rapidly pulled shorewards. They soon landed, and by expressive signs the officer in charge gave us to understand that he was prepared to take us all on board, but that we must make haste, as the vicinity was much too dangerous to linger in longer than was absolutely necessary. Not one word of each other's language did we understand, yet we found no difficulty in getting at one another's meaning sufficiently near for all practical purposes. To my amazement, however, the skipper, the mate, and four others, refused to avail themselves of the opportunity to escape. They said they did not want to go to Havana, where the barque would land us, preferring to sail in the pinnace to Sisal and take their chance there. When the French officer realized this, he looked as if he thought the small party refusing to come with him were mad. But after an outburst of volubility, quite wasted upon our misunderstanding, he shrugged his shoulders and retreated towards his boat, followed by all who were ready to go with him. His men had made good use of their time by getting a goodly quantity of birds and eggs collected, and now disposed themselves, with a perfect uproar of chattering, in as small a compass as they could, while our fellows took the oars and pulled away for the barque. Looking back, I saw the little group of our late shipmates standing watching us from the beach: a sight so pathetic that I could not help bursting into tears, quite forgetting that it was entirely in accordance with their own desires that they were thus abandoned.

082

We could have put in several months on that barren patch of sand quite happily.

We soon reached the ship, swarmed on board, and swung the boat up to the davits in a twinkling, while the officer who had brought us—the chief mate—held an animated colloquy with the captain on the poop. From the expressive gestures used, we had no doubt but that they were discussing the incomprehensible resolve of our captain and his followers. They terminated their conversation by mutual shoulder-shruggings, as who should say, "But what would you, my friend? they are English, whose ways are past finding out." Nothing could be more cordial than our reception by all hands. The big long-boat was cleared out for our sleeping-place, as the barque's fo'lk'sle accommodation was too limited to admit any more than at present occupied it; and a bountiful meal of *fazhole blanc*, a delicious *purée* of haricot beans, good biscuit, and *vin ordinaire* was served out to us.

CHAPTER VI.

TO HAVANA AND AFTER.

This seems to be an appropriate place for noticing how, at less cost, the Frenchmen fared so much better than in any sailing ship I have ever been in. The Board of Trade scale of provisions for the Mercantile Marine must strike every landsman as being a most absurd compilation. On four days of the week each man is entitled to one and a half pounds of salt beef, including bone, accompanied by half a pound of flour, except on Saturdays, when half a pint of rice *may* be given, or nothing. The other three days each bring one and a quarter pounds of salt pork and one-third of a pint of split peas. Every day there is an allowance *per capita* of one pound of bread (biscuit), an eighth of an ounce of tea, half an ounce of coffee, and three quarts of water; and each week twelve ounces of sugar and half a pint of vinegar is allowed per man.

What scope is there here for any variety or skill in cookery? Even supposing that the beef and pork were in any way comparable with the same articles on shore—which they cannot be in the nature of things—such a diet must soon become infernally monotonous. But the very best ship's beef and pork is not nice; the second best is nasty; and what will pass an inspector, is often utterly unfit for men to live upon entirely for any length of time, while it would be considered loathsome ashore. And what can be done with half a pound of flour? Lacking *anything* else, except a few hops, obviously the best thing to do is to make bread, which is a little more palatable than the flinty outrage on the name of food that is called ship's biscuit. What is usually done is to make "duff." This is really boiled bread, with the addition of some skimmed grease from the coppers in which the meat is boiled. As an act of grace, but by no means of necessity, a pannikin (pint) of molasses is doled out for all hands on duff days, but the crew are not allowed to forget that they have no claim to this dainty by Act of Parliament.

On pork days pea-soup is made, or "yellow broth," as sailors call it. But pease and water with a flavouring of pork (not too much lest the soup become uneatable from salt) needs a stretch of courtesy to be called soup. A little, very little, addition of vegetables would make it palatable, but "'tis not i' the bond." And even if so, do you think, reader, you would feel contented with fat pork and pea-soup for dinner three times a week for four months on end? For breakfast and supper (tea) there is biscuit and beef, or biscuit and pork, washed down with the result of the modicum of coffee or tea. And that is all. For very shame's sake, a minority of shipowners do provide a few extras: such as butter, an occasional mess of tinned meat, and a few preserved potatoes and pickles. But these are the exception and not the rule. Moreover, whenever these additional helps are given, the men are always reminded that they have no right to them, that no owner need give anything more than the bare pound and pint of the Board of Trade scale.

Contrast this with our living on board the Bordeaux barque *Potosi*. In the first place the bread, which was in large puffy cakes, became, under the slightest moisture, as easy to eat and as palatable as baker's bread. This alone was an enormous boon. Breakfast, which, like all other meals, was taken by all hands at once, was hardly a meal in our sense of the term. It was only a cup of coffee (exceedingly good), some bread, and about a gill of cognac. Luncheon at noon consisted of half a pound of meat, free of bone, and some preparation of vegetables, bread, and half a pint of wine. Dinner at four p. m. was a grand affair. The changes were rung upon haricot beans, lentils, vermicelli, macaroni, and such legumes cooked with meat and flavoured so that the smell was intensely appetizing. Bread, and half pint of wine. And there was abundance, but no waste. Yet I am persuaded that the cost was much less than that of our authorized scale of provisions, about which it is difficult to speak with patience. It will, I think, be admitted that where men are shut up to a life of such monotony as the seaman's calling must necessarily be, their food ought at least to have some consideration. The meal-hours form almost the only breaks in the day's sameness, and if the food be poor in quality and without variety, it is bound to engender bad feeling and a hatred of those of whose fault it is the outcome. This by way of apology for such a lengthy dwelling upon the subject, if any be needed, though I have always felt that its importance is great enough to merit much more attention than it commonly receives.

We had a very pleasant passage. The barque was a wonderfully handy vessel, and her equipment was so good that it excited the wondering admiration of all our men. The discipline was quite naval in its character, and the day's duties went on with the regularity of clockwork. Of course we could not understand the language, and were, in consequence, unable to know whether there was the same amount of grumbling commentary forward, upon the sayings and doings of the officers, as is almost universal in British ships, with the exception of "Blue-noses" (Canadian vessels). But it was admitted by all of us that the crew seemed well content and heartily willing, and that she was indeed a model ship. My scanty knowledge of Spanish came in useful, for the captain spoke that language about as well as I did. On his discovering this fact he sent for me, and, by dint of patience, succeeded in learning from me such facts as he wished to know, rewarding me with many a tit-bit from his table, as well as some very useful gifts of clothing, which, as I was almost naked, were most acceptable.

Arriving at Havana, we were handed over to the British consul, leaving the friendly Frenchmen with much regret and three hearty cheers, which they returned with interest *à la Française*. We were no sooner clear of her than they began to get under way again, and, by the time we were on the wharf, she was once more heading for home. By the orders of the consul we were marched up to a "fonda," or eating house, facing the Plaza de Armas, which we understood was to be our home during our stay. A plentiful meal was set before us, but we did not appreciate it much, every dish being saturated with the flavour of garlic. But as two bottles of wine were apportioned to each individual, the meal was a merry one, all hands declaring that bread and wine would suit them down to the ground. A bundle of cigars were distributed by a benevolent-looking old stranger, who introduced himself as the shipping-master, and spoke excellent American, being, as he informed us, a native of New Orleans.

After a smoke, we were conducted to a large paved room at the back of the premises, which was simply furnished with a couple of huge tables and sundry benches, and had in one corner an unprotected well. Here we were told we must spread such bedding as we had, and make ourselves as comfortable as we could, until our proper dormitory was vacated by the recruiting party that at present occupied it. The said party were by no means an inviting crowd. They swarmed about the big chamber we were in, looking fit for any villainy, and ostentatiously displaying their vicious-looking bowie-knives. All our fellows had been deprived of their sheath-knives upon first coming ashore, under the plea that the carrying of weapons was unlawful, though we were the only unarmed people I saw in the city during my stay. However, we had no choice of quarters, so we proceeded to spread such ragged blankets as we possessed upon the flagstones against one of the bare walls, and in due time ranged ourselves thereon. Owing, I suppose, to the unusual quantity of wine they had drunk, all our men were soon asleep, and when some one took away the smoky kerosene lamp, the place was pitchy dark, except where the silver bars of moonlight, streaming through the unglazed holes in the walls, divided the blackness into rigid sections. I could not sleep. The novelty of the situation, the strange smells, and an indefinable fear of that truculent crowd of armed men, kept all my senses at highest tension. There was no door, and, through the opening in the wall, dark shapes of men came and went softly on Heaven knows what errands. I had reached a condition of mind when I felt as if I must scream to relieve my pent-up feelings, when I saw some figures bending over my sleeping shipmates as if searching for something. By this time my eyes had become able to distinguish objects in the surrounding gloom, and I found that there were at least twenty men in the place.

Terribly frightened, and hardly knowing what I did, I roused the carpenter, by whose side I lay, and whispered hoarsely in his ear what I had seen. The word was passed along, and in a few minutes we were all afoot and straggling out into the moonlight-flooded courtyard. There we stood like a flock of startled sheep, irresolute what to do. But some of the knife-carrying gentry emerged after us, and began whetting their weapons on the blocks of stone laying about—portions of a ruined wall. This significant hint decided us, and we passed out into the silent street, feeling to the full that we were strangers in a strange land. Lights of any kind there were none, and the intense brilliance of the moon cast shadows as solid as does the electric glare. A few yards of uncertain wandering, and we were lost. There seemed to be no one about, and yet I could have sworn I saw dark shapes gliding along in the inky shadows. And presently I fell headlong over something in the road, my outstretched hands striking with a splash into a pool of mud. A cold thrill ran along my spine when I found I was lying across a corpse, and that the sticky paste on my hands was red. We quickened our steps after that, keeping in the middle of the streets, but as ignorant of our direction, or our purpose, as if we had been a herd of swine devoid of instinct. At last, from sheer weariness, we sat down upon the steps of some large building, and drooped our heads. As if he had risen from the ground, a "vigilante" (watchman) appeared, bearing a short spear, from the upper third of which dangled a lantern. "Vamos, perros!" he growled, prodding those nearest to him into instant wakefulness. No one needed a translation, or a second bidding to "Begone, dogs!" So we tramped wearily along, our bare feet bruised by the littering stones. As often as we dropped for a brief rest, one of those ubiquitous sereños moved us on again to the same monotonous epithet of contempt. I often think what a queer-looking procession we must have been. My only garments were a flannel singlet and a pair of canvas trousers, so stiff that they creaked woodenly as I trotted along. Cap or boots I had none. The rest were in much the same plight, though none were quite so naked as me. Going along a narrow lane, whereof I read the title, "Aguacallè," on a building at the corner, I slipped off the hummocky sidewalk into a slough of soft slush up to my armpits, and was dragged out by my next friend with a new covering of such evil odour that I had to keep a respectful distance from my companions thenceforth. Finally we emerged upon what seemed to be a wide common or piece of waste ground. Here at last we were permitted to squat unmolested. Fear of scorpions, centipedes, and snakes, kept me from sleep; but all my companions lay sound in strange attitudes, under the full glare of the moon, while I watched, wondering if the night would ever end. At the first glimmer of dawn I aroused my companions, who were all reeking with dew, and we made for the streets again, going as straight back to our lodgings as if we knew the road. When we entered, the warriors had all gone. No one belonging to the establishment was astir, so we cast ourselves down on our rags and slept like stones until roused at eight o'clock by the servants. Until eleven we dozed on the benches, or in whatever corners we could find, when a plentiful breakfast revived us in spite of the garlic.

After our meal the vice-consul paid us a visit. He listened gravely to our complaints of the accommodation we had found. Then he invited us to accompany him to the consul's office. On our arrival all hands were shown into a large, bare room, while I was called upstairs to undergo a searching cross-examination by the consul as to what clothes the men had saved, the incidents of the shipwreck, etc. I suppose he thought that so young a boy would be more likely to tell a true tale than those artful rogues of sailors, as he seemed to regard them. He was not at all kind or sympathetic: that was no part of his business, I suppose; but as he was writing an order upon a slop-seller for some clothing for us, a handsome young lieutenant from an English man-o'-war came in. His eyes fastened upon me at once, and, after a hurried question or two of the consul, he came to me and spoke pitifully, giving me two dollars out of his pocket as a solid token of his sympathy. Then the consul had all hands in and harangued them, telling them to be sure and keep sober (which, as they were penniless, was rather uncalled-for advice), and by no means to stray away from the immediate vicinity of the shipping-office. They would be sure to get a ship in a day or two, he said. Dismissing us with a curt good-day, he retired, while we followed the vice-consul to the clothier's. Here the men received each a rig-out of cheap garments, but I was treated much better; why, I do not know. After all the men had been served and had returned to our lodging, I was furnished with quite a nice suit of clothes, with good underclothing, patent leather shoes, and broad-brimmed Panama hat. A brilliant red silk sash was given me by the shopkeeper as a present, and, thus glorified, I felt quite transformed. With many cautions as to my behaviour, the official bade me good-day, and I was left to my own devices. And then began one of the strangest experiences of my life. Wherever I went, people looked kindly at me, and spoke to me as if they were interested in me. I entered into shop after shop to spend some of my money, but found it impossible, for the shopkeepers insisted upon giving me what I asked for without payment, and often added to my store of cash besides. When at last I returned to the fonda, I was loaded with cigars, fruit, pastry, and all sorts of odds-and-ends, so that my shipmates were loud in their welcomes. By nightfall we were all in a very contented condition of mind, and, when the landlord politely requested me to inform my friends that our sleeping apartment was prepared, we felt that our comfort was complete. But our joy had a tremendous setback when we were shown the said bedroom. It was a long lean-to shed erected against an ancient wall of rubble that had never known contact with a whitewash brush. The floor was of dried mud. Along the centre of its whole length ran an open ditch, which carried in a sluggish stream all the sewage of the house. On either side of this foul *cloaca* were ranged "charpoys," a sort of exaggerated camp-stool, which constituted the entire furnishing of this primitive bed-chamber. It was well ventilated, although there were no windows, for daylight was visible in many places through gaps in the boarding of the outer wall and roof. Many and vigorous were the comments passed upon the filthy hole, but there was no suggestion of raising any complaint, as all felt that it would be useless, and, at any rate, the place was our own, and we could barricade the door. So spreading our blankets upon the charpoys, we turned in, and were soon oblivious of all our surroundings.

Next day, in the course of my wanderings, I entered the fine billiard room of the Hotel St. Isabel and chummed up with the marker. I was well acquainted with the game, having learned how to mark in one of the strange by-paths of my nomad life before going to sea. And this knowledge now came in usefully, for the marker was a one-armed man who was often sorely bothered by the management of his three tables, especially when the players were lively American and English skippers. I was made heartily welcome, being helpful, in a double sense, from my knowledge of Spanish as well as my acquaintance with the game. From that time forward the "Fonda del buen gusto" saw little of me, and that little at uncertain intervals. I had a comfortable chamber, the best fare the hotel afforded, while as for money, the customers supplied me so liberally that my pockets were always full. As I could not spend it, most of it found its way to my shipmates, for I never came across one without handing some of it over. The idea of saving any never dawned upon me, and, when all my old shipmates were gone afloat again, I could always manage to find some English-speaking mariners to whom I was welcome company for a ramble round town.

The time flew by on golden wings. All my former miseries were forgotten in my present luxurious life, and I blossomed into that hateful thing, an impudent boy uncontrolled by anybody, and possessing all the swagger and assurance of a man. Such as I was, however, I attracted the attention of a gentleman who held a most important post under government as a civil engineer. He was a fairly constant visitor at the hotel when in Havana, and our acquaintance ripened into a strong desire on his part to adopt me, and save me from the ruin he could see awaited me. His only son, a young man of three-and-twenty, was his assistant, the two being more like brothers than parent and child. Having made up his mind, he fitted me out with an elegant suit of clothes made to his liking, and one day took me in his carriage to see the consul and arrange matters. To his intense surprise and disgust the consul flatly refused to sanction the affair, telling him that he was responsible for my return to England, and that, as I had admitted that my father was alive, any inquiry after me, which resulted in the discovery that I had been allowed to remain in Cuba without my parent's consent, would make matters very unpleasant for him. All attempts on Mr. D.'s part to shake this decision were fruitless. The consul refused to discuss the matter further, and closed the conversation by warning me that I was liable to severe punishment for absenting myself so long from the home (?) where he had placed me. What I felt I cannot describe. Mr. D., with a deeply dejected face, bade me good-bye, his duties calling him into the interior next day. He gave me twenty-five dollars as a parting present, and advised me to get a ship as soon as possible for home. It may readily be imagined that I had no hankering after the sea again. The pleasant, aimless life I had been leading, the inordinate petting and luxury I had grown accustomed to, had made me look upon ship-life with unutterable loathing, and I secretly determined that if I could avoid it I would never go to sea any more.

About this time a terrible epidemic of yellow fever set in. So great was its virulence, that even the never-ending warfare between the royalists and insurgents slowed down, and instead of a ragged regiment of wastrels being despatched into the mountains about twice a week, the authorities were hard put to it to collect recruits at all. The great bell of the cathedral tolled unceasingly. All night long the rumble of the waggons over the uneven causeways sounded like subdued thunder, as they passed from house to house collecting the corpses of the victims. The harbour was crowded with vessels denuded of their crews, and from every masthead flew the hateful yellow flag. It was heart-breaking to see and hear the agony of the sailors being taken ashore to hospital. They knew full well that there was hardly a glimmer of hope that they would return. The Chinese, who acted as nurses, were destitute of any feeling of humanity, and the doctors were worked to death. The nuns, who gave their lives nobly, could do little but minister such ghostly comfort as they knew how; but the net result of the hospital treatment was, with hardly an exception, death. Yet, in spite of the scourge, and general paralysis of trade in consequence, life, as far as I could see, went on much the same as ever. The inhabitants seemed determined to put a brave air on, whatever their inner feelings might be, and I declare that I saw very little to frighten me. One can get used to anything, especially when one has not learned to think. Several weeks passed away, and I was still free, though not quite so flush of money, for the customers at the hotel were necessarily fewer.

One day I was taking a stroll down by the deserted wharves, when I noticed a peculiar glow in the sky. It came from the heart of a gigantic cloud that draped half the heavens, and seemed as if it hid hell behind it. Fascinated by the sight, though my heart thumped furiously, I waited on the wharf and watched its development. The cloud spread until the whole dome was covered in by it, and the fierce glare took a strange greenish tinge. All around the edge of the darkness ran an incessant tangle of vari-coloured lightnings, and a continual rumble of thunder seemed to make the earth vibrate. Suddenly the storm burst. Jamming myself into a corner between some posts, whence I felt sure no wind could dislodge me, I waited and watched. For the first few minutes I thought I should have died of fright. Torrents of water, like the fall of a sea, were lashed into foam as they fell, and all torn into gleaming fragments by innumerable flashes flying in every conceivable direction. An overpowering smell like burning sulphur pervaded all. As for the wind, its force must have been frightful, judging from its effect upon the shipping and houses; but where I stood only a very strong gale could be felt, such as no seaman would think extraordinary. This lasted about an hour (but I cannot say much for time), and then the rain ceased. What a scene of horror the bay presented! Vessels of all kinds drifted aimlessly about, wrecking each other, and covering the boiling mäelstrom of the harbour with their *débris*. Overhead a louder roar occasionally made me look up to catch sight of a flying roof like a cloud fragment fleeting through the murky air. A large Yankee schooner was torn from her anchors, and lifted on to a ledge beneath the Moro Castle, which jutted out of the perpendicular cliff about a hundred feet above high-water mark. There she remained upright, with her bottom stove in like Columbus's egg. Of all the vessels in the harbour, the only ones that survived without serious damage were the warships, which, with topmasts housed and cables veered out to the clinch, were all steaming full speed ahead, and, even then, hardly easing the tremendous strain on the latter.

Taking advantage of a lull I emerged from my corner, drenched to the skin, of course, and so cramped from my long crookedness, that at first I could hardly feel my feet. As hurriedly as I could I made my way towards the hotel, finding the roadways almost blocked with ruins. The hotel had escaped much damage, and I was received with open arms, soon forgetting all my fears in a good meal and cheerful talk. In spite of the havoc it had made, the general feeling was one of thankfulness, it being taken for granted that the hurricane would be found to have swept away the far more dreaded "Yellow Jack." And this was literally true, for not a single fresh case was reported from that day forward. Business revived with a bound, for there was much work to do everywhere, shipwrights especially commanding almost any wages they liked to ask. About a week after the hurricane, I was standing watching the transport of a huge steam-launch over an isthmus to the dockyard, when I felt a hand on my shoulder. Turning sharply, I saw the yellow visage of the vice-consul, who was accompanied by a man in uniform, to whom he gave me in charge. I was fairly caught, and without further delay, in spite of my vehement protestations, I was put into a boat and taken on board a large barque, the *Sea Gem* of St. Andrews, N. S. The captain, a kindly-looking old gentleman, heard my impudent remarks in amused silence, until he thought I had gone far enough. Then he stopped me with a quiet, "That'll do, my lad, you don't want a rope's-ending, I'm sure." I had not lost all sense, so I pocketed my grievance and crept sullenly forward.

CHAPTER VII.

OFF TO SEA AGAIN.

The *Sea Gem* had suffered greatly from the hurricane, but, by dint of strenuous effort on the part of her agents, was now fairly seaworthy again. The ravages of pestilence, however, had left her almost unmanned, the only survivors being the second mate, the carpenter, and a couple of American negro youths. The new captain, I learned from the carpenter—who had taken me under his protection—had been retired for some years, occupying a fairly well-paid post ashore in Havana. But tempted by a lucrative offer from the agents, and greatly longing to return home again, he had accepted the post of master of the *Sea Gem.* He had succeeded in collecting another crew to take the vessel home; but they were, indeed, a motley crowd. Three Austrians, a Montenegrin, a Swede, a Frenchman and two more negroes made up the complement forward, all of whom spoke a barbarous dialect of Spanish among themselves, although the Austrians also conversed indifferently in some Slav tongue as well as in Italian. There was as yet no chief mate, but another American negro had been secured for cook and steward.

No cargo being procurable, we were to proceed in ballast to Mobile for cotton, and thence home. I had not yet lost hope of being able to escape before sailing; and the carpenter, who seemed to be greatly amused by my company, rather encouraged me in the idea. Strangely enough, nobody seemed to trouble about me, and I foolishly sulked about all day, doing nothing but brood over the possibility of getting away. At last a chance presented itself. All the members of the new crew were taken ashore to the consul's office to sign articles, and I, of course, went along. I had still a good deal of money, and, as soon as I had signed, and been ordered by the captain to go down to the boat and await his coming, I demurely obeyed, and bolted in a contrary direction as soon as I had turned the street corner. I was free. True, I had an uneasy feeling that at any moment I might be arrested for desertion; but I refused to entertain it, and hurried up town to the Hotel St. Isabel. Here I got a shock. My old friend the billiard marker was gone, and the new man did not look upon me at all favourably. My other acquaintances in the hotel, too, appeared anxious to avoid me, as if they had been warned not to give me harbourage there. So I wandered forth disconsolately, feeling as if the place was quite strange to me. In the course of a long ramble I fell in with a young American seaman who was outward bound, i. e. hard up, but as full of fun as if he had just been paid off. We had a great time together for a couple of days, getting as far away as Matanzas, and using up my stock of dollars at an alarming rate. The third day we were a bit weary of skylarking about, and decided to return to his boarding-house and have a good night's rest. When we arrived there it was past closing time, and the place was all dark and silent. It was a big corner building, springing straight from the roadway, with flat walls, up to a height of about fourteen feet, where a balcony ran right round the building. To rouse the landlord was more than we dared; so, after much scheming, we managed to find a light cart under a shed, which we dragged from its place and up-ended under the balcony. My chum, who was very tall, climbed up the shafts and scaled the balcony, then lowered his long sash to me. I was speedily by his side, and together we sought and found his room, which opened on to the balcony and was luckily unoccupied. Feeling secure, our love of fun overcame weariness, and after a boisterous pillow-fight we strolled out on to the balcony again. Just then a sereño loitered round the corner and uplifted his voice, "Ave Maria purissima, sin pecado concebida. Doce hora; noche sereña!" As the echoes died away, he caught sight of the cart standing where it ought not, and proceeded to investigate. Moved by the same spirit of mischief, we hurried to the chamber, and found a big jug of water, which Zeke carefully poured upon the head of the muttering vigilante. The effect was amazing. Raving like a lunatic, he assaulted the great door with feet and spear-butt, making an uproar that speedily aroused everybody within earshot. Our house hummed like a hive, and, before many minutes, we heard the hurried tramp of feet along the uncarpeted corridors, and the babel of many voices—the drenched official's shrilly predominant. Presently they entered our room, to find us just awaking from a sound sleep! and blinking at the lanterns like owls. So deep had been our slumbers, that it was some time before Zeke could explain how I came to be there; but the landlord, whom I recognized as an old acquaintance, was quite easily satisfied about me. Clearly we were not the offenders, and the search-party passed along, leaving us to enjoy a frantic jig at the glorious disturbance we had aroused. How the affair was settled I never heard, for the next day was my last of liberty.

Zeke went down to the shipping-office to look for a ship in the morning, leaving me to my own devices. After an hour's ramble up town, I began to feel a miserable reaction, helped on doubtless by the fact that I had shared my last dollar with my chum, and couldn't for the life of me see where any more were coming from. Presently I turned into a café and called for a cup of coffee (I had not learned to drink anything stronger). While I sat moodily sipping it, a drunken, disreputable-looking man of about forty, roused himself from one of the tables, and, coming over to where I was, addressed me in broad Scotch. With maudlin tears he assured me that he was the chief mate of the *Sea Gem*, and that he must get on board that day, but how he did not know. He dared not go out for fear of being arrested; would I take pity on him, and see him on board? He must have been in a queer state of mind, for I was but a boy of thirteen, and small for my age. My pride was touched, and I readily assented, leading him carefully down to the wharf, and engaging a boat for him. There I would have left him, but he held on to me like a bear, swearing he would be lost and undone without me, so I had to go off with him. When we got alongside, the second mate appeared at the gangway, and lowered a bowline, which I slipped over the helpless creature's head and under his arms. Thus he was hauled on board like a sack of flour. Then the second mate sternly ordered me to come up. I refused. But he quietly said, "Well, then, I must come and fetch you." That was sufficient; I mounted the side, and said good-bye to Havana.

That a rope's-ending awaited me, I felt sure; but instead of that, the captain called me into his cabin, and gave me a most fatherly talking to. His kindness made me feel bad, and I promised him forthwith to be a good boy, and forget my vagabond, independent way of living ashore. Patting me on the head, he dismissed me to make my peace with the second mate, who was very angry with me indeed. He received my apologies in silence, and, although never friendly, I had no cause to complain of his treatment afterwards. Of the mate I saw nothing for two or three days, for, although we left Havana the next morning, he was in such a woeful condition, after his long debauch, that he could not leave his berth. When he did appear he seemed to have forgotten who I was. His manner to me was extremely brutal; in fact, he was a brute all round—although a lively regard for his own skin made him careful how he treated the curious crowd of "dagoes" forward. They were not at all a bad lot, and, considering their limited vocabulary, got on fairly well with the work of the ship. The little Frenchman, in particular, was like a bundle of watch-springs. When he once comprehended an order, it was delightful to see him execute it. But his desperate attempts to understand what was said were quite pathetic. He spoke a mixture of Spanish and French, which the others did not well understand; and at last he pitched upon me as the only one he could hold anything like a conversation with, though how we managed it I have now no idea.

Everybody liked the old man. He was so genial, so simple, that it was a pleasure to see him. But I am afraid he would have had a bad time of it with a crew of Britishers. They appreciate a tight hand, and are quick to take advantage of anything like easy-going on the part of their officers. This polyglot crowd, however, gave no trouble; and, in spite of the bungling stupidity of the mate, who never seemed to get quite clear of the after-effects of his big drunk, things went on oiled wheels.

We were drawing near our port, when one afternoon, during a fine wholesail breeze, there was a sudden gloom which rapidly overspread the sky. Somebody was keeping a bad look-out, doubtless, for before any sail could be reduced, a squall of wind and hail struck the vessel, throwing her on her beam ends. It was so sudden that, although all halliards and sheets were let fly at once, not a yard would come down, the ship lying over at too great an angle. And above the roaring of the wind, and the flapping of the flying canvas, the ominous rumble of the stone ballast rattling down to leeward could be plainly heard. The deck was like the wall of a house, and, when I saw the foaming sea rising up on the leeside as high as the hatches, I felt sure she was turning bottom up. By God's mercy, we had an old suit of sails bent, which the wind stripped from the yards and stays like muslin. Great sheets of canvas flitted away into the darkness to leeward, while the flying running-gear cracked like volleys of musketry. Gradually as the pressure weakened she righted, regaining as even a keel as the shifted ballast would allow, and we were safe. But there were many pale faces besides mine, the old captain especially looking terribly shaken up.

Every stitch of canvas that had been set when the squall burst was gone, and, as the weather gradually settled into a strong gale, there was a desperate night's work ahead. In our position, with a great deal of land about, it was imperatively necessary to get sail set; but before that could be done it had to be "bent," that is, secured to the yards. Such a task as this tests the capabilities of a crew very well. In a man-of-war, where they can send a man to every roband, and a couple to each earring, the job is fairly easy; but in a merchant-ship it means almost superhuman labour, from the scarcity of hands. I shall not attempt to describe the process, which bristles with technical details, that cannot be grasped without a corresponding idea of the conditions of work aloft in bad weather. Suffice it to say that by midnight the two lower topsails, foresail, and fore-topmast staysail were set, and the hands, thoroughly exhausted, allowed to rest a while. It was my first experience of bad weather at sea, and I thought regretfully of the ease and comfort of my late life. But a kind of philosophic determination not to cry over spilt milk, which has attended me all my life, came to my rescue, and prevented me from being too miserable.

The poor old captain, however, was severely tried. Evidently his fortitude and ability were less than he had imagined. He looked worn and decrepit, a settled anxiety gave him a haggard appearance, and all hands pitied him. The fine weather had entirely forsaken us, nothing but fierce squalls and incessantly shifting winds prevailing until we made Dog Island, at the entrance to Mobile Bay, under the lee of which we came to an anchor. Our troubles were even then not over, for a gale sprang up almost immediately, which raised so ugly a sea that the lively vessel almost plunged bows under. All hands but the captain and myself were aloft, furling the sails forward. I stood alone by the windlass, ready to slack or make fast such running-gear as I was called upon to look after, when, with a tremendous bound, the ship reared herself high in air forrard, snapping the sorely-tried cable, the released links of which flew aft over the windlass-barrel with a deafening crash and shower of sparks. Everything was at once dropped aloft, the hands came sliding down backstays at their best gait, and in less than five minutes the other anchor was let go. Cable was veered away to ninety fathoms, and fervent hopes expressed that she would hold, for night was almost upon us, and our position was dangerous in the extreme. Happily the wind hauled soon after, the sea became smooth, and we rode in comparative comfort till noon next day, when a powerful tug came down and towed us up among the shipping to a secure berth.

A fine fleet of ships lay here, all loading cotton for Liverpool. Nor, in spite of the number of vessels, was there any delay in commencing our cargo, for the next day, after mooring, a gang of stevedores came on board and set to work, with characteristic American energy, to prepare the hold. Our captain left us for Mobile City in the same steamer that brought them, returning with the first load of cotton, but only to bid us farewell. He called us all aft, and, with a quivering lip, informed us that he did not feel equal to taking the ship home. Therefore he had determined to make way for a better man, who would be with us in a few days. He thanked all hands for the way they had treated him, and then, shaking hands all round, got into the boat and was rowed away to an upward-bound steamer, which lay alongside our nearest neighbour, the *Mary Durkee.* A hearty cheer followed him, which, if it lacked the simultaneous volume peculiar to Britons, was certainly no less sincere.

Then the cotton began to come in. The great loosely pressed bales, weighing some six hundredweight each, were whipped on board like magic by a single-purchase steam-winch on board the steamer, and tumbled into the hold as fast as they came. Below, operations commenced by laying a single tier of bales, side by side across the ship, on the levelled ballast, leaving sufficient space in the middle of the tier to adjust a jack-screw. Then, to a grunting chantey, the screw was extended to its full length, and another bale inserted. The process was repeated until at last long wooden levers were attached to the iron bars of the screw, and the whole gang "tallied" on until the last possible bale was squeezed into the tier, which was then almost as solid as a beam of timber built into the ship. It was a point of honour among stevedores to jam as many bales into a ship as she could possibly be made to contain, and restraint was often needed to prevent the energetic workers from seriously injuring vessels by the displacement of deck-planks, stanchions, bulkheads, and even beams.

On deck there was much to do. A winter passage across the Atlantic was before us. The vessel had been greatly neglected in Havana, and a great deal of sail-making had to be done. The mate, having obtained a demijohn of "bug-juice" from one of the cotton-steamers, was constantly drunk; so that all the work devolved upon the austere second mate, who toiled early and late to keep matters in hand. Owing to the docility of the crew, this was possible; but he was greatly relieved when one fine morning a tall, determined-looking man with a sallow face, heavy black moustache, and nasal twang arrived on board, and announced himself as "Captain Jones, come to take command." Within half an hour of his arrival, he had been all over the ship, had interviewed every member of the crew, and had repeated at least a dozen times that he was a "down Easter," and proposed to "run this packet Yankee fashion." With an intuition I have always had, I determined at once that he was carrying a good cargo of liquor; and it was as well for the besotted chief mate that this was so, for he would not otherwise have been so friendly with him, I'm sure. His rounds completed, he retired to the "saloon," catching sight of me as he went, and appointing me cabin-boy on the spot. My first duty was to call the mate into his presence. There and then the two of them, seated *vis-a-vis*, began to drink themselves speechless, while I stood in attendance, filling up their glasses until they could no longer hold them. At last they rolled off their seats, and lay across one another insensible. I retired and informed the steward, who lifted his hands despairingly, exclaiming, "Fo' de good Lawd, dis gwine ter be ole hell erfloat. One on 'em's bad nuff, but skipper en mate bofe: wa' we gwine ter do *I* doan know." But Captain Jones' carouse only lasted a couple of days. At the expiration of that time he "sobered up," and, though looking very demoralized, went about the ship like a man that knew his business thoroughly and meant doing it. Strangely enough, he allowed the mate to go on as he had been doing, never interfering with him in any way.

When two-thirds of our cargo was in, Captain Jones went up to the city again. During his absence the stevedores quitted work and left us for the Christmas holidays. By Christmas Eve there was not a steamer left in the bay, and an aching sense of discontent manifested itself all through the fleet. Not to speak of any festive provision, there was an actual dearth of fresh stores of any kind, as no vessels had been down for several days. Boats came and went from ship to ship on the same errand, seeking wherewithal to make a Christmas dinner; but there was no hope, all were alike unprovided. Gloom sat on every face as the prospect of a salt-junk dinner on Christmas Day grew more definite, and the language used about the matter was altogether improper and unseasonable. But, just as dusk was stealing in, a solitary schooner was sighted coming into the bay from the river under a press of canvas, which, in spite of the light breeze prevailing, drove her along at a good pace. It was quite dark by the time she reached us, and much to our surprise dropped her anchor close aboard of us. As soon as she swung to the wind the voice of Captain Jones hailed us from her deck, crying, "Send a boat aboard!" He had no sooner spoken than a perfect chorus arose about him: the squealing of swine, the cackling of geese, and the shrill war-cry of turkeys. Blessed discord! filling us with visions of feasting too delightful for speech. There was no delay in getting the boat afloat, all hands being full of eagerness to assist.

After receiving the skipper, the boat made a tour of the anchorage, Captain Jones standing up as each ship was passed, and shouting the good news at the top of his voice. Then returning to the schooner, the boatmen laboured like Trojans to transfer the stock to our deck. Besides the poultry and pigs, there was a huge pile of fresh beef, vegetables, and enough drinkables to furnish a carouse for the combined crews of the whole fleet. The transhipment was barely completed when customers began to arrive. Soon we were the centre of a flotilla of boats, whose crews lined our rails while the skippers examined the provisions. All the lamps in the ship were lighted and hung about, and, a rostrum being erected, Captain Jones began his auction. It was the strangest scene I ever witnessed on board ship. Roars of laughter punctuated every remark of the auctioneer, and, assisted by swiftly circulating bottles of strong waters, the fun raged furiously until long past midnight. Then, as the last of the visitors departed uproariously, our excited crowd quickly calmed down, and quiet reigned until a late hour on Christmas morning. Of the subsequent feast there is no need to speak. Sufficient to say that it laid over all my experiences on board ship, for our skipper, having cleared a goodly sum by his "cuteness" and enterprise, could well afford to be generous; and he was.

Four or five days elapsed before our stevedores returned, and the work of shipping cargo re-commenced. But once they got to work again no more time was lost. A week more saw every crevice, wherein it was possible to jam, by the most violent means, a bale of cotton, utilized, and even then the skipper growled because the time of year made it impossible for him to risk carrying a few bales on deck. At last the day came on which Captain Jones was to make his last journey to town to clear the ship for sea. Before he went, he called all hands aft and offered to buy such clothing as they required for the homeward passage. Being almost destitute of "dunnage," I ventured to put in my plea for a little, but was grievously disappointed. He would not buy me a rag, telling me that I was not a wage-earner but a passenger, and he couldn't afford to spend money out of his own pocket. Two days after we weighed for home.

We had fairly good weather as we were swept through the tortuous Florida Straits by the rush of the Gulf Stream, which, whether you will or not, carries you to the north-east at the rate of a hundred miles in twenty-four hours. But we were hardly clear of the land before a fierce north-westerly gale came howling down upon us, and my sufferings commenced in real earnest. For although I was supposed to be cabin-boy, I had to be on deck almost as much as I was in the cabin. The mate seemed to take a curious sort of pleasure in hazing me about, as if he had some personal grudge against me, although I never could understand why. I was so bitterly cold-footed that I stole a pair of the captain's stockings—I had nothing but a pair of patent-leather shoes—for footwear. They (the stockings) were very old, and I soon wore out the feet, which I cut off at the ankles, sewed up the openings, and put them on again. This ingenuity led to disaster, for springing up on the after-house one day by the side of the captain, who was leaning against it, he saw his initials on my leg. Investigation followed, in which I pleaded my sufferings from cold and his refusal to get me anything to wear in Mobile. My excuse was, of course, unacceptable, and, although he did not beat me, I was forbidden the cabin precincts any more, and compelled to go barefoot for the remainder of the passage.

I was now in the mate's watch, and that worthy treated me with studied brutality. I scarcely ever came within reach of him but I got a kick—he seldom struck me with his hands.

As we got farther to the eastward the weather grew worse and worse. Gale succeeded gale with hardly a lull between, but our vessel being in such fine trim, we were decidedly better off than as if she had been deep in the water. At last, however, we fell in with a regular hurricane. Every stitch of canvas was taken in but a storm-staysail, made of the heaviest canvas woven, under which we lay-to until she gave a tremendous weather-lurch, and, rolling to leeward with a vicious jerk, the triangular patch of sail blew clean out of its bolt-ropes. From that time we lay under bare poles for eighteen hours, during much of which I sat on the poop beside the tiller, hauling back the slack of the wheel-ropes, more dead than alive from the wet and cold. Never having seen such a storm at sea before, I was dreadfully frightened, until I saw how unconcernedly the sea-birds hovered about us. Then I reasoned that if those tiny things were so secure, surely a big ship like ours must be much more so. Unsound as my conclusion was, it comforted me, and I had no more fear. A few days of light fine weather succeeded this storm, during which everything was made ship-shape again aloft. The captain was a prime seaman, and, having completely left off his drinking, managed everything in first-rate style. But he never forgave me for my theft, nor did he ever check the mate for his ill-usage of me.

One lovely afternoon, to the surprise of all hands, the order was given to shorten sail. There was not a cloud in the sky, and a gentle south-westerly breeze was wafting us along about four knots an hour. But, as the work of furling the upper canvas proceeded, the rumour went round that the "glass," as seamen always term the barometer, was falling very fast. It may have been, but for twenty-four hours we lay under lower topsails and courses, not a trace of change in the serene weather prevailing. In the first watch of the next night there stole over the sky a gloomy shade, which deepened until the heavens were black. Not black as night, or black as ink, but as if a pall of black velvet had been suspended over the sea, scarcely higher than the mastheads. The wind died completely away. The water was smooth as oil, and so still that not a creaking rope or rattling sheave disturbed the deathlike silence. When the look-out man struck four bells, the sound seemed to wound like a sword-cut, so sharp and unnatural was its clangour. This state of things lasted for about three hours. Then, gradually, tiny threads of light ran waveringly in every direction, as if the solemn dome of darkness above was cracking, and revealing an immense glow above it. The brilliant crevices widened, grew longer and more vivid, until the whole firmament was aglow with flashes of intensest light, while all our spars were outlined in lambent flame. This display lasted for about an hour, then faded away; the gloom disappeared, and the deep blue sky, studded with innumerable stars and unflecked by a single cloud, extended from horizon to horizon. This beautiful weather lasted for another twenty-four hours, and then a gentle westerly breeze sprang up, which gradually freshened, until we were flying along homeward at tremendous speed, carrying every stitch of canvas the ship could stagger under.

Meanwhile the mate's treatment of me got worse, until one night he dealt me a savage kick, which hurled me off the poop on to the main deck, where I lay insensible for some time. Although no bones were broken, I had received such severe injury that I was unable to walk for two days. During my confinement I made a desperate resolution, and, as soon as I resumed work again, carried it into effect by boldly approaching my merciless tyrant, and telling him that I was a consul's passenger, as he very well knew. I promised him that if there was any law that could reach him, I would endeavour to have him punished for his cruelty. And now I said, "You can kill me if you like, I don't care." Much to my surprise, he weakened at once, and for the remainder of the voyage I was freed from his cowardly attacks.

The brave westerly wind that was hurling us homeward acted as usual. That is to say, it strengthened until, slowly and reluctantly, sail was reduced to the two lower topsails and reefed foresail. The ship was so buoyant that the mountainous seas which surrounded her, and often rose upon either side to such a height as to make it appear as if we were racing through a deep green valley, never broke on board. But the skilful, courageous steering required could only be performed by a few selected members of the crew. Several men had to be suddenly relieved of the task, for their nerve failed them at sight of the mighty green walls soaring above their heads, and they were within an ace of letting her broach-to. This terrible calamity, which has been the end of so many fine ships, occurs when the vessel swings broadside on to a great sea, which either smashes her up or rolls her over. In the most favourable cases much damage is bound to follow. We saw one sorrowful instance of it in a brig, which we flew by, helpless to aid. She was just sinking, the doomed crew clinging to the weather rigging as if to put off their inevitable fate for a few fleeting minutes. A huge sea rose between us, hiding her from view, and when we soared on the crest of the next one, she was gone like a foam flake.

Thus we ran until the colour of the water told us we were nearing the land, and soon we saw through the flying spindrift the lonely outpost of the Fastnet rock, with its sturdy lighthouse, which looked to me like a beckoning finger. Then mist-wreaths and snow-squalls shut out everything from view, except a barque, which, apparently going to Liverpool like ourselves, kept steadily on about a mile in front of us. So exactly did we keep in her wake that it looked as if we were following her lead. The weather got thicker, but the gale was unabated, and still we flew before it. Suddenly we were all startled by the report of a gun, and out of the fog on the starboard bow loomed the figure of a lightship with three ball-crowned masts. Our leader had disappeared. As we passed the lightship she fired another gun, and a lift in the fog showed the name on her side—*Coningbeg*. Still we kept on, all hands watching the skipper's troubled face. But a sudden roar of "Breakers right ahead!" sent all hands flying to the braces. Hard down went the helm, and round came the ship on her heel, the spray from the heavy following sea flying high over our topsail-yards, while the tender vessel heeled over until the lee rail was under water. Not a moment too soon, for the furious roar of the baffled breakers sounded deafeningly, as their fleecy crests boiled and foamed under our lee only half a dozen cables-length away. Slowly, slowly we clawed off that ugly reef. For more than an hour the issue was in gravest doubt; then hope began to revive as the good ship's weatherly qualities became manifest, and it was plain to all that we were drawing clear. The breeze now began to take off a bit, and more sail was made. Without any further incident, we ran steadily up-channel to Point Lynas, where we got a pilot and a tug, which by daylight brought us safely to an anchorage in the Mersey. We only anchored for an hour or two, waiting for high water, when we were coaxed into the Brunswick Dock, and made solidly fast on the side next the street. As soon as ever I could do so unobserved, I slipped down a fender lanyard and touched England with my feet, feeling a delightful thrill as I did so. Why, I did not know, but the fact remains. A homeless, friendless waif, with no prospects before me, no one to welcome me, I rejoiced to be in England again, as if I, too, felt it good to be at home.

120

A huge sea rose between us, hiding her from view, and when we

soared on the crest of the next one she was gone like a foam flake.

CHAPTER VIII.

STRUGGLES IN LIVERPOOL AND LONDON.

In a very short time all hands had left the ship but myself. A decrepit old man arrived from somewhere to act as watchman; but he took no notice of me, and I made no advances. Not a word had been said to me by anybody when they left the ship, and I was greatly in doubt as to whether I was supposed to clear out like everybody else. But I was very sure that I did not know where to go, and so I coiled myself up in my bunk and went to sleep, as it was getting late. When I woke it was morning. A heavy fall of snow had covered everything during the night, and the outlook was as desolate and dreary as could be imagined. Making my way aft, I found the cabin all locked up; so that, though I was ravenously hungry, there was no chance of getting anything to eat. The ancient watchman was fast asleep in the galley, into which I stole to warm my freezing bare feet. As soon as I got the chill out of my bones I returned to the fo'lk'sle, and found, to my delight, an old pair of boots that one of the chaps had discarded. With these and some rags I covered my aching feet, and then, mounting on the rail, looked long and eagerly shorewards. Presently I made out, over the window of a small shop, the legend, "Brunswick Dock Eating-house," and noted with satisfaction a feather of smoke curling from one of the chimneys belonging to the building. Hardly stopping to think, I slipped down a rope and ran across the road, knocking boldly at the door. A ruddy-faced little girl about my own age opened it, and said, hesitatingly, "What d'you want?" Trying to look big, I said, "I'm a sailor belonging to that ship there, an' I want to come an' lodge here till I'm paid off." With a doubtful glance at my beggarly outfit, she said, "I'll go and call aunty," and ran off upstairs. There was a glorious fire roaring in a great open fireplace at the end of the low flagged room, so, without waiting permission, I entered, and seated myself on a bench close to the bright blaze. In a few minutes a sharp, business-like woman came down. In response to her keen questions I told my story, carefully avoiding any reference to my "passenger" status on board. Apparently she was satisfied, for in a very short time I was supplied with such a breakfast as had long haunted my hungry dreams. Rashers of toasted bacon, boiled eggs, new bread-and-butter, fragrant coffee—it was just heavenly. All my miseries were forgotten in present joys, and I ate and ate until, suddenly looking up, I saw the little girl gazing at me with awe. No wonder she was astonished. The way I was demolishing the food was a sight to see. But, meeting my eye, she blushed crimson, and gabbled something in a strange tongue (which I afterwards learned was Welsh) to her aunt, who stood also looking at me with a good-humoured smile on her face.

Being warmed and fed, two satisfactory experiences to which I had long been a stranger, I was in no hurry to leave such comfortable quarters for the bleak outer world. But during the morning I ran over to the ship, and finding there the cook, I learned that she was to be paid off the next day. I determined to present myself with the rest at the shipping-office, although my hopes of getting any money were very faint. Still I knew enough of the world to be certain that, without money, I should not be allowed to remain at my present lodgings. So at the appointed hour I marched up to the Sailors' Home, meeting with a cordial welcome from my shipmates, especially the little Frenchman. Better still, as each of them received their money, they very kindly gave me a little, the total amount thus contributed being twenty-two shillings. Then came my turn to appear at the pay table. My heart beat fast with apprehension as I faced Captain Jones, my head only just appearing above the counter. His words were gruff and his manner unkind, but I believe he was moved with pity for my forlorn position, for he actually gave me two pounds ten shillings, pay at the rate of one pound a month. I was so glad that I knew not what to say, but I hastily retreated lest he should change his mind and take the money away again. As fast as my legs would carry me, I ran back to the boarding-house to exhibit my wealth to the landlady. I had never had so much money of my own before, and was proportionately elated, the thought of how much I needed it never entering my head. The landlady immediately suggested that I should treat her and her crony from next door, who was in conversation with her, at which proposition I felt quite a man, and inquired loftily what the ladies would take. A little drop of "Donovans" appeared to be the favourite liquor, a totally unknown beverage to me, but I should have agreed had it been champagne. The little niece was dispatched for it, as well as a couple of bottles of ginger-beer for us, who were too young and wise to thirst for "Donovans"—which I knew, as soon as it arrived, to be rum.

To do my landlady justice, she interested herself in getting me some decent clothing, and promised to keep me on what remained of my money until I got another ship or some employment ashore. But getting a ship, I found, was an impossible task. My diminutive size and weakly appearance obtained for me only derision when I ventured to ask for a berth on what I considered likely-looking craft, and it soon appeared hopeless to look in that direction any more. Help came from an unexpected quarter. Next door to my lodging-place was the workshop of a figure-head carver, who was a young, energetic man of great skill, and very intimate with my landlady. He was kind enough to employ me in his business, where I soon became useful in sharpening tools and roughing-out work for him and his brother to finish. He paid me sufficient for my board and lodging, which, considering that he was teaching me his trade, was very generous. Here I was quite happy, for my new master was kindness itself; and I believe I was really quick to profit by all I was taught, so as to be worth my pay. But my evil genius pursued me still. His brother became jealous of the attentions I received, and, after I had been with them a couple of months, quarrels between them on my account were of almost daily occurrence. This unsatisfactory state of things culminated in my getting knocked senseless one morning by my enemy during his brother's absence at a job. When Mr. R. returned he was alarmed at my appearance, for I had an ugly cut on the head which made me look quite ghastly. A tremendous row followed, the upshot of which was that Mr. R. sorrowfully informed me that he was obliged to send me away before serious harm was done. He advised me to return to London, where I was better known(?), and gave me ten shillings to pay my fare thither. I took his advice forthwith, finding no difficulty in getting a half ticket to Euston, where I arrived with two shillings and sixpence in my pocket.

The well-known streets looked strange to me after my long absence. In fact, I felt more in the way than ever. I knew nobody that could or would shelter me, and I had got out of the way of street life. Husbanding my scanty store of coppers as well as I could, I haunted Thames Street in the hope that I might pick up a coaster at the King's Head, where, in those days, skippers of small craft used to get most of their crews. There is a cook-shop with a tank of pea-soup in the window, where for a penny I could always get a bellyfull of the thick, comforting stuff—the best value for money in the grub line that I knew of, and I was no bad judge. It—the tank—used to be cleaned out every three days, and a fresh jorum of soup made. On the first day it was comparatively thin; on the second, being filled up without removing the solid matter settled at the bottom, it was better; but on the third day you could almost cut it—a spoon would stand upright in it. And, anxious to clear it out, they gave bigger penn'orths. I often used to go without on the second day, so that I could have two separate portions on the third; after which I felt as bloated as an alderman after a civic feast. But the pence failed, and I picked up very few more; so that, though I slept in any hole or corner I could find, to avoid the expense of lodgings, the time soon came when I was face to face with starvation again. Then a bright idea occurred to me, so obvious that I wondered why it hadn't struck me before. I had my discharge from the *Sea Gem.* I would seek a kindly boarding-master, and ask him to keep me till I got a ship, paying himself out of my advance. I knew better than to go to the so-called "Sailors' Home." They don't take in hard-up seamen there. It is only a home for those who can pay down for their accommodation.

With my fortunate idea burning in my mind, I hastened down the West India Dock Road, attacking the first house I saw with "boarding-house for seamen" painted up over it. The proprietor, an old bo'sun, grumbled at my request a good deal, but he took me in, God bless him! More than that, he got me a ship three days after by means of his influence that way, and once again I was freed from the misery of being masterless. The vessel in which I was to sail was a splendid barque, reminding me strongly of the luckless *Discoverer*, and about the same size. I shall call her the *Bonanza*, for reasons of my own, though that was not her name. She was bound to a port in Jamaica, with a general cargo for new owners, and with a new captain and officers. When we came up to sign on at "Green's Home," I found, to my delight, that I was to have twenty shillings a month. Like all the rest, I received a month's advance, out of which my boarding-master paid himself, and provided me with a "donkey's breakfast" (straw-bed), hook-pot, pannikin, and plate; a knife, and a suit of oilskins. So *he* didn't rob me to any great extent. He also gave me a few odds and ends of clothing, which had been left by boarders, out of which, being a fair hand with my needle, I managed to botch up enough garments to change. I bade him good-bye with hearty feelings of gratitude, which he fully deserved, and took my departure on board my ship.

CHAPTER IX.

BOUND FOR JAMAICA.

All hands had been ordered on board in the afternoon, the tide serving about five p.m., but from some unexplained cause we did not sail at the time appointed. This delay led to complications, for although the crew had, for a wonder, come on board fairly sober, they all rejoiced at the opportunity afforded them of a last carouse. By some mysterious means some money was obtained; all hands departed for the purlieus of Shadwell, with the result that at ten o'clock the officers were scouring the slums hunting for them. It was a hopeless task, as the event proved, for by midnight only two had been found, and they were both helplessly drunk. They were dragged on board like bundles of rags, and hoisted into their bunks, where they remained in peace. That tide being lost, the officers had a few hours' rest, turning out again about four a.m. to renew the search. Meanwhile the vessel was shifted into the Shadwell Basin, ready to start the moment her crew were on board. The morning broke cheerlessly enough with a light fall of snow, gradually increasing to a blinding mist of white, through which occasionally a little party came dragging some oblivious mariner, who had spent his respite in filling himself with whatever fire-water he could obtain. At last, weary of waiting, the skipper determined to go on, although he was still two men short. Accordingly the warps were cast off, the tug backed in and took hold of us, and away we went down the river through the thick veil of snow that made the "mud pilot's" job both difficult and dangerous. There was another boy besides me, a burly fellow of sixteen, who very soon made it clear to me that I was not going to lead a pleasant time with him. He had come from the *Warspite*, and knew nothing of the ways of merchant-ships, which gave me a little advantage over him in one way. But he was well provided with plenty of warm clothing, by the bounty of the Marine Society, while I was so thinly clad that the piercing cold benumbed all my faculties, and I crawled about like a snail, making a very bad impression upon the officers. Our arrival at Gravesend came as a blessed relief, for there was a good hot meal of fresh food ready as soon as the anchor was down. And as all the seamen were in a deep, drunken slumber, Bill, my colleague, and myself had a mighty feed all to ourselves, after which we turned in, and slept unmolested till supper-time. The skipper had gone ashore to get a couple of men in place of the defaulters, and did not return till after dark. He brought two sober seamen with him, who looked as though they had been outward-bound for a very long time. Their cheeks were quite hollow with hunger, and they had hardly more clothing than they stood in. Yet they were both able men, proving indeed the best seamen on board. After they had eaten a good meal, they were set to keep anchor-watch turn about, until at midnight all hands were called to man the windlass.

I wish it was possible to give my readers an idea of the misery involved in this operation under such conditions. First of all, the officers were obliged to drag the sodden sleepers from their lairs; then to shake, if possible, some gleam of sense into them, some faint idea of what was required of them. After nearly an hour's struggle, the miserable men were at last mustered on the fo'lk'sle head at the windlass levers, where, exposed to the full fury of the bitter wind, they cowered more like sheep than men. Their feelings, as the drink died out of them, and the cold searched their very vitals, must have been horrible. Occasionally one of them would slip down gently from the fo'lk'sle and disappear, only to be hunted up again by the vigorous boatswain, who kept a watchful eye upon any would-be skulkers. More by dint of the bo'sun's energy, I believe, than any vitality in the limp crew, the anchor was at last lifted, the hawser passed to the hovering tug, and away we glided ghost-like down-stream. Ben, the big boy, and myself were pretty well fagged out with hauling back the big links of cable, and stowing them in neat fakes abaft the windlass; but the bo'sun believed in keeping boys on the go, so we got no time to think about being tired. Luckily for us the wind was dead on end, so that it was useless making sail. All hands were kept busily employed clearing up the decks, getting the running-gear into its proper places, and generally preparing the ship for independent travelling. By daylight the weather grew better, the wind veered to the eastward a little, and the fore-and-aft sails were set. So we drew slowly round to the North Foreland, where the tug slipped our hawser; all sail was set, and we were fairly started on our voyage. As I got a little warmth into my stiffened limbs, I won back some of the good opinion I had forfeited by my clumsy, spiritless movements of the previous day. Being sent aloft to loose some of the square sails, I was cheered by hearing the elderly mate remark quietly, "That's a smart little boy," and I must confess I was not displeased to note that Ben only succeeded in drawing down maledictions on his head for his clumsiness and general inability to do what was required of him. There was a vengeful gleam in his eye, as he saw how inferior he was in smartness to myself, which boded no good to me, and from the first day out he never lost an opportunity of doing me an ill turn.

The captain was a fine, manly specimen of a seaman, with glowing red hair and beard, and a voice of thunder. Fiery tempered, yet easily pacified, he was also one of the most energetic of men, and I never saw a skipper better liked by his crew. The mate was a middle-aged man, at least ten years the captain's senior, rather slow and sedate, but a thorough seaman and navigator. The bo'sun, who was acting second mate, was an old shipmate of the skipper's, and quite his equal in energy. He was one of that fast-decaying type of seamen, a Blackwall rigger, to whom every detail of sailorizing was as familiar as eating his breakfast. Besides this, he was a born leader of men, who would enforce his will regardless of consequences. No man durst give him "slack lip" on pain of being instantly knocked endways; a feat of which, by reason of his size and strength, he was fully capable. As a result we were a well-disciplined crowd, from whom no growling was heard whatever the work imposed. There were eight A.B.'s, out of whom only three were foreigners; but not one of them calls for any special description from me. They all had the bad old idea that boys were born slaves, who must do all the dirty work on deck, and when below be content with their leavings, wait upon them hand and foot, and take uncomplainingly all the ill-treatment it was their prerogative to bestow. Being at the bottom of the scale, I had a wretched life. For I was no match for Ben, who unfailingly passed on his share of blows to me, so that I was seldom without some visible marks of ill-usage. But the food was certainly above the average. The skipper had the provisioning of the ship, and, being a just man, he did not do as so many would have done under the same circumstances: starve the men to fatten his own pocket. What with the decent meals, and the masterfulness of the bo'sun, she was a contented ship, and more work was done in a day on board than I have ever seen before or since. As usual on this passage, fine weather prevailed, the wind being so steady that for days together we never touched a brace. This was taken advantage of by the skipper to practically refit the ship, all hands being kept at work all day long splicing, turning-in blocks, serving shrouds, fitting new running-gear, and doing rigger's work generally. At night they all slept, with the exception of the helmsman, the look-out man, the officer of the watch and a boy, who had to keep near the officer to carry his commands to the sleepers should the need arise. Really I was kept so constantly at work that, for all I saw of the sea and its marvels, I might as well have been ashore. Except at night, and then I was always half asleep through getting so little legitimate opportunity for rest.

Twenty-eight days flew rapidly past without a single incident worth noting, the same blue sky overhead, and steady breeze astern, until one morning the beautiful shores of Jamaica loomed up ahead. A few hours later we sailed in between the points of a sheltering coral reef to an anchorage in the pretty little harbour of Falmouth, pompously announcing our arrival by the firing of a four-pounder gun as the anchor was dropped. While we were furling sails and clearing up the decks, visitors were arriving from the four vessels in harbour as well as from the shore, so that by the time work was over our decks were thronged. The skipper seemed a prime favourite here, judging by the number of people who came to see him and congratulate him upon his new command—the largest vessel that had yet entered the little port. There were high times forrard as well as aft, for canoe-loads of good things were brought, and all hands invested recklessly on credit, forgetting that as yet they had no money owing to them by the ship. Not only eatables but sundry bottles of new rum made their appearance, which potent fluid soon made things exceedingly lively in the fo'lk'sle. Matters culminated, of course, in a free fight, which so alarmed me that I crept into a corner under the heel of the bowsprit, out of the way of the revellers. There I went to sleep so soundly that it was morning when I again emerged at the hoarse cry of the boatswain calling us to "turn to."

The darkies here were even merrier than my old friends of Demerara. Such a jovial, musical lot I never saw. Living from hand to mouth on the coarsest food, and with the oddest assortment of rags for clothing possible to be imagined, they really seemed to be perfectly happy. The feeblest joke was sufficient to send them into convulsions of laughter, and the gift of an old shirt or pair of pants would keep them on the broad grin for a couple of days. My life was so consistently miserable from harsh treatment, that I continually envied them their careless existence, wondering all the time how they managed to be so jolly under what I often saw to be painful circumstances. To crown my misfortunes I fell ill. After suffering for two or three days, I was sent ashore to hospital. Then I was thankful for what I had thought the climax of my misery. For in the hospital I was allowed to do pretty well as I liked. There was no discipline, no rule of any kind. The doctor, as we called him (I think he must have been the dispenser), was a mulatto, or quadroon, with a comical notion of his vast importance, but a kindly young fellow enough. Sometimes I had medicine; but only by accident, I believe. At any rate, I soon got better, and rambled about the great building or played on the beach outside with the darky boys of about my own age, forgetting that such a place as the *Bonanza's* fo'lk'sle existed. At last I began to hope that the captain had forgotten my existence, having some dim idea, I suppose, that I might be allowed to spend an indefinite time in this pleasant way. But I was to be rudely undeceived. One day, when I was presiding with much importance over a game at cricket (much I knew about it), with twenty or thirty youngsters of almost as many shades of colour around me, I suddenly heard my captain calling me, with an angry note in his voice that boded me no good. He had come up from the town to inquire about me, and had caught me unaware. "You lazy young sodjer!" he cried, "this is how sick you are, is it? I'll give you a lesson for this! Get down to the boat!" The thought of returning to the ship was so terrible to me that I actually dared to ask him to let me go—to discharge me. In a voice that shook with fear and anxiety I told him how I had been treated, and implored him not to take me back with him. I believe he was half-melted, but his anger at what he thought was my skulking got the better of him. "Serve you very well right," he said. "I'll give you a rope's-ending myself when I've got time. Now be off with you, straight down to the boat." With that he strode on to the hospital, while I, feeling as if I was going to the scaffold, trudged through the sand down to the landing-place. In about an hour he returned, but said no word more to me as the boat danced over the wavelets back to that hateful prison. It was "knock-off" time, and I busied myself in sweeping up decks with all the alacrity I could muster, until I was free to fetch my many masters their tea from the galley. They hailed me with many sarcastic queries after my health, and the noble time they supposed I had enjoyed ashore at their expense, commiserating Ben exceedingly for having been obliged to do my work, as they said, while I had been loafing ashore. Happily I got over the evening without anything worse than hard words being thrown at me. Some grievance or another had excited the anger of a big Irishman, and he soon monopolized all attention by a recital of his wrongs. It appeared that the bo'sun had "got a down on him," in his opinion; but if the bo'sun thought that he, Mike, was going to be played with, that was just where he was all adrift. He, Mike, was a blank Fenian, so he was, an' he'd just shwim in blood before he was put upon by any blank dock-walloper that ever mooched around Blackwall, so he would. In the fervour of his harangue he omitted to notice how he had raised his voice; but he was presently reminded of it by the voice of the bo'sun at the fo'lk'sle door, calling, "Mike, I want you a minute!" There was complete silence in a moment, which reigned until the bo'sun repeated his words, with the quiet addition, "You don't want me to fetch you out, I s'pose?" Then Mike protested feebly that it was his watch below, that he was having his supper, that various reasons, in fact, prevented him from emerging. Like a tiger the bo'sun leapt into the crowded space. There was a medley of arms, heads, and legs, a hubbub of inarticulate noises, but out of it all the bo'sun and Mike emerged on deck. How they got there, I don't believe any one knew. I heard the bo'sun imploring Mike to stand up to him like a man, and Mike piteously reminding him that he was by no means his match, that he was twenty years older (which was nearly true). "Very well, then," said the boss, "not so much of your slack next time. If you're an old man, behave like one, an' don't open your mouth so wide, in case anybody jumps down your throat." There was peace after that. Not even a word was said to me when I ventured to crawl into the raffle of rags which was my bunk.

At daylight next morning all hands were called to get under way. In the cabin the skipper had been entertaining a large party of friends, who had been keeping up an extensive carouse all night. Uproariously they departed their several ways as we toiled at the windlass, while boats from all the other vessels in port came and fastened on to us to assist us out from between the reefs. Such aid was absolutely necessary unless the miserably slow method of warping out by a kedge-anchor was resorted to. For in these West Indian ports there is invariably, during the night, a gentle air from the land, which soon after daybreak dies away to a complete calm, lasting perhaps an hour, and succeeded by the invigorating "doctor," or sea-breeze. This latter soon gathers strength and blows more or less forcibly all day long. In consequence of this it becomes imperative to gain an offing before the "doctor" begins, in order that the vessel may be able to fetch off the land in the teeth of an increasing breeze.

Having assisted us to get about two miles out, the boats cast off from us, and with many hearty farewells returned to port, taking with them our pilot. A stark calm succeeded as usual, during which all hands lounged about and whistled for a breeze, until some of the keener observers noticed that the strong undertow was sweeping us rapidly towards a long spit of sand that stretched seaward, about three miles to the northward of us. Presently the mate's anxiety constrained him to approach the captain, who, with flushed face and abstracted air, was pacing the poop, and suggest that the anchors might be prepared for letting go. Strange to say, the skipper received this hint with a bad grace, answering his officer so abruptly and angrily that his words were distinctly audible all over the ship. The mate, whose age and experience, apart from his other undeniably good qualities, entitled him to very different treatment, bowed and retired, evidently much hurt. A short period of silence followed, while the vessel, her sails hanging as if carved in stone, and her hull motionless, as if in dry dock, was being carried along over the now visible coral bottom at the rate of nearly four knots an hour. At last the bo'sun, unable to contain himself, strode up to the captain and said boldly, "Cap'n——, if you don't anchor this ship'll be ashore in another ten minutes." "Get off my poop, you impudent rascal! How dare you come an' speak to me like that! For two pins I'd put you in irons. D'ye think I don't know my duty? I never heard such cheek in my life!" and he stamped with fury. But the bo'sun simply said, "Well, don't you say you wasn't warned, that's all," and, turning on his heel, left the angry, unreasonable man to himself. By this time all hands were fully possessed of the idea that only a miracle could save the ship, for the reef seemed to be actually touching the keel through the clear water which was carrying us so swiftly over it. And the idea of the vessel's loss filled me with unholy joy. No one could realize how terribly I dreaded the homeward passage, and, now that deliverance seemed so near, I could hardly restrain my feelings. Slinking into the empty forecastle, I waited breathlessly for the crash I felt sure was imminent. It came, a long grinding sensation, like a boat grounding on a pebbly beach magnified a thousand times. Almost delirious, I danced about the place, in the middle of which unpardonable exercise I was discovered by the bo'sun. Outraged beyond speech, he dealt me one savage kick, which put all dancing out of my power for many a day, and for the present stretched me motionless on the deck. Not, however, to lie there long, for hearing my name shouted outside, I dragged myself up, mustering all my energy, and hobbled off to obey the call before some worse thing should befall me.

I found all hands toiling like ants, getting out anchors and hawsers, and doing all that experience could suggest to free the vessel from the position of danger into which she had been brought so recklessly. But the calm was over, the sea-breeze had commenced, and was increasing so fast that already the hitherto placid sea was beginning to foam. Breakers, too, born of the jagged reef so close to the surface, were rolling in steadily, although as yet they were of puny height and weight. Being at so short a distance from the port we had left, our plight was plainly visible to those on shore. Consequently, in a couple of hours, every boat of sufficient size in the place was alongside. Scores of willing hands plied every means by which good might be done, but the steady increase in wind and sea, driving directly shoreward, mocked all efforts at heaving the ship off. There were no steam vessels either in Falmouth or the adjacent ports, so that, when every purchase that could be got upon the anchors and cables laid out astern was brought to a standstill, that branch of the work was perforce abandoned.

Then the cargo was attacked at all three hatches, everybody working as if their very lives depended upon their labours. The negroes especially seemed to regard the whole affair as a gigantic spree, for without abating one jot of their labours, they yelled, sang, danced about, and behaved generally like a pack of schoolboys just let loose without any supervision. As the day wore on the wind increased to a strong gale, and the rollers attained so formidable a height that at times they lifted the vessel bodily from her jagged bed of rock, letting her fall again with a crash that threatened to shake all her stout timbers apart. After each of these blows she seemed to slide seawards a little, but all her buoyancy was gone—the stern went down at an increasing angle, and the water rose in the hold so freely that it was evident there were some serious gaps in the hull. Still the work went on. Drogher after drogher left us filled with salvage, while others crowded as near as they dared to receive the bags, cases and bundles, that were constantly being hurled overside. By nightfall all our own crew were worn out, and transferred to one of the small craft which clung to our side receiving the salved cargo. Each man secured what he could of his poor belongings, but I, being unable in the scramble and confusion to get hold of the few rags composing my stock of clothing, contented myself with carrying off an old wide-awake hat containing five blind kittens. The anxious mother kept me close company, much to the amusement of the toiling darkies.

All through the night the wind maintained a most unusual force, and hour by hour the work of salvage became increasingly difficult. Every package had to be dived for into the blackness of the hold, which was quite full of water up to the hatch-coamings. Great torches of tarred rope, lashed to conspicuous points, roared and flared in the gale. By their uncertain glare the black toilers darted hither and thither with astounding energy and a deafening incessant tumult of wild song. Every one was mother-naked, and their ebony skins shone like those of a school of gambolling porpoises. At each tremendous lift and heave of the doomed vessel all hands would make a frantic rush to the side, leaping with blood-curdling yells into the waiting droghers. But the instant it was seen that she yet survived the shock, back they all came and attacked the cargo with renewed vigour. At last a bigger breaker than ever came along, rearing its hoary crest against the paling sky. Reaching the vessel, it enwrapped her in masses of shining foam, lifting her at the same time with such power that for half a minute she seemed all afloat. As it receded, the ill-used hulk, as if loth to leave its embrace, slid along the reef with a rending crash, nor stopped until all that remained visible of her was the jibboom, pointing upward to the sky like a warning beacon. In the whirl of weltering foam left by her sudden exit, the droghers danced like mad things, all having been cut adrift as the yelling crowd sprang from the sinking ship. As nothing more could possibly be done for the present, the little fleet made sail, and stood in towards the town with their spoil. In every conceivable and inconceivable position the utterly wearied negroes lay about asleep, regardless of the flying spray or such minor inconveniences as being trampled upon by the crews. I found a snug corner out of everybody's way, and there, cuddling my cats, I, too, fell into sweet oblivion. When I awoke, the vessel was just taking the beach in front of the town. The sun was only just rising, but all the population of Falmouth appeared to be there, and intensely solicitous for our welfare. We were immediately taken to the "hotel," only a few hundred yards away, and all manner of creature comforts pressed upon us with kindly persistence, as if we had been adrift for a month. Suddenly I realized that I was quite a centre of attraction—the fact of my having rescued the kittens appearing to appeal to all the visitors in a way that I should hardly have believed possible. But, indeed, our reception generally was so kind that we were all in danger of being spoiled. Within the memory of the oldest inhabitant no wreck of such importance had occurred near the port, and consequently, I suppose, we reaped the benefit of long-suppressed benevolence.

146

At each tremendous lift and heave of the doomed vessel all hands would make a frantic rush to the side.

CHAPTER X.

ADVENTURES OF A SHIPWRECKED CREW.

The hotel to which we had been brought upon our arrival was, although the only one in the place, far too small to stand the strain of such an influx of visitors as we were, as far as sleeping accommodation went. Therefore arrangements were made for our lodgment in an empty house in town, while for all meals we were to return to the hotel. To this sheltering place we were escorted by a delighted band of darkies, who insisted upon carrying such traps as we possessed, and also worked like bees to sweep and cleanse the house. Such bedding as we had was spread upon the floor in a big front-room, and in Oriental fashion; with the sailor's ready adaptability to circumstances, we made ourselves comfortable. We had plenty of company, for the whole coloured population made holiday and visited us. Few came empty handed, the majority bringing such gifts as they thought would please us: mostly fruit, tobacco, and rum. There was such abundance of the latter, that by dinner-time there was a universal debauch, from which I gladly escaped. Making my way down to the beach I found the work of salvage in full swing, for the hull of the ship had broken apart so much that the floatable cargo was coming ashore in great quantities. Puncheons of rum, bundles of walking-sticks, cakes of bees-wax and innumerable cocoa-nuts were heaped in scattered piles upon the beach, each of which was guarded by some one, whose allies were either scouring the shores or paddling furiously after some piece of flotsam apparently worth pursuit. Everywhere I found friends. Such a godsend as this had not fallen to the lot of the dusky Falmouthians before, and they were willing to recognise even the humblest member of the crew as in some sense a benefactor. When I got tired of roaming about the beach, I sought the hotel for something more satisfying than fruit, and was received by the host's buxom daughter, Marian, with great delight. She had taken charge of my hatful of kittens, and showed me, with manifest pride, how comfortable the old cat and her blind progeny had been made. Ungrateful puss would hardly recognise me, her changed circumstances had made her forget old but humble friends.

Noticing that I limped considerably, Marian inquired anxiously whether I had cut my foot, which made me smile, since, not having worn boots for months, my natural soles were almost as hard as tanned leather. But I admitted that there was something hurting me a great deal, upon which she peremptorily ordered me to sit down while she had a look. A short search resulted in her finding the place, which she proceeded to investigate with a needle, and presently drew therefrom a bag about as large as a marrowfat pea, which she opened, and showed me was full of tiny eggs. "You'se had dem chigoes mighty bad, chile," she said, "but I gwineter put stop to 'em right now." With that she went and fetched a tub of warm water. After bathing my feet thoroughly, she searched most carefully for more of these pests, finding two other nests, full like the first, of eggs, but which had caused me only a slight itching sensation. Having removed all she could see, she made a vile compound of tobacco-ash and kerosene, which she rubbed into the wounds, causing me exquisite pain. It took all my fortitude to keep from screaming, and I was unable to prevent a few big tears dropping. With many strange words of endearment she assured me of her sympathy, but declared this heroic treatment to be the only way of effecting a radical cure. I have no doubt that she firmly believed in her treatment, and I must admit that in the end it was certainly effectual; but it was so harsh that I was quite crippled for over a week. During this miserable time I was a close prisoner in our empty house, being generally alone during the day, while through most of the night the drunken antics of my shipmates kept me in constant terror. Nevertheless there was some slight consolation, for by some means it had got about that I could sing, and I was sent for by the officers of the garrison to warble some of my simple ditties for their amusement. As I was unable to walk, the messengers made a rude litter, upon which they carried me to the hotel, where I was propped up in an armchair while I sang. The generosity of the officers provided me with plenty of money, unfortunately of no service to me, since I dared not refuse the constant demands of my shipmates, who, of course, had none of their own. I made two or three friends among the better-class people in the town, who gave me quite a respectable bag of half-worn clothes, and also promised their aid in other directions.

At last, after the lapse of three weeks, during which time a perfunctory sort of inquiry into the loss of the vessel was held, and the captain acquitted of all blame, it was decided to send all the crew round to Kingston, whence we might get shipped home. A small schooner was chartered for this purpose, as no steamers ran round the island; and after considerable delay, provisions for three days were put on board, and we set sail, doubtless much to the relief of those worthies who had been obliged to feed such a hungry horde as we were. But, to our great disgust, we found at the first meal-time that, in addition to the stock of food being disgracefully small, it consisted solely of ship-biscuit, yams, and salt beef of the worst sort. If the kind providers of this outfit could have been affected by the maledictions of our party, they certainly would not have survived the first day of our voyage; after that, the subject dropped from very monotony. Calms and light airs prevailed, and all faces began to lengthen when, on the evening of the third day, the cook announced that the last of the supply of food was before us for supper, while our passage was only beginning. Luckily a young shark was caught, making us a meagre breakfast. Then hunger stared us in the face. We were at least fifteen miles off the land, with a dead calm, and nothing but water left to supply the needs of fourteen hungry men. No fish came to our hooks, no vessels came near us, and, as there was nothing whatever to occupy the men's minds, the subject of food-supply was soon discussed threadbare. Then, as often happens among crews similarly situated, the possibility of there being a Jonah among us was mooted, and called forth an amazing variety of opinions and reminiscences. Unhappily for me, the bo'sun was indiscreet enough to let out the story of my behaviour at the time of the vessel's striking on the reef. He told it laughingly, referring, with a good deal of satisfaction, to the swinging kick he had dealt me, the bruise from which had not even then disappeared. But the effect of his statement upon those ignorant and frightened men was most strange and significant. They accepted it without question as positive proof: first, that all their misfortunes were due to the presence of a Jonah among them, and, secondly, that I was that Jonah!

It may be found difficult of belief that, among the crew of a London ship in the year 1871, such a thing should have been possible; but I solemnly declare it to be true that they at once decided that unless I were cast overboard they would never reach Kingston. I was immediately seized by them and commanded to say my prayers quickly, as I had only a few minutes to live. I looked at those cruel, brutish faces and saw no gleam of pity; I cried for mercy in incoherent terms while they only scowled. With trembling lips, and scarcely beating heart, I tried to do as they told me—say my prayers; but my senses were fast leaving me, and I do not really know what I did say. Then one of them tied my hands behind my back with a bit of fishing-line; and this act first seemed to awaken the three negroes, who were the crew of the schooner, to the fact that murder was intended. It almost drove them crazy with fear and horror. Regardless of the odds against them, they rushed to my rescue, only to be beaten back with the assurance that little would make my tormenters serve them the same. The bitterness of death was almost past, when, to my unbounded amazement, and renewing all my hopes of life, help came from the most unexpected quarter. The bo'sun, who, I do not think, had realized himself how far in earnest they were until then, suddenly bestirred himself, making one stride across the deck to where I lay, hardly conscious. Oh, how god-like I thought him! The scene returns to me across the chasm of years as vividly as a photograph. His manly figure, erect before my poor little shrinking body, and the sweep of his strong right arm as he drove those bloodthirsty pagans back, will never fade from my mind. "That's enough now," he said, "ye —— idiots. Did ye think I was goin' ter let yer drown the kid? S'elp me, ef I thought yer really meant it, damfi wouldn't drown two or three of ye meself, ye yelpin' cowardly scum!" For a short minute or so they faced him, their eyes glaring with the lust of superstitious cruelty, and then (it should be remembered that there were ten of them) they slank away, muttering blasphemies between their clenched teeth. With a bitter laugh of derision he stooped and cut my hands adrift from the lashing, and then resumed his pipe as if nothing extraordinary had happened. It hardly needs saying that I cowered close to his side, nor did I once get out of arm's length of him during the remainder of that passage.

Happily for us a breeze sprang up, sending the schooner bustling along at a good rate into the harbour of Savannah Le Mar, where we arrived late that evening. By some means or other, which I don't understand, considering our penniless condition, a good supply of yams, salt fish, and water was obtained, and we set sail again at about ten p. m. by the light of the incandescent moon. Our troubles were at an end for the time, the wind holding strong and fair; so that in less than forty-eight hours we were running in swiftly past Port Royal and up to the wharves at Kingston.

It probably had never occurred to any one of us to doubt that when we arrived there it would be all plain sailing for us. As shipwrecked seamen, and in a British port, we naturally supposed that all we needed to do was to march in a body to the Sailors' Home, show our credentials, and be received with the warmest of welcomes. And the rest of our stay, until ships were found for us to go home again in, would, of course, be one delightful round of eating, drinking, and sleeping, varied by such amusements as the place afforded. Accordingly, every man shouldered his belongings, and off we marched, guided by friendly darkies, to the Sailors' Home, which we entered with the air of proprietors. It was a fine, large building, with a double row of verandahs and an air of coolness and comfort extremely grateful to us after our miserable trip in the schooner. We were received with great courtesy, and shown to the dormitory, which, with its rows of clean beds and white mosquito-curtains, looked like fairyland. We were told that breakfast would be ready in a few minutes; so all hands had a good wash, hastening down grubwards at the first stroke of the welcome bell. There appeared to be scarcely any other boarders; at any rate, there were none visible then. Coffee and bread were brought, and then a white man came, who introduced himself as the superintendent. He called our attention to the fact that there were three tariffs here, according to the kind of food desired, and wished to know which of them we would choose. The bo'sun replied that, as we were the guests of our country, we might as well have the best, and added that, as we were somewhat sharp-set, the sooner we got it the happier we should be. "Oh," said the official; "if that's the case, I'm afraid I can't take you in. I've had no orders; and our rule here is payment in advance." Blank amazement overspread every face, and half a dozen voices volubly attempted to explain the situation. But to all remarks, remonstrances, and objurgations, the superintendent was adamant. He had no doubt it was all true enough; but he had no instructions on our behalf, and, until he had, we could either pay or go. When asked who we ought to apply to, he was blandly ignorant; but it was increasingly evident that he wanted us gone very badly.

157

For a short minute or so they faced him, their eyes glaring with the lust of superstitious cruelty.

Well, there was no help for it, and so, breakfastless and dispirited, we started off again to the town, intending to go to the shipping-office, as the only place we could think of. In a foreign port we should, of course, have gone to the consul at once; but here, under our own flag, no one knew what to do. Our escort of negroes grew quite imposing as we trudged along, and the news of our reception passed from mouth to mouth. Floods of advice were poured upon us by our sable friends, and offers of hospitality also without limit. Indeed, had any of our crowd been orators, there seemed to be all the materials necessary for a very decent riot. But, peaceably enough, we reached the shipping-office, where we asked humbly if we might see his high-mightiness the shipping-master. After keeping us waiting for nearly an hour, this gentleman came out, and in bullying tones demanded our business. Our spokesman, the bo'sun, laid our hard case before him in a most respectful manner; but before he had finished his story the shipping-master cut him short, roughly telling him that we had no business to come there whining, and that he had nothing to do with us. And with that he ordered us out of the office. Utterly amazed and dispirited at this treatment, we retired. Upon reaching the street we were surrounded at once by the friendly darkies, who made good their previous promises by carrying all hands off to breakfast in their several huts, talking and gesticulating violently all the time. Fortunately I remembered that I had a letter of introduction to a gentleman in the town; so, refusing all offers of hospitality, I hurried off to present it. I was not very cordially received; but a note to the superintendent of the Sailors' Home was at once given me, which procured me instant admission to that institution, with a right to the best entertainment they could give.

Meanwhile the crew had formulated a plan of campaign, romantic enough, but promising well. It should be remembered that Port Royal, at the entrance to Kingston Harbour is, or was, one of our most important colonial naval stations. A huge old line-of-battle ship, called the *Aboukir*, was then the guard-ship, and lay moored opposite the dockyard at Port Royal, several miles from Kingston. A deputation of two, one of which was the bo'sun, determined to board the guard-ship and lay the case before the commodore, feeling, like all British seamen abroad, that, although not to be lightly approached, the captain of a British man-o'-war could always be depended upon to see justice done to any sailor, however humble. Accordingly, they availed themselves of a friendly fisherman's canoe, and immediately set out on their long paddle down the bay to Port Royal. At the same time the elderly Irishman before spoken of, volunteered to tramp out to Spanish Town, the residence of the Governor of Jamaica—a distance of about ten miles, as nearly as I can remember. He said he was well used to the road, having tramped between nearly every seaport in England. And so, while the majority of the crew lay around in the shade discussing the situation over and over again with a deeply interested crowd of darkies, male and female, the messenger fared forth. The Port Royal deputation reached their goal first, and, climbing up the steep side of the great guard-ship, saluted, and asked to see the commodore. They were promptly conducted aft before this officer, who listened patiently to their yarn, and did not interrupt them in its recital. When they ceased speaking, he said, "Is that all, my men?" "Yes, yer honour." "Then go forward and get some food at once, and, when you have done so, the second lieutenant will return with you. You shall be cared for. Good morning." With a salute they retreated, and, not being hungry, received a tot of grog instead. Then, to their astonishment and delight, they saw a natty little steam-launch alongside, into which they were invited to descend. A smart young lieutenant in full uniform joined them, the white-clad crew jumped in, and away they went back to Kingston. Long before they arrived at the landing-place the anxious watchers had descried them, and, when they touched land, there was quite an excited crowd ready to welcome them. Straight to the shipping-office went the lieutenant, and at his brief request the shipping-master was immediately forthcoming. Without wasting a word the lieutenant came to the point, demanding to know whether his commanding officer had been rightly informed by these men of the state of their case. As the facts were undeniable there was little reply. Sternly, scornfully, the young officer reminded the discomfited official of his obvious duty to British seamen in distress, with an expression of wonder at its being necessary for him to do so. "You will be good enough to see all these men's wants immediately attended to, and a passage home found for them at the earliest possible opportunity. The commodore trusts he will hear no more complaints of a like nature." Then, turning on his heel, the lieutenant bade our delighted fellows good day, returning to his launch amid the cheers of the darkies. A clerk was at once sent with the men to the "Home" with instructions to the superintendent, and the trouble was over.

Not so those of the unfortunate shipping-master, who must have been heartily sorry for his foolish behaviour. For late in the afternoon our other messenger returned in state from Spanish Town in one of the governor's carriages, accompanied by a secretary who bore a message from the governor that made the shipping-master quake. He could only return an abject apology, with an assurance that the shipwrecked crew were now well cared-for, and that nothing on his part should be lacking for their comfort. But, though we heard no more of the affair, I doubt very much whether the shipping-master did. From the stir the event made in Kingston, I am inclined to think it was a long time before he was permitted to forget it.

For about a fortnight I had a rattling good time in Kingston. Confident in the assurance that I should not be forgotten whenever a chance presented itself of getting away, I cast all care to the winds, and set about enjoying myself all I knew how. Moonlight fishing-excursions in ramshackle canoes to sheltered coves around the great harbour, long rambles in the wonderful brakes and jungles with darkies, that, though men in years, were children in their fresh enjoyment of everything; singing-parties along the beautiful beaches in the silky evenings, and all with never a thought of to-morrow—oh, it was heavenly! I scarcely saw anything of my shipmates. I didn't want to. My new associates, although black, were full of kindliness, and as pleased with me as I was with them; what wonder that I avoided, as far as I could, any intercourse with men whose presence only reminded me of miserable days better forgotten. Out of the many incidents that are mellowed by time into a haze of half recollection, one grotesque affair stands out sharply, and even now makes me quiver with laughter as its vivid details reappear. A favourite pastime with the *élite* of the coloured population was to gather in large numbers, dressed in all their finery, upon an old disused pier, whose crazy piles and beams actually swayed with a stronger breeze than usual. Upon this ancient structure, when the day's work was over, the young men and women would frisk or loll about, according to their humour; but their chief amusement was the singing of chanties, camp-meeting hymns, and, in fact, anything with a rousing chorus in which all hands could join. On the night in question, song had succeeded song until somebody sent an electric thrill through the whole gathering by starting the negroes' great anthem of freedom, "Marching through Georgia." You could hear the pulses of that great crowd beat while they waited breathlessly for the last word of the sonorous verse; and then, in one tremendous burst of melody, every one lifted up heart and voice, while from far-away fishermen on the bay and labourers on the hills the inspiring chorus rolled on. As verse succeeded verse the enthusiasm rose to fever-heat; every one sprang to their feet, waving their arms and stamping in unison until the crazy structure upon which they stood trembled to its ancient foundations. It was a wonderful sight, having its ludicrous side, doubtless; but the high seriousness, and irrepressible energy of the actors, prevented all desire to laugh. Suddenly, in the height of the chorus, there was a rending crash, and the entire fabric collapsed in one chaotic heap of disjointed timbers and shrieking humanity into the placid waters beneath. No one was hurt, for the tide was high, and every darky swam like a fish; but the scene of mad merriment on the beach, as one draggled figure after another emerged from the wreckage, was indescribable. Not until long after midnight did the peals of laughter entirely cease, for they rose again and again in all quarters of the town, as the participants rehearsed the scene to those who had not been fortunate enough to witness it.

I had begun to feel as if I had always lived there, and the thought of leaving had quite disappeared from my mind, when one day I received a note from the gentleman to whom I had brought the letter of introduction, telling me to go on board a large steamer, which had arrived at Kingston that morning, as he had seen the captain, and made arrangements for me to be allowed to work my passage home.

CHAPTER XI.

AN EVENTFUL PASSAGE HOME.

Now that the time of my departure drew near, the same old feeling of reluctance to leave a place to which I had become accustomed came upon me with its usual force. Possibly because I was never very long in one place, I have always, except in one instance, felt loth to begin wandering again; and, even now, my mind often turns regretfully to the many ports I have visited, and quite a painful longing seizes me to see them all again. Therefore I am afraid I did not feel nearly as grateful to my friend as I ought to have done; but, fully realizing how dangerous it was for me not to take advantage of this offer, I made myself as presentable as I could and hurried on board. The captain, a big, burly gentleman in a smart uniform, received me with a sharp glance, and dismissed me at once with a curt "All right; go and tell the chief steward I've sent you to him." I thanked him, and left the presence, very much in awe of the gorgeous surroundings and great size of everything, so different to all my previous experience of shipboard. She was a fairly large steamship for those days, I suppose of nearly three thousand tons; but to me she was vast beyond conception. When I entered the saloon, I felt utterly crushed beneath the splendour of the place—oh, how small and shabby it would look now, beside the floating palaces of to-day!—and I hardly dared to tread upon the thick carpet which was laid, the vessel being in harbour. When I found the chief steward, he cross-examined me pretty sharply as to my qualifications, etc.; but, being short-handed, he was glad of even such help as I could give, and promptly set me to work. Now, for the first time, I became acquainted with the toilsome routine of housemaid's duties which have to be performed by the steward's staff of a passenger steamer: endless dish-washing, knife and silver-cleaning, floor-scrubbing, and metal-polishing. And all the work had to be done by a staff of four, exclusive of my insignificant self; so that the chief steward had no time to play the gentleman at large that he so often appears where the manning is on a more liberal scale. Indeed, but for the second steward—a dapper Chinese, rejoicing in the most unappropriate name of "Hadji"—I don't think we could ever have kept things straight. But Hadji was a host in himself. Never in a hurry, always looking well-groomed and smart, the amount of work that this wonderful little man got through in a day was marvellous. Not more so, however, than his history, of which one episode will suffice as a sample. While working on board a large steamer of this same employ lying in Colon, there was a terrific explosion on board—whether of gunpowder or nitro-glycerine I have forgotten. Men, decks, fittings, were hurled skyward amidst a vast cloud of smoke, and the fragments fell in an immense area, extending for hundreds of yards around the unfortunate ship. When the first alarm had subsided, the stewards of an adjacent vessel returned to their tasks below, and found Hadji on the saloon table, having crashed through the skylight in his descent, but unhurt, and apparently unaffrighted. It was not easy to imagine what would disturb his smiling *sang-froid.* If in a gale of wind a heavy sea found its way below, causing the utmost hubbub and terror among the passengers, whether by night or day, Hadji would appear in the thick of the *mêlée*, calmly setting everything and everybody to rights, his pleasant smile most reassuring to behold.

But, in my admiration for this invaluable Celestial, I am forgetting current events. The day we were to sail, I was much astonished to see all my old shipmates march on board, having been sent by the shipping-master for a passage to England in his anxiety to avoid another interview with the offended powers. They were passengers in the sense that no work was expected of them; but they lived and messed with the crew. However, as we were at different ends of the ship, we did not come in contact at all, for which I was grateful. Yet, strangely enough, I got into my first and only scrape on board through them. The waste of food from the saloon table was very great; but my instructions were to throw all broken meats into a "dog-basket" at washing-up time, with all sorts of dirty odds and ends, which basket was presently emptied over the side. I managed to obtain a clean basket, into which I turned all such broken victuals as I considered worth saving, and, watching my opportunity, I carried this provender forward to my shipmates, who I knew were getting only the usual miserable fare. In this benevolent work I was discovered by the chief steward, who "clouted my ear," as he termed it, and threatened me with all sorts of pains and penalties if

I dared to so offend again. So from thenceforth all the good food not wanted aft went overboard as before.

We were bound to Liverpool *via* Port-au-Prince, in the island of Hayti, and, from a few words let fall by the passengers, I gathered that it was just possible we might see some "fun," as they termed it. I did not then know that Hayti was in the throes of a successful revolution against the sovereignty of Spain and France, which eventually resulted in the establishment of two republics in the island; one-half calling itself the republic of Hayti, the other that of St. Domingo. At that time the long struggle must have been drawing near its close, for on land the triumphant negroes had things all their own way, while at sea the fleets of France and Spain played at what they were pleased to call a blockade. Whether any vessels trading with Hayti paid any attention to the alleged blockade, I do not know; certainly we did not. Nothing at all in our proceedings would have suggested to any one that we were making for a blockaded port. Even when, as we steamed briskly up the long V-shaped gulf, at the apex of which Port-au-Prince lies, we sighted two grimlooking war-ships lying at anchor on either side of the fairway with steam up, no more notice was taken of them than the usual curiosity evinced by passengers at a strange sail. As we passed between them we could see that one was French, the other Spanish, by their ensigns flying. We rendered the usual sea-courtesy of dipping our flag, but of that no notice at all was taken by them. Doubtless, as usual, they felt none too amicably disposed towards the all-pervading *Anglais*. Right onward we steamed into the harbour, and alongside the Company's hulk, where such scant cargo as could be collected awaited us. The only other vessel lying there was a long, low steamer of perhaps 700 or 800 tons, whose raking, schooner-spars and funnel, and the light grey-blue that everything was painted, to say nothing of the miniature stars and stripes that floated from her flag-staff, spelt "Yankee filibuster" as plainly as if she had been lettered with those words in characters two feet wide. There was no sign of life on board of her, except a mere suggestion of bluish smoke, that curled slowly from her funnel, telling of banked fires below. For some time she was an object of the greatest interest to all on board, until other matters occupied all our attention.

The town was in a pitiable condition. What with the long rebellion and civil broils, in addition to the careless, happy-go-lucky fashion in which the farce of government was carried on, whole streets were in ruins; business was at a standstill, and even the few merchants who still clung to the remnants of their trade were in despair. It was no place for white men, anyhow. The negro was master of the situation. He had fought long and savagely for his independence, and now that he had got it he was drunken with it as with brandy. That careless white man who omitted, from any cause, to salute in the humblest manner any functionary of the Government of the hour, however ludicrous in appearance, speedily found himself in serious trouble, out of which he did not easily extricate himself. And since new officials were constantly emerging from the rag-tag and bob-tail, the only wise course was to salute *every* black man, no matter how menial his capacity might be. One never knew whether the road-mender of to-day might not be a general of division to-morrow, having power of life and death even while wanting a decent pair of trousers.

A party of our fellows were allowed to go ashore, by a serious error of judgment, and, as they strolled carelessly along one of the principal thoroughfares, they met a company of soldiers so scarecrow-like that they simply stood and roared with laughter. This had been crime enough, but the sailor-men must needs aggravate their offence. The officer in command, swelling with rage, demanded their salute. Instead of complying they indulged in some ribaldry, in which his get-up, as well as that of his ragged regiment, was held up to ridicule in effective fashion. This behaviour could not be tolerated. They were surrounded, overpowered, and dragged off to the "calabozo." Then, when they saw what their folly had led them into, they repented sorely. It had been worth any amount of "ko-tow" to have escaped from such a fate as now befell them. The lock-up was apparently an ancient cow-byre, standing like an island in a lake of sewage, which, under that blazing sun, sent up a steam of putridity into the heavy air. Through this foul morass they were dragged with every indignity their exulting captors could devise, and there, more dead than alive, they were left for twenty-four hours, when the captain managed to overcome the stubborn attitude of the sable authorities, and induce them to accept a substantial fine. When they were released and brought on board they looked like resuscitated corpses, and every article of clothing they wore had to be flung overboard. The doctor examined them with gathering anxiety upon his face, but his only comment was "The sooner we're out of this hell-hole the better."

Fortunately we were to sail in the morning, for every one was feverishly anxious to be gone. That evening a passenger embarked, who came alongside in a canoe paddled by two negroes, bringing with him several weighty chests. He was a well-dressed black man, with an air of nervous anxiety; and he hovered around, while his baggage was being hoisted on board, as if he dared not trust it out of his sight. When it was all safely embarked and carried below, to a muttered accompaniment of growls at its weight, the canoe and its sable crew disappeared into the darkness, while the passenger also hid himself, and rarely appeared thenceforward.

At daybreak all hands were astir, the firemen working like sooty gnomes down in their gloomy pit to get steam up, while dense volumes of smoke poured from our funnels, gladdening the eyes of all hands. Amidst the universal activity we yet found time to notice that the thin coronal of vapour hovering above the smoke-stack of the filibuster was also getting more palpable, and the knowing ones winked at each other meaningly. At last a hissing from our steam-pipe betokened full pressure in the boilers, the "old man" mounted the bridge, and all hands took their stations. "Cast off fore and aft!" shouted the skipper. Willing hands released the heavy hawsers from the bitts, and, with a rattle of steam-winches and cheerful yells from the crew, we moved slowly away from the hulk, the ensign and "house-flag" being run up at the same time. Then, to our breathless amazement, the filibuster, apparently of her own accord, stole from her position and came gently alongside, a tall, romantic-looking figure mounting her bridge as she did so. So close did she come that the figure on the bridge was able to step nimbly on board of us. He was a spare, elegantly-built man, dressed in a well-fitting suit of grey silk, with an immense white Panama sombrero on his head. He was strikingly handsome, having a dark, oval face, with a heavy black moustache and Velasquez beard, while his black, brilliant eyes, wide set, seemed to take in everything at a glance. Shaking hands cordially with our captain, he said a few words inaudible on deck; then the pair descended from the bridge, and, joined by the mate, entered the chart-room. They remained there for a couple of minutes with the door closed, and then, coming out again, the Yankee leapt on board his own vessel, while our two officers took their stations—the captain on the bridge and the mate forward. Our engine-room bell clanged the order, "Full speed ahead," and, as the engines responded, our good ship vibrated from stem to stern under their impulse. Without any apparent effort the Yankee kept her place by our side, not a soul visible on board, except the tall figure lolling calmly on the bridge, meditatively puffing at a big cigar.

The decks being cleared, there was, for a brief space, nothing to do; so all hands, including passengers, crowded the rails, watching with breathless interest the two war-ships which lay in grim silence where they were when we entered the harbour. Not a word was spoken, and the clanging chorus of the massive machinery below seemed many times louder than we had ever heard it before. The scene was sufficiently impressive to fix itself permanently in the memory of every one on board. There was not a breath of wind, the water of the widening gulf lying like another sky before us, tinted in innumerable shades by the floating clouds and the richly-coloured hills on either hand. Every thrust of the pistons drove us nearer those two surly sentinels laden with potential destruction, which we all well knew might, at any moment, be let loose upon us. But there was much comfort in an occasional glance at the splendid old red ensign flying gallantly overhead, for everybody on board felt how much might and majesty it represented. Nearer and nearer we drew to the point midway between the war-ships, that now began to show a thickening cloud of smoke at their funnels, and a white feather of escaping steam. At last we were fairly between them. Suddenly the silent Yankee alongside straightened himself, made us a sweeping bow, and said, "A thousand thanks, captain. Farewell, ladies and gentlemen, and a pleasant passage. G'lang ahead!" At his word a gong boomed below, and the lithe vessel sprang forward like an unleashed greyhound, the pitchy fumes from her funnel filling the clean air with the stench of burning petroleum. Boom! boom! went two big guns from the men-of-war as they both started in chase, while from the filibuster's masthead the flag dipped as if in ironical courtesy. Many shots were fired after the daring craft; but although the fountains cast up by the massive shot apparently played all around her, none actually reached her. And as she certainly steamed nearly two knots to their one, she was soon hopelessly out of range. Recognising this, they gave up the chase. I suppose, according to the rules of romance, they should now have intercepted us; but this is fact, not fiction, and so it must be admitted that they paid not the slightest attention to us, but returned to their old position. Despite our good rate of speed, in less than four hours there was nothing visible of our *protégé* but a long grimy streak in the bright blue sky.

Under ordinary circumstances such an adventure would have afforded an inexhaustible topic of conversation during the remainder of the passage, but unhappily, a much more serious matter soon claimed everybody's attention. Those truly awful words, "Yellow fever," began to circulate in terrified whispers, while the merry, genial doctor's face looked terribly solemn. There was little suspense. The very next day the first victim died—one of the men who had spent the night in that unspeakably filthy calabozo at Port-au-Prince. Ordinary prudence forbade any delay in disposing of the poor remains. In less than an hour after death came the solemn little meeting, the bare-headed group at the gangway, the long white bundle on a hatch at an open port, the halting, diffident reading of the old sublime Service, and then the hoarse s-s-s-s-h, and the sullen plunge into unknown depths.

177

Everybody on deck was terrified at the apparition of a mother-naked giant, armed with the cook's axe.

The destroyer made such strides that a large tent had to be rigged over the main hatch as an open-air hospital, and there the brave, unwearying doctor laboured day and night at his hopeless task. There was no discrimination, except as far as the passengers were concerned—perhaps because they were better seasoned to the climate. At any rate none of them were attacked; but of the ship's company, officers, engineers, firemen, sailors, and stewards all gave tithe to death. The disease was terribly swift in its operation. One Friday morning our bo'sun's mate, a huge, hirsute Irishman, suddenly complained of his head. This was at eight a.m. At ten a.m. he was in the hospital grinding his teeth in delirium. A few minutes after everybody on deck was terrified at the apparition of a mother-naked giant, armed with the cook's axe, which he had snatched from beside the galley door, rushing madly about the decks. Not many seconds elapsed before he was alone, striking furiously at everything in his way, while the foam flew from his gaping mouth. Having made the round of the deck aft, he came to the weather side of the wheel-house, within which the quarter-master was calmly steering quite unconscious of what was happening. Suddenly the maniac caught sight of him through the side window, and immediately rained a torrent of tremendous blows upon the stout teak door. Poor Teddy fled out of the lee door, and up into the main rigging just as Carney burst in. Then all was quiet. After a while some one was courageous enough to creep along and peer in. There was Carney, lying at full length on the grating, having fallen upon the upturned edge of the axe, which had sunk deep enough into his chest to have let out a dozen lives. The place was like a slaughter-house. That afternoon one reading of the Service sufficed for three burials, two more men having died while the maniac had possession of the deck.

Naturally there was little levity on board. Cooped up with such an awful scourge none felt inclined for merriment. But the ordinary routine of work went on without a hitch. My shipmates were set to work on full wages to supply the places of the dead, and, although they did not relish doing firemen's duty, they were not sorry to have the prospect of a little money when they reached home, supposing they were still alive. My turn came. One morning at five o'clock, when, as usual, I was called to begin my day's work, I lifted my head to rise, but it fell again like a piece of lead. A feeling of utter helplessness had seized my whole body, although I could not say I felt ill. But not even the awe in which I stood of the chief steward could overcome my want of strength, and I humbly said, "I'm not able to get up, sir." Instantly alarmed, the steward fetched the doctor, who, after feeling my pulse, etc., pulled me out of the bunk, and set me on my trembling legs, telling the steward to put me to some work that did not require any running about, but on no account to allow me to sit down. His orders were strictly obeyed, but how I got through that dreadful day I cannot tell. I felt as if I would gladly have given the whole world to be allowed to lay down for a little while, and several times my legs doubled up under me, letting me sink in a heap on the pantry deck, but there was no respite allowed me. This stern treatment was completely successful, for by supper-time I felt quite strong again, and I was troubled no more by any recurrence of those alarming symptoms. What was the matter with me, I never knew; but undoubtedly I owed my life to the doctor's wisdom, much as I hated his treatment at the time. Day after day dragged on, each bringing with it a death for some one of our diminishing number, while the doctor, worn almost to a shadow, still battled with the enemy with unabated vigour. His chief task was with those who had won through the crisis, to nurse them back to strength again. Beef-tea with brandy was his sheet anchor, and this potent reviver he was continually administering in tiny doses, while commenting cheerily on its marvellous virtues, to his wasted patients. Then, as if to fill up our cup of misfortunes, the engines suddenly stopped. The boilers were old—in fact, too old for safe use—and one of them had sprung a dangerous leak. The engineers attacked the trouble with that stolid heroism for which their class is famous, although, from its prosaic nature, little is thought or said about it by a world that loves its heroes to glitter with pomp and circumstance, and to do their great deeds upon some conspicuous stage. Down beneath the boilers, where the narrow limits compelled them to lie at full length, half roasted by the fierce heat, and scalded from head to heel by the spurtings of boiling water, they laboured with hardly a pause for a day and a night. They succeeded in the almost incredible task of patching up the leaky source of our speed, doing moreover their work so well that, although our rate of going was greatly reduced, the repairs held good until we reached port.

The joyful day arrived at last when the faithful doctor was able to announce that the yellow fever had left us, and that, unless some of the convalescents died of weakness, there would be no more deaths from that scourge. It was high time. In the short period of twenty days we had buried thirty men, every one of whose deaths was distinctly traceable to that foul den in Port-au-Prince. Happily the weather held fine, and the wind held to the south-west, so that we were able to help her along with the sails, until one morning a thrill of delight ran through the ship at the sight of green water alongside, sure sign of our nearness to the Channel. Presently that solitary sentinel, the Fastnet, hove in sight, and soon behind it we saw the green hills of Ireland. All our miseries were now forgotten, and there was a general air of joyful expectation mixed with deep thankfulness that we had been spared. That afternoon our negro passenger, whom we had hardly seen during the passage, made his appearance on deck. He was evidently seeking the captain, for, as soon as he caught sight of him, he hastened towards him and the two went straight into the captain's state-room. From thence there soon issued strange noises as of a foreigner under strong excitement, while now and then the deep tones of the skipper chimed in as if he were speaking soothingly. Suddenly the door was flung open and the captain called for the mate. That officer responded promptly, but did not succeed in hushing the din. On the contrary, the shrill voice of the black man rose higher than ever, until he was fairly yelling with fury. The mate blew his whistle, and, when the bo'sun appeared in answer to it, he received an order to bring the carpenter with a pair of irons and three or four men. The reinforcements manhandled the excited negro, hauling him with scant ceremony on deck, and bundling him forward into an empty cabin, wherein they locked him and left him to his own reflections. This mysterious affair caused much excitement among both passengers and crew, but it was not until after the vessel had been in dock some days that any explanation was forthcoming. It appeared that, according to *his* story, the negro had been First Lord of the Treasury, or whatever grandiloquent title they had bestowed upon their keeper of the funds, and, seizing a favourable opportunity, he had levanted with quite a large sum (he said $100,000). Getting safely on board he had committed his loot to the care of the captain and mate, who, however, most unaccountably forgot all about it when he claimed it coming up Channel. Finding that he could by no means recall it to their memories, he went temporarily mad—insane enough, at any rate, to institute proceedings against them for its recovery. His story, which I have given above (with the exception of the way in which he obtained his wealth), was simply laughed at, and he was fain to revert to his original profession of scullion or some such occupation.

The passage up Channel was uneventful. The hateful yellow flag (quarantine) was hoisted as we entered the Mersey; but, as soon as the Health Officer boarded us, we learned that there would be no delay in docking, yellow fever being innocuous in our favoured land. So the dock gates swung wide and we passed in to our berth, the vessel being in two hours deserted by everybody except the night watchman and me.

CHAPTER XII.

ADRIFT IN LIVERPOOL ONCE MORE.

That night I slept soundly, heedless of to-morrow; but when the day dawned the problem of what I was to do confronted me, and a very awkward question it was. For I was still so puny in size and so delicate-looking that I knew it would be no easy matter to persuade any one to employ me. Besides, I was penniless. I had little clothes but what I was wearing, and I felt sure no boarding-master would take me in on the chance of my paying him out of my advance-note here. My only hope was that I might be allowed to work by the ship, at a small weekly wage, until I had earned enough to pay for a week's board, either in the Sailors' Home or some boarding-house where they would try and get me a ship. That hope was soon dashed when the chief steward appeared. With unnecessary gruffness, as I thought, he told me that I was not wanted, and the sooner I got ashore "out of it" the better. Hadji was kinder. He gave me a cheerful smile, a hearty shake of the hand, and half a crown, besides wishing me luck. In a few minutes I stood outside the dock gates with all the town before me, but not a friend or even an acquaintance, as far as I knew, within its limits. Conscious that I had no time to lose, I wandered about the docks until I was weary, speaking to every likely looking officer on board the various ships I visited, and getting nothing but plenty of good-natured chaff as well as outspoken comments upon my childish appearance. Yes, I got one good meal; so that when night fell, and I sought a great heap of hay in the Cobourg Dock that I had noted as a promising place to spend the night, my precious piece of silver was still unbroken. I slept soundly, though none too warm, my long stay in the tropics having thinned my blood. At daylight I crept stealthily from my nest and recommenced my tramp, but it was fruitless. Then I remembered the wood-carver, and thought I would look him up again. But there was another name over the shop, and I saw that another business was being carried on there. I did not like to go into my old boarding-house next door, feeling sure that I should be unwelcome with only two shillings and sixpence in my pocket and no prospects. I went to the Sailors' Home and told my story, but they refused to take me in—as indeed I had fully expected they would.

For the next week I roamed about those wretched docks, getting more and more discouraged every day, until, at last, I was afraid to ask for a berth in case I got a cuff as well as a refusal. Finally, when I had been reduced to picking scraps out of the gutter, I resolved to go to the workhouse. How such an idea entered my head I can't imagine, but it did, and seemed feasible too. So off I started up Brownlow Hill, but the strains of a German band arrested my none too eager progress, and, all hungry as I was, I stayed to listen. Perhaps the music cheered me up; at any rate, while listening, I determined to go to my old boarding-mistress and offer my services to her in return for a shelter and such scraps as she could spare. She received me ungraciously enough; but I pleaded hard, having learned well the hard lesson of not to take "no" for an answer without a struggle, and eventually she agreed. The place was a poor kind of cookshop, the staples of which were penny bowls of broth and tea for the poverty-stricken dock labourers, with twopenny plates of potato-pie for the better-off. I honestly earned my keep, and more; but business getting slack, she told me plainly that she could not afford to keep me much longer, and she would allow me a couple of hours a day for a week to look for a ship, at the end of which time I must shift for myself again. I was not altogether sorry at this chance, slender though it was. Every day I hunted diligently about during the time allotted me, and, after four days, I succeeded in getting a job as cabin-boy on board a German barque, the *Greif* of Rostock. The captain had his wife and little daughter on board, neither of whom spoke a word of English; but the captain said he had just discharged an English boy, who had pleased them very well, and whose name of "Dan" I was in future to answer to. I took up my new duties with zest, doing my best, not only to give satisfaction in my work, but to master the (to me) awful difficulties of the German language. For a time I succeeded admirably, except that the ladies called me "schoufskopf" (sheep's-head) far more frequently than Dan, being irritated, I suppose, by what they considered my stupidity in not being able to understand them. The only person on board who seemed inclined to be hard upon me was the mate, a huge North German, who never missed an opportunity of giving me a blow, apparently by way of keeping his hand in. Therefore, I exercised all the ingenuity I possessed in keeping out of his way—no easy task—for, as soon as my work in the cabin was finished, I was always called on deck to lend such a hand as I was able. And I could not help noticing that, in spite of the difficulty I had always found in getting a berth, whenever I did succeed in finding one there was never any trouble in keeping me fully employed. So matters progressed in fairly even fashion for three weeks, while the *Greif*, which lay in the Huskisson Dock, was taking in a general cargo for Demerara. I made fair progress with the language, and was certainly something of a favourite with the bo'sun, the cook, and the sailors. I began to hope that I should succeed at last in making myself comfortable, as well as necessary, in some way, to the comfort of others; and only my dread of the mate gave me any uneasiness. But one morning the cook took advantage of some brief leisure I had to get me to chop some firewood for him. Gaily I started to obey him, using one large piece for a block, and was halfway through my task, when the axe struck a knot, glanced off, and entered the deck, making an ugly mark. The next moment I received a blow under the ear from behind which stretched me bleeding and senseless on the deck. When I came to I felt very sick; but there was such an uproar around me that I speedily forgot my own trouble in my anxiety to know what was the matter. The mate stood, white as chalk, the centre of an angry little crowd of the men, one of whom, a tall, fair Swede, was fairly raving with excitement, and seemed by his threatening motions to be hard put to it to keep his hands to himself. Gradually it dawned upon me that all this row was about me. The mate had struck me brutally and unjustly for what was a pure accident, and his cruelty had actually caused the whole crew to resent his action. This was really one of the strangest experiences I ever had. I have been beaten innumerable times in all sorts of vessels, but only once was a voice ever raised on my behalf besides this occasion, and that was by Joe, the Yorkshireman, against my uncle in my first ship. That a mixed crew of Germans and Scandinavians, on board a German vessel, should raise a protest against the ill-treatment of an English boy, was an unheard-of thing, especially when it is remembered that in those days brutality to boys at sea, except in American ships, was the almost invariable rule.

I was more frightened at the consequences of the mate's action than anything else, especially as it looked as if there would be a regular riot directly. Before, however, any blows were exchanged, the captain arrived. His presence acted like magic. He made no noise, but just pushed his way into the centre of the disturbance, speaking quietly to the men, who at once dispersed to their several duties. Then he turned to me, and said, in the same passionless voice, "Ashore mit you. If I findt you hier in den minutes more, I schlings you oferbordt." I did not linger. In less than five minutes I was out of the ship, and again in the unenviable position of being masterless. There was a change in my hitherto persistent bad luck, however. Strolling dejectedly round the dock, I came to the very biggest sailing-ship I had ever yet seen. When I had done admiring her enormous proportions, my attention was caught by a new spar, which lay upon the quay nearly ready for going aloft. I walked round it wondering, with all my might, whatever kind of mast it could be. At last I stopped, and, according to a lifelong habit of mine, began thinking aloud. "T'aint a schooner's topmast, 'cause there's three sheave-holes in it; nor yet a barque's mizzen-topmast, for the same reason. N'ther ain't a ship afloat as 'ud carry sech a stick fur a to'-gallanm'st, nor yet fur a jibboom. *I* never see sech a spar 'n *my* life." "You give it up, then, I suppose?" said a grave voice behind me. Turning sharp round I confronted a tall, distinguished-looking gentleman, who was regarding me with an amused smile. "Yes, sir," I said, "I thought I knew all about ships' masts; but I can't think what this one can be for." "Well," he replied, "I'll enlighten you. It's my ship's foreto'-gallanmast, and that third sheavehole that puzzled you so much is for the skys'le-halliards. Now do you see?" I thanked him and said I did; but I was none the less surprised that any ship could carry such a mighty spar so high up. And then, by a happy inspiration, I told him my story, right down to the last episode. He heard me in silence, and, as soon as I had finished, turned and went on board, telling me to follow him. Gladly enough I obeyed, until we reached the quarter-deck, where we found the shipkeeper. Telling him to find me something to do, the captain then turned to me, saying, "I shan't be able to take you to sea with me, for all our gear is so heavy that we never carry any boys; but while the ship is in Liverpool you may stay on board doing what you can, and I will pay you twelve shillings a week, out of which you must keep yourself. Now, be a good boy, and I'll see what I can do for you when we sail." I was hard put to it to express my gratitude; but he cut me short by walking away, and leaving me to realize my extraordinary good fortune. As soon as he was gone, I hunted up the shipkeeper, who had taken himself off somewhere, and asked him for a job. He was an easy-going individual, not over fond of work himself, or given to expecting much from any one else. So he said, "Oh, I can't be bothered just now. You scull round a bit 'n have a look at the ship, 'n I'll fine yer sutthin to do bimeby." That was good enough for me. For the next two or three hours I exhausted all my powers of admiration over this magnificent vessel. She was called the *Jorawur* of London, and built frigate-fashion, with imitation quarter galleries, which added to her already great appearance of size. She belonged to a school that has now departed, whereof the *Superb*, *Calcutta*, *Lady Jocelyn*, and *Hydaspes* (the last two converted steamships), were conspicuous examples. She carried thirty-two A.B.'s and six petty officers, so that she was well manned, even taking her great size and enormous spars into account. But alas! years after, I saw her bought by a firm of Jewish ship-knackers, who razeéd her taunt spars, sold the yards off her mizzenmast, turning her into a barque, and finally sent her to sea with *seven* A.B.'s forrard. No one was surprised when she took entire charge of the poor handful of men before she got clear of the Channel. God help them! they could hardly get her yards round, much less shorten sail. She was eventually picked up, almost derelict, and towed into Falmouth, where the ill-used crew promptly refused to do any more in her, and were, of course, clapped in gaol therefor, with that steady application of the rights of owners so characteristic of our seaport magistrates. But this is digression.

"Knock-off" time came, and with it the exodus of all the motley crowd of riggers, painters, and stevedores who had been busy about the ship all day. Seeing them depart homewards I remembered, with some misgivings, that I too could only be considered a day-worker, and might also be required to clear out, but whither? So I sought the shipkeeper, and timidly approached the question whether I might be allowed to stay on board. I found him very glad to have some one who would relieve him of the necessity of keeping so close to the ship as he had been doing. He at once gave me the free run of the cabin, and hastened to "clean himself" preparatory to a cruise down town. I busied myself in hunting up such odds and ends as lay about the staterooms available for bedding, and before long had rigged myself quite a cosy nook, near the glowing stove, which, as the weather was cold, was very comforting.

My friend having departed, I was left quite alone on board the huge vessel; but this, so far from giving me any uneasiness, was just in my line—I was more than contented. I found the keys of the pantry and store-room, where my eager search soon discovered plenty of cuddy bread (biscuits), half a chest of tea, sugar, oatmeal, sago, and arrowroot. There was nothing else eatable or drinkable. This find, however, gave me great delight. I felt no apprehensions now that I should have to spend much in food—a fear which had somewhat daunted me before, seeing how badly I wanted to save all my wages to get myself a few clothes and pay for a week's board in the Sailors' Home when the *Jorawur* sailed. Another expedition to the galley provided me with a saucepan, with which I at once proceeded to make myself a mighty bowl of arrowroot, thinking, in my ignorance, that not only was it very nice to eat, but that it must be most strengthening as well. How could I know that it was only starch? A couple of biscuits and the half-gallon of arrowroot (plenty of sugar in it) made me feel at peace with all the world, if even I was in rather an inflated condition. Fed and warmed, with a good roof over my head, and a fairly comfortable bed (if it *was* composed of rags), I only wanted one thing more to be perfectly happy. And even that was forthcoming—a book. "Bleak House" lay in one of the pantry drawers waiting for me, I felt. Putting the lamp handy and replenishing the fire, I settled down luxuriously into my nest, all my troubles forgotten in present bliss.

When the shipkeeper came on board I don't know, for when I awoke it was morning—five o'clock. I jumped up, hustled my bed out of sight, and lit the fire. While it was burning up I went on deck for a wash, returning sharp-set to a good breakfast of tea and biscuit, after which I felt ready for anything that might come along. By the look of the shipkeeper when at last he appeared, his last night's excursion had been anywhere but in the paths of virtue. But his amiability was unimpaired, and it was in quite a deprecatory tone that he requested me to "pop across the road" and get him a drop of rum, as he didn't feel very well. Whether it was my alacrity in obeying his request, or the speed with which I afterwards got him a cup of tea, I don't know, but thenceforth our relations were of the pleasantest kind. I wished, though, that he hadn't found me quite such a miserably cold job; for that forenoon he set me to clean out the row of 400-gallon tanks in which the sea-stock of fresh water was carried, my slender body being easily able to slip in through the "man-hole"—a feat that was really impossible to him. Now, some of these tanks had over eighteen inches of water in them: all had enough to come well above my ankles. As it was late autumn I got chilled to the marrow, for, as I must needs bale all the water into buckets and pass it up to him through the man-hole, I soon got wet through. Then I had to scrub and sluice vigorously to get the thick coating of rust off, in which process I became very much like a piece of rusty old iron myself. As each tank was thoroughly cleansed, a pail of limewash was handed in to me with a big brush, and I gave top, bottom, and sides a liberal coating of it. In consequence of this occupation my appearance was filthy beyond words; but I did not mind that, until, one day, having come on deck for something, I met the captain. Looking at me with an expression of the liveliest disgust, he said, "Dirty little beast!" This cut me to the quick, as being both unkind as well as utterly undeserved. However, I made no defence. One of the earliest lessons inculcated on board ship is "no back answers," and the boy of gumption loses no time in understanding that the less he says, by way of excuse, the better for his welfare. Much injustice is thus suffered, of course, but there is apparently no help for it. From that day forward I carefully avoided the captain, lest he should discharge me—a fate which I dreaded.

The peculiar diet beginning to pall, even upon my palate, I hit upon a plan which, however indefensible morally, gave me then no qualms, while the results were extremely gratifying. The gang of painters who were re-decorating the cabin brought their meals with them, and I supplied them with tea out of the half-chest in the storeroom, receiving in return a portion of their food. By this means I still kept my wages intact. The only money I spent while on board was on one unlucky Saturday. Fired by the description of a savoury dumpling, filled with bacon and kidney, which I read in the late steward's cookery book, I slipped ashore and bought the necessary ingredients. On Sunday morning I tried my hand, and, having succeeded in making the dumpling, dropped it clothless into a saucepan of boiling water, made up a roaring fire under, and hungrily awaited the result. Rigidly repressing an eager desire to peep into the pot, I watched the clock until the specified time had elapsed. Then, my fingers trembling with excitement, I lifted the lid and peered through the dense steam. A greyish soup with a villainous burnt smell greeted my sight; my dumpling had melted. Crying with vexation and disappointment, I turned the mess out into a dish, but I couldn't eat it. It was too bad even for me. So I fell back upon sago, and made no more experiments in cookery.

The inevitable day drew near when the ship was to sail. Her cargo of salt (for Calcutta) was nearly all in, the riggers had bent the sails, and a smart steward took charge of the cabin, ejecting me summarily. I took refuge in the forecastle that night, and the next morning, having made myself as presentable as I could (I *was* a queer-looking little scarecrow), I waylaid the captain and besought him to ship me for the voyage. Giving me a half-laughing, half-pitying look, he said, "No, my boy, there is no duty here light enough for you; I cannot take you to sea with me. But I will take you up to the Home, and tell them to get you a ship. You shan't have to prowl the docks again if I can help it." I thanked him, but ventured to say that I should have liked much better to sail in such a splendid ship as the *Jorawur*. He seemed pleased, but shook his head decidedly, and in a few minutes we were ashore, making for the Sailors' Home. Arriving at the great building, the captain immediately made for the office, and sought an interview with the superintendent. As soon as that gentleman appeared I was brought forward, and introduced to him, with a brief summary of my adventures and present position. My good friend the captain concluded his remarks by paying down a fortnight's board for me, at the same time expressing a hope that they would find me a berth as speedily as possible in some outward-bound ship, so that I should for some time at least be beyond the reach of homeless destitution. The superintendent readily promised his aid, and, bidding me good-bye, the kindly captain returned to his duties, happier, I hope, for the knowledge that he had done me a really good turn, for which it was highly improbable I could ever repay him.

I was at once handed over to the care of one of the stewards, who led the way up a seemingly interminable series of staircases to a cubicle on the fourth floor. The place was built in tiers of galleries, running right round a large central space lighted from above, and paved at the bottom. This covered-in quadrangle was used as a promenade, smoking-room, and lounge by the inmates, while it was, of course, possible to take in a complete view of the whole interior from any one of the seven galleries. Before we arrived at my berth, the steward was in possession of most of my story, and began to regard me with more friendly interest than I looked for, seeing that no "tip" was to be expected from me. He seemed surprised when, in answer to his inquiry for my "dunnage," I told him I had none but what I stood in; and at once promised that he would see what he could do by way of beating up a few duds for me—a promise he faithfully kept. Then he ushered me into the snug little chamber, with its clean bed and handy lockers, and, giving me a key of it, left me to my own devices.

CHAPTER XIII.

THE DAWN OF BETTER DAYS.

At last I felt as if I was standing on firm ground. Here, a solvent boarder in this great institution, with thirty-six shillings in my pocket, of which no one knew but myself, and with the superintendent pledged to get me a ship, there did seem a prospect that the days of my waifhood were over and done with. I looked around me at the comfort and cleanliness of my little room, I thought of the precarious existence I had been suffering, and I felt very thankful. Outside my door was a row of big basins, well furnished with soap, jack towels, and abundance of water. Off went my clothes, and I fairly revelled in a good wash. I had barely finished when the clangour of a great gong startled me. I rushed to the railings, and looked over to see a general move of the inmates from all quarters towards one goal. Instinct informed me that this strange noise was a summons for dinner; so I hastened to join the throng, and presently found myself in an immense dining-hall filled with long tables, at which a steady stream of men were seating themselves. At one of these tables I took my place, in joyful anticipation of a good dinner, when suddenly a sharp "Hi!" from the head of the board arrested my attention. It was the steward in charge, who stood waiting to serve out the food. He had spied a stranger. As soon as he caught my eye, he said, "What flat are you on?" Now the barges in Liverpool are known as "flats," and, jumping at the conclusion that I was suspected of being a bargee-boy, I replied with much heat, "I'm not on any flat; I've just left a two-thousand-ton ship!" Surely never did a more feeble unintentional joke meet with a warmer reception. My neighbours roared with delight, and, as the words were repeated from table to table, very soon the whole vast chamber reverberated with merriment. Utterly bewildered, I sat speechless, until it was explained to me that the galleries in the Home were called "flats" too. They were lettered for convenience of distinction, and the steward's query was in order to assure himself that I occupied a room on the flat under his charge, as, otherwise, I had no right at his table. That little matter was soon cleared up, and feasting began. Never in my life had I sat at such a board. Every one ate like giants, and mountains of food vanished, washed down by huge cans of ale, served out liberally by the attendants. I am ashamed to remember how I ate; but the blissful thought that this sort of thing would be a regular incident of each day heightened my enjoyment. The meal over, diners wandered forth again in very different style to their entrance of half an hour before. Hardly knowing whither I went, I sauntered along one of the galleries, when suddenly the words, "To the Library," caught my eye. No longer undecided, I hurried in the direction indicated, and found a really fine room, most comfortably furnished, with roaring fires and an enormous number of books. There were only three people in it; indeed, it was never well patronized. I found a volume of Captain Cook's Travels, coiled myself up in a big armchair, and passed at once into another world. Thenceforth, during my stay, that peaceful chamber was my home. Except for a little exercise, sleep, and meals, I scarcely left it, and, long ago though it is, I can vividly remember how entirely happy I was. Occasionally I heard, through the mighty void that separated me from the outer world, a ringing shout of, "Where's that shipwrecked boy? Anybody seen that shipwrecked boy?" as the huge doorkeeper, standing in the centre of the quadrangle below, bellowed for me. The said shipwrecked urchin was far too comfortable to desire any change in his present circumstances, and, it must be confessed, did nothing to assist the authorities in their efforts to get him a ship. To tell the truth, whenever I must needs go out, I used to watch my opportunity and evade the officials downstairs. I had tasted the sweets of life and was loth to return to the bitter.

During my seclusion in the library, however, I made the acquaintance of several officers of ships, through whose kindness I obtained quite a respectable lot of clothes, so that I was able to reserve my precious little hoard to purchase sea-stock with when the inevitable day came. But, in the meantime, I saw as little of Liverpool as I possibly could. Apart from my love of the library and its contents, the town was hateful to me. Its streets seemed to scowl at me, and every turning reminded me of misery. But one day, as I was darting across the quadrangle on my return from some errand, a long arm shot out from behind a pillar and grabbed me. Panting with my run, I looked up and saw the form of the doorkeeper towering over me. "Why, where ha' you been stowed away all this time, you young rascal?" he said.

"Here have I ben shoutin' myself hoarse after you, an' never a sight of yer could I get. Come along!" And with that he marched me off to the shipping-office in the same building, and handed me over to one of the clerks, who immediately brought me before a jolly-looking captain who was just engaging his crew. What he said I don't remember; but, in a few minutes, I had signed articles as boy at twenty-five shillings per month on board the *Western Belle* of Greenock, bound to Bombay, and sailing two days after, at eight in the morning, from the Alfred Dock, Seacombe. I received a month's advance like the rest, half of which I had to pay for a week's board, as I had been three weeks in the Home. But with my well-kept little hoard I had sufficient to buy my oilskins, bed, hookpot, pannikin and plate, soap, matches, knife, etc., so that I was better off, in those respects, than I had ever been before.

Early on the morning of the appointed day, in company with several others of the crew who had been lodging at the Home, I was escorted across the Mersey by the official belonging to the institution, whose business it was to see us safe on board. Like all my companions, I had not the slightest idea what sort of a craft I was going in, except that she was a ship of 1225 tons register. This, however, is one of the most common experiences of the sailor. Of late years it has become more the practice for men to cruise round and choose a ship, handing their discharges to the mate as a sort of guarantee that they will be shipped when she signs articles. But, even now, thousands of men take a leap in the dark, often finding themselves in for a most unpleasant experience, which a little forethought on their part would have saved them. When forethought is a characteristic of the sailor, his lot will rapidly amend. That, however, is almost too much to hope for.

We soon arrived at our ship's side, finding her to be an old American-built soft-wood ship, fairly comfortable looking, and with a house on deck for the crew instead of the villainous den beneath the top-gallant-forecastle, far in the fore-part of the ship, which is the lair of seamen in most English ships. I was told off to the petty officers' quarters, or "half deck," a fair-sized apartment in the after part of the forward deck-house, with bunks for eight, and separated from the men's berth by the galley and carpenter's shop. There was no time to take stock. She was moving, all hands being on board, and, for a wonder, not so drunk as usual.

She was rapidly warped down to the dock gates, where one of the powerful tugs, for which Liverpool has long been justly famous, awaited her—the *Constitution.* The hawser was passed and secured, the ropes which held us to the pier cast off, and away we went down the river at a great rate—our voyage was begun. Much to the discomfiture of our fellows a large ship, the *Stornoway*, came rushing past us, bound into dock, having just finished the long round we were beginning. The sight of a "homeward bounder" is always a depressing one for Jack who is just starting again. And it is usually made harder for him by the jocular remarks of the fortunate crew, who shout of "bright pots and pannikins and clean donkey's breakfasts" (straw beds), usually throwing some of their rusty tinware overboard, at the same time, to give point to their unkind remarks.

There was little time though for thought, despondent or otherwise. We were rapidly nearing the bar, upon which the rising wind was making a heavy sea get up, and our jibboom had to be rigged out. What this means is, I am afraid, impossible to make clear to a landsman. The amount of work involved in getting the long, heavy spar into position, with all its jungle of standing rigging, which looks to the uninstructed eye a hopeless mass of entanglement, is enormous. When, too, it has to be done as the ship is dragged relentlessly through a heavy head sea, as was now the case, the difficulty and danger is certainly doubled. Yet it must be done, and that speedily, for none of the upper spars on all three masts are secure until what seamen call the "head gear" is set up, to say nothing of the urgent necessity which may, at any moment, arise of setting the head sails, as the jibs are termed collectively. So rapidly did the sea rise, and so powerful was the tug, that before long heavy masses of water began to come on board, and several ugly lumps came over the forecastle head, half drowning the unfortunate men, who, in poor physical condition, were toiling at the head gear. Some of them were, of course, compelled to work right over the bows, where, as she plunged along, the boiling foam now and then surged right over their heads. Under these circumstances some disaster was inevitable. It came. Suddenly I saw the boatswain leap from the forecastle-deck aft, a distance of some twenty feet, yelling, while in the air, "Man overboard!" There was hardly a minute's delay before the tug stopped, and everybody gave a sigh of relief to see that the unfortunate man had caught one of the life-buoys thrown to him.

He placed his hands upon the edge of the buoyant ring, which rose edgeways and fell over his head, making him perfectly safe. But he was so eager that he got his arms through, and, with both hands on the buoy, tried to raise himself higher. Unfortunately he succeeded, and immediately overbalanced, his head going down while his legs hung over the sides of the ring. Burdened as he was with oilskins, sea-boots, and much thick clothing underneath, it was impossible for him to regain his position, and when the boat from the tug picked him up he was quite dead. Steaming back alongside of us the skipper of the tug reported the sad fact, suggesting that he might as well take the body back to Liverpool when he had finished towing us. This was of course agreed to, and the towage resumed. But no sooner had the news of our shipmate's death reached us, than there was a rush to the forecastle by our crew, to divide the dead man's belongings—a piece of barbarism quite uncommon among seamen. They made such a clean sweep of everything, that when the captain sent to have the deceased seaman's effects brought aft, all that was produced would hardly have filled a large handkerchief, although he had brought two great bags and a bundle on board with him. So passed from among us poor Peter Hill, a steady middle-aged seaman, leaving a widow and two children to mourn their loss, and exist as best they could without the meagre half pay he had left them.

After this calamity the speed of the tug was reduced until the jibboom was rigged and the anchors secured. Then the impatient tug-skipper tried to make up for lost time. Green seas rolled over the bows as the bluff old ship was towed through the ugly, advancing waves at a rate quite beyond anything she could have done unaided. She strained and groaned as if in pain, while the severity of her treatment was attested by a long spell at the pumps, the quantity of water she had in her giving rise to many ominous mutterings among the crew. At last the Tuskar was reached, the topsails and lower staysails were set, and the tug let go of us, much to our relief, as the motion at once became easier. Then came the muster and picking for watches, when the grim fact became apparent that we were grievously undermanned. There were but twelve A.B.'s and one ordinary seaman forward, four tradesmen, *i.e.* bo'sun, carpenter, sailmaker, and painter, with three boys in the half-deck, steward and cook. Aft were the captain and two officers. Under any circumstances this would have been a very small crew for a ship of her size;

but, to make matters worse, she was what sailors call "parish rigged," meaning that all her gear was of the cheapest—common rope, that with a little usage grew swollen and clumsy, often requiring the strength of one man to pull the slack of it through the wretched "Armstrong patent" blocks, and not a purchase of any kind to assist labour except two capstans. Already we had gotten a taste of her quality in setting the scanty sail she now carried; what would it be, later on, when all sail came to be made, we could easily anticipate. The crew were, as usual, a mixed lot. There was an elderly Yankee bo'sun's mate answering to the name of Nat, who, in spite of his fifty years, was one of the best men on board; a smart little Yorkshireman, very tidy and quiet; and two Liverpool-Irishmen—dirty, slovenly, and obscene always—Flanagan and Mahoney. They, I learned afterwards, had come home a fortnight before from the East Indies with a fairly good pay-day, which they had never seen a copper of, having lain in one continuous state of drunkenness in a cellar, from the evening of their arrival, until the vampires who supplied them with liquor had somehow obtained a claim upon all their wages. Then, when the money was drawn, the two miserable fools were flung into the gutter, sans everything but the filthy rags on their backs. A jovial darky from Mauritius, with a face whose native ugliness was heightened by an extraordinary marking from smallpox, kept all hands alive with his incessant fun. He signed as Jean Baptiste, which sacred appellation was immediately anglicized to Johnny the Baptist, nor did he ever get called anything else. There was also a Frenchman from St. Nazaire, who, though his English was hardly intelligible, had sailed in our country's ships so long that he had lost all desire for anything French. He was also a fine seaman, but the wrong side of forty. A taciturn Dane, tall and thin, but a good man as far as his strength went, was also of our company; and a brawny, hairy Nova Scotiaman, John Bradley, able enough, but by no means willing to exert his great strength. Lastly, of those whom I can remember, came Peter Burn and Julius Cæsar. When the first-named signed in Liverpool, he looked like a hale old sea-dog about fifty, worth half a dozen young, unseasoned men. Unfortunately for us, he had come out of the experienced hands of Paddy Finn, a well-known boarding-master renowned as a "faker-up" of worn-out and 'long-shore sailors. Rumour had it, too, that he had recently married a young woman, who had eloped with several years' savings, leaving him without any prospect but the workhouse, until Paddy Finn took him in hand for the sake of his month's advance. Be that as it may, it was almost impossible for any one to recognise in the decrepit, palsied old wreck that crawled aft to muster, and answered to the name of Peter Burn, the bluff, hearty old seaman that had signed on so boldly two or three days before. Julius Cæsar was a long, cadaverous lad, willing and good-natured, hailing from Vermont, but so weak and inexperienced that you could hardly feel him on a rope. The other three men have entirely faded from my memory.

Of the petty officers with whom I lived, it only needs just now that I note them as all Scotch, belonging, like the skipper and mate, to the shores of the Firth of Forth, with the exception of the painter. He was a Yarmouth man, really an A.B., but, in consequence of his great ability in decorating, mixing paints, etc., given five shillings a month extra, with a bunk in the half-deck. There was no sea-sobriquet for him, like "Bo'sun," "Chips," "Sails," or "Doctor," so he was called by his rightful surname, "Barber." The cook, or "doctor," was a grimy little Maltese, not quite such a living libel on cookery as usual, but dirty beyond belief. I said there were three boys in the half-deck, but that statement needs qualifying. The eldest of the trio was as good a man as any on board the ship, and deserves much more than passing notice. He had been, like myself, a London Arab, although never homeless; for his mother, who earned a scanty living by selling water-cresses, always managed to keep a corner for him in her one room up a Shoreditch court. But Bill was far too manly to be a burden to his mother a day longer than he could help, so, after trying many ways of earning an honest crust, he finally managed to get taken on board the *Warspite* training-ship, whence he was apprenticed in the *Western Belle* for four years. He was now in his third year of service, a sturdy, reliable young fellow of eighteen, not very brilliant, perhaps, but a first-class seaman: a credit to himself and to his training. The other boy, besides myself, was a keen urchin about my own age, on his first voyage, of respectable parentage, and with a good outfit. Whatever his previous experience had been I don't remember; I think he came straight from school. Anyhow, he was artful enough to early earn the title of "a young sailor, but a d—-d old soldier," which concise character sums up all that a seaman can say as to a person's ability in doing as little as possible. Captain Smith, our chief, was a jolly, easy-going Scotchman of about sixty, always good-tempered, and disinclined to worry about anything. He had his wife and daughter with him, the latter a plain young lady of about twenty-two. Both of them shared the skipper's good qualities, and the ship was certainly more comfortable for their presence. Mr. Edny, the chief mate, was a splendid specimen of manhood, a Scotchman about thirty-five years of age, with coal-black hair and eyes. He was the most hirsute individual I have ever seen, a shaggy black mane, longer and thicker than any Newfoundland dog's, waving all over his chest and back. Mr. Cottam, the second mate, was a square-built, undersized man from the Midlands, the bane of my existence, but a prime seaman who loved work for its own sake.

CHAPTER XIV.

DUE SOUTH

Perhaps an undue amount of space has been given to particularizing the *Western Belle's* crew, but my excuse must be that this was my first big ship (the steamer didn't count), as well as my first long voyage. To me it was the commencement of a new era. Hitherto I had not been long enough on board any one ship to take much interest in either her or her crew. The changes had been so numerous and rapid, that while I was certainly accumulating a large stock of varied experiences, I was unable to put them to much practical use, because I remained so small and weak. But now I knew that, barring accidents, I was in for a twelve-months' voyage; I should cross the "line" four times, round the Cape twice, and return a regular "Sou'-Spainer," looking down from a lofty height of superiority upon other sea-boys who had never sailed to the "Suthard."

When the watches had been picked I found myself under the second mate, whom I dismissed rather summarily at the close of the last chapter, because I shall have a great deal to say about him later on. For the present it suffices to note that my evil genius must have been in the ascendant, for "Jemmy the Scrubber," as we always called Mr. Cottam behind his back, was a regular tyrant, who spared nobody, not even himself. The men of his watch took things easily, as usual, knowing full well that he was unable to coerce them; but I was helpless in his hands, and he did not fail to let me know the fact. There was some compensation for me in having Bill Smith, the sturdy apprentice before mentioned, as my watch-mate, for he was both able and willing to lend me a helping hand whenever possible, although of course he could not shield me from the amiable weaknesses of Jemmy the Scrubber. Still, his friendship was very valuable to me, and it has endured unto this day.

At the outset of the voyage I found, that if I had never earned my pay in my life before, I was going to do so now. When there was one hand at the wheel and one on the look-out, there were four A.B.'s, Bill and myself, available to make or shorten sail. Consequently it became the practice to send me up alone to loose whatever sail was going to be set during the night, and I would go up and down from one masthead to the other while the men did the hauling on deck. Then when the job was finished the men retired to their several corners, more often than not into their bunks in the fo'lk'sle, leaving me to coil up all the ropes and then return to my post aft in front of the poop, ready to carry Jemmy's orders when he gave any. She was a very heavy-working ship, as before noted, making the ordinary duties of trimming sail for such a handful of men most exhaustive; but, in addition to that, the food was so bad that it reminded me strongly of the *Arabella*. Yet so usual, so universal, was this shameful condition of things, that there was no more than the ordinary quantity of "growling"; no complaints brought aft; and things went on pretty comfortably. Of course she leaked—"made a good drop o' water," as sailors say—but still in fine weather the pumps would "suck" in ten minutes at four-hour intervals. But sail she couldn't. A Rochester barge would have given her two miles in ten, and as to "turning to windward"—that is, zig-zagging against a contrary wind—it was a mere farce. She made so much leeway that she just sailed to and fro on the same old track till the wind freed. Therefore it was a weary time before we got down as far as that dreaded stretch of stormy sea known to seamen as the "Bay," although it extends many a league Atlantic-wards from the Bay of Biscay. Here we battered about for several days, against a persistent south-westerly wind that refused to let us get south, until at last it freshened into a bitter gale, accompanied by the ugly cross sea that gives this region such unenviable notoriety. Under two lower topsails and reefed foresail we wallowed and drifted, watching with envious gaze the "flyers" gliding homeward under enormous clouds of canvas, steady and dry, while we were just like a half-tide rock, swept fore and aft by every comber that came hissing along. Here I got a narrow squeak for my life. I was coiling up the gear in the waist when she lurched heavily to windward, just as a green mass of water lifted itself like a hill on that side. Before she could rise to it, hundreds of tons of foaming water rolled on board, sweeping me blindly off my feet and over the lee rail. Clinging desperately to the rope I held, I waited, swollen almost to bursting with holding my breath, but quite unconscious of the fact that I was overboard. At last she rolled to windward again, and I was swept back by another wave, which flung me like a swab into the tangle of gear surrounding the mainmast, little the worse for my perilous journey. And thus she behaved all that night, never free from a roaring mass of water that swept fore and aft continually, leaving not a dry corner anywhere. Sundry noises beneath the fore-hatch warned us that something heavy among the stores had broken adrift; but it was impossible to go down and see, not only for fear of the water getting below, but because of the accumulated gas from the coal, which, unventilated for days, would only have needed a spark to have blown the ship sky-high. Towards morning, however, the weather fined down. As soon as possible the fore-hatch was taken off, and there we found in the 'tween decks a mess awful to contemplate. The whole of our sea-stock of salt beef and pork in tierces had broken adrift, together with two casks of Stockholm tar, and had been hurled backwards and forwards across the ship until every barrel was broken in pieces. There lay the big joints of meat like miniature islands in a sea of tar, except that, with every roll of the ship, they swam languidly from side to side in the black flood. All hands were set to work to collect the food—it was all we had—hoist it on deck, and secure it there in such fashion as we could. Then it was scraped clear of the thickest of the tar, the barrels were set up again and refilled with the filthy stuff, into the midst of which freshly-made pickle was poured. It was not good food before, but now, completely saturated with tar, it was nauseous beyond the power of words to describe. Yet it was eaten, and before long we got so used to the flavour that it passed unnoticed. This diversion kept all hands busy for two or three days, during which the weather was kind to us, and we gradually stole south, until the steady trade took hold of us and helped us along into settled fine weather.

By this time all hands had settled down into their several grooves, determined to make the best of a bad bargain. One thing was agreed upon—that, except for her short-handedness and starvation, she was a pretty comfortable ship. There was no driving, no rows; while the feminine influence aft made itself felt in the general freedom from bad language that prevailed on deck. But we were not yet low enough in numbers, apparently. The old man, Peter Burn, who shook so much that he was never allowed aloft, became perfectly useless. He had been an old man-o'-war's man, living, whenever possible, a life of riot and debauchery, for which he was now called upon to pay the penalty. At a time of life when many men are not long past their prime, he was reduced to childishness—a very picture of senile decay. His body, too, in consequence, I suppose, of the foul feeding, became a horrible sight upon the opening of more than forty abscesses, from which, however, he seemed to feel no pain. Strange to say, his rough shipmates, who of course had to make good his deficiency, showed no resentment at the serious addition to their labours. With a gentleness and care that could hardly have been expected of them, they endeavoured to make the ancient mariner's declining days as comfortable as the circumstances would allow, and I am sure that nowhere could the old fellow have been more carefully looked after.

She was an unlucky ship. Her slow gait, even with favouring winds, was something to wonder at; but, as if even that were not delay enough, we met with a most abnormal amount of calms and light airs—hindrances that would have made some skippers I have known unbearable to live with. But Captain Smith was one of a thousand. Nothing seemed to ruffle his serene good-humour. It must have been infectious, for the conditions of food and work were so bad that a little ugly temper added thereto would certainly have caused a mutiny. As usual I, unluckiest of urchins, was about the worst-off person on board. Jemmy the Scrubber, unable to imbue the rest of his watch with his own restless activity, gave me no peace night or day. Woe betide me, if, overcome by sleep in my watch on deck at night, I failed to hear his first call. With a bull's-eye lantern in one hand, and a piece of ratline stuff in the other, he would prowl around until he found me, and then—well, I was wide-awake enough for the rest of that watch. In the half-deck I was treated fairly well, except in the matter of food, and even that got put right in time. I have often wondered since how four men of good standing, like our petty officers, could deliberately cheat two boys out of their scanty share of the only eatable food we had; but they certainly did. Every other day except Saturday was "duff" day, when the modicum of flour allowed us was made into a plain pudding by the addition of yeast and fat. The portion due to each made a decent-sized plateful, and, with a spoonful of questionable molasses, furnished the best meals we got. Now the duff for the half-deck was boiled in a conical bag, and turned out very similar in shape and size to a sugar-loaf. It was brought into the house in a tin pan not wide enough to allow it to lay flat, so it stuck up diagonally. The sailmaker always "whacked it out," marking off as many divisions as there were candidates. So far so good. But when he cut off his portion, instead of cutting fair across the duff, he used to cut straight down, thus taking off half the next portion as well, owing to the diagonal position of the duff. Then came the bo'sun, who of course followed suit, and the others likewise, until the last two "whacks" falling to the share of the boys was really only the size of one. For a long time this hardship was endured in silence, until one day, at the weekly apportionment of the sugar, much the same sort of thing took place. Then Bill Smith broke out, and there was a rare to-do. Our seniors were dreadfully indignant at his daring to hint at the possibility of their being unfair, and, for some time, I feared a combined assault upon the sturdy fellow. All their tall talk, however, only served to stiffen his back, and, in the result, we got our fair share of what was going.

Hitherto I had not seen any deep-sea fishing; so, when one day a school of bonito came leaping round the bows, and the mate went out on the jibboom end with a line, my curiosity was at fever-heat. How ever I endured until eight bells I don't know. Once or twice the wrath of Jemmy was kindled against me for inattention, and I got a sharp reminder of my duties. At last eight bells struck. I had the dinner in the house in a twinkling, and in another minute was rushing out along the boom to where the mate had left his line while he went in to "take the sun." The tackle was simplicity itself, consisting solely of a stout line about the thickness of blind-cord, with an inch hook firmly seized to its end, baited with a shred of white rag. My fingers trembled so that I could hardly loose the neat coil the mate had left, for below me, gambolling in the sparkling foam beaten forward from the bluff bows, were quite a large number of splendid fish, although they did not seem nearly as large as they were in reality. At last I got the line free, and, bestriding the boom-end with my legs firmly locked between the jib guys, I allowed the lure to flutter away to leeward, jerking it gently so as to imitate a leaping squid or bewildered flying-fish. Splash! and the graceful curve of my line suddenly changed into a straight; I had hooked one. In a perfect frenzy of excitement I hauled madly, scarcely daring to look below where my prize dangled, his weight fairly cutting my hands. At last I had him in my arms, but such was the tremendous vibration of his massive body that, although I plunged my thumbs through his gills, I was benumbed from head to heel. All feeling left me, and my head was beginning to swim, when I bethought me of plunging him into the folds of the jib, which was furled on the boom. With a flash of energy I accomplished this, falling across the quivering carcase half dead myself. But before he was quite dead I had recovered, and, prouder than any victorious warrior returning from the hard-won field, I bore him inboard. I was received in the half-deck as a benefactor to my species, for had I not provided twenty pounds of fresh food. How welcome my catch was can hardly be comprehended by those who have never known what it means to subsist upon beef and pork, which when dry turns white and hard as salt itself, with the flavour of tar superadded, and that for many weeks. The first flush of excitement over, attention was called to my gory appearance. I had not noticed it before, but now I found that I was literally drenched in blood, black-red from the chin downwards. What of that? I had caught my first big fish, and nothing else mattered. Out I went again, succeeding in a few minutes in hooking another. But one of my watchmates must needs come interfering, and take it away from me, in spite of my protests. I was actually bold enough to tell him that the way he was carrying it was unsafe—the idea of me, with my five minutes' experience, dictating to an old "shellback" like Bradley. I was right though, for, when half way in, the fish gave a convulsive plunge and fell, leaving his gills in Bradley's fist. I didn't say anything, but, like the parrot, I did some tall thinking. All the fish left us instanter, attracted doubtless by the blood of their mutilated fellow; so, sulkily coiling up the line, I came in. There was a plentiful supper at four bells, and, though I should now pronounce the flesh of a bonito as dry and tasteless, then it was sweeter to me than I could express. While it was yet in my mouth, yea! ere it was chewed, retribution overtook me. I heard the watch on deck setting sail forward, and more conversation ensuing upon the performance than usual. Suddenly a shock-head thrust itself into the half-deck. The voice of Cæsar said ominously, "Tom, th' mate wanse yer!" With a thrill of dread crawling up the roots of my hair I obeyed, following the messenger forrard. There stood the port watch, grouped round the mate, gazing upward at the sail they had just been setting, the jib. Well they might. From head to tack down its whole length ran ghastly streaks and patches of gore, a sight that made my flesh creep. "Did *you* do that?" said the mate in an awful tone. There was no need for any answer; my guilt was manifest. Vengeance lingered not, and, in a few minutes, the *manes* of my first fish were propitiated. Lamely I retired to complete my supper with what appetite I could muster, and to vow that the next fishing I did I would take a sack out with me. But the evidence of my offence was permanent, surviving the bleaching of sun, rain, and spray throughout the whole of the voyage. My waspish little tyrant, the second mate, could hardly rope's-end me again for the same fault; but he made it an excuse for robbing me of a goodly portion of each day-watch below, keeping me on deck sorting the carpet-thrums of which he was for ever making hearthrugs. Oh, how I did hate his fancy-work and him too. But I dared not complain or refuse, although at night I was always getting into trouble for going to sleep, which I really couldn't help.

CHAPTER XV.

EIGHT WEEKS' CALM.

Leisurely as our progress had been hitherto, we had always managed to make some Southing each day. But now ensued a time unique in all my experience. What our exact position was I do not know; but I fancy it must have been somewhere near the Equator in the Atlantic. When the faltering, fitful breezes first failed us, a long succession of rain deluges set in, which at first were most heartily welcome. For, like many other ships of her class in those days, the *Western Belle's* store of water-tanks contained barely enough of the precious fluid to suffice us for half the voyage, even upon the regulation allowance of three quarts per man each day. Rain was depended upon to replenish them in time, and on such voyages, of course, seldom failed to afford a bountiful supply. Now, however, it fell for whole days in one solid, roaring downpour that, in spite of the many openings by which the decks were drained, filled them so that it was possible to swim from poop to forecastle in fresh water. Everybody turned out all their belongings that were washable, and a regular carnival of soap and water took place. Then the ports were opened and the decks cleared of water. It still poured over the front of the poop like a small Niagara, and from thence, as being the cleanest, we refilled all our tanks. Still the flood came down without a break, until the incessant roar became awe-inspiring. Many of the crew spoke of it as passing all their experience, even hinting at the possibility of another flood. It was so heavy that the experiment was successfully tried of scooping up drinkable water off the sea-surface, which was like a mill-pond for its level, although all a-foam with the falling torrent. The ship lay as nearly motionless as it is possible for a ship to be out in mid-ocean. For Coleridge's simile of "A painted ship upon a painted ocean" is only a poet's licence, and grates upon a seaman as the sole picture in that wonderful work which is not literally true. Admiral Wharton's remark that "In all the incalculable mass of the ocean not one particle is ever absolutely at rest," may strike most people as strange; but it is sober truth, and therefore it is impossible for a vessel at sea ever to be perfectly motionless.

Gradually the massive downpour abated, the sun peeped out, and the sodden decks and gear dried up. But there was no breath of wind. And as Captain Smith was a practical man, with all his patience, he decided to utilize this otherwise barren time in carrying out a scheme he had purposed leaving for some long spell of waiting in Indian harbours. We had on deck three huge, rough spars—long logs, in fact. These were loosed from their lashings and lifted on to the gallows, whereon the boats usually rested. A big rip-saw was produced—the only time I ever saw one on board ship—and the strange spectacle was witnessed of a ship's deck being turned into a saw-pit, sailors into sawyers. Thick slabs were sawn off the spars, after which the carpenter, and a couple of men who could handle axe and adze, set to work to fashion them into topsail-yards. Meanwhile, the rest of the hands toiled like beavers, unbending sails, sending down yards, and overhauling standing rigging, until the old ship looked as if she were in some snug dock corner being dismantled. All day long this work went on, no one knowing or caring whose watch on deck it should be, and at night the weary workers lay around promiscuously, sleeping away the hours of darkness in calm certainty of being undisturbed. This curious interlude in an ocean voyage developed strange faculties in our men. The iron bands, which form part of the fittings of a ship's yards, were, owing to the skipper's desire to have heavier spars, found to be too small. No matter. An impromptu forge was rigged up on a barrel filled with sand, a most ingenious bellows was made by somebody, and, as if born and bred in a smithy, the bo'sun and two hands manipulated that ironwork in such workmanlike fashion that it answered its purpose as well as if turned out of a Blackwall foundry.

For many days this work went on, with apparently no more notice taken of its strangeness than as if it were the normal course of events. But gradually the deathly stillness of our surroundings, the utter absence of the faintest air of wind, or sign of any other vessel in a similar plight, began to tell upon everybody's nerves. Men took to gathering in twos and threes in the evenings to recount their experiences of lengthened calms, and the yarns they had heard of bygone tragedies connected with ships that had strayed into windless seas. Even the busy working-hours could not prevent the men from gazing uneasily over the side where the familiar, smiling face of the sea was undergoing a mysterious change. There is about the deep sea, even in the hottest weather, a delicious atmosphere of cool cleanliness, a searching purity, such as the earth can never yield, giving one the fixed idea that to this vast, unpollutable limpidity the nations owe their health. In some dim fashion this thought is present with all sea-farers, however dense and unnoticing they may be. Therefore, when that familiar freshness was found to be giving place to a stale, stagnant greasiness to which a mawkish, uninvigorating atmosphere clung, what wonder that uneasiness—all the more difficult to bear quietly because undefinable—became generally manifest. Adding to the sense of eerieness, was the fact that old Peter was failing fast. I have already mentioned how willingly his share of the common burden was borne by his shipmates, and how loyally they tended him, even though such service as he needed could not be spoken of without offence. But now his mind had completely gone. He lived in some misty past, about which he babbled unceasingly. Often, in the still evenings, all hands would gather round him, listening in perfect silence to his disjointed reminiscences of desperate deeds in the way of duty, of long-drawn-out debaucheries in filthy rookeries of home ports, as well as the well-known hells at Hong Kong, Calcutta, or Callao. They were strange scenes, those dog-watch gatherings, nothing distinctly visible but the red glow of the pipes—except when the sudden glare of a match, struck to light fresh tobacco, shed a momentary gleam over the group of haggard, bearded faces, each beclouded with an unwonted shadow. In the midst, a placid stream of sound, Peter's voice prattled on, its lurid language in the strangest contrast to the gentleness of his speech. Still the days dragged on and the faces grew longer. All the refitting was finished, and only the ordinary routine of ship-life was left to be carried on. Happily those duties are always, in the hands of capable officers, sufficiently onerous to prevent time ever hanging heavily. One of the strangest of all the strange notions current ashore about sea-life is that sailors have nothing to do but watch the ship go along, except during stormy weather. One would have thought that the never-ending, ever-beginning round of work in a house that is properly kept would have taught all landsmen and women that the great complicated machine called a ship would demand at least equal labours to keep it fit and in working order. But "watch and watch" was now restored, which, of course, threw a great deal of additional time upon the men's hands, since they could still sleep through the night, if they chose, without fear of being disturbed. So for hours, when unemployed, men took to hanging over the rail, watching, with an unnatural curiosity, the myriads of strange creatures that, lured from their silent haunts in the gloomy middle-depths of the ocean by the long-enduring stillness above, came crawling about, blinking glassily with dead-looking eyes at the unfamiliar light. Truly it was an uncanny sight. Not only fish of bizarre shape abounded, but vast numbers of great medusæ—semi-transparent simulacra of all the hideous things that ever haunted a maniac's dream—crawled greasily about us, befouling the once clear blue of the sea, and coating its sleek surface with stagnant slime. And, deeper down, mighty shadows passed sluggishly to and fro, filling the gazers with wordless terror as the days crept wearily away and those formless apparitions gradually chose higher levels. Overhead the sweet fathomless azure of the sky paled as if in sympathy with the silent sea. Cloudless, indeed, but overspread with a filmy veil of strange mist, that, while it robbed the sun of its glare, seemed to enclose us within a dome of heat, unventilated and stale. When night fell, instead of cool refreshment—such as comes, even in tropical calms, after sunset at all ordinary times—there arose a foul odour of decaying things that clung clammily to the palate like a miasma. The densely populated ocean beneath palpitated with pale fire, the gleaming of putrescence. Instead of the usual brisk movement seen among the glowing denizens of the deep, everything crawled languidly, as if infected with some universal pestilence. Moon and stars lost their strong silver glow, and were no longer reflected in the smoothness beneath as if shining in another heaven. And at moonrise, when the fantastic mist-wreaths writhed about the horizon, the broad red disc of the moon would be distorted into many uncouth shapes, or patterns of strange design were drawn across her paling surface.

At last, one night, when old Peter was holding his usual levee, he suddenly raised his voice, and authoritatively demanded that his auditors should bear him on to the forecastle head. They instantly obeyed, lifting him tenderly upon his mattress, and laying him gently by the side of the capstan. Then all hands gathered round him in the darkness, only the glow of the pipes fitfully illuminating the rugged countenances. Slowly the moon rose, but sent no silvery pathway across the sea, until suddenly, as if with a great effort, she broke through the hampering mist-wreaths that seemed to clog her upward way. A pure, pale beam shot right athwart our vessel, lighting up the little group of watchers on the forecastle, and lingering as if lovingly upon the withered, weather-scarred face of our ancient shipmate. As it did so he smiled—a patient, happy smile—his lips unclosed, and, with a sigh of relief like a weary child, he died.

Breaking the steadfast silence came the mate's mellow cry, "Square the mainyard!" As the men rose to obey, a gentle breath, welcome as the first thrill of returning health, kissed the tanned faces. Slowly the great yards swung round, a pleasant murmuring as of a mountain rivulet arose from the bows, and the long calm was over. In quiet attendance upon the dead came the sailmaker, with a roll of worn canvas under his arm in which the poor, shrivelled remains were reverently wrapped and neatly sewn up. A big lump of coal was found and secured to the feet, and the long parcel was borne gently aft to the gangway. There in the moonlight we all gathered, while the skipper, with faltering, unaccustomed voice, read the stately words of the Burial Service, all hands standing like statues as they listened to what all admit to be one of the most solemn as well as majestic selections known in our splendid language. Suddenly there was a pause; the skipper raised his hand, and those who supported the plank on which the worn-out tabernacle of old Peter lay, gently raised its inner end. There was a subdued s-s-s-h as the white fardel slid slowly seaward, followed by a sullen plunge. All rushed to the side, where an ascending column of green light marked the descent into those calm profundities of our dead. An almost inaudible sigh of relief escaped from every lip, as if a well-nigh intolerable burden had been removed. Undoubtedly that was the predominant feeling, intensified by the fact that a sweet breeze was now blowing steadily. In the blue dome above, the moon and her attendant stars were shining with their full splendour, and from the now sparkling face of the surrounding sea the sickly mist was rolled quite away.

Thenceforward, although our progress was wretchedly slow, of course, we were little troubled by calms. But our tribulations were not yet all over. Barber, the painter A.B., was taken ill; so ill as to be quite useless, nor did he ever again that voyage recover sufficiently to resume his place as an active member of the crew. And other men were grievously tried by scurvy, which, though in a mild form, was painful and weakening. How it was that they were no worse, I cannot think, for the food was bad enough truly for the development of that malignant disease in its worst form. But, somehow, we worried along in dogged fashion, every one showing rare patience under their unmerited sufferings.

And so, in laborious fashion, we crept southward and round the Cape without any bad weather worth mentioning, until well to the eastward of that justly dreaded point. Then one night we had a narrow escape from serious disaster. It was our (the second mate's) watch on deck from eight to midnight. We were jogging along before a light south-westerly breeze, at about four knots, the weather being singularly fine for those latitudes. Down in the cabin the skipper, his wife and daughter, and the mate were playing cards, while the second mate, with a carelessness most unusual with him, was hanging over the open scuttle, absorbed in watching the game. Rees, the old Frenchman with a Welsh name, was on the look-out, and I heard him muttering and grumbling because the officer of the watch was oblivious of the fact that an ominous-looking cloud was rising in the northeast, or almost right ahead. Presently from its black bosom faint gleams of lightning showed themselves, while the subdued murmur of the breeze we had became hushed in an unnatural quiet. With a quickness that seemed miraculous, the threatening cloud ahead overspread the sky, and still the second mate did not realize what was coming. As all sail was set, the position began to look so threatening that all the watch took the alarm, and gathered in the waist, ready for the sudden emergency imminent. Presently the wind dropped dead, its sudden failure arousing the supine officer, who, lifting his head, took in the situation at a glance. But before he could issue an order, there came a smart patter of rain, followed immediately by a roar as the north-east wind, like a savage beast, leapt upon us, taking us flat aback. Then there was a hubbub. Up rushed the skipper and mate, shouting for all hands. Everything was let go at once; but the sails, jammed backward against the masts, refused to allow the yards to come down. The ship began to drive astern most dangerously, nor could she be got round by any means. Presently she dipped her stern right under, taking a sea in over the taffrail that filled the decks fore and aft. It was now a question of minutes with us. If she could not be got round she would certainly go down stern foremost, for again and again she drove her broad stern under the rising sea as the now furious gale hurled her backwards. The feeble efforts of the crew seemed utterly unavailing against the mighty force of this sudden tempest. But, providentially, a huge sea caught her on one bow, flinging her head off far enough for the wind to grip the head sails. Round she spun upon her heel like a top, and in another minute the shreds of the rending sails were thundering above our heads as they flew to fragments. In an indescribable uproar, wherein the howling of the gale, the reverberations of the thunder, and the crash of our yards were all mingled, the ill-used vessel sped away before the wind as if fleeing for her life. An almost continual glare of lightning shed an unearthly light over all, by which the havoc that was being wrought was plainly to be seen. How that night's work was ever accomplished I have no idea. But when morning dawned we were fore-reaching under the three lower topsails and fore topmast staysail, the fluttering rags of what remained of our lighter sails being secured in some haphazard sort of fashion to the yards. We had escaped the doom of many a fine ship, whose crew have paid the penalty of carelessness with their lives. It was long, however, before we overtook the labour which those few hours involved us in. For many days we jogged along under easy sail, getting farther and farther to the northward every day, happily for us, and so putting a greater distance between us and bad weather.

CHAPTER XVI.

UP THE INDIAN OCEAN TO BOMBAY.

At certain seasons of the year the minds of mariners navigating the Indian Ocean are always, more or less, upon the tension of expectancy concerning the possibility of their encountering one of those tremendous meteors known as cyclones. A keen watch is continually kept upon the mercury in the barometer for any deviation from its normal ebb and flow, which occurs with the greatest regularity in the tropics during settled weather. For these truly awful storms are so justly dreaded, by even the bravest seaman, that no danger of navigation claims more attention. The possibility of meeting, or being overtaken by one, bulks largely in the dog-watch discussions among the foremast hands, and he who has successfully braved an encounter with a cyclone, speaks with an authority denied to his fellows who have never had such a painful experience. Even to me, juvenile as I was, an almost deferential hearing was accorded when I spoke of my Havana experience—the hurricane of the West Indies, the typhoon of the China seas, and the cyclone of the Indian Ocean being only different names for the same mighty atmospheric convulsion. Happily, our leisurely progress northward was unattended by any such deeply perilous adventure as the encounter with a cyclone would have been. Doubts were freely expressed as to the probability of the *Western Belle* weathering one at any time, but especially under our present short-handed conditions. Every day, therefore, that passed seeing us nearer port was noted with delight, as lessening our chances of utter extermination. And when at last we passed the latitude of Cape Comorin and entered the Arabian Sea, there was a distinct lightening of faces and a tendency to make little of the weary passage now gradually nearing its end. We did not see a vessel of any description, during our journey from the Cape, until within two hundred miles of Bombay, neither did we sight any land. But one morning, to my amazement, I saw a vessel nearing us, unlike any I had ever seen before—except in pictures. She had a hull like the half of an egg cut lengthways, and was propelled by an enormous white sail of lateen shape, or almost like one of our jibs. She could not have been more than ten or fifteen tons capacity, and how she stood up under such an immense spread of sail was a mystery. She came flying along like a huge sea-bird, shooting up almost in the wind's eye, and presently, graceful as an albatross, rounded-to under our stern and "spilled" her sail. Seated in the after part of this queer craft were two or three dignified-looking men in white raiment, with the peculiar stiff headgear affected by Parsees. One of the black, unclad natives forming her crew hooked on to our fore-chains, and, with an agility I should have hardly believed possible, one of the white-robed visitors seized a rope flung over the side and skipped on board. Speaking correct English, he saluted the mate, who stood at the gangway; then hastened aft, and, making a low salaam to the skipper, solicited the honour of being our "dubash," or general purveyor, while we were in harbour. To his great disappointment, however, Captain Smith was an old Bombay trader, and always employed the same dubash; so that, after a few compliments, our visitor politely took his leave, hoping for better luck next time.

Thenceforward we met many native craft, or "buggalows," as they call them, lumbering along the coast on various errands, all characterized by a general makeshift appearance that made me wonder how ever they dared brave the dangers of the sea at all. But that is a peculiarity of all Eastern native craft. They are things of shreds and patches, and look as seaworthy as a waggon with a worn-out tarpaulin set. Most of them creep along shore pretty closely, and, at night, lower their wooden anchors down about twenty fathoms, furl sail, and turn in—or, at least, go to sleep. She is pretty safe to fetch up somewhere, and time doesn't matter. If she gets run down by some bustling ship or another, it is Kismet, and not to be helped.

At last we drew near Bombay—that Liverpool of the East—the first sight of which is so amazing to an untravelled Briton. I was almost stupefied with wonder at the mighty stream of traffic, the immense fleet of ships that lay at anchor in the magnificent harbour, and the beauty of the great city. We had shipped a white pilot, who, being anxious to get up to the anchorage before dusk, and make one job of the mooring, was "cracking on" to an exceedingly stiff breeze, making the old ship heel over alarmingly. Suddenly I heard my name called. Running aft, I was met by the second mate, who, handing me a coil of line, ordered me to go up and reeve the signal halliards in the mizzen truck. Now, I should premise that, like all American-built ships, we carried very long "royal poles," or bare tapering extensions of the masts above the highest part of the rigging. Ours were extra long—some sixteen feet or so—and crowned at the top, which was not much thicker than a man's wrist, with a flat piece of wood about as large as a cheese-plate, in one side of which was a sheave for the signal halliards or flag-line. I started aloft boldly enough; but when I reached the base of the pole, and saw to what a height its bareness towered above me, while the staggering ship lurched to leeward and the foaming sea roared a hundred and twenty feet below, my heart failed me, my head swam, and all my scanty stock of strength left me. For some time I sat with my legs clutched round the pole, just clinging, without power to move. Then I heard the voice of the second mate pealing up from the deck. "Hurry up there with those halliards!" Strange as it may appear, although I felt that I was going to certain death, my fear of him was so great that I made the attempt. Pulling myself up, I shut my eyes and murmured a prayer. Trembling in every nerve, but fighting against my benumbing weakness, I actually struggled to the top. As I write, the cold sweat bursts from every pore, for I feel again the terrible agony of that moment. Opening my eyes, I thrust at the opening of the sheave with the end of the line; but it was knotted, and would not go through. I *had* tried and failed, and with my last flash of energy I grasped the pole again in both arms, and slid down on to the eyes of the royal rigging. Here I clung for a few minutes to recover myself, and to be violently sick; then, feeling as if the bitterness of death was past, I descended to the deck, walked up to Mr. Cottam, and said, "I have tried, and I can't do it, sir—not if you kill me." He stared at me blankly for a moment. Then turning away, as if the situation was beyond him, he called my constant chum, Bill Smith, and gave him the job. He, being strong as a bear and agile as a monkey, very soon managed it; not without considerable grumbling at Jemmy for sending a "weakly kid" like me on such an errand. The whole episode may seem trivial; but I frankly declare that having, in my experience, faced death many times, I have never felt such terror as I did then.

We made a "flying moor" in fine style, in spite of the great fleet of ships surrounding us, the sails were furled, decks cleared up, and all hands dismissed forrard to meditate upon the successful close of our passage of seven months from Liverpool. Soon everybody's attention was drawn to a large ship near by, whose crew were weighing anchor, homeward bound. It was the *Stornoway*, the vessel we had seen towing into Liverpool as we left. She had discharged and loaded in Liverpool, made her passage out, and now, having discharged and loaded in Bombay, was returning again. Such differences there are between sailing ships.

The morning brought a chattering crowd of coolies carrying little shallow baskets and short hoes. At first, the idea of discharging two thousand tons of coal by such childish means seemed absurd, and, when a start was made, impossible. For the poor wretches—men, women, and children—did not appear to have the faintest idea of working, or to possess enough strength to do more than carry their attenuated bodies about. But they were formed into lines, from the hatches to the gangways, and, while some scratched the coal into the baskets with the hoes, the rest passed them from hand to hand to a monotonous chant of "Jal marck ooday, jal marck oodayleeallah, jal marck ooday." The spelling, of course, is phonetic, and I haven't the faintest idea what it meant. So mechanically did they "puckarow" those baskets, that often one would pass from the hatch to the gangway empty, the coolie on the rail going through the motions of tilting it over into the lighter and returning it. In any case, I do not think the average weight of coal passed in a basket was seven pounds. Yet somehow the lighters got filled. There was such a number of coolies, and the passing was so incessant, that it was bound to tell. The crew, apart from the discomfort of the all-pervading coal-dust, had a very good time, as little work being required of them as possible. And, while a plentiful allowance of fresh meat and vegetables was provided by the ship, there was also a bumboat in attendance that kept the men well supplied, at their own cost, with fruit, eggs, etc. I was fortunate enough again to be book-keeper, receiving in return as much fruit as I wanted.

Except on Sundays, matters went on in a very humdrum style, the only incident out of the common being a picnic excursion to the rock-temples of Elephanta. But I have no intention of describing such places, that, indeed, are as well known to readers as the Isle of Wight. My object is a totally different one. On Sundays I should think the bulk of the trading population got afloat, and came ship-visiting. If our ship's deck was a fair sample of those of the rest of the fleet, there could have been little merchandise left in the bazaars. From the cabin to the forecastle the decks were almost impassable for the piles of curios of all kinds—clothes, cigars, birds, etc. The bulk of the stuff was dreadful rubbish, almost worthless, in fact; yet, owing to the ignorance of sailors of what can be bought in decent shops at home, the trash fetched high prices, at least double what really good articles of the same style and place of origin could be bought for in London. And, in addition to that, by a system nothing short of robbery, each man was charged two shillings and fourpence for every rupee he drew against his hardly earned wages, while at that time the rupee was quoted officially at one shilling and eightpence. Who pocketed the eightpence, I do not know; but I shrewdly suspect that it was considered, like the backsheesh levied from the tailor and the bumboat-wallah, the captain's legitimate perquisite. I have known a captain pocket fifty rupees off a bumboat bill of two hundred and fifty, and, of course, the keen-witted Hindu based his charges to the men on the expectation of such a tax; so that Jack was robbed on every hand, unless he sternly made up his mind to spend nothing "in the country." And, as not one in a hundred sailors have such resolution as that, there are some very pretty pickings out of their scanty wages.

The time sped swiftly away, and soon the coal was all out and most of the stone ballast in. No cargo was obtainable for us in Bombay, so we were ordered to proceed to Bimliapatam on the Coromandel coast, and after that to Coconada to complete. But, before our departure, the time-honoured custom of giving the crew twenty-four hours' liberty must be observed. Consequently the mate's watch duly received twenty rupees each, and, dressed in their best, started for the shore one morning at eight o'clock. All of them returned the following morning except Bradley, the hirsute Bluenose who lost my fish for me on the passage out. But oh! what a pitiful, dirty, draggled lot they were. And, in spite of their miserable condition, they must needs get up several fights among themselves in order to crown the delights they had been indulging in ashore. It was quite out of the question to allow the second mate's watch ashore that day; and this decision nearly caused our first serious row, so eager were the other half of the crew to go and do even as their fellows had done. But as there was nothing to prevent the petty officers going, they all furbished up and started, taking us two boys with them. My chum Bill Smith was of the party; but as soon as we landed he went off with me, being far too old a hand to be led by anybody. Of course, poor fellow! having no wages, he had contrived to earn a little by washing, etc., and every copper was carefully hoarded for the Bombay bazaars, where, he informed me, better bargains in clothes could be got than anywhere in London. Up and down the crowded lanes of the bazaar he led me, driving away with contumely the pilots who offered to personally conduct us for a consideration, and fingering the goods of the various shopkeepers with the air of one who is bursting with wealth. At last, finding a booth to his mind, he entered, and forthwith selected a great heap of things: such as soldier's trousers, woollen shirts, dungaree jumpers and trousers, towels, caps, soap—in fact, a regular outfit. At last the middle-aged Mussulman who ran the show began to look suspicious, and said, "You got plenty rupee, Johnny?" "I've got all I want, Johnny," said he. "Gimme jar o' ginger. *Ginger*, mind; none o' yer m'lasses." The ginger was brought and added to the heap. Then Bill said, "Now, then, Johnny, how much for the lot?" A portentous calculation ensued, which occupied, I should think, twenty minutes. At last the account was made up—forty-five rupees. Without moving a muscle of his face, Bill immediately replied, "I'll give you ten." Horror, amazement, indignation, chased one another over the countenances of the shopkeepers. At last one of them found words. "You make plenty laugh, Johnny; speakee barabba one time. Gib forty rupee." "Not another pice," said Bill, pulling out his money and counting it ostentatiously. Well, the antics those two natives did cut, to be sure! They worked themselves up into a foaming rage, they cast their turbans recklessly in the dust; in such English as they could command they reviled their tormentor and all his relations to the remotest degree, and finally came down to thirty rupees. That, they swore with sudden solemnity, was absolutely the bottom figure, at which they would lose at least five rupees on the transaction. "Oh, very well," said Bill, "then I'm off." And, rising, he said, "Come along, Tom." Out we went, and strolled leisurely along the alley for about a hundred yards, when suddenly one of the merchants came flying after us, and, with many smiles, besought Bill to return and "speakee barabba" now. Back we went, and the game began again. I got thoroughly weary of it at last; but Bill's patience was inexhaustible. He was rewarded, finally, by their absolute submission to his terms, when, to my consternation, he refused to have the goods unless they gave him a large bottle of pepper as backsheesh. Surely, I thought, this will so disgust them that they will assault us. But no; after another quarter of an hour's haggling they yielded the last point, and, laden like a sumpter mule, Bill took his triumphant departure.

By this time I had seen more than enough of the steaming hubbub of the bazaars. But Bill had more business to transact; so we parted company; and I wandered away alone, gazing with wide-eyed wonder at the innumerable strange sights to be seen in this great humming city. No one molested me, although many curious glances were cast at me by groups of languid natives, of all shades, as I trudged along without any definite idea whither I was going. At last, utterly weary, I found myself down at the water's edge again. The afternoon was getting on, and I should soon have to return on board; but as I had still two rupees, I thought I would like a trip up the harbour to Mazagan, or beyond it. Full of my project, I chartered a canoe with two men in it to take me for a sail, bargaining, as well as I was able, in my ignorance of the language, for a two hours' sail, ending on board my ship. We started, and, for perhaps half an hour, I thoroughly enjoyed myself, as the canoe glided along right up past the P. and O. moorings and the Arsenal. Then, when we were clear of the shipping, my boatmen suddenly stopped and began an animated discussion with me, which was somewhat complicated by the fact that neither of us understood the other. Eventually I became convinced that they wanted more money, and their previously mild behaviour grew certainly more aggressive. I felt very nervous, but struggled to conceal the fact, speaking boldly, as if accustomed to be obeyed. Finally I produced my money, and turned my pockets inside out to show that I had no more. Upon seeing this they held a long conversation, during which the canoe drifted idly and I sat upon thorns. At last, much to my relief, they turned the boat's head towards the anchorage again, and, without another word, paddled homeward. Arriving at about a cable's length from the ship they stopped, and demanded their money. But I, having seen the stalwart figure of the mate standing on the forecastle head, stood up, and, with all the voice I could muster, shouted, "*Western Belle*, ahoy!" Mr. Edny heard me and waved his hand. This move on my part evidently disconcerted them, and they paddled vigorously for the gangway. As soon as the canoe touched the side, I sprang up and told Mr. Edny what had happened. He asked me what I had promised them. I told him one rupee. Taking eight annas from me, he went down the gangway and offered it to them. When they set up a perfect storm of protests, he just pitched the piece of money into the canoe and pushed it away from the side, returning on board without taking any further notice. Needless to say, I was heartily thankful to be well out of what at one time looked like an ugly scrape.

Next morning the liberty men returned on board in the usual condition, but Bradley was not with them. That night, however, he paid us a visit by stealth, coming up the cable and rifling several of his shipmates' chests of whatever was worth carrying off. Then he went ashore again unperceived, showing what a very slack watch was kept. There was consternation in the forecastle when the robbery was discovered, and a good deal of wild talk; but Bradley was something of a "bucko," and I very much doubt whether any of them would have said much to him had he been there in person. Three days longer we remained at anchor, although apparently quite ready for sea. On the second morning Bradley returned, and climbing on board, walked aft and coolly asked the mate for a rupee to pay his boatman with. Being curtly refused and ordered forward, he stripped off the filthy white shirt he was wearing, and rolling it up, flung it over to the dinghy-wallah, bidding him to "Kinnaree jao, jildee" (get ashore quick). With this the poor beggar was perforce content, making off hurriedly. Bradley then made for his bunk, saying no word to any one until the afternoon, when he bade Julius Cæsar go and tell the skipper that he was very ill. This message actually made the old man angry. He came forward and gave the defaulter a piece of his mind; but being evidently impressed by the look of the man, who had been gutter-raking in all the filth of "coolie town" for three days, he sent for the harbour doctor. That worthy, after examination, gave it as his opinion that there was nothing the matter with the fellow but bad gin and want of food, assuring the skipper that he would be all right as soon as we got to sea.

Next morning we got under way and sailed, not without another protest from Bradley, of which no notice was taken, as the medical officer, who was then paying his final visit, adhered to his opinion. We took a favourable wind at the harbour's mouth, and slid gently down the coast under easy sail, the vessel being "tender" from scanty allowance of ballast. But the weather was lovely, the wind fair, and everything promised a delightful trip.

Bradley, however, steadily got worse. Presently an angry-looking eruption of pimples burst out all over his body, even the inside of his mouth being invaded. Then my purgatory commenced. No one would have anything to do with him, although he was quite helpless. He was shifted out of the forecastle up on to the forecastle-head, and a sort of tent rigged over him to keep the sun off. Then I was told off to attend to him. The horror of that time will never leave me. He was, as I have before noted, with the exception of the mate, the most hairy man I ever saw, the black shaggy covering of his arms and legs being at least an inch and a half long, while his chest and back were more like a great ape's than a man's. Therefore, when all those pimples grew until they were large as a finger-top, and so close together that not a speck of sound flesh was visible, the task of washing him, which I had to perform alone, was really an awful one. I must draw a veil over the further development of those horrible pustules.... Happily for the patient he became delirious and apparently insensible to pain. How I kept my reason I don't know; but I thought, and still think, that it was a frightful ordeal for a youngster under fourteen to endure for a whole week. I had nothing else to do; no relief, except my ordinary watch below, during which he was left quite alone. On the eleventh day after leaving Bombay we entered Bimliapatam Roads, and just as we did so death mercifully came to his rescue and mine. The carpenter botched up a rough coffin, into which the unrecognizable heap, with all its bedding, was hurriedly bundled, taken ashore, and buried at the foot of the flagstaff without any ceremony whatever. No one seemed to know what the disease had been; but I can only say that having seen lepers in all stages of disfigurement, and many other cases of terrible pestilential ravages, I have never seen anything so awful as the case of William Bradley.

CHAPTER XVII.

ON THE COROMANDEL COAST.

Freed from that horrible incubus, I had now leisure to look about and enjoy the varied scenes that presented themselves. The place we were lying at was, I suppose, a typical native coast village, a big hill facing the anchorage having a rock-hewn temple upon its sea-front. There was no harbour or shelter of any kind, so that vessels lay all ready for sea in case of bad weather setting in. All cargo was brought off in the crazy "massulah" boats, which have been so often described by visitors to Madras, and are the only craft able to stand the rough usage of the surf-beaten beach. The fishermen went out on primitive contrivances of three logs lashed together without any attempt at hollowing out or fashioning bow and stern. Kneeling upon the two outer logs in the centre of the crazy thing, the poor wretch would paddle seaward until out of sight, his sole equipment a palm-leaf basket secured just in front of him, and containing his fishing-tackle. Neither food nor water could be carried, yet in this miserable condition they would remain out for many hours, at the mercy of every wave that came along, and often being rolled over several times in succession. The catches of fish they made were always pitifully small, it seemed to me, sometimes consisting of only a couple of dozen large prawns, though how they caught *them* out there was a mystery to me.

Our cargo was an assorted one. Jaggery, or palm sugar—looking like bags of black mud, and almost as nice to handle,—buffalo horns and hides, cases of castor oil, bags of myrabolums (a kind of dye-nut), and sundry other queer things came off to us in small quantities at a time, and were flung on board in a most haphazard fashion, owing to the constant swell, which made the boats tumble about alongside vivaciously. All the stowage was done by the crew under the direction of Jemmy the Scrubber, who proved himself as capable a stevedore as he was a seaman. No one went ashore except the skipper while we lay there, and he would gladly have avoided the necessity, if possible, since it usually meant a thorough drenching. On the whole, we were by no means sorry when the news came that we were to leave and proceed down the coast to Coconada. As we were always ready to sail, there were none of the usual preliminaries; we just hauled in the fenders, hove the anchor up, and started. Here our skipper's local knowledge was of great service. For we hugged the coast closely all the way down, keeping a favourable wind, which brought us into Coconada Bay in a few hours, while the *Andromeda*, a big Liverpool ship that sailed at the same time for the same port, stood off the land, got into bad weather, and did not arrive for twenty-eight days. She had also sustained severe damage to both ship and cargo.

While Coconada was evidently a much more important place than Bimliapatam, we saw nothing of the town, for we lay a long way off in the centre of a huge bay. We were near enough, though, to hear the various cries of the wild beasts, among which the hideous noise of the hyenas was especially noticeable. Our unhappy painter, who had remained in Bombay hospital during the whole of our stay there, was again so ill that he had to be landed here. But, getting convalescent, he and a fellow patient went for a stroll one day, and, wandering out of the town, they met a hyena. Barber was so scared that he fainted right away, but the other man found sufficient vitality to scramble up a tree. He had not got very high, though, before weakness overcame him, and he fell, breaking his leg. When Barber came to there was no trace of the hyena, but he and his fellow were in a pitiable plight. There they would doubtless have stopped, and had their bones picked clean by the morning, but for a party of friendly coolies who came along, and, seeing their condition, fetched a couple of "palkees" and carried them back to hospital again.

Here, then, we remained for three weeks, filling the hold with a miscellaneous collection of Indian produce, of which cotton, linseed, and myrabolums formed the staple, until the great capacity of our ship for cargo was effectually satisfied, and she was jammed full to the hatch coamings. Then all hands, released from their stifling labours below, bent their energies to getting ready for sea. Meanwhile, although our crew were certainly a most patient set of men, their discontent at the short-handedness, which ever since leaving home had pressed so hardly upon us all, gathered to a head, culminating in a visit of all hands to the quarter-deck with a request to see the skipper. Genial as ever, Captain Smith appeared, his ruddy face wearing an expression of benign wonderment at the unusual summons. "Well, what is it, men?" said he. Then stepped forward an elderly Yankee, who had been a bo'sun's mate in the American navy, a shrewd, intelligent man with a rich fund of native humour, and a prime favourite fore and aft. "We've taken the libbaty, sir, ov comin' aft t'ask ye ef it's yeur intenshun ter sail 'thout shippin' enny more hands?" was his reply. "Well, in the first place, Nat," answered the skipper, "there's no hands ter be got here, an' besides, in sech a easy-workin' ship as this is, there's no hardship in bein' a cupple o' hands short." "The good Lawd fergive ye, sir!" exclaimed Nat; "ef thishyers a heasy-workin' ship, what mout ye reckon a *hard*-workin' one 'ud be like? Why, cap'n, it takes two men to haul thro' the slack ov th' braces, an' it's all a man's work to overhaul the gear of a to'gantsle. 'Sides, sir, yew know it takes all hands to shorten her down to the taupsles, 'n what we k'n do with her in a squall—well, I hain't fergot thet plesant evenin' off the Cape, ef yew have." At this vigorous reply the old man could only laugh to show his appreciation of the home-thrusts it contained, but with native shrewdness he changed his base, still preserving his cheery good temper. "Mind ye, I don't say we ain't short-handed," he said—"very short-handed; but we're gettin' out ov the Bay o' Bengal 'fore the sou-west monsoon sets in, 'n yew know 's well 's me that it's fine weather 'mos' all the way ter the Cape once we cross the line. 'N if we git enny dirt offn the Cape I'll keep her under easy sail, 'n let the 'Gulhas current sweep her roun', 'n then we'll jest be home in no time. Yew leav' it t' me. We hain't been eight months together 'thout knowin' each other, 'n yew all know yew k'n depend on me to do the best I k'n ter make ye comfortable. But I *can't* get any hands in this God-forsaken place if we only had two left forrard." That speech settled it. If Captain Smith had been an irritable man, inclined to put on airs of outraged dignity because his crew asked him a perfectly reasonable question, and to rate them like a set of fractious children, there would have been an instant refusal of duty on the part of the men, followed by much suffering and loss on both sides, for the chaps were thoroughly in earnest. But the skipper's frank good-humour and acceptance of the situation disarmed them, and they returned forward with minds made up to see the voyage out as best they could. Next day we weighed anchor and sailed for London, the windlass revolving to the time-honoured tune of "Good-bye, fare-you-well; hurrah, my boys, we're homeward bound."

Just prior to our departure we received on board some two or three hundred fowls and two goats, which, added to about twenty pigs—mostly bred on board, two large dogs, two monkeys, sundry parrots and two cats, made the ship bear no bad resemblance to Noah's Ark. None of these animals had any settled abiding place; they just roamed about the decks whithersoever they would, except on the sacred precincts of the poop, which were faithfully guarded by one of the dogs, who allowed no intrusion by any of the grunting, clucking, or chattering crowd. But this state of things was a great trial to all concerned. For one of the cardinal necessities of British or American ships is cleanliness, which is secured by copious floods of salt water, and vigorous scrubbing every morning. Under present conditions keeping the vessel clean was manifestly impossible, the crowd of animals even invading the men's quarters, as well as every nook into which they could possibly squeeze themselves. There was a great deal of dissatisfaction forward at this state of things, and fowls were continually flying overboard, being chased and smitten by angry men, who found everything under their hands befouled and stinking. Still the nuisance was unabated until we were ten days out. Just off Cape Comorin we got our first stiff breeze of the homeward passage, and very soon, in accordance with her invariable custom, the old ship began to take sufficient water over the rail to flood the decks fore and aft. Then there was a commotion in the farmyard. The watch, up to their waists in water, splashed about collecting the squawking chickens, and driving the bewildered swine into a temporary shelter, rigged up under the topgallant forecastle. Next morning at least four dozen dead fowls were flung overboard, in addition to many that had fled blindly into the sea on the previous day. This loss so disgusted the skipper that he ordered all hands to be fed on poultry until the stock was exhausted. At first this benevolent (?) command gave a good deal of delight, but when the miserable, leathery carcases, boiled in salt water, unclean and unsavory, were brought into the forecastle, there was almost a riot. A deputation waited upon the captain to protest and demand their proper rations of "salt horse." They were received by the skipper with a very ill grace, and the usual senseless remarks about sailors' fastidiousness in the matter of food were freely indulged in by the "old man," who seemed quite out of temper. We got no more Coromandel poultry, though, which was a blessing, albeit they were served up to the cabin as usual. Being prepared in a civilized fashion, I suppose, the officers found them eatable. But in various ways the flock of fowls diminished rapidly, much to our relief, and gradually the decks began to assume their normal cleanliness. The pigs, numerous as they were, could be kept within bounds forward; in fact, the dogs rarely permitted them to come abaft the foremast. As for the two goats, they grew so mischievous, gnawing the ends of all the ropes, and nibbling at everything except iron, that orders for their execution went forth, and since no one would eat them, their bodies were flung overboard.

CHAPTER XVIII.

HOMEWARD TO LONDON.

As Captain Smith had foretold, we were having an exceedingly fine-weather passage. All the way down the Indian Ocean we were favoured with pleasant breezes, fair for our course, and glorious weather. Every care was taken to make the work as light as possible for the small crew, although we in the starboard watch were sorely exasperated by the second mate's devotion to sand and canvas—a mania that had given him his well-earned sobriquet of "Jemmy the Scrubber." If he could only have his watch slopping about with a few buckets of sand and rags of old canvas, rubbing away at the dingy interior of the bulwarks, that with all his attentions never *would* look white, he was in his glory. But oh! how we did hate the messy, fiddling abomination. It made our discontent the greater to notice that the mate's watch scarcely ever touched it. Like a sensible man, Mr. Edny preferred to have one thoroughly good scrub down at lengthy intervals, going over the whole of the paint in one day, to scratching like a broody hen, first here and then there, in patches, and never making a decent job after all. It kept the watch in a chronic state of growl, which was only prevented from breaking out into downright rebellion by the knowledge that the second mate was always in hot water aft, although, owing to his seven years' service in the ship, the skipper and mate allowed him to have pretty much his own way. Apart from this, things went on smoothly enough. Many a time did Jemmy, with only such assistance as Bill and I could give him, set and take in the lighter sails without disturbing the rest of the watch, who were fast asleep in their several bunks. They knew this well, and consequently never turned out, even upon the most urgent necessity, without a chorus of growls at the second mate, although he never took the slightest notice of them.

So we slowly lumbered homeward in uneventful monotony, until one morning we made the land about East London, and congratulated ourselves that we were near the southern limit of our journey home. Still the weather was kind to us. No envious southerly gale battered us back from the Cape we were striving to get round, and presently we found ourselves in the embrace of the great Agulhas current that for ever sets steadily round the Cape westward. Homeward bounders have reason to rejoice when they enter the limits of this mighty marine river, for, in spite of contrary winds or calms, they are irresistibly carried on the way they would go at a rate that is the same for the bluff-bowed sea-waggon as for the ocean-flyer. And one day, to my intense delight—for I had heard a tale from Bill—the wind died completely away and the water became as smooth as a mirror. Every bit of line in the ship that could by any possibility serve as a fishing-line was ferreted out, and fishing commenced. At first only the favoured few, whose lines were fifty or sixty fathoms long, got a look in, bringing up from the bank far below us some magnificent specimens of cod. Then, as the fish followed their disappearing comrades up, the shorter lines came into play, and the fun became general. It was a regular orgie of fishing. At least three hundred splendid fish of various kinds, but chiefly cod, rewarded our efforts, the subsequent feast being something to date from. Better still, the weather being cool, we were able to salt down a large quantity for use later on, so that we had fish for nearly a month afterwards. After about eight hours of this calm a gentle south-easterly breeze sprang up, which persisted and strengthened, until, with the dim outlines of the high land behind the Cape of Good Hope on our starboard quarter, we were bowling cheerily along under every rag we could muster, our head pointing north-north-west, homeward-bound indeed.

Then the work that must be undertaken in every respectable ship on the "home-stretch" came with a rush. Setting up rigging, rattling down, general overhaul of running and standing gear, chipping iron-work and painting it with red lead, scraping bright woodwork, etc., etc., kept us all busy, although we were allowed watch and watch all along. In most ships it is the custom while in the south-east trades, homeward-bound, to give no afternoon watch below in order that the bulk of the "redding-up" may be done before crossing the line. But for several reasons our skipper did not think it advisable to tax his scanty crew too much. As for attendance on the sails, we might have been a steamship for all the work of that kind required—the "south-east trades" being notoriously steady and reliable in the Atlantic, while the north-east trades are often entirely wanting. So we had trades, from the Cape to the line, that did not vary a point in force or direction for three weeks; and, if she would have steered herself, she could have made that part of the passage unmanned. The time literally flew by, being delightfully punctuated every Sunday by a glorious feed of roast pig—two of our large stock of home-bred porkers being sacrificed each Saturday, and fairly apportioned among all hands.

St. Helena was sighted ten days after losing sight of the African land—a huge black mass, towering to an enormous height, as it seemed to me. We approached it very closely, purposing to report ourselves there, but not to anchor. Coming round under the huge crags of the southern end with all sail set, we had a splendid view of the cliffs, rising sheer from the sea, whereon the gliding shadow of our ship was cast in almost perfect resemblance. Who was responsible for the neglect, I do not know, but suddenly down a gorge in the mountain rushed a fierce blast almost at right angles to the wind we were carrying, and making the canvas shake and flap with a thunderous noise. There was a great bustle to get sail off her, but unfortunately she paid off rather smartly, and *crack* went the mizzen-topmast before the sails came down. A piece of gross carelessness! for no coast of that kind should ever be approached under sail without all due precautions for shortening down. Neglect of such preparation has caused the loss of many a fine ship and countless boats, with appalling sacrifice of life. It was the only spar we lost during the whole of that voyage.

By the time we had got the kites off her we had opened out the great gorge, in which, as if it had been dropped from the cliffs above, lies the town, the houses appearing curiously jumbled together. We were so close in that the great ladder, credited, I believe, with a rung for every day in the year, which leads up on to the cliffs from the town, was plainly visible. Only one ship, the *Noach VIII.*, of Rotterdam, one of the regular old Dutch East Indiamen from Java, was at anchor, for even then the prosperous days of St. Helena as a sort of ocean "half-way house" had departed, never to return. We spelt out our name and ports of departure and destination with the length of passage, our information being duly acknowledged from the flag-staff. In a few minutes more we were again in the grip of our faithful friend the south-east trade, and feeling that another important milestone was passed on our long journey. Placidly, equably, we jogged on, four days afterwards sighting and signalling to the barren volcano-scarred island of Ascension, the exclusive domain of men-o'-war, for whose behalf a large naval establishment is maintained in highest efficiency. Another landmark left behind. Onward we sped with freshening trades and increasing speed until we were actually in eight degrees north latitude, so kindly had the fair wind we took off the pitch of the Cape favoured us. But our good fortune still held. Instead of at least a week of the detestable doldrums we fully expected, we had only one day's detention before the north-east trades swept down upon us, and away we went, braced sharp up on the starboard tack to the north-westward. And now for a while, all the tarry work being done, all hands were transformed into painters, and varnishers. Within and without also, as far as the wash of the sea alongside would allow, we painted and polished, until the grimy, once shabby old packet looked quite smart and shining. The second mate was right in his element. He begrudged himself necessary rest, and often looked angrily at the sun when setting, as if he felt he was being defrauded out of a few minutes more of his beloved labour. Never surely was there a man who loved work for its own sake better than he. Never had a ship a more energetic seamanlike officer. Yet he was by no means appreciated aft, although his worth was undeniable. And as so often happens, he was doomed to be a junior officer all his life, for he could not do the simplest problem in navigation without making the most ludicrous mistakes. However he "passed" for second mate was a mystery known only to the examiners. Mainly, I believe, by his untiring efforts, all our painting operations were successfully completed before we reached the northern verge of the tropic, where changeable weather began to appear. But, when once the paint was on, he was like a hen with one chick. His eager eye was ever on the watch for any unfortunate who should dare to sully the whiteness of the bulwarks within, or heave anything overboard carelessly that might mark the glossy blackness outside. But his great carnival was yet to come. One morning shortly after four, under his directions, I lugged up from the fore-peak a number of lumps of sandstone, which he busied himself till daylight in shaping into sizable blocks, while I pounded the smaller pieces into sand. Promptly at four bells the watch were gathered aft, and "holystoning" commenced. This delightful pastime consists of rubbing the decks, along the grain of the wood, with blocks of sandstone, the process being assisted by scattered sand and water. For three days the decks were in a continual muck of muddy sand, and

Jemmy's face wore a steady, beaming smile. When, at last, all the grit was flooded away, the result was dazzling. The decks were really beautiful in their spotless cleanliness. Then, to my unbounded amazement, no sooner were they dry, than a vile mixture of varnish, oil, and coal-tar, was boiled in an impromptu furnace on deck, and with this hideous compost the spotless planks were liberally besmeared. I felt personally aggrieved. "Why"—I could not help asking my chum Bill—"why, in the name of goodness all this back-breaking holystoning only to plaster such a foul mess on the decks immediately afterward?" "Preserves the wood," was the sententious reply, and it was all the answer I could get. Certainly the poop was varnished only, which made it a golden hue until the first water was poured on it. After that it always looked as if a lot of soapsuds had been poured over it and left to dry.

But with this final outrage on common sense, as I couldn't help considering it, our ship-decorating came to an end. Henceforth the chief object in view apparently was to preserve, as far as possible, the spick and span appearance of the vessel until she reached home. Those beautiful decks, especially, were the objects of Jemmy's constant solicitude. He found some nail-marks one day left by somebody's boots, and one would have thought the ship had sprung a leak like a well-mouth by the outcry he made. As far as possible work was confined to the fore part of the ship, and beside the ordinary routine little was done but the plaiting of rope yarns into sennit—always a kill-time. But we were now so far north that the variable weather of the North Atlantic began to give us plenty of occupation in the working of the ship. Fortunately we were not long delayed by contrary winds. The brave westerlies came to our assistance, driving us along in fine style and at increasing speed, until one day through the driving mist we sighted Corvo, one of the northern outposts of the Azores. It was fortunate that we did so, for thenceforward thickening weather and overcast skies prevented any observation of the heavenly bodies, and "dead reckoning" was our only means of knowing the ship's position. Now Captain Smith, though thoroughly at home on the Indian coasts, had a great dread of his own shores, and as the distance from land grew less he became exceedingly nervous, until at last, when by his estimate we were well up Channel, he dared no longer run as fast as the following gale would have driven him, but shortened sail, much to every one else's disgust. Ship after ship came up astern, passed us, and sped away homewards, while we dawdled through those crowded waters, running the risk of the fair wind blowing itself out before we had gained our port. Before we had sighted land or light it came down a thick fog—a regular Channel fret—which is a condition of things dreaded by all seamen on our dangerous coasts. We hove-to, keeping the foghorn going with its melancholy bray. Thus for six mortal hours we lay helplessly tossing in the fairway, listening to the miserable discord of foghorns, syrens, and whistles, but unable to see the ship's length away from us. The anxiety was exceedingly great, for at any moment we were liable to be run down by something or another, whose commander was more venturesome than ours. Suddenly out of the gloom came a hoarse hail, "D'ye want a pilot, sir?" A sweeter sound was never heard. Without a moment's hesitation the old man replied, "Yes, where are you?" He had hardly spoken before the dim outlines of a lugger came into view close alongside. "Are you a Trinity pilot?" asked the skipper. "No, sir, but I can run you up to him," replied the voice. "How much?" queried the captain. "Five pounds, sir!" came promptly back. "All right, come aboard!" said the old man, and all hands crowded to the side to see our deliverer from suspense. "Heave us a line, please, sir!" came up from the darkness, where we could see the shadowy form of the big boat tossing and tumbling in the heavy sea. The main brace was flung out to her, and, as she sheered in towards us, a black bundle seemed to hurl itself at us, and in a few seconds it stood erect and dripping on deck—a man swathed in oilskins till he looked like a mummy. Only pausing to dash the water out of his eyes, he shouted, "Square the mainyard!" and walking aft to the helmsman ordered him to "Keep her away." A minute before all had been miserable in the extreme, and the bitter gale roaring overhead seemed to be withering all the life out of us. But what a change! The man seemed to have brought fine weather with him; the perfect confidence that every one had in him dispelling every gloomy thought. The lesson of that little episode, so commonplace, yet so full of instruction, has never been forgotten by me. It is so palpable that I dare not enlarge upon it.

Meanwhile one of the lugger's crew had followed his chief, and was busy begging tobacco, meat, and anything else the steward could find to part with. When he had got all he could, the lugger sheered in again, and he tumbled back on board with his booty. Very soon the fog cleared away, and as soon as it did so we saw the light on Dungeness close aboard. We ran up to the pilot's cruising ground and hove-to, burning a blue light as a signal, while our friendly hoveller pocketed his five pounds and departed, well pleased with his four hours' earnings. These men get called some very hard names, and may perhaps occasionally deserve them; but as long as sailing-ships exist they will be found, as we undoubtedly found one, a very present help in time of need, and the salvation of many a fine ship.

The Trinity pilot was some time making his appearance, for there were many ships about, and we must needs wait our turn. But in due time we were supplied, the yards were again squared, and away we went around the Foreland. Presently there was a welcome sound of paddle-wheels, and up came a tug anxious for the job of towing us up to London. But our captain's Scotch economy forbade him to take steam while there was so much fair wind going for nothing; and the subsequent haggling was almost as protracted as Bill's celebrated feat in Bombay. At last, after two or three departures of the tug in fits of irritation, a bargain was struck, and the ever-welcome command came pealing forward, "Get the hawser along!" No need to call all hands. Everybody came on the jump, and that mighty rope was handled as if it had been a lead-line. In a wonderfully short time the end was passed to the tug, a severe turn was taken with our end round the windlass bitts, and with what the sailor calls "a fair wind ahead," we went spinning up through the intricate channels of the Thames estuary. All hands worked with a will to get the sails clewed up and unbent from the yards, as it was now daylight. Such a morning's work had not been done on board for many a day, for was not the end of the voyage here. As for me, I was continually in hot water, for I could not keep my eyes off the wonderful scenes through which we were passing. It was my first home-coming to London by sea, and on the two previous occasions of leaving, I had either no heart to look about me or I had come down at night. Just stopping at Gravesend long enough to exchange pilots, since the sea-pilot never takes a ship into dock, we sped onward again, the tug straining every nerve to save the tide. Soon everything was ready for docking, and all hands were allowed to "stand by," resting until we should reach Blackwall.

The East India Docks at last, with the usual little group of expectant yet nonchalant officials and the loafers in the background. Are we going to dock at once, or will she tie up in the basin? As anxiously as if docking was going to take a month were these questions bandied about, so eager were all the fellows to get ashore. Joy!—she is hauled in to the side of the basin, made fast temporarily, and the mate, with a merry twinkle in his eye, says the closing benediction, "That'll do, men." By this time the voracious crowd of boarding-masters' runners, tailors' ditto, and unclassified scoundrels were swarming on board (it was before the beneficent regulations were passed forbidding these gentry to board an in-coming ship), and the forecastle was a perfect pandemonium. But one by one the chaps emerged with their dunnage, and were carried off in triumph by one or other of the sharks, until, the last one having gone, we of the half-deck were left in peace. And now I *was* home what was I going to do? I felt like a stranger in a strange land, and it was with a sense of great relief that I accepted an invitation to stay by the ship for the present.

CHAPTER XIX.

A CHANGE OF NATIONALITY.

Much as I longed for my liberty, the certain sense of a home afforded by the ship was so comforting that I was in considerable dread of the time when, as I supposed, I should be paid off and sent adrift like the rest of the crew. Therefore it was with joy that I received the welcome news from the mate that I might remain and work by the ship, and that my wages would be fourteen shillings a week, out of which I was to keep myself. The future, which had begun to worry me greatly with its possibilities of misfortune, owing to my still insignificant size, now took a decidedly roseate hue. My arch-enemy (as I considered him), the second mate, became quite amiable, even condescending to inform me that the plenteous kicks and cuffs he had bestowed upon me had all been prompted by a sincere desire for my best interests, and that, before I was much older, I should thank him heartily for his rigorous treatment. In this latter prophecy he was grossly in error, for I have never been able to find any excuse for the brutality of a man to the helpless who chance to be in his power, whether human or brute.

Pay-day came and I received my account of wages, finding that I was entitled to nine golden sovereigns. At the appointed hour I made my way up the East India Dock-road to Green's Home, where I foregathered with most of my shipmates, who were dogged by villainous-looking men as closely as if they were criminals out for an airing. While waiting, they made frequent visits to the public-house at the back of the office, which fairly hummed with the accumulated rascality of the neighbourhood. But for the danger of actions for libel, I would tell some pretty little stories of what I have seen in some of the highly respectable (see evidence before the Licensing Committees) liquor-shops in "sailor town." But I must refrain, comforting myself with the knowledge that such tales have already been better told elsewhere. When at last my turn came, and I received that little pile of gold—more money than I had ever seen at one time before—I was almost afraid of being the possessor of so much wealth. And knowing well, as I did, the risk I ran if any one got an inkling of my riches, did not lessen my fears. I did not think of the Post Office, strange to say; but, in a few minutes, formed a resolution to lay all my money out in a stock of clothes—which, indeed, I was urgently in need of—and depend upon my weekly earnings from the ship to keep me. The thought of losing my employment never seems to have dawned upon me. Full of my project, I started for Aldgate; but brought up sharply at the Baths before I had gone a hundred yards. A nice warm bath—what a luxury! In I went and enjoyed myself immensely. In about half an hour I was out again and walking briskly westward, when I stopped to make some trifling purchase—to find my money gone, purse and all. On the instant I turned and rushed back to the Baths, flew past the doorkeeper, and up the corridor towards the bath I had recently left. The door stood wide open, and there was my purse on the seat, with the money intact. I grabbed it and drew a long breath, the first, it seemed to me, since I missed it. Going out, I met an angry man at the door, who was anxious to know what I thought I was up to, and so on. A shilling assuaged all his curiosity and lit up his lowering face with sudden smiles. Clutching my purse, I made all the haste I could to Messrs. Moses and Sons, arriving there with a sigh of thankfulness. I didn't feel capable of owning so much money, much less taking care of it. A gorgeously attired individual strode forward with an ironical air of courtesy as I entered, and, bowing low, wished to know my pleasure. Ah! if I was going to spend all my money, here was at least a chance to taste the sweets of that power which its possession brings. With all the hauteur I could assume, I said, as I swelled my four feet of stature in opposition to the shopwalker's majestic presence, "I want an outfit, something plain and substantial; say about nine or ten pounds." And as I spoke I secretly emptied my purse in my pocket, and drawing out a few sovereigns nonchalantly, I passed them through my fingers and dropped them into another pocket. Out of the corner of my eye I watched my gentleman's face. All his sarcastic attitude vanished, and for the time he was my obsequious, humble servant. But oh! how shamelessly he made me pay for his attendance. Even after this lapse of years I blush to think how I was taken in—the shoddy rags which I received for my gold, and the swelling pride with which I ordered them to be sent down to *my* ship. When I left the huge shop I felt quite an important personage, although I had but five shillings left out of my year's wages. Still, such as they were, I had a complete stock of clothing, including a chest and bedding, oilskins and sea-boots; in fact, such an outfit as I had never owned before. When I returned on board I informed Bill of my purchases. He applauded my resolution, but blamed me for not keeping a little money in case of an emergency—he always did himself, he said. For a fortnight, however, I found no reason to regret my precipitate action. Then, on a Saturday afternoon, came the stunning intelligence that, as there was no more work to be done, I was no longer wanted. Fortunately I had saved enough out of my weekly wage to pay for a week's board; so I immediately made my way to my old boarding-house in the West India Dock-road, and was received with open arms. I paid my twelve shillings down manfully, telling the master that I wanted a ship as soon as possible. After finding out by cross-examination that I had been paid off with nine pounds, he was much less cordial. In fact, he grumbled a good deal; but finally promised to do his best to get me a ship at once. Fortunately (as I thought at the time), before the week was out, I got a berth on board a large American ship—the *Pharos* of Boston, which was lying in the South-West India Dock, loading general cargo for Melbourne. As she was only about half full, I begged permission to come and work on board for my food, so that I should not get into debt at the boarding-house. The mate, who engaged me, readily granted my request; in fact, he seemed to take no interest in the matter. So I took up my quarters on board, becoming great friends immediately with the amiable old mulatto steward, who, besides being a most valuable servant, was a deeply religious man according to his lights.

And now my lines were cast in truly pleasant places. I had heard of the good times enjoyed by boys in American ships—such floating hells for their crews as a rule—and my experiences at present fully bore out the truth of my information. But I very soon saw that all was not right on board. The mate was utterly neglectful of the cargo, spending most of his time tippling in his berth with all sorts of visitors. The second mate, a stalwart youth of twenty, busied himself constantly with the rigging, studiously avoiding any encroachment upon the mate's province of attending to the shipment of the cargo. The captain rarely appeared. He was a very old man, with an awful scowl, and, although bearing himself erect, and smart-looking, was evidently long past the efficient performance of his duties. The only other members of the crew on board were the carpenter, a Finn of about sixty years of age, and the cook, a garrulous Dane, who spent most of his time yarning at the galley door with a huge knife in one hand as if it were his sceptre. A good deal of drinking went on about that galley, and often at knock-off time the stevedores had much ado to get ashore, so drunk were they. At last the mate left—how or why I do not know—and from thenceforward no pretence was made of tallying in the cargo at all. Not until three days before she was advertised to sail did we get another mate, a prim little man, who had been long master of English ships, and looked like a fish out of water on board the *Pharos*.

Shipping day came, and, leaving the second mate, steward, and carpenter (who were on the original articles) on board, the rest of us went down to a shop in Ratcliff Highway to "sign on." It was a Jew tailor's, of all places in the world, and never shall I forget my astonishment at the sight it presented. When we got there the shop was full of as motley a crowd of scallawags as one could collect anywhere. Apparently they were shipping in some other American ship, from the scraps of conversation I heard. Presently one of the fellows asked a question of the sturdy-looking Israelite behind the counter. Looking up from his book, that worthy said fiercely, "Get out!" The man hesitated, and muttered some reply. With a howl like an enraged tiger the tailor snatched up a pair of shears and sprang over the counter after him. There was a regular scuffle among the crowd for a few seconds, as the thoroughly scared candidate rushed for the door, just succeeding in making his escape as the vengeful Jew reached the pavement. In another second the tailor was back at his book as if nothing had happened. But I noticed that nobody asked any more questions, except one man, whom I took to be the captain of the ship signing on. After some little confusion the first crowd took their departure, and another assortment took their places, ready to sign in the *Pharos*. The whole proceedings were an utter farce, though with a semblance of legality; but what surprised me most of all was that each man received, whether he wanted it or not, two months' advance in the form of a promissory note, payable at this shop three days after the ship left Gravesend. Only three out of the whole crowd signed their names, the rest modestly made their mark, and the tailor wrote down such fantastic designations as his fancy suggested. Then one of his assistants marshalled us all together like a flock of sheep, and convoyed us to the office of the

American Consul-General in the city, where, in wholesale fashion, we were made citizens of the United States of America. The ceremony was no sooner over than we were told to go, but sharply reminded of the hour of sailing. Our guide mysteriously disappeared, leaving us to find our way back to sailor-town as best we could.

To my surprise and gratification I found myself shipped as an ordinary seaman, at thirty shillings per month, three pounds of which I already held in the form of a "promise to pay." I immediately hastened to my boarding-house to get the said paper converted into money, but, as I didn't owe him anything, the master refused to touch it, and further favoured me with his opinion that I shouldn't find anybody who would give me more than ten shillings for it. Somewhat alarmed at this, I hurried to various places where they professed to discount seamen's advance notes, finding to my amazement, that he had spoken the truth. Then I suddenly remembered an old acquaintance with whom I had become friendly, and who, being a tradesman, might be able to change my note. Off to him I hurried, finding him both able and willing; so I got my three pounds in full. But I afterwards learnt that the highest amount any of the sailors had been able to get for their notes of six pounds had been two pounds ten shillings, and of this a goodly portion had to be taken out in clothes. And this I was told was because of the uncertainty attaching to the payment of these notes when they were presented. Under such conditions there was little room for wonder that cases of disappearance of the men who had obtained these advance notes were frequent. It was no unusual thing for half of a crew to be missing when a vessel sailed, when, of course, those who had given anything for the notes lost their money beyond hope of recovery.

Although it seems premature to say so, I feel bound to add that the friend who cashed my note received his money, when it was due, without question. Seven of the men who signed on with me did not turn up on sailing-day, so that we left the dock shorthanded to that extent. We anchored at Gravesend, however, and a scratch lot of "hard cases" were found to make up our complement. For three days we lay at the Red Buoy below Gravesend, while I wondered mightily at such delay, foreign altogether to my notions of the despatch of Australian packets. But finally a huge lighter painted a brilliant red came alongside, and immediately the order was issued for all fire or light of any kind to be extinguished, as we were going to ship gunpowder. As soon as the officers were satisfied that there was no danger from a stray spark to be apprehended, the transhipment began, and soon fifty tons of explosives were transferred to the square of our main hatch, in cases and kegs, from which a good deal of loose powder was leaking. The stowing completed, the hatch was securely battened down for sea, the lighter left, and the order was given to man the windlass. Hitherto I had been agreeably surprised to see how quietly the work went on, altogether a different state of affairs to what I had expected on board a Yankee ship. But the reason was not far to seek. Vicious as the captain looked, he was utterly helpless to inaugurate a reign of terror on board, for he had no truculent set of officers to back him. The mate was a quiet, elderly man, looking as unlike a seaman as possible, and certainly was not the man to develop into a bully. The second mate was too young, although as smart a man as ever stepped, to tackle the whole crew single-handed, even had he felt disposed; and, of course, the ancient carpenter counted for nothing. Half the crew were exceedingly hard citizens, who looked as if all the ways of "Western Ocean blood-boats" were familiar to them; the other half were Norwegians and Swedes, who were unable to speak English, and ready to endure any kind of brutality, at whoever's hands it might be presented. Poor wretches! had they but known it, they were fortunate, for the worst that befell them was being treated as boys by the hard-bitten members of the crew, and made to wait on them hand and foot. On deck their lives were easy enough and the food was really good.

In order to save the skipper trouble, I suppose, we had a Channel pilot on board to take the ship as far as Portland. He, poor man, was sadly out of his element with the skipper, whom he early described, to the half-dozen passengers we carried, as an unmitigated hog. Still there was no open breach between them until we arrived off the Wight. Then when the pilot altered the course (we had been coming down in mid-channel), too close in with the land, the old man walked up to the helmsman and sternly ordered him to resume the course he had been steering, right down the centre of the Channel. Of course there was an explosion. The pilot protested in no measured terms against his behaviour, saying that, as his contract was performed, he was anxious to be put ashore. The captain, however, treated him with cool insolence, assuring him that he wasn't going one mile out of his way to land him, and the utmost he would do would be to put him on board any homeward-bounder we might pass near enough. This nearly drove the pilot frantic. We could hear him all over the ship. But, for all the impression he made upon the venerable Yankee, he might as well have saved his breath. Then there was trouble with the passengers. They had been led to believe that they would be sumptuously fed and waited upon, the charterers in London having painted in glowing colours the comforts sure to be met with in so large a ship for seven passengers. Now, however, they found that even the cooking of their food was a privilege for which they must fee the cook, the steward was forbidden to wait upon them, and they were entirely thrown upon their own resources. When they complained to the captain he calmly told them that their difficulties were no concern of his; he had quite sufficient annoyance in seeing them occupying his saloon, which he could assure them was intended for the reception of a very different class of people to them. Happily they were all fairly well used to roughing it, and so they sensibly set about making the best of their very bad bargain, and thenceforward ignored the scowling skipper altogether. The unfortunate pilot was kept on board five days, and finally put on board a homeward-bound Mediterranean steamer that we spoke half-way across the Bay. As he went over the side he hurled his opinion of the skipper back at him, his voice rising higher and higher, until he was no longer audible, to the huge delight of passengers and crew alike.

CHAPTER XX.

THE PASSAGE TO MELBOURNE.

We were now fairly on the voyage, and it must be confessed at the outset that the work of the ship, in spite of the paucity of officers, went on with automatic regularity. No disturbance of any kind marred the general peace, all hands seeming well content to do their duty quietly, although fully aware of the weakness of the afterguard. My own position was a queer one. Although I was on the articles as an ordinary seaman, and slept in the forecastle among the men, neither of the officers ever gave me any work to do, and I was compelled in self-defence to fall back upon my old friend the steward for something to occupy my time. I had all my food with him, and whenever I could do so without fear of being discovered by the captain, he allowed me to perform a few small offices for the unfortunate passengers. Before we had been a fortnight out, a circumstance, which I dare not hint at the nature of, compelled me to give up my quarters in the forecastle and take refuge in the cabin, where I spread my nightly couch under the saloon table. The captain never seemed to notice my existence at all, at which I used to wonder much; but feeling that obscurity was not a bad thing for me, I kept out of his way as much as possible. I do not think it would be possible to find a more perfect representation of Bunyan's "Pope" than he was. Whenever he looked at one of the men his scowl was shocking, almost murderous, and he was continually snarling at the mate for not using violence towards them. But the first gale we encountered revealed a new and still more unpleasant side of his character. Although the ship was new, and staunch as faithful building could make her, her equipment in all details of the very best procurable, I was astonished to see how rapidly sail was reduced, as if she had been the veriest poverty-stricken old hulk that ever was sent to sea to sink. Long before the gale attained its height she was "fore-reaching" under a main lower-topsail and storm staysails, and he, the commander, like an unquiet spirit, was prowling incessantly about the cabin, or pacing restlessly in front of the wheel. In one hand he held a large plug of tobacco, from which his trembling fingers tore leaf after leaf and crammed them into his mouth until it would hold no more. Then he would pause for a moment at the lee rail and disgorge, only to resume his feeding an instant later. He even consulted the poor old steward, asking him, in quite familiar tones, whether he thought the gale was taking off, although at other times he spoke to him rather more brutally than a costermonger would to his donkey. But the crowning act of almost lunatic fear was to come. I was doing something in his beautiful state-room, when I heard him descending the ladder. I could not get out without passing him, so I hid myself behind a curtain, feeling sure that he would not remain there more than a minute. Peeping cautiously out, I saw him standing gazing fixedly at a large print of the Lord's Prayer that adorned one of the panels. Presently he burst out into the most terrible blasphemies: guttural cursings that sent cold chills of horror chasing one another over my scalp. Then he began to moan pitifully, as if in pain, and suddenly, to my intense relief, he hurriedly went on deck again. I fled in to the steward, shaking from head to foot, and told him what I had heard. "Doan tak' no notice, honey," said the kind old fellow. "I guess he's a-gettin' mighty ole 'n scared, so's he don' know haef wat he sez. Ennyhaow, we cain't he'p his cussedness, 'n de good Lawd ain't a-gwine ter mek us pay fer him. I knows Him better'n dat. Don' yew lissen t'im no mo', sonny, ef yew kin he'p it." Little need to tell me that, I thought. There was really nothing extraordinary in the gale. Even the passengers, apart from the discomfort of their surroundings, were unmoved by it, for the splendid vessel behaved herself grandly, hardly shipping a drop of water. Gradually the wind took off; but not until every trace of bad weather was out of the sky was any attempt made to set sail again. And when at last orders were given to loose the topsails and staysails, the captain seemed half afraid of his own temerity, although two or three vessels passed us with every stitch set, their crews lining the bulwarks to stare at us in wonder as to why we were thus wasting the fine fair wind.

This cautious navigation, however, troubled nobody but the passengers; and even they were less disturbed by it than they would have been had they known anything of the ship's position. But that no one in the ship knew, with any certainty, except the old fellow himself; for he navigated the vessel, and did not allow the mate to take an observation, treating him in this matter, as in all others, with a contempt almost too great for words. Why, no one could tell; for Mr. Small was a good officer and seaman, keeping the ship in perfect order, and attending to all his duties in a most exemplary way. The only reason that could be imagined for the captain's behaviour to him was that he had none of the loud-voiced bully about him, and utterly refused to beat, kick, or swear at any member of the crew. One thing was especially noticeable: neither of the officers ever went forward of the men's quarters after dark, unless absolutely compelled to do so in the course of trimming or setting sail. This reluctance, on their part, to venture into what they had come to look upon as the men's part of the deck, was of the greatest assistance to the crew in the pursuit of their nefarious schemes of plunder, which were carried on here to a greater extent than I have ever heard of elsewhere. It has been already noticed that a good deal of drunkenness was indulged in before the vessel left the dock, owing to the previous mate's total neglect of duty, and this was principally focussed about the galley. Now, it so happened that the stock of kindling-wood fell very low, and this furnished an excellent excuse for the cook to be much in the fore-hold, seeking such stray pieces of dunnage-wood as he might burn. He was a poor cook, but a superlatively ingenious robber. For, finding that the 'tween decks held little worth his attention, he wrought unceasingly to get the lower hatches lifted—a tremendous task, from the massive weights stowed on top of them. At last he succeeded in getting into the lower hold, and laying open the vast accumulation of valuable cargo that lay beneath. Having done this he informed the "hard-case" members of his exploit, and considerately arranged the fastenings on the fore-hatch so that they could get below when they listed. Thenceforward that forecastle was a scene of luxury such as I believe has never been equalled in a merchant ship. Wire chandeliers, fitted with massive wax candles, lit up the usually darksome house, the burning of costly cigars filled it with aroma, liquors of every kind were drunk from tin pots, and at meal-times all sorts of canned meats, seasoned with various condiments, tickled their palates. Yet, strange to say, there was no drunkenness. One man, the ringleader in this systematic robbery, possessed sufficient force of character to actually prevent any of his shipmates from "giving the show away," as he termed it. In consequence, this eating and drinking of luxuries went on for fully three months, and never a whisper of the goings-on reached the officers' ears. Even the passengers shared in the plunder. Their stores, besides being of bad quality, were so limited in quantity and variety that they were glad to purchase from the sailors a little of their spoil, asking no questions as to its origin. As the various cases were emptied the cook broke them up, carried the fragments into the galley and burnt them, so that no trace was left of the depredations.

The nightly excursions below were attended with awful risk. In the first place the men possessed no dark lantern, so that they carried naked candles flaring in their hands as they crawled through the restricted spaces between the cargo and the deck overhead. And, on first entering the lower hold, they had to make their way over hundreds of drums of naphtha. These were all sealed, it is true; but had there been one leaky can in that temperature over which a naked light passed! More than that, in their investigations the marauders penetrated as far aft as the stern, passing among little heaps of loose gunpowder which had sifted through the hatches of the between-decks, and writhing over kegs of blasting-powder which were stowed right across the vessel amidships. At first they did this unthinkingly; but when they realized it they still went on as before. No doubt this statement of mine will stagger many who have found no difficulty hitherto in accepting my word that this book contains absolutely nothing but the truth, and is a record of my personal experience. Nevertheless, I solemnly declare that I have not deviated one iota from the simple facts of the case. What is strange to myself about it is that I did not, could not, then realize what frightful danger we were continually in; but ever since, when I recall the events of that voyage, the cold sweat starts out upon me and I tremble violently.

True to his traditions the old man kept north as soon as we were well round the Cape, afraid to run the easting down in the usual latitudes because of the stern vigour of the brave west winds. Consequently, we dawdled along with variable winds and dirty weather, never keeping a steady breeze for more than a day or two at the outside. But, as the longest passage must come to an end at last, when nearly four months had elapsed since leaving London, a rumour ran round the ship that we were on the meridian of Cape Leeuwin, the south-westernmost point of Australia. This put all hands in an exceedingly good humour, and incidentally had strange consequences. Not that she had ever been an uncomfortable ship, except for the mate and the passengers. There was never an angry word or a growl heard. Orders were executed with as much alacrity as if there had been half a dozen belaying-pin-wielding officers prowling about, ready to knock any skulker senseless on the instant. No doubt this was owing to some strange under-current of feeling about their nefarious proceedings on the part of the crew, as if they could, in some measure, set-off their wholesale robbery by the prompt, cheerful obedience they paid to all orders. But, as I have said, the report of our nearness to port sent a glow of unusual cheerfulness through the ship. Under its influence the prime mover in the plundering felt so benevolent that he actually went and fetched a bottle of brandy out of his chest, and, hiding it in the breast of his jumper, brought it to the old carpenter as he sat solitary in his berth at the after-end of the forward-house. Chips was profuse in his thanks, earnest in his protestations that he would be *very* careful not to take too much and so let the officers into the secret. No sooner was he left alone, however, than, pouring himself out about half a pint of the glowing "Three Star," he drank it off at a draught. His age fell from him like a shed garment. With a strange glitter in his eye he seized the bottle again, and treated this new man that had entered into him to another jorum like the first. Then, on the instant, all the contumely that he had so long and patiently endured from the skipper rushed into his mind—a hateful burden of memories too heavy to be longer tamely borne. Flinging wide his door he stepped on deck and solemnly marched aft, high determination apparent in every motion of his transformed body. Halting before the cabin door, he shouted, "Cap'n Collier, ye mouldy-headed old son of a gun, come out here! I'm jest goin' ter lam de measly ole hed off'n ye!" The rest of his harangue was unfit for publication. Sufficient to say that, in spite of his deficient acquaintance with the English language, he showed himself marvellously fluent in all the quaint profanity of which Americans are the acknowledged masters. Thrice was he forcibly removed to his berth by the two officers, redoubling his efforts to induce the captain to appear, and thrice he burst forth again and clamoured for the old man's blood. At last, seeing that nothing else would suffice, he was put in irons, his feet were lashed together, and, thus bound, he was cast into his bunk to "sober up," while the second mate searched his berth for the *fons et origo mali.* He soon found it, and brought it aft to the captain. Then a close examination of the fore-hatch was made, revealing the fact that it was unlocked, although the cook swore that he *had* always locked it before he returned the keys to the second mate. However, it was now made secure, and the keys brought aft and given to the captain. Neither of the officers remembered, though, that a spacious ventilator through the fore-part of the house led directly down into the hold. This was accordingly left unfastened, and every night one or other of the unhappy foreigners were compelled to slide down it and pass up such stores as they could lay their hands on. And so the game went merrily on.

Meanwhile the weather holding fine and the wind fair, we drew rapidly nearer to the end of the passage. For my part, easy as my lot had been, I was thoroughly sick of it. I had never been aloft all the passage, nor had I been allowed to take any part in the ordinary work of the ship. Consequently I felt as if I were losing all my knowledge of my business, and I had gloomy forebodings of my sufferings in the next ship. Moreover I felt very uneasy in my mind as to the probable outcome of the goings-on in the forecastle and galley. I had been so much amongst it that I felt sure it would be difficult for me to clear myself if it came to court, and as each day passed I felt more and more certain that there would be a wholesale arrest as soon as the vessel arrived. Therefore I was thoroughly unquiet, longing for the passage to end, yet dreading the arrival in port. But, so far as I could see, these dismal reflections troubled the crew not at all. The seasoned hands had evidently prepared a plan of campaign, and had made ample provision for a lengthy tramp up-country, by stocking their bags with such preserved foods as they fancied. In addition each man had a fine gun, out of a case they had found, and a goodly quantity of cigars and spirits. Such utter recklessness, in the face of their probable wholesale arrest before the ship came alongside the wharf, was hard to understand; yet so they acted.

At last the long-looked-for light on Cape Otway was sighted, and before a splendid westerly breeze we sped through Bass's Straits, and northward for Port Phillip Heads. Without any hindrance, except to take up a pilot, we raced onwards until we reached the anchorage off Williamstown, where, with the red flag flying at our mainmast head in token of the dangerous nature of our cargo, we brought up and furled all sail, 155 days out from London. It was the longest passage that any vessel had made for years, and great was the astonishment manifested by all who boarded us to hear of it. None of them could understand how it was that so fine a ship could possibly have taken the time, especially as another ship, belonging to the same owners, and admittedly a much slower vessel, had been in port a fortnight, having left London one month after us. Captain Collier told the reporters a terrible tale of the severity of our passage, which did great credit to his imagination, but left his veracity derelict. Four days passed at the Williamstown anchorage before we finally got rid of our powder—days of utter misery for every one concerned in the depredations, for they were in momentary expectation of the arrival of a police-boat with orders for their arrest. To this day it is a mystery to me why this did not happen. Of course the skipper could not know how far the robbery had gone, but that "broaching of cargo" had been indulged in he must have been well aware. But he was so utterly contemptuous of all things English, that he may have felt quite indifferent as to what became of Englishmen's property. As his ship was chartered by a London firm it was doubtless their loss. At any rate, he did not trouble himself to order any examination of the hold, or make any inquiry into the suspicious circumstances that had taken place on the passage. At last, all being ready, we weighed anchor and were towed over to the Sandridge Pier. We arrived there late in the afternoon, so that by the time we were moored it was dusk. The decks were cleared up, and all hands sent to supper. About an hour afterwards every man forrard, with the exception of the young foreigners, who had hardly learned English, shouldered their bags and walked ashore. The old man was parading the poop as the row of deserters marched up the pier, but he either did not or would not see them. So they disappeared, and we saw them no more. Nor did we hear of them again, although two days afterwards a reward of four pounds each was offered for their apprehension—a piece of folly almost inconceivable in its fatuity. Of course the cook had gone along with them, the danger of his position far outweighing the loss of twenty pounds in wages which he thus forfeited.

As far as I was concerned, things ran along as smoothly as heart could wish. But I was unsettled, nor could all the kindness of the worthy steward avail to satisfy me. Theoretically, I ought to have been exceedingly comfortable. I had literally nothing to do but avoid the skipper; I had thirty shillings a month as wages, abundance of good food, and I was on the best of terms with every soul on board but one. Yet, somehow, I longed to be out of it all, and could not bring myself to face the possibility of going to sea again in the ship. I took to frequenting the large coasting-steamers, which used to lie at the shore end of the pier, and at last made great friends with the chief cook of one of them: the *Wonga Wonga.* This worthy was a herculean negro, rejoicing in the name of Sam White, which, as a piece of charcoal would have made a white mark on him, was somewhat inappropriate. At the close of a delightful evening spent in his company on board the *Wonga Wonga*, I made bold to ask him if he could get me a passage to Sydney with him. Oh, there could be nothing easier than that, according to him; it was only necessary for him to speak the word, and he could take half a dozen friends up with him. But it was usual to make him a small present. I, of course, had no money; but I timidly offered him a gold scarf-pin, which had been given me by the passengers as a present (I afterwards learnt that it was worth fifty shillings). He was graciously pleased to accept it, and told me to bring my dunnage along at once. In a fever of excitement I returned on board the *Pharos*, and packed up all my belongings, now swollen to a goodly heap by the many articles of clothing given me by the passengers when they left. When I had completed my packing, I could scarcely drag the great pile of chest, bag, and bundle along the deck, and I dared not ask any one on board to help me. But I had plenty of resource; so I hooked on the yardarm cargo-tackle to the lot (all well lashed together), and after a struggle succeeded in hoisting it high enough to swing on to the wharf, having first seen that the watchman was comfortably dozing in the galley. Very carefully I lowered my precious cargo on to the pier, then crept ashore, and dragged it under a railway truck, while I went back to the *Wonga Wonga*, and enlisted the services of the cook's mate to come and carry it up to their ship, and place it under Mr. White's care. Then I got my final instructions. I was to return on board the *Pharos*, and remain there till the next day at dinner-time, when I must hasten on board the steamer, where Mr. White would receive me, and in an hour I should be on my way to Sydney. Making my grateful acknowledgments, I returned on board, and upon a heap of old canvas slept dreamlessly until morning.

CHAPTER XXI.

I BECOME A COLONIAL COASTER.

Surely never morning contained so many hours as did this one. Never before, in all my varied experience, had I felt time to be so leaden-footed. For, do what I would, the thought that at the last moment some hindrance would arise and prevent me from following all my earthly possessions would not be put aside. My good old friend, the steward, noted my nervous condition, and at last called me into the pantry and asked me, in kindly, serious tones, what was the matter. In a few broken words I told him all, so fully did I trust him. He was silent for a couple of minutes, then he said, "Well, Tommy, my boy, I'm sorry you'se gwine; but I couldn't wish to keep ye here. It's no place for ye. And, alldough I'm 'fraid I'm not doin' de right ting to let ye go, I cain't fine it in me heart to stop ye. I only hope you'll be a good boy an' do well, and I shall pray God to bless ye. I don't s'pose you've got any money, so here's ten dollars for ye. Don't let anybody know you've got it, or you'll be sure to get it stole; an' if de times should be bad in Sydney it'll keep ye fur a while. Good-bye, my son." And with that he kissed me. That broke me all up. I declare that, never since I lost my dear old aunt, had I ever felt the genuine thrill of human affection as I felt it then at the touch of that good old coloured man, whose memory I shall cherish as long as I live.

At last the whistle sounded for dinner, and, almost immediately after, I heard the hoarse notes of the *Wonga Wonga's* warning that she was ready to depart. Like an eel I glided over the side, and off up the pier I ran, catching a glimpse between the trucks of the grim figure of Captain Collier as he prowled up and down the sacred limits of his poop. When I reached the steamer, she was in a great state of bustle. A host of passengers with their baggage were embarking, and it was one of the easiest of tasks to slip on board unnoticed. I rushed below to the cook's quarters, finding him in the thick of preparations for the saloon dinner. Hardly looking at me, he uttered a few hurried instructions: the purport of them being that I must creep down through a dim alleyway into the chain-locker, and there remain until he should send for me. At the same time he gave me a hunk of bread and meat. Then it dawned upon me that I was nothing but a "stowaway" after all, especially as he whispered a final command to me not to mention his name upon any account. It was a shock indeed, but there was no place for repentance; I had burned my bridges. So wriggling through the dark crevice he had indicated, I wormed my way along until I reached the chain-locker, where I made myself as comfortable as the rugged heaps of chain-cable would allow. Overhead I heard, as if at an immense distance, the hurry-scurry of departure, and presently, that all-pervading vibration following the deep clang of the engine-room gong that told me we were off. Satisfied, so far, that I was unlikely to return, I went to sleep, and, despite the knobby nature of my couch, slumbered serenely. How long I had thus been oblivious of my strange surroundings I don't know, but it suddenly occurred to me that some one was pulling my legs as they protruded beyond the bulkhead of the chain-locker.

"Sailor-man, by his boots, sir!" said a gruff voice, answered by another, "All right, rouse him up!" Roused up I was accordingly, and, sliding forward, I confronted an elderly man in uniform, whom I took to be the mate, and a stalwart fellow in a guernsey—apparently a quarter-master. In answer to their inquiries, I told them that I had run away from an American ship at Sandridge, and, being anxious to get to Sydney, had stowed away. "Why didn't you come and ask me for a passage?" said the officer. "I didn't dare to risk a refusal," I answered. "Don't you know you can be punished for stowing away?" queried my interlocutor, severely. "No, sir," I replied, "an' I don't care much. I'm satisfied to know that, unless you head me up in a beef-cask and throw me overboard, I shall get to Sydney anyhow." At this impudent reply he frowned a little; but being, as I afterwards found, one of the best-tempered men in the world, he merely said, "Well, come along on deck and we'll see if we can't find you something to do."

Thenceforward I was regarded as one of the crew, and very pleased I was to find things turn out so comfortably. On the third day out we arrived off Sydney Heads, and went up the magnificent bay to the city amid scenes of loveliness that I do not believe can be surpassed by any harbour in the wide world. Mr. White had kept me at arm's length all the passage, apparently prepared to deny all knowledge of me should I show any signs of discovering our bargain to any one; but now, as we neared the A.S.N. Company's wharf, he called me to him and endeavoured to make me believe that my good treatment was entirely owing to his having interested himself on my behalf. I didn't believe a word he said, but I had thoroughly learned how unwise it was to make enemies needlessly, so I pretended to be grateful for his protection. He inquired what my plans were, and, finding that I had none, offered me the hospitality of his home until he should be able to find me a berth in one of the steamers. This offer I accepted, feeling glad to have somewhere to go to as well as to avoid the necessity of breaking into my little stock of money. So we parted for the time on the best of terms, and I returned to my work until knock-off time, when it was understood that I was to accompany him ashore. While I was washing I was agreeably surprised to be called by the mate, who with great kindness presented me with a sovereign, and promised to do his best to get me a berth as lamp-trimmer. He also gave me some good advice as to the company I got into, warning me to beware of the larrikins that infested certain quarters of the town. I thanked him as earnestly as I was able, telling him that I was going to lodge for the present with one of the crew, and, bidding him good-bye, went down the gangway and through the warehouse to wait for the cook as we had arranged. He soon joined me, followed by his two mates bearing my chest, which was put upon a lorry and conveyed up town. I found his wife a kindly, slatternly white woman, and his home a weather-board house in Lower York Street, with hardly any pretensions to comfort. Still, I reasoned, it would do for the time as well as any other place I should be likely to find, and, from the stories I had heard of "down town" Sydney, was probably a great deal safer.

I spent a week ashore wandering wherever I had a mind to, and seeing the beautiful place thoroughly; but I made no acquaintances. One thing was early impressed upon my mind, and subsequent experience only confirmed my belief, that Sydney was the most shamelessly immoral place I had ever seen. That, of course, was twenty-seven years ago, so may not be at all the case to-day. At the end of the week I was overjoyed to get a berth, without anybody's assistance, as lamp-trimmer on board a pretty little steamer, called the *Helen M'Gregor*, that ran regularly between Sydney and the town of Grafton on the Clarence River, calling at Newcastle and sundry places on the river *en route*. By closely observing the duties of the "lamps" on board the *Wonga Wonga*, I had been fairly well prepared to take such a berth; but I thought, with a bitter smile, how little my sailorizing would avail me now. Still, the wages were two pounds ten shillings per month, the same as the A.B.'s had been paid on the outward passage, so I was well content.

My lamp-room was a mere cupboard by the side of the funnel, on deck, and just abaft the galley. To do my work I had to kneel on a hot iron plate in front of the said cupboard, exposed to whatever weather was going. But the cook had all my sympathies. In his tiny caboose he had to prepare meals for seventy or eighty people, while all his pastry-making, butchering, etc. (for we carried live sheep and fowls with us), must needs be done on deck. Now the vessel, though exceedingly pretty to look at in harbour, was utterly unfit to cope with the tremendous seas that sweep along the eastern shores of Australia. Somewhere, in one of Henry Kingsley's books (the "Hillyars and Burtons," I think), he speaks of a little steamer climbing one of those gigantic seas like a bat clinging to a wall. That was a common experience of ours. Her motions were frightful. I have seen every soul on board sea-sick while she crawled up, up, up one mountainous wave after another, plunging down into the abysses between them as if she would really turn a complete summersault. Everybody was black and blue with being flung about, and the passengers, who had perforce to be battened down in the sweltering saloon, or second cabin, suffered misery untellable. Yet even that wretchedness had its ludicrous side. To see our fierce little hunchback cook astride of a half-skinned sheep, to which he held on with a death-like grip, his knife between his teeth and a demoniacal glare in his eye, careering fore and aft in a smother of foam, surrounded by the *débris* of the preparing dinner, made even men half dead with fatigue and nausea laugh. But it was terrible work. As for me, I got no respite at all at night. For I had to keep the lamps burning; and she thought nothing of hurling both the big side-lanterns out of their slides on deck, or shooting both binnacle-lights at once into the air, leaving the helmsman staring at a black disc instead of the illuminated compass-card. And often, as I painfully made my way forrard with the side-lights, after a long struggle with wetted wicks and broken glass, she would plunge her bows under a huge comber, lifting a massive flood over all, which seized me in its ruthless embrace and swept me, entangled with my burden, the whole length of the deck, till I brought up against the second-cabin door right aft, with a bang that knocked the scanty remnant of breath out of my trembling body. Down in the engine-room the grey-headed chief-engineer stood by the grunting machinery, his hand on the throttle-valve, which he incessantly manipulated to prevent the propeller racing the engines out of their seats whenever she lifted her stern out of the water and the screw revolved in thin air. For the old-fashioned low-pressure engines had no "governor," and consequently, no automatic means of relieving the terrific strain thrown upon them in such weather as this. And the firemen, who *had* to keep steam up, though they were hurled to and fro over the slippery plates like toys, were probably in the most evil case of all.

She must have been staunchly built, for she bore the fearful buffeting without any damage worth speaking of, except to the unfortunates who were compelled to attend to their duties under such difficulties. And after the gale blew itself out, and the glorious sun mounted triumphantly in the deep blue dome above, the scene was splendid beyond description. We always kept fairly close in with the land, except when crossing a deep bight, and the views we obtained of the magnificent scenery along that wonderful coast were worth enduring a good deal of hardship to witness. We arrived off the entrance to the Clarence River just at dark, and, to my great astonishment, instead of going in, sail was set, the fires were damped down, and we stood "off and on" until daylight. As soon as there was sufficient light to distinguish objects on shore, we stood in; all passengers were ordered below and everything was battened down. All hands perched themselves as high as they could on the bridge, upper-deck, and in the rigging, while we made straight for the bar. These precautions had filled me with wonder, for I knew nothing of bar harbours. But when, on our nearer approach, I saw the mighty stretch of turbulent breakers rolling in mountains of snowy foam across the river's mouth, I began to understand that the passage through *that* would mean considerable danger. Every ounce of steam we could raise was on her, and the skipper, a splendid specimen of a British seaman, stood on the bridge, the very picture of vigorous vigilance. We entered the first line of breakers; all around us seethed the turmoil of snowy foam, with not a mark of any kind to show the channel, except such bearings as the skipper knew of on the distant shore. Perched upon the rail, a leadsman sounded as rapidly as he could, calling out such depths of water as amazed me, knowing our draught. Along came an enormous wall of white water, overwhelming the hull and hiding it from sight. "Lead—quick!" yelled the skipper above the thunder of the sea; and Joe screamed, "Two, half one, quarter less two." Ah! a long and grinding concussion as she tore up the ground, then along came another mighty comber over all. When it had passed we were over the bar and in smooth water, only the yeasty flakes of the spent breakers following us as if disappointed of their prey. A very few minutes sufficed to dry up the decks, and the passengers appeared well pleased to be in the placid waters of the river and at peace once more. What a lovely scene it was! At times we sped along close to the bank, while a great stretch of river extended on the other side of us a mile wide, but too shallow for even our light draught. On gleaming sand-patches flocks of pelicans performed their unwieldy gambols, and shoals of fish reflected the sunlight from their myriad glittering scales. Turning a sharp bend we would disturb a flock of black swans that rose with deafening clamour in such immense numbers as to darken the sky overhead like a thunder-cloud. And, about the bushes that clothed the banks, flew parrots, cockatoos, and magpies in such hosts as I had never dreamed of. For an hour we saw no sign of inhabitants; then, suddenly, we sighted a little village with a rude jetty and about half a dozen houses. All the population, I suppose, stood on the pier to greet us, who came bearing to them in their lonely corner a bit of the great outside world. Our skipper, though noted for his seamanship, was equally notorious for his clumsiness in bringing his vessel alongside a wharf, and we came into the somewhat crazy structure with a crash that sent the shore-folk scurrying off into safety until it was seen to be still intact. We were soon fast, and all hands working like Chinamen to land the few packages of goods, for we had a long way to go yet and several other places to call at. Our discharging was soon over, the warps cast off, and, followed by (as I thought) the wistful looks of the little community of Rocky Mouth, we proceeded up the river again. Occasionally we sighted a homestead standing among a thick plantation of banana trees, each laden with its massive bunch of fruit, and broad acres of sugar-cane or maize. From amongst the latter as we passed rose perfect clouds of cockatoos and parrots, screaming discordantly, and making even the dullest observer think of the heavy toll they were levying upon the toiling farmer. Again and again we stopped at villages, each bearing a family likeness to the first, but all looking thriving, and inhabited by well-fed, sturdy people. Just before sunset we arrived at Grafton, having passed but two vessels on our journey up—one a handsome brigantine, whose crew were laboriously towing her along at a snail's pace in a solitary boat, and the other a flat-bottomed stern-wheel steamer of so light a draught that she looked capable of crossing a meadow in a heavy dew. There was a substantial jetty built out from the steep bank, to the end of which, after considerable fumbling about, we moored. The only house visible was a rather fine dwelling whose front verandah overlooked the jetty from the top of the bank. But, when work was done for the evening and I climbed up the bank, I was surprised to find quite a considerable town, with well-laidout streets and every appearance of prosperity. There was little inducement to remain, however, and I soon hurried on board again to enjoy some grand fishing over the side.

Here we remained for a week discharging our cargo and reloading with maize, cases of preserved beef and mutton, and bags of tin ore. Just before sailing we received a good deal of farm produce, including several hundred bunches of bananas, for which there was always a good demand in Sydney. In order not to miss a tide we sailed sometime before daylight one morning, and, when about twenty miles down the river, ran into the region of a bush fire. As we had to hug the bank rather closely just there, we had an anxious time of it, the great showers of sparks and sheets of flame reaching out towards us as if determined to claim us, too, among their victims. The sight was terribly grand; the blood-red sky overhead and the glowing river beneath making it appear as if we were between two furnaces, while the deep terrific roar of the furious fire so near drowned every other sound. All hands were kept on the alert dowsing sparks that settled on board of us, and right glad was everybody when we emerged into the cool and smoke-free air beyond. After that we had a most humdrum passage all the way to Sydney.

I made at least twenty trips afterwards, all very much alike in their freedom from incidents worth recording here—except one, which made a very vivid impression upon me of the hardships endured by settlers in that beautiful country. It had been raining steadily for several days, making our transhipment of cargo a miserable operation; and it was noticed by all of us, as we lay at Grafton jetty, how rapidly the river was running. Before dark one evening the skipper ordered the warps to be cast off, and we hauled out into the fairway, anchoring there with a good scope of cable. All night long the rain poured down harder than ever. When daylight broke, so thick was the obscurity caused by the deluge of rain, that we could hardly make out the familiar outlines of things ashore, even at that short distance. But we could both feel and see that the river was now a torrent, bringing down with it massive trees and floating islands of *débris* torn from the banks higher up. Towards noon the rain took off, and revealed to us a disastrous state of affairs ashore. The river had risen over twenty feet; so that we now floated on a level with the top of the bank, and might have steamed over the wharf at which we had lain the previous evening. It became necessary for our skipper to go ashore, although it was a most dangerous task navigating the boat through that raging, tumultuous current. But the sight of those poor folks' plight in the town made us forget all else. The turbid flood was everywhere; all the houses standing like islands in a muddy sea, and boats plying busily to and fro, carrying loads of stricken people who had seen the labour of years destroyed in a night. And all down the river the tale was the same: homes, crops, stock—everything that had been slowly and painfully accumulated by years of self-sacrifice—buried under the all-devouring flood. It was too pitiful for words. How terribly true those words of warning returned now which I had read some months before in one of the Sydney newspapers, "Beware of the rich alluvial soil along the banks of rivers." As far as I remember, but little notice was taken of the matter in Sydney; for there had been a great flood on the Hunter River, much nearer to them, at about the same time, and that seemed to occupy most of the public attention. So many pathetic incidents were witnessed by us on that trip that it would be invidious to make a selection, even if it were not outside the scope of my purpose to do so; but one scene, from the intensity of its pathos, has haunted me ever since. A certain homestead on the shores of a lovely bend of the river, some twenty miles from Grafton, was one of the most familiar of our landmarks. The man and his wife were a splendid couple, full of energy and ability, and they had, by their own unaided efforts, made such a home of this out-of-the-way corner as gladdened the eyes to look upon. Whenever we went up or down there the worthy couple would be surrounded by their vigorous group of sunburnt youngsters, shouting greetings to us as if we were all old friends. At this particular season they had a more than ordinarily fine crop of sugar-cane, for which they had already received a good offer from the manager of a new sugar-mill erected in one of the reaches above Grafton. When we passed down after the flood, there, on a heap of muddy rubbish, sat the man, his head bowed on his knees and his children crouching near in the deepest wretchedness. Blowing our whistle, as usual, we roused him; but after a momentary glance his head fell again. All was ruin and desolation, utter and complete. Even the grove of banana trees that used to embower his house had been swept away. And his wife was nowhere to be seen.

Twenty miles down the river we ran into the region of a bush fire.

CHAPTER XXII.

PROSPERITY PALLS UPON ME.

As I grew better acquainted with the conditions of life on board the coasting steamers, I became extremely dissatisfied with my treatment on board the *Helen M'Gregor.* For while I had the usual duties of a lamp-trimmer to attend to, I was also compelled to work at all hours as one of the crew, while the heavy weights I was ordered to handle were far beyond my strength, and several times I was severely hurt. So that at a fitting opportunity I left her, taking up my abode with a shoemaker, who had a large connection among steamer-hands, and for two or three weeks led the unprofitable life of a gentleman at large. This was bad for me in many ways. The company I was thrown amongst was doubtful; I did not then know how much so, and, although I did not get involved in any of their shadier exploits, I began to drink pretty heavily, and, to put it briefly, go to the devil generally. This career was fortunately put a stop to by the emptying of my purse, which compelled me to get employment again.

My next ship was one of the finest on the coast, the last new vessel of the Australasian Steam Navigation Company's (A.S.N.) fleet, which was called the *Wentworth.* To my juvenile ideas she was a floating palace, everything on board being on a grand scale as compared with the little *Helen M'Gregor.* The mate was a huge Scotchman named Wallace, rough as a bear, but very just and straightforward. When he engaged me, he gave me to understand that my duties consisted solely in attending to the lamps and polishing the ornamental brass-work about the deck, and that I was on no account to do anything else or take orders from anybody but himself or the captain. This, added to the fact that my wages were now to be three pounds ten shillings a month, made me feel quite an important personage—in fact, I was almost "too big for my boots." Everything on board was so excellent in quality, and so well managed, that I felt great pride in my ship, and I determined that, as I had only one master to please, I would do all I could to succeed. The first thing I resolved was that no ship in harbour should have such dazzling brass as mine, and, after I had polished it all, I used to go round the other ships and look at theirs. If there was one that I thought looked more brilliant than mine, I would come back and go over my polishing again until I was satisfied, and so I gradually got the reputation of being smart at brass-cleaning anyhow. I lived entirely alone in a little cubicle by my lamp-room, which was a spacious apartment, well fitted and quite sheltered from the weather, being on the main-deck. In return for trimming the cook's lamps, I received all my meals from the saloon messes, and thus I lived better than I have ever done before or since. Not that the men fared indifferently. The food supplied to them was of the best quality, and as for quantity—well, they had steaks, chops, and potatoes, with unlimited baker's bread, for breakfast; roast joints and potatoes for dinner, and for supper the same as for breakfast. The waste was shameful. The first two or three hands to arrive on the spot where they took their meals, would cut all the brown off a ten or twelve-pound joint. When the laggards came along, if the appearance of the meat was not to their liking, which was usually the case, they would just fling it over the side and go to the galley for more. The cook dared not complain, as the officers always took the crew's part. This partiality was owing to the system obtaining, whereby a contractor ashore supplied all provisions at so much per head, finding cooks and stewards himself. And any suggestion upon the part of his servants that food was being wasted was always fiercely resented by every member of the crew, who would immediately accuse them of trying to fatten their employer at the sailor's expense. The result was that as much food was wasted each passage as would have supplied another ship of the same size.

Those were the palmy days of Australian coasters. A.B.'s received £7 per month, and one shilling and sixpence per hour overtime when in harbour, while the day consisted of eight hours only. Firemen got £10, and trimmers £8 per month, with overtime in addition like the sailors. And, in justice to them, it must be said that they seemed to value their privileges, and did not behave in the senseless way that deep-water sailors usually do. They spent a lot of money on dress and theatre-going, it is true; but many of them owned house-property or land. Nor was their life a hard one. There was none of that tremendous drive and tear seen on the American coast, where high wages are paid—as if the officers are determined to get the last ounce of energy out of every man because he was well paid. No; take it all round, it was the most comfortable sea-service that ever I saw or heard of, and I never ceased to wonder at it, or imagine that it was much too good to last. From all reports that have reached me of late years, my ideas on the latter point seem to have been well founded, for I hear that neither pay nor conditions of service are in any degree comparable with what then obtained.

As for me, I led a gentleman's life. Called at daylight to take in the lamps, I was able to finish all my work before ten a. m., and from thenceforward I was my own master. So heavily did the time hang when at sea, that I took in washing from both sailors and firemen at the rate of three shillings and sixpence per dozen, and thus earned a lot of extra money. Unfortunately, I had no ideas of thrift; and so, although I must have been in receipt of at least thirty shillings weekly, I never saved a penny. My earnings used to leak away as if all my pockets were sieves. But, on the other hand, the comfortable life, abundance of good food, and freedom from ill-usage, had such an effect upon my hitherto puny body, that I began to look and feel as if I was capable of doing a good day's work, and should, therefore, not now be ashamed to ask for employment. I no longer felt like a sailor, nor did the prospect of a return to the old life ever enter my head—in fact, I am afraid I never thought of the future at all. My life was very pleasant; and there was nobody in the world who cared a row of pins what became of me—what more natural than that I should, like any other pampered animal, live contentedly in the present?

Our usual trip was between Sydney and Melbourne, and it generally occupied from eight to ten days. Anything more delightful than the ordinary run along the coast would be hard to imagine. I got to know every landmark between the two ports as intimately as one knows the route between his work and his own street-door. But, although I was always interested in the Australian scenery, I felt delighted to hear one trip that we were bound to Auckland next voyage. I had heard so much of New Zealand that I had got to regard it as a sort of fairy-land—a group of Islands of the Blest. We left Sydney on Christmas Eve for our Auckland trip, much to the disgust of everybody on board except myself; but as we carried the mails no delay could be allowed. The next day we were, of course, out of sight of land, steering straight across that stretch of the Pacific that lies between Australia and New

Zealand; the sea was like a lake of glowing oil, and the sky a fleckless dome of deepest blue, with one mighty globe of molten gold hanging in its midst. Festivities began early—so early, indeed, that by dinner-time some of the fellows were getting very frivolous. There was a Gargantuan feed, of course; and, after that—well, it was surely expecting too much of human nature to suppose that steam would or could be kept up as usual. At any rate it wasn't. It went down, down, down, until, by four p.m., the propeller was just feebly revolving, the vessel making no more than two knots at the outside. By dusk I verily believe that the only two sober males on board were the captain and myself. Drunkenness reigned supreme in saloon, stokehold, and forecastle. By-and-by the screw stopped altogether, and we lay almost motionless. A few of the more vigorous revellers made spasmodic efforts to "keep it up"; but gradually the "fun" fizzled out, and general sleep succeeded. How long it lasted I don't know, for I turned in as usual; but in the morning she was going again, though at no great speed, it is true. The only redeeming feature about the whole orgie was the absence of quarrelling. General good-humour prevailed everywhere on board, and not a word was said in recrimination after the resumption of work. A day late, we sighted the Three Kings—those solitary rocks off the north point of New Zealand that stand up so sternly out of the blue waste about them. When we made them out, it was in the tremulous lovely light of dawn—beautiful beyond expression in those latitudes—and their rugged outlines stood out sharply against the tenderly tinted sky, through that lucent atmosphere, like the shadows cast by an electric beam. Then, as the sun sprang into the smiling heaven, they were gilded, and became like some fantastic ruin in black marble fringed with fiery rays and floating on a sea of many-coloured flame. A few hours' run brought us to the Gulf of Hauraki, up which we steamed amidst some of the most beautiful scenery in the world. As we glided onward to where, apparently, a huge mountain completely blocked up the apex of the gulf, a lovely island was pointed out to me on the starboard hand as the earthly paradise of Sir George Grey—Tiri-tiri. Here I was told it was his custom to receive troops of his Maori friends, and entertain them for days, mingling with them without the slightest consciousness of any difference of rank or colour between him and them. No wonder they loved him, and will hand his memory down to their remotest descendants as the great white chief who loved them and justice.

Nearer and nearer we drew to Rangitoto, the frowning peak that loomed heavily right in our path. At last, when within a very short distance of it, we made a sharp turn, and, skirting a reef that extended some distance from its base, we presently opened up Auckland Harbour, which, if not so picturesque as its approaches might have led one to expect, had all the merits that a good harbour should have—pre-eminently, the chief one of being safe with all winds. In a few minutes we were alongside the wharf, and besieged by an eager crowd who had been anxiously awaiting us, as we were so much over our time. As was my constant habit, I began at once to inquire as to the fishing possibilities of the place, learning, to my intense delight, that the harbour literally swarmed with fish of all kinds, and that even from the wharf they could be caught in enormous quantities. That settled my spare-time occupation for me. During our three visits to the city, although our stay lasted a week each time, I only went "up town" twice, and then strictly on business. My beloved sport claimed all my attention. For some reason, perhaps to avoid accidents, the authorities did not permit fishing from the wharf in working hours. So at daylight, enthusiastic fishermen like myself would gather along its lee edge, where the furious current boiled and bubbled around the piles, and eagerly try to "jag" a few of the tiny mackerel that clustered in shoals wherever there was an eddy. As soon as one was caught he would be impaled on a large hook, fastened to the end of a long, stout line, and cast out into the current without any other gear attached. As the line "slithered" through one's fingers an eager watch was kept where the bait might be expected to be. Presently, like a bar of silver, a huge fish would leap into the air, and it was pull for your life. There was no finesse, no sport, in the angler's sense of the term, but I doubt if any angler ever enjoyed his fishing more than I did. This particular kind of fishing, however, always had to cease at six o'clock, that is, when work began. At other times I fished on the bottom from the ship, and was often at a serious loss to know what to do with the enormous numbers I caught. But even then I did not realize how vast were the shoals of fish in the harbour, until one day I took an oar in a boat conveying a pleasure party from our vessel down the bay. When near the reef which fringed Rangitoto Mountain, the numbers of kauwhai (a fish much like an overgrown mullet, and averaging four or five pounds in weight) were so great, that each dip of the oar slew them until the water around us was reddened with their blood. They were a fish of most delicate flavour, and would have commanded a high price in any civilized fish-market. But the people of Auckland seemed quite indifferent to the piscatorial advantages they enjoyed.

So in this pleasant, easy-going fashion the months passed away, until one day we left Sydney for Melbourne in the teeth of a southerly gale. It was hopeless to expect that we should make any progress; but I was told, that because we had the mails on board, we were bound to "show willing." We managed to get round the South Head, and there we stuck; the engines doggedly pounding away, green seas coming over all, passengers all sea-sick, and we not gaining an inch against the fierce wind that roared up from its icy breeding-place in the Antarctic regions. At last the "governor" carried away, and all attempts to repair it were ineffectual. This, coupled with the fact that night was coming on, determined our skipper to run back and anchor in Watson's Bay, just behind the North Head, for shelter. The word was given, and she spun round as if rejoicing to be freed from the enormous strain she had been undergoing. As we drew rapidly near the mouth of the harbour the sight was one of the grandest conceivable. From the summit of the North Head—a gigantic cliff over four hundred feet high—fountains of spray shot up forty or fifty feet into the air, the incalculable pressure of those tremendous waves, rolling up against it from their thousand-league journey, having forced the reluctant sea upwards through the interstices of that massy cliff to such a stupendous height. We flew in through the entrance and immediately all was still. As we rounded to in the quiet little bay and dropped anchor, it was almost impossible to realize what a tormented waste of boiling sea we had just left, since here we lay perfectly motionless, without a ripple on the waters around. As it was dusk I prepared the "riding-lamp," which is always suspended from the fore-rigging of a vessel at anchor; but, for some stupid reason of my own, I did not place it in its position. Then I forgot all about it. The captain was the first to discover its absence, and, blowing his whistle for the chief officer, he reproved him sternly for his inattention to this important detail. Smarting at this, the mate called me and asked why I had not put the light up. I made some idiotic excuse, telling him that it was already lighted and awaited his orders. He was almost speechless with rage;

but controlled himself so far that he presently said calmly, "Well, go and hang it up." I did so promptly, and soon thought no more about it. There was just this shade of excuse for me—that I had never been anchored in a fairway before, since I had been a lamp-trimmer, except up the Clarence River, and there the gangway-lamp sufficed.

We resumed our voyage on the morrow, and returned to Sydney without incident worth remembering. On the first morning after our arrival the mate called me, and, giving me the balance of my month's money, discharged me. Not a word was said, but I felt sure of the reason, and did not feel sufficiently courageous to try and appease him. Nevertheless I was very sore, for I knew that, while I had had one of the best ships on the coast, I had also done my work thoroughly well, for over and over again the mate had commended me upon it. I slunk ashore like a beaten dog, not caring what became of me, and, returning to my old lodgings at the shoemaker's, set about spending my little stock of cash in reckless fashion. It did not last long, of course, and I was soon fain to look for a ship; but, strange to say, I hadn't the heart to try for another berth as a lamp-trimmer. It suddenly occurred to me that I would like to go "home" again. That is one of the most incomprehensible things imaginable to me. Never, during the first thirteen years of my life at sea, did I have any home in England, or one friendly face to welcome me back there. Yet, however well I was treated in foreign countries or in the Australasian colonies, I always felt a longing to get back to my own country again; and the sight of my home-land never failed to make a lump come in my throat and raise a feeling of wordless love for her in my breast. Why a homeless waif should thus love his native land, I do not profess to understand; but it is a solid fact, and one that has to be reckoned with, since I do not for a moment suppose that I am any different to the ordinary run of people.

In consequence of this strange longing to see the white cliffs of England once more, I neglected the intercolonial steamers altogether, and spent much of my time hanging about Circular Quay watching the proceedings on board the splendid clipper-ships that lay in that beautiful cove discharging their outward cargoes of merchandise, or filling their capacious holds with the wool, tin, copper, and meat of the Colonies for transhipment to the mother country. But, owing to a diffidence that has always afflicted me, I did not venture on board any of them to ask whether my services were required, although I was now a sturdy youngster, well able to do a day's work and looking like it. One day, as I was prowling round one of the outlying wharves, I got into conversation with a burly Londoner, who was second mate of an old barque lying there, apparently waiting for freight, which was not forthcoming for any such out-of-date craft as she was. This individual informed me that his ship was in want of two ordinary seamen, and that if I would go to a certain hotel (*Anglicè*, public-house) in the vicinity, I should find the skipper there, and that he would probably engage me at once if I was willing. This was by no means the kind of ship that I had proposed going home in; but I was heartily weary of being ashore doing nothing (my money was all gone), so I turned my steps towards the skipper's haunt at once. I found it without any difficulty—indeed, the place was fairly well known to me by sight—and, entering, I inquired of a red-faced man (who, in his shirt-sleeves, with unbuttoned vest, was leaning over the bar from the inside, smoking a "churchwarden" pipe) if he could tell me where I might be likely to find Captain Bunker. He turned a liquorish eye upon me, and murmured, between the puffs of smoke, "What might ye be wantin' of him?" "I'll tell him when I see him," was my ready reply; at which he removed his pipe and laughed most unmusically, much to my annoyance, as I did not feel like being made game of. At last he said, "I'm Captain Bunker, m' lad; whadjer want of me?" For a moment I stared at him incredulously; and then, the conviction dawning on me that he was speaking the truth, I told him my errand. Immediately he assumed a magisterial air, and began to cross-examine me as to my qualifications, etc. My replies being satisfactory, he then tried to cut me down in the wages. But I held out for three pounds per month, and, strange to say, succeeded in getting his consent to give it to me; but not before he assured me that, if I couldn't fulfil what he was pleased to call the duties of an ordinary seaman, he would stop my pay altogether. As, in addition to my confidence in my own abilities, I knew that he was talking nonsense, I made no complaint about this; and he drew me a glass of ale to clinch the bargain. Then he told me I might go on board and consider myself one of the crew, and that he would "sign me on" with the other new hands in a day or two.

CHAPTER XXIII.

ANOTHER QUEER SHIP.

Having thus satisfactorily arranged for my future during some months, at all events, I lost no time in getting on board my new ship, finding her fairly comfortable, although the crew's quarters were under the top-gallant forecastle—that abominable place that no men should ever be housed in. She was called the *Harrowby*, a barque of some five hundred tons, and, as nearly as I could judge, about twenty years old. She had been absent from England nearly two years, having been running backwards and forwards between the Colonies and Mauritius for some time, and was now, in the absence of any other freight offering, going in ballast to Rangoon for a cargo of rice to the United Kingdom. Of her original crew but half was left: the captain, mate, and second mate aft, two apprentices, the carpenter, and three seamen forward. The mate was a tall, wiry, red-headed Cumberland man, stern and morose, but a good seaman, and inflexibly just. The second mate was so fat and easy-going that he looked more like an East-end Jew tailor than a sailor; but he was a very jolly fellow, knowing his business well, and thoroughly independent, so that he stood not the slightest in awe of his superior officers, but did pretty much as he liked. The two apprentices were gentlemanly lads, whose parents had paid heavy premiums for their indentures in this old tub, where they were just loblolly boys, at every one's beck and call, no one pretending to teach them anything, and kept on precisely the same level as the crew, except that they had a little pigstye of a berth to themselves beside the carpenter's in a house on deck. Poor lads! they were bitterly disillusioned, and full of projects for showing up this shameful neglect when they got home again. At this time one of them was acting as cabin-boy, and the other was playing at cook, with such casual direction as he could get from Hansen, an old Danish seaman. But, generally speaking, the hands went ashore to dinner and chalked their bills up to the skipper's account. The old carpenter was a philosopher in his way. Nobody interfered with him, and he just muddled along from day to day, finding himself enough work to keep him from being actually idle, and coming forrard every evening for a smoke and a yarn with old Hansen, who, with a lanky Irishman and a pimply faced young cockney, formed for the present the whole of the crew forrard.

To my amazement I learned that for nearly a fortnight the vessel had been ready for sea, but the old man was so enamoured of his snug quarters behind the bar of the little pub, that he could not tear himself away. Nobody seemed to care very much. They killed time in a variety of ways, making believe to do some work, but principally occupied in "dodging Pompey." This state of things was broken into by my advent. Whether the act of engaging me had recalled Captain Bunker to a sense of his duty or not, I can not tell; but in the course of a couple of days we were joined by an elderly Yankee A.B., rejoicing in the name of Oliver Peck, an ex-mounted policeman, whom we always called Joe; a tall, merry Suffolk man, who was the very incarnation of good-humour; a white-faced Scotchman, who said he had been chief cook of a huge steamship called the *Mikado*, and had just shipped with us as cook to work his passage home; another ordinary seaman, like myself, a Londoner, but twice the man I was; and a delicate, artful little fellow, about my own age, who shipped as cabin-boy. Now we had a full crew, and soon the skipper made his appearance on board, marching us up to the shipping-office with him in great pomp and putting us all on the articles. Having once broken the spell that had bound him to the pub, he kept free, remaining on board that night, and hauling off into the channel at daylight ready to sail. But while we were actually getting under way a boat came alongside, bearing a lady in deep mourning and an official, who mounted the side, and solemnly presenting the skipper with a piece of stamped paper, informed him that he had come to stop the ship until all charges due to Mrs. Blank, landlady of the St. Margaret's Hotel, for board, lodging, and refreshments supplied, had been settled. The old man made a ghastly attempt to smile, but the thing was too palpable. Besides, all his crew were witnesses of his attempt to pay the widow with the "foretopsail sheet," as sailors say, and, hugely as *they* enjoyed the spectacle, he looked as if he had been suddenly attacked by *cholera morbus*. There was no help for it; he had to pay up, although how he did it I don't know. At any rate he succeeded in satisfying the bailiff, who bade him an elaborate farewell and descended to the boat, where the widow was volubly holding forth, in our delighted hearing, upon the many delinquencies of our skipper. The news of the settlement of her claim only seemed to add fuel to her fire, and, as long as she was within hearing, she continued to favour us with a minute account of the many acts and deeds of meanness of which Captain Bunker had been guilty. As the shrill sounds grew fainter, I could not help thinking that it was an inauspicious commencement for our voyage; and, in accordance with an old mental trick of mine, began to run over in my mind the probable state of my feelings had I been in the skipper's place. There was quite a little spell of silence after the boat's departure, during which all hands looked first at one another and then at the rubicund face of the skipper, which bore a peculiar vacant smile, but not the slightest symptom of shame. At last the uneasy quiet was broken by the harsh voice of Mr. Messenger, our chief, shouting, "Man the windlass!" In an instant we were all busy again, and did not cease our labours until the old barque, under all canvas, was gliding gently down the beautiful bay towards the wide Pacific.

At first my hopes were high that we should be going north about, for, in addition to a strong desire to avoid the unpleasantness inseparable from working to the westward through the Great Australian Bight, I was anxious to see something of the East Indian Archipelago. But the thought of Torres Straits, with its intricacies and baffling currents, was evidently too much for Captain Bunker's courage or confidence in his navigating ability, for we made the best of our way to the southward as soon as we were well clear of the Heads. At the picking of watches I found myself, much to my satisfaction, under the second mate, who seemed to have some little liking for me as his townsman. My watch-mates were the Yankee, Oliver, the ex-policeman, and the Suffolker. As I could steer, and, except for being rather a light weight on a rope, was well up to my work, we felt pretty well manned on our side. But the mate's watch came worse off, as their "ordinary" could not steer. Oh, it was weary work after my late life of ease! The deadly slowness of our progress, too, down the coast I had been used to skirt with the regularity of a railway-train, was hard to bear. And, in addition to all this, I soon found that my poor three pounds a month was rankling in the skipper's mind, and he was determined to try and reduce it if possible. I got a friendly hint or two from the second mate, who, although he liked me well enough, certainly did not intend to openly side with me against the old man. In most matters, it is true, he treated the skipper with such scant courtesy that I was amazed, but he put in no word of backing for me. A fortnight passed away, and we had all fairly shaken down into sea-life, while I, by strenuous efforts, had managed to recall all my previous experience and use it, with the added benefit of my additional strength. What troubled me most were the stun'sails. Studding-sails, as the word should be spelt, are the *betes noire* of seamen. Modern vessels have practically discarded them, happily for their crews; but such vessels as the *Harrowby* cling to them as long as they live. They are temporary sails, which in fair weather are set at the ends of some of the yards, thereby extending the spread of canvas (when they are carried on both sides) to nearly double its normal width. They are set by means of booms, which slide along in two hoops screwed into bands on the yards. These booms vary in size, of course, with the ship, and also with the height at which they are carried; but even a top-gallant stun'sail-boom, the size of an average scaffold-pole, which has to be rigged out by one man, or even a boy, is a quite heavy enough piece of timber to have loose on your hands, or hand (since you *must* hold on), while swaying on a footrope some eighty or ninety feet above the deck. Then the sails themselves, with their complicated gear, require deft handling to get them adjusted in their lofty positions, and as the upper ones need to be taken into the tops, there is some fancy gymnastic work involved in handling them, which generally falls to the boys. But when they *are* set, if there is any wind worth mentioning, and the vessel does not steer well, the helmsman has a bad time, for their gear being necessarily slight and simple, catching them aback is apt to bring them down by the run in a raffle of ropes, torn canvas, and splintered booms. These delights on a dark, wet night cannot be explained; they must be endured to be appreciated. No doubt a ship with stun'sails set below and aloft, flying along with a steady breeze just abaft the beam, the golden sunlight glancing on her canvas, and making her look like a mountain of snow, while the sparkling wavelets leap around her or are churned into lovely wreaths of dazzling foam by the eager sheer of her cutwater, makes a magnificent picture, and one that will be soon only seen in pictures. But when one remembers the cruel toil and deadly danger attached to these "flying kites," as sailors term them, one can only feel devoutly thankful that their day is done. Unfortunately, in the *Harrowby* we were continually harassed by these wretched things, which was the more aggravating as she was a dull sailer, to whom they made not a shadow of difference as far as any acceleration of her speed went. But we accepted them grumblingly, as sailors do any other crook in their never very straight lot. Nevertheless I felt pretty sure that, sooner or later, I should suffer in some severe way from them, and the fulfilment of my forebodings was not long delayed. We got a heavy breeze from the north-east off Cape Leeuwin, and the skipper, laudably anxious to get round that awkward corner and up north into finer weather, carried on all the sail the old barkey could stagger under, including topmast and lower stun'sails. Now the *Harrowby* steered none too well at the best of times, for she was fitted with the old-fashioned chain and barrel steering-gear, that made a two hours' trick at the wheel a fairly stiff ordeal for a youngster like me. By dint of the hardest trying, however, I had managed so far to get along without more than an occasional growl from the skipper to the effect that I was making a devilish bad course. At last, on the night in question, I came aft at four bells, fully equipped in oilskins, for it was raining as well as blowing. As I reached to take the spoke from Oliver, he muttered, "Yew'd better shed them oilskins, er she'll sweat yer hull soul out. She's kickin' like a broncho." I took his advice, preferring to get wet than to be hampered by too many coverings at such a task. It was as dark as the inside of a coal-sack, so that there was nothing to steer by but the compass and the "feel" of the wheel, which every sailor knows is not conducive to keeping a straight course, as the compass, however lively, never moves at the same moment the ship's head does, and consequently you can't meet her with the helm as quickly as when the stars or clouds are visible and indicate her slightest movement. Besides, the "old man" was on deck, and, before I had time to get into her present peculiarities, he was at me with, "Now, then! mind y'r weather hellum. Where th' —— er ye goin' with the ship? Meet her—meet her! Blast your eyes, meet her! Goin' to sleep—er what?" and so on. I might have done fairly well but for this brutal nagging; but now I certainly steered badly, and the thought of wiping her up into the wind and bringing all that raffle of stun'sails and gear down about the ears of the watch on deck made me as nervous as a cat. However, I sculled her along somehow—about two points each way, I reckon—the "old man" keeping up a running commentary all the time, until suddenly, along came a howling big sea, hitting her on the weather-quarter and sending a dense mass of spray right over the quarter-deck, drenching my tormentor and twisting her up into the wind till the weather-leech of the lower stun'sails began to flap. Down sprang the second mate to my assistance, and hove the wheel up so that she spun off the wind again like a weather-cock. "Oh, we can't have any more of this!" yelled the old man. "That —— fellow's no good. 'Nother hand to the wheel!" "'Nother hand to the wheel!" roared the second mate; and I declare I wasn't sorry, though my pride was sorely hurt at the injustice of the thing. The Suffolker came aft, good-humoured as was his wont, and smiled pleasantly as he took the wheel from my clammy hands. He favoured me with a sly wink, too, as much as to say, "Now you'll see some fun!" As I went forrard along the lee alley-way, the old man followed me, saying. "I'll log ye to-morrow. I'll show ye how ter come aboard my ship on false pretences." This did my business, and I turned savagely round, saying, "I *can* steer as well as any man in the ship if I'm let alone, and you know that. You only want an excuse to stop my wages——" Further remarks were drowned in a tremendous roar of tumbling water and cracking spars as the ship flew up into the wind, taking a mighty mass of black sea over all, and bringing the stun'sails down with an uproar truly terrific. "All hands on deck! Tumble up, there! Shorten sail!" screamed the skipper, fairly dancing in his excitement. Well, there *was* a mess, and no mistake! It took us three hours of hard struggle before we got her clear and shortened down, and during that time there were as many curses levelled at the old sinner as would have sunk the British Navy if their weight had been proportionate to the wishes of their utterers. For my part I was speechless with delight, for I felt if ever a poor fellow was vindicated promptly it was me. The diversion gave us all sore bones, though; and when, at last, we got below, we were almost too weary to growl. Stripping off our drenched rags we tumbled into our bunks, and slept so soundly that the two hours and a half left of our watch seemed only like five minutes. I took my usual trick at the wheel again without comment; but after breakfast, to my amazement, I was called down into the cabin. The skipper solemnly read to me an entry in the Official Logbook to the effect that on the night of ——, in lat. —, long. —, it having been found that I could not steer, I was sent from the wheel as unfit for my work, and, in consequence, my wages were reduced to one pound per month. This libel was signed by the second mate as a witness. I was then invited to sign it; but I refused, saying that the entry was false, and appealing to the second mate to support my protest. He, standing behind the skipper, gave me a reassuring wink which cheered me mightily, and after bandying a few more compliments with the skipper, I was told to "Get out of my cabin." The events of the past night were the subject of a good deal of comment forrard, and the general conclusion arrived at was that the old man was no good, and any deference or politeness towards him might usefully be dropped in future.

But something happened that day which, although in no wise the skipper's fault, made the feeling of insubordination ten times stronger than it otherwise would have been. Hitherto we had been living fairly well upon fresh meat and vegetables, although the cooking was very bad. The pasty-faced Scotchman who had shipped as cook *might* have been cook of the *Mikado* as he said; but, if so, he had certainly forgotten the most elementary portion of his duties. Having just come to an end of the fresh provisions, he informed us pompously that he was going to make us "duff" to-day, "An', ma wurrd," said he, with an air, "a'll gie ye somethin' ye *can* eat! Ye dinna ken whatn' duff's like aboord ther win'jammers." As may be imagined, we were in high glee at the prospect of such a notable benefit as high-class duff would be. The last stroke was hardly off the bell at seven bells before I was at the galley with the kid, my mouth watering in anticipation of this superlative duff. But it strikes me that the subsequent proceedings were important enough for a new chapter.

CHAPTER XXIV.

DEEP-WATER AMENITIES.

The cook stood by the galley stove, swelling with conscious dignity, as of a man whose position is unassailable—above criticism. "Now then, cook!" I cried, "where's that duff?" For all answer he seized his "tormentors"—a sort of miniature pitchfork—and began jabbing them down into the seething copper. "Look out, cook!" I said, in terror, "you'll bust the duff-bag, won't you?" No answer deigned he, but presently, with a mighty heave of both hands, he produced a square grey mass of something unlike anything edible that ever I had seen. This he dumped into the kid without a word, and waved his hand to bid me begone. Too much amazed to speak, I bore the ugly thing into the fo'lk'sle, setting it down in the midst of my expectant watch-mates, and silently retired to my corner in hungry anticipation of some fun presently. Joe approached the kid, knife and plate in hand, but on seeing the contents, drew back with a start and an exclamation of "What the —— is *that*?" "Duff, the cook calls it," I murmured softly. "Well, I'll be —— if ever I see or smelt anything like it in all my life," said he; "but p'raps it eats better'n it looks, so here goes." So saying, he attacked it with his knife, but only succeeded in removing some sodden, sloppy morsels from the outside of the lump. Upon the stuff itself he could make no impression; it was like a piece of indurated gutta-percha. Heavens! how he did swear. Then Oliver had a try; but in a minute he, too, was reciting the commination service. For the mess was hopeless. It was nothing but a mixture of flour and water, without yeast or fat, which had been roughly moulded into a square, and, without any covering, had been dropped into a cauldron of boiling, dirty sea-water. Of course it had hardened and toughened, as well as attracted to itself all the suspended grime in the water, until it had emerged the outrageous abomination before us. The men's wrath was really too great for ordinary bad language; they wanted to kill somebody. Presently Joe snatched up the kid and rushed to the galley with it, but the cook had wisely retreated to the cabin. Thither the furious men followed him, shouting in strident tones for him to "Come out of that!" they wanted to speak to him. Of course the old man showed himself first, blustering grandly about the impudence that thus invaded the holy calm of his cabin. This precipitated matters, and in about a minute there was a furious row. It culminated presently in Joe hurling the kid and its slippery contents right into the cabin, and striding forward with a savage string of oaths to the effect that not another stroke would *he* do until he got something that he could eat. Quiet reigned for a brief space, until presently Harry, the cabin-boy, poked his nose round the fo'lk'sle door, saying with a grin, "Cook's awful sorry he spiled the duff, but he's coming forrard presently with a tin o' soup and bully as soon's the old man's back's turned. Don't go fer him, pore beggar! he's nearly frightened to deth." The wrath having been mostly diverted to the skipper, this proposition was not unfavourably entertained, and in due time the cook sneaked forrard with a hang-dog air, a huge tin of preserved soup under his apron. And so it came to pass that peace was patched up for the time, although this outbreak of hostilities made the way plain and easy for a succession of rows, until the skipper's authority was a thing of naught. To make matters worse we actually fell short of provisions. This was a most scandalous thing to happen, for we were only six weeks out from Sydney, where all sorts of ship's consumable stores were both excellent and cheap. And we were informed by one of the apprentices that he knew for a fact that the owners had ordered Captain Bunker to provision the ship fully in the colonies for this very reason. We were stinted in everything; but by the connivance of the cabin-boy, Harry, who used to leave the pantry door unlocked, I made many a nightly raid upon its contents, such as they were. Many a time I had to crouch in its dark recesses, while the old man, prowling about on his bare feet, was peering in and inquiring querulously, "Who's there? I thought I heard somebody!" The instant his back was turned I would bolt for the fo'lk'sle, with my cap full of sugar or the breast of my jumper full of cuddy biscuits, or whatever spoil was comeatable. These nocturnal depredations were a source of endless delight to the second mate. His fat sides would shake with silent laughter as he watched the stealthy glidings to and fro, and heard the mutterings of the suspicious skipper, who never dared say a wry word to him. One night, at the wheel, I was telling him how savagely hungry I was, when, to my amazement, he replied, "Well, there's a meat pie on the swingin' tray, why don't ye go an' pinch it?" "What?" I said in a horrified whisper, "an' have the old man come out an' catch me! Why he'd put me in irons for a month." "G'way," he muttered scornfully, "he'd never hear ye. No man thet smokes ez much ez he does is a light sleeper. You ain't got pluck enough, that's what's the matter with *you*. Yew'd rather go hungry than run a little risk." The fact was, I didn't trust him any too much, for it occurred to me that it might fall in with his notions of fun to see the old man come out and muzzle me in the very act of embezzling that pie. His next move, however, completely dissipated all my fears. For he rolled off the hen-coop, where he had been lolling, and disappeared below, returning in a few minutes with the information that he had lashed the old man's state-room door-handles together, so that he couldn't get out if he did wake. I immediately resigned the wheel to him, shot down into the darkness, and had that pie on deck before you could count ten. I sat on the break of the poop and ate it, while the second mate steered as well as he could for laughing at the precipitous disappearance of the pie. When I had concealed it all, I replaced the empty dish on the swinging tray, and returned to the wheel. Then the second mate cast adrift the lashings on the door, and all resumed its normal calm, preceding the hurricane at breakfast-time, when the loss was discovered. But there was no breach of confidence, and the vanished pie took its place among the unsolved mysteries of life for Captain Bunker.

As we crept closer and closer to our port, favoured by fine weather, discipline disappeared altogether as far as the skipper was concerned. Work still went on as usual out of deference to the officers, with whom the chaps felt they had no quarrel, but if the old man opened his mouth he was sure to be insulted by somebody. I have not told—indeed, I dare not tell—a tithe of the things that were said to him; the only persons preserving any show of deference towards him being old Hansen and the boys. The officers, of course, did not openly flout him—they just ignored him, while he almost cringed to them. And then one day, a week before our arrival off the mouth of the Irrawaddy, Harry came forrard and told us something that made sport for all hands for the rest of that voyage. Everybody was hungry now, fore and aft, the commons being woefully short. But at the usual time for taking the forenoon sights for longitude, the skipper being in his state-room with the door shut, Harry went to call him, supposing him to be asleep. After knocking two or three times, Harry heard a muffled voice within saying, "Go away, I'm at my devotions." Such a statement took Harry's breath away for a moment, but yielding to an uncontrollable impulse, he stooped and peeped through the keyhole. There sat Captain Bunker, a square tin of biscuits between his knees, a pot of jam open by his side, and his mouth bulging with the delicate food. Harry had seen enough; and in ten minutes it was all over the ship. From that time forward, "Don't disturb me, I'm at my devotions," was heard whenever it was possible to drag it in, until the monotonous repetition of the phrase became wearisome as a London catch-word. It annoyed the skipper almost to madness; but that only gave delight to the men, who felt that at last they had got hold of a cheap and effective way of repaying him for the hardships they were enduring through him.

We were favoured with splendid weather, although the north-east monsoon, being almost "dead on end"—that is, blowing right from the direction in which we had to go—made our progress exasperatingly slow; and as the scanty stock of bad provisions got lower and lower the gloomiest anticipations prevailed. But we managed to reach Elephant Point before we were quite starved, and with the utmost joy received a white pilot on board, who, finding that he was likely to hunger if he had to make any lengthened stay with us, used all his skill to get us into port quickly. There were some fine screw-tugs plying on the Irrawaddy, but, of course, we could not avail ourselves of their assistance, the towage being enormously high, and our old man most anxious to curtail expenses to balance his waste in other directions. So we were treated to an exhibition of backing and filling up the river on the flood, just as the old Geordie colliers do to this day up the Thames: a feat of seamanship requiring a great deal of skill for its successful accomplishment. Of course the tide will carry a vessel up the river, but it is necessary to keep her under control, and, with the wind blowing straight down the river, the only way of doing this is to stand across the stream, say on the starboard tack, with all sails full; then, when as far as possible has been sailed, to haul the yards aback, and go stern foremost back again. In this manner we worked up the noble stream, finding ourselves at the turn of the tide within a few miles of our destination, at a spot known as Monkey Point. Here we anchored for the night, the rushing of the swift ebb past us keeping up a continual undertone of energy, and straining our cable out taut as if we were stemming a gale. All manner of bloodthirsty insects boarded us in battalions, lured in our direction, doubtless, by the smell of fresh supplies of food, and through their united efforts we spent a most miserable night. So much were we tormented, that when daylight called us to resume our journey we were languid and worn-out, hardly able to tear the anchor from its tremendous hold upon the thick, elastic mud forming the bed of the river. We got under way at last, however, and then another couple of hours brought us up to the anchorage off the city, where a great fleet of steamers and ships lay loading rice, mostly for India, for the relief of a famine which was then raging.

We moored with an anchor ahead and another astern, as is usual in crowded anchorages, so that the vessel, as I have before explained, swings round and round as if moored to a post, taking up little more room than her own length. In many respects this was the strangest place that I had yet visited, the pointed spires of the numerous pagodas rising out of the dense leafage giving the city a truly Eastern appearance, while the lofty shining summit of the great pagoda dominated everything else. As soon as the work of furling sails and clearing up decks was done—as the skipper had hurried ashore—we were allowed the remainder of the day to rest, and, rigging up an awning over the forecastle, we proceeded to enjoy ourselves. Here the boats are propelled by the boatmen in exactly the same way as a gondola is, and the way those fellows managed their cumbrous craft in the swift current was something compelling all our admiration. The native vessels, too, that came majestically gliding down from far up country laden with rice for shipment, were the most interesting that I had yet seen. They were of large size, some of them carrying fifty tons of cargo, and roofed in by a deeply slanting covering of bamboo mats to protect the cargo. Both stern and bow rose in a graceful curve, while the stem often towered high in air—a perpendicular beam of teak most richly carved into elaborate designs of the quaintest and most eerie character. A tiny deck aft accommodated the steersman, who with great effort manipulated a gigantic oar working through a hole in the stern, also richly carved and decorated in some cases with gilding. But the men—the yellow, almond-eyed Burmese—not satisfied with the prodigious amount of labour expended on the adornment of their craft, decorated their own bodies so elaborately that it was difficult to understand however they could have borne the tedium of the tattooing, to say nothing of the pain. No people in the world carry the practice of tattooing to such artistic lengths as the Burmese universally do. Every man we saw had a magnificent series of designs covering his trunk to the waist, executed in vermilion, and representing flowers, animals, and graceful whorls filling in any spaces too small to allow of anything else being tattooed there. From the waist to the knees they were tattooed in blue, the designs being plainer and not so artistic as above. They were a jolly, cheerful lot; but dignified, too, having none of the exuberance of the negro about them.

Just across the river, opposite to where we lay, was a great saw-mill, where a herd of a dozen elephants were gravely occupied in drawing teak-logs from rafts in the water up through the mud, and piling them in stacks well above high-water mark. They worked in couples, and seemed to need no directing what to do. Two or three natives lounged about among them; but every effort they made was apparently the result of their own initiative as far as could be seen. They worked in couples—sedately, ponderously; but the sum-total of their labour was quite in keeping with their huge bulk. One enormous beast was apparently the foreman (our fellows called him the bo'sun). He roamed about leisurely, bearing in his trunk a couple of yards of massive chain, which he flourished now and then as if it were a scourge which he would use upon his toiling charges should he see fit to encourage them to more strenuous effort. But as we stared at the strange sight with intense interest, there was a jet of steam from the mill, a deep whistle sounded, and on the instant every elephant dropped whatever he had in his trunk and, with quickened steps, made for his quarters. It was "knock-off time."

Work proceeded in a very easy-going fashion, for the captain had taken up his quarters on shore and did not return for several days, being supposed by all of us to have entered upon a steady course of spree. We got the hold ready to receive the cargo, and did such other duties as were required of us, without any undue strain upon our energies, while our bumboatman kept us well supplied with all such luxuries, in the way of fruit, soft-tack, eggs, etc., as sailors delight in in Indian ports. Matters proceeded in this way until one day an order came off from the skipper that an anchor-watch must be kept. This meant that, instead of one man keeping watch all night, and being free from any other duty, every man must take one hour's watch in addition to his day's work. Now, this sort of vigil is only kept during a temporary anchorage, never as a harbour duty; and, consequently, there was an instant refusal to obey unless the day's work was shortened. The officers, having no authority to do this, refused to entertain the idea, and the result was that no regular watch was kept at all. Two or three nights passed until, in the midst of a tremendous storm of thunder, lightning, and rain, I was roused by old Hansen with the words, "Tom, id's your vatch, und de olt man's 'longside, kigging up de fery teufel 'cause dere's nopody avake." I was lying on the forecastle head under the awning, nearly stifled with the heat; and, muttering a blessing upon the old man, I pulled off my sole garment, and sallied forth into the black, steaming deluge in the costume of Adam before the fall. As I reached the gangway the old man just climbed on board; and at that moment a flash of lightning revealed everything as if in full noonday glare—especially my shining white skin. He was just angry drunk; and the sight of me standing there, naked and not ashamed, nearly made him split with rage. He howled like a hyena for the mate, who, startled beyond measure, came rushing out of his cabin into the flood. Turning savagely to him, the skipper, almost unintelligibly, demanded the reason of this disgraceful state of affairs—pointing to me, standing, like Lot's wife, under the incessant play of the lightning. It was an irresistibly funny tableau. Over the rail peered the black faces and glaring eyeballs of the Hindu boatmen who had brought the skipper off, their impassive faces showing no sign of the wonder they must have felt at these unprecedented proceedings. The hissing downpour of rain descended pitilessly, its noise almost drowning the infuriated voice of Captain Bunker, who, foaming with rage, berated the saturnine mate. Every other second we were all invisible to each other—the darkness engulfed us. Then a rending glare of white light revealed us all again, standing as if posing for our portraits. The mate tired of it first, and, turning to me, said grimly, "Go an' get some close on. Y'ought ter be 'shamed o' yerself comin' aft like that." I instantly retreated forrard, while the old man, still raging, followed the mate as he returned to his cabin without deigning a word of reply. I rigged myself hurriedly and came aft again, prepared to keep the rest of my watch under the poop-awning in such comfort as I could. But I had hardly lit a cigar (the rupee a hundred sort), and settled myself cosily in the skipper's long chair, when that restless man emerged from the companion and strolled towards me. I did not stir—indeed, it was too late, since I was caught. I could only brazen it out. At first I feared his rage would choke him, for he gasped as if the flow of eloquence was literally strangling him in its frantic efforts to find a vent. Suddenly he made two steps towards me, gurgling as he did so, "Git off my poop or I'll kick ye down the steps!" I sprang lightly out of my seat and stood on the defensive, saying nothing, but backing cautiously to the ladder, which I descended with my face towards him. I heard no more of him afterwards, for my watch was soon over, and my relief, one of the apprentices, came on watch at once. Next day there was a regular inquiry into the vexed anchor-watch question; and, after much heated discussion, it was arranged that we should resume work one hour later each morning and keep regular watch one hour each through the night. As soon as this was settled our worthy chief departed on shore again; and there, to our great relief, he remained.

CHAPTER XXV.

PROCEEDINGS AT RANGOON.

Freed from the annoyance of the captain's presence, we were by no means an unhappy crowd. Lying in such a crowded anchorage there was plenty of sight-seeing, and the coming and going of vessels was incessant, owing to the demand for rice to feed the famishing millions on the other side of the Bay of Bengal. Besides that, we youngsters often got a run ashore when the mate or second mate wanted to go up town, which was pretty frequent, as there was no restraint upon them. To while away the time of waiting on the pier for them we used to have great fun with the boatmen, who squatted there sucking their eternal hubble-bubbles and chattering continually. Many a queer yarn, in queerer gibberish, did I hear from those good-natured fellows, only understanding about one word in ten that they said, and averaging the rest; so that I have no doubt that a comparison between my idea of a story and the story itself must have been exceedingly funny. But one day, when surrounded by a knot of Hindus, I suddenly remembered that when I was quite a child I had read in *Chambers' Miscellany* a number of stories of Hindu mythology, all of which were as fresh in my memory as the alphabet. Accordingly I commenced to repeat the "Avatar of the Fish" in such broken English, and occasional native words, as I thought would best convey my meaning. The effect was wonderful. Usually undemonstrative, they seemed fairly startled out of all their reserve, and over the ring of eager black faces wave after wave of conflicting expressions chased one another, while broken ejaculations burst irrepressibly from their parted lips. As the well-known names of Rama, Vishnu, Siva, Ganesh and Co. rolled trippingly off my tongue, their delight knew no bounds; and when at last I halted for lack of breath, they were ready to give me anything they possessed. Thenceforward I was a prime favourite among them. Well for me that it was so, for very shortly afterwards an event happened that nearly brought my career to a premature close. I had been shaking hands with them all round, and boy-like, had been showing off my strength by squeezing their delicate hands in mine, extorting from them all sorts of queer grimaces and expressions of wonder at my strength of wrist. Presently a Mussulman joined the group. He had just come up from the water, where he had been bathing, after having his poll shaven. Clad only in a waist-cloth, his torso was fully revealed, its splendid proportions showing a development that many a pugilist would have envied. Our proceedings did not appear to please him, for he wore a most diabolical scowl, which, as he was anything but handsome, gave me a serious disrelish for his company. But suddenly, as if by an uncontrollable impulse, he thrust out his hand to me, making signs for me to try my strength on him. I would have refused, but pride forbade; so I placed my hand in his and waited for his grip, determined to show no sign even if the blood should spurt from my finger-tips. We stood facing one another thus for almost a minute, when, without warning, he lifted my arm high, and at the same time thrust me backwards towards the edge of the wharf, which was thirty feet above the mud (the tide being out) and totally unprotected. Another second and I should have been over, when the whole crowd of boatmen rushed at him, and, dragging him off me, forced him to retreat up the wharf shorewards. Mad with rage I seized a log of wood and rushed after him; but the remainder of my friends surrounded me, and implored me not to pursue him, as I should certainly be killed. And, indeed, as soon as I cooled down somewhat, the justice of their contention was evident, for in those tortuous alleys one might be attacked from a dozen differing directions at once, and never see the aggressor. Therefore I felt glad that I had not been allowed to have the way my mad folly would have led me, and thankfully meditated upon my undoubtedly narrow escape. The affair made a deep impression upon me, for it was the only time in all my experience that I was ever attacked abroad.

The loading of our vessel proceeded very slowly, which was not to be wondered at, since all the energies of the shipping people seemed to be absorbed by the demands of the big steamships that were incessantly carrying rice to Calcutta because of the famine. But, slow as it was, it gradually approached completion, and the important question began to occupy all our minds: Were we going to get any liberty or money? Since the night of the skipper's surprise-visit, we had only seen him once, and that was when he returned on shore the next morning. The officers were warily approached upon the subject, but they knew no more than we did of the skipper's movements or intentions. At last, after a prolonged council of war, it was decided to send him a letter, signed by one of the A.B.'s on behalf of the rest. But then the difficulty arose: who was to write the important document? Not one of the men was capable of doing so—in fact, I was the letter-writer in ordinary for all hands. So I was approached as to my willingness to do what was required. I readily consented, only stipulating that I should be held blameless in the event of trouble ensuing. "Oh, of course," said they all, "we wouldn't let you take the blame." Well, I wrote the letter, and, although I was no hand at composition, I remember that it was exceedingly terse and to the point. With a good deal of pride I read it to the assembled conclave, and all agreed that it was a model of what such a letter ought to be. But when it came to signing the document, I was disgusted to find that each man was anxious that some other fellow should have the honour. All professed readiness to take the responsibility, but when it came to putting their names to paper they hung back. At last, to my secret amusement, the old Dutchman, Hansen, said, "Oh, all righd, put my name to id; I tondt care for te oldt man nodt a liddle pidt." It struck me at once that the old fellow had no idea of the vigour of the language used, but that was none of my affair. So "Hans Hansen" was appended to the letter; it was enclosed in an envelope, and sent per the "dubash" to the "British Burmah Bar," where the old man was living. In a perfect fever of excitement I awaited the result. It was not long delayed. Shortly after dinner the skipper came on board in a perfect fury, and, before he had got his foot over the rail, yelled for Hansen. The poor old Dutchman paddled aft, shaking like a feather-vane in a gale of wind, and, when he got to where the old man was standing, he looked as if his legs would double up under him. Good heavens! how the skipper did rave. Seeing who he had to deal with he just spread himself, so to speak, and, much to his satisfaction, succeeded in scaring Hansen nearly to death. Suddenly my name was called, and, in a moment, I recognized that I had been given away. Well, I had to face the music; so I determined to put the best face I could upon the matter, and, in any case, to show no cowardice. I strolled quietly aft, and received the old sinner's broadside with a perfectly unmoved front. He threatened me with prison—almost hanging—for the unparalleled crime I had committed; but I smiled sweetly, and, as soon as I could get in a word, I told him he couldn't do anything to me at all. Then he changed his tactics, and tried to wheedle me into saying that the men had compelled me to write, and begged me to tell him whose composition it was. Having by this time grown bolder, I told him that I was the author, and that I felt proud of it. This so enraged him that he ran at me foaming and screaming to me to get out of his cabin. But, even then, his prudence did not desert him, for he never ventured to strike me, and both the officers remained strictly neutral. And, after all, the desired end was attained for every one except myself, for the next day liberty was announced, with cash to the extent of twenty rupees each. But from this I was to be excluded. However, after the other fellows had gone, my fellow ordinary seaman and I were told by the mate that we might go too, if we chose, but that he had no money to give us. We had a couple of rupees between us, enough to get ourselves something to eat, so we gladly availed ourselves of his permission and were soon ashore.

From the first hour of our arrival I had looked with longing eyes upon the mighty mass of the Golden Pagoda, and never ceased hoping that I might be able to see it near at hand; and now I determined to lose no time in realizing my desires. Bill wanted to go down town, and hunt up some of our shipmates for the purpose of borrowing a little from them; but I dissuaded him, and, after a bottle of beer each, and the purchase of a fistful of cigars for the equivalent of twopence, we trudged off. There was no mistaking the way, for the road was broad and the pagoda itself was our guide; but I have ever since rejoiced that I did not know how far it was, or I certainly should never have visited it. The fierce sun glared down upon the white dusty road so that it was like walking in an oven; gharries and ekkas rolled tantalizingly by, and our throats became like leather. But we persevered, and after I am afraid to say how long, we came at last to the imposing avenue of colossal black marble monsters leading to the first plateau. Immensely broad flights of steps led up to an enormous platform, around which we roamed, bewildered by the wonderful array of uncouth monsters grouped everywhere. Then up more steps on to another plateau from whence sprang the central mass, a sort of pyramid without angles, and rising in broad steps of masonry which, flat at first, gradually sloped upward until they were lost in the glittering cone of the towering summit. Around the base of this vast structure were small temples like porticoes leading to the interior of the main building; but far as we could see, each of them was self-contained, and no entrance to the central edifice was visible. I made many inquiries whether that great pyramid was solid, or contained chambers of any sort; but the answers I got were so conflicting that I could come to no conclusion at all. The strangest feature of the whole wonderful place was the number of elaborately decorated bells of all sizes which hung about, some of them on the most flimsy erections. They emitted, when struck, tones of the most silvery sweetness, such as I have never heard from bells (except specimens from the same country) before or since. And presently we came upon one in a secluded corner that must be, I should think, one of the largest bells in the world, although I have never seen any mention of it in books or articles where big bells are spoken of. It was hanging under a sort of conical shed, suspended from a gallows built of huge baulks of teak, but its lip was only about eighteen inches off the ground. It was covered with inscriptions—in Burmese, I suppose—but had no other enrichment. Curious to hear its tone, I struck it with a large deer-horn, of which there were many lying about; but there was no response. Harder and harder I struck, until at last Bill hove a massive fragment of stone against it with all his force; but still not a sound could be heard—no, not so much as an iron wall would have given back. Baffled in sampling its tone, we tried to measure it roughly, and found that with outstretched arms we could reach round it in four times. This would make its circumference about twenty feet. Then, lying flat on my back, I tried to measure its thickness of metal; but my arm was not long enough—it was much thicker than I could reach in from outside. Its height I should estimate at twelve feet; but that is very rough, since we had no pole. Altogether a grandfather of bells. Gilding was going on in all directions, the workmen perched upon flimsy bamboo scaffolding in all sorts of precarious positions; and I remember trying to calculate how much gold it must take to keep so great a place brilliant. I did not then know that the gold-leaf was one of the principal offerings made by worshippers, although, when we presently entered one of the temples, and witnessed the worship, the strangeness of the proceedings ought to have enlightened me. Yellow-garbed, close-shaven Phoongyees were squatting all over the pavement of the building, apparently absorbed in reverent adoration of the row of idols ranged along the inner end of the place. Yet, at the same time, more workmen were busily engaged in gilding the idols themselves—one, especially, was plastering the face of the central figure with it, until it shone in that dim hall like a setting sun. I was speechless with wonder at what seemed such a strange mixture of irreverence and worship. While I stood silently gazing at the strange scene, a voice near me said, in most perfect high-bred English, "I suppose you don't believe in this, do you?" I turned sharply; and there at my elbow stood a Chinaman, simply dressed in white silk, with purple cap and shoes. A delightful subtle scent exhaled from his robes, and a gentle smile played about his calm, intellectual face. In fact, "gentleman" was writ large upon him; but I could not grasp the idea that it was he who had spoken. As soon as my bewilderment had passed a little, I said, "Was it you that spoke just now?" He nodded, and repeated his question. "Of course not," I answered; "neither do you, I should imagine?" With the slightest possible shrug of his shoulders, he said, "Why not? I do not claim to be wiser than the myriads of my ancestors whose faith it was. What sufficed them may surely content me." "But," I replied eagerly, "you have evidently studied in some English-speaking country, and you must have read our books. Did they not alter your opinions as to the wisdom of your ancestors?" "I have taken my B.A. degree at Cambridge," said he, "and I am fairly conversant with Western literature; but upon religious topics I do not profess any opinions. The subject is far too vast for me to attempt to take up, since it would necessarily mean the exclusion of all others; and I have much to do. Consequently I accept unquestioningly that form of religion in which I was born, taking the line of least resistance. But I must bid you good day, hoping you will enjoy your visit." And before I could say another word he was gone. I felt very small and ignorant beside this exquisite Oriental, whose gracious manners and beautiful voice have haunted me ever since, and, although I am fully conscious how poor a figure I must have cut beside so gifted and highly educated a man, I have never ceased to regret that I did not have a longer enjoyment of his pleasant company. While I still stood musing over this strange encounter, a heavy hand was laid upon my shoulder, and, turning sharply round, I was confronted by our second mate, whose ill-fitting clothes, gross, animalized face and boisterous behaviour, formed a complete contrast to the dainty gentleman who had just quitted my side. "Hullo!" he said with a sneer, "what you doin' ere, hay? Goin' ter turn Me'ommedun?" I made some jesting reply, looking anxiously meanwhile at his cigar, and then at the silent row of priests, in grave doubt as to how they might take his noisy behaviour in their sacred building. But they were apparently used to it, for they took not the slightest notice. "Got 'ny money?" he queried with a grin, knowing pretty well how unlikely it was. Upon my telling him how poorly we were off, he kindly gave me two rupees and then went on his way.

355

"I suppose you don't believe in this, do you?"

As I had by this time had quite enough of sight-seeing, besides being hungry and thirsty, I started to look for my chum; and, after some search, found him sitting in a shady angle of the great flight of steps, intently watching the impassive figure of one of a long row of mendicants that lined the side of the way up to the temple. He was quite happy, and very much interested in the queer offerings that he had seen made to the beggar whom he had been studying. Shreds of tobacco, a few grains of rice, and other trifles unfamiliar to us, but of the tiniest possible value, were being dropped into his basket by the native passers-by, in response to the mellow note which resounded from a triangular piece of metal which he held suspended from a stick, and occasionally tapped with a bone. "Goin' ter give him anythin', Bill?" I asked. "'Oo? Me? Wot djer tek me for? Lazy ole swine! I bet 'ees got a —— sight more brass 'n you er me'll ever 'ave. No bloomin' fear!" It may have been fancy, but certainly I thought I saw a gleam in that beggar's filmy eye as if Bill's contemptuous words were quite understood by him. "Well," I said, "I'm goin' ter give 'im a tanner fer luck." And, as I spoke, I fished out four annas and dropped the little piece of silver into his cup. I turned to go immediately; but he stretched forth a skinny arm, offering me a withered, blood-red flower, and murmuring some (to me) utterly unintelligible words. Now, I would not willingly hurt any one's feelings gratuitously; so I smiled cheerfully back, accepted his flower, and saying, "Bote accha; Salaam, ole stockin'," skipped off down the steps, followed grumblingly by Bill. As we went, I told him of the second mate's gift. He immediately suggested taking a gharry back. I was in no wise loth to agree, for the remembrance of our morning's trudge was anything but pleasant. But, when we arrived at the place where the vehicles were grouped, those infernal gharry-wallahs were all so independent that they wouldn't bate a pice of three rupees for the trip. As this was quite out of the question, we took the road again with heavy hearts and aching feet: Bill cursing, in choicest Bermondsey, niggers in general and gharry-wallahs in particular. For about half a mile we trudged along, when, suddenly turning a slight bend in the road, we sighted a gharry ambling along with one door open. A bright thought seized me, and, whispering to Bill my idea, we hurried noiselessly after the slowly-moving carriage. As soon as we got near enough, we saw that the driver was soundly asleep upon his box, the reins dangling loosely from his fingers, and the old horse plodding along at his own sweet will. Gently we popped into the crazy old ambulance, quietly closed the door, and lounged back like two plutocrats. I don't think I ever enjoyed a ride more, for, slowly as we went, we arrived at the gharry-stand in Phayre Street all too soon to suit me. Before the gharry stopped we opened the door, and, quietly as we had entered, were stepping out, when that unlucky Bill caught his foot in the step, and, catching at the door to save himself, gave the whole concern a heavy lurch. This effectually roused the driver, who jumped down off his box and demanded his fare. Bill was furious (at being caught, I suppose), and was proposing to slay and eat the fellow, whose yells speedily brought all his chums round. As I was getting nervous I offered him eight annas, at the same time trying to pacify my burly shipmate, who was carrying on like a madman. Fortunately a white policeman came along, before whose dignified approach all the clustering natives stood respectfully back. To him I told the exact facts of the story. Without a word he took the eight annas from me, gave it to the hack-man, and uttered the single word "Jao." The effect was magical. The crowd melted away, and we were at liberty to resume our journey. The rest of the day passed uneventfully enough. We had a splendid dinner in one of the bazaar dining-rooms at a rupee each, washed it down with a bottle of Bass, and, after sundry cigars, strolled leisurely down the pier, and sat there enjoying the coolness of the evening, until, feeling tired of shore, we hailed the ship, and were fetched on board by the two apprentices. A quiet night's rest succeeded; but the morning brought diversions. The ex-policeman came on board quietly enough, as befitted a man accustomed to discipline; but the rest, with the exception of old Hansen, who returned early on the previous day, were in a parlous state. Two did not return; and, later, news came that they were safely in chowkey, having covered themselves with glory by routing a whole brigade of native police who tried to arrest them, and caused grievous bodily harm to several white constables who had finally carried them off. One of them was the jolly Suffolker, who had thus falsified all my previous estimates of his amiability;

the other was Mick, the long Irishman, at whose outburst nobody was surprised. It is hardly necessary, perhaps, to say that no work was done that day, except a little clearing up decks, for which of course we boys were available. But, towards evening, the repentant revellers began to realize the extent of their folly, and to appear, in some measure, ashamed of themselves. Just at sunset a police-boat arrived bringing Mick, a deplorable object, his clothes hanging from him in festoons, and his flesh caked up with dried filth and blood. He was certainly much the worse for wear, but filled with an unholy delight at the thought of the glorious time he had enjoyed. It appeared, however, that the behaviour of Charley the Suffolker had been so outrageous, and his refusal to return to his ship so decided, that the authorities—lenient, as they undoubtedly were, to sailors—were compelled to give him a month's hard labour. Upon hearing his sentence he lifted up his voice and shouted, "Hooray!" to the great annoyance of the magistrate, who had him incontinently man-handled off to the cells.

CHAPTER XXVI.

HOMEWARD-BOUND IN DIFFICULTIES.

And now—our cargo being all on board, sails bent, and hatches battened down—we began to look forward to the homeward passage. But our anticipations were in no sense pleasurable, for, although we had certainly lived well while in port, we had as yet received no stores for sea use, and we were in grievous doubt as to the intentions of our commander in this respect. At last, when we were fully prepared to refuse to proceed unless we saw some reasonable prospect of being fed while at sea, a boat-load of stores came off, accompanied by a new recruit to take the place of Charley, who was busy mat-making in Rangoon gaol. He was an old acquaintance of mine, having been cook of a barque called the *Gemsbok*, which lay at Auckland during one of my visits—a fair-haired, happy-go-lucky Englishman; but a very poor sailor, however able he might have been as a cook. He had not been half an hour on board before he had joined us in solemn condemnation of the scanty stock of provisions he had accompanied on board, declaring that we should all be starved before we got home, unless we made a wonderfully rapid passage. But, with the carelessness of sailors, we allowed our opportunity of protesting to slip by; and next morning, we unmoored and dropped down to Monkey Point, ready to proceed down the river. For some unexplained reason we lay here all day doing nothing, although everything was as favourable as it could well be for our departure. Towards evening, when all hands were sitting on the top-gallant forecastle, enjoying the cool and smoking the universal cheroot of Burmah, the devil entered into Mick, and induced him to sneak down into the forecastle and search for something to drink. He succeeded in discovering a bottle of square gin—the cayenne and turpentine brand at twelve annas a bottle—in Hansen's chest, which, as is customary in all ships' fo'lk'sles, was left unlocked. Knocking the neck of it off immediately, he poured the contents into a hookpot, and, at one draught, swallowed about a pint of the horrible stuff. Another drink nearly finished it; and in a few minutes he returned to our midst, not drunk, but a raving lunatic. For a little while we were highly amused at his antics; but presently, yelling, "Well, so long all!" he rushed to the rail with the evident intention of flinging himself overboard. Bill—the other ordinary seaman—and I rushed at him, dragged him back, and, after a severe struggle, got him to lie down. Then commenced such a night of labour as I have never experienced before or since. Every device that his mad cunning could suggest did he try in order to take his own life. We got not a moment's rest. Sometimes he would feign to be asleep; but, the moment we were off our guard, he would be at it again, startling us almost out of our wits, and giving us a fearful struggle before we could get him quieted again. None of the others would relieve us, or lend us a hand—nay, they cursed us for a pair of idiots that we did not let him go, with a wannion on him. How could we? Although we bitterly resented the utterly uncalled-for toil, we dared not relax our vigilance: both of us feeling that, if we did, his blood would be upon our heads. And, to add to our miseries, a land-breeze brought off mosquitoes and sandflies in myriads, so that, in our exposed condition, we were stung almost beyond bearing. At last, just as the first streak of dawn appeared over the jungle, he dropped off to sleep in reality. Before we had time to snatch the briefest doze came the strident voice of the mate, "Man the windlass!" Of course Mick was excused—he was ill; but we, poor wretches, who had been engaged in a life-and-death struggle with him the whole night through, were compelled to work as if we had enjoyed our lawful night's rest. And we were so weary! Hardly able to crawl about from our tremendous exertions, and continually blackguarded for our lack of smartness, it was with no kindly feelings towards Mick that we dragged ourselves forecastlewards at breakfast-time, when, the ship being under way and pointed down the river, we had a short spell of leisure. Of course he sat up and looked for his breakfast, confound him! As I handed him his coffee, I said, "A pretty fine dance you led Bill and me last night, Mick!" "Fhwat the divil d'yez mane?" growled he. I told him as frankly as I could; and, as soon as I had done, he said, "Well, I alwuz tought yez wur a pair ov —— fules, an' now oim —— well sure ov ut. Fhwy'nt yez let me go, —— yer dhirty sowls t' hell?" I answered him never a word; but swore solemnly to myself that, come what might, I would never again move one inch to protect a drunken man from the consequences of his own act, and I have devoutly kept that oath.

Our progress down the river was but little faster than the flow of the tide, for there was not sufficient breeze to keep the sails full, and we all noticed that the old man seemed to be in an unusual state of nervous agitation. A tiny pillar of smoke astern seemed to attract most of his attention; so palpably, indeed, did he watch it, that we began to whisper among ourselves that he had been paying somebody with the "fore-topsail sheet" again. And the event proved that we were right in our surmise, for before long a steam-launch overtook us, and a peremptory order was given from on board of her for us to lay the foreyard aback. Our pilot immediately complied, the launch sheered alongside, and a red-uniformed official climbed on board. His first act was to present the skipper with a piece of paper. But that worthy had no need to read it; he knew well enough what it contained. Then a white man, very well dressed, came on board, and began slanging the miserable captain in rare style. He had been at his old games again; eating and drinking—especially drinking—at somebody else's expense during the whole of our stay in port, and then trying to get away without paying his bill. This time, however, matters looked serious for him, for he had very little money, and his bill amounted to one hundred and fifty rupees. There was a tremendous amount of haggling done before the hotel-keeper would accept a compromise; but at last, a number of bolts of new canvas and several coils of rope were transferred to the launch, and with these, I have no doubt, the creditor was very well paid indeed. But what excuse the skipper would hatch up to satisfy his owners about those missing stores we could none of us imagine. Undoubtedly he placed himself completely in the power of every one on board by his mean and dishonest behaviour. As if we had only been waiting for his discomfiture, no sooner had the launch left us than we squared away to a spanking breeze, which took us well clear of the land before nightfall, fairly started on our long homeward passage.

And now we all pursued a definite course of action. It was unanimously agreed that the skipper had fairly put himself out of court, and that to him no respect whatever was due. The officers, on the other hand, who did their part well under these trying circumstances, were treated by every one with that deference which was their right, and consequently the work of the ship went on in seamanlike fashion. We were fortunate, too, in getting out of the Bay of Bengal before the setting in of the south-west monsoon, when the weather is unspeakably vile. Steaming weather, variable winds, and frequent deluges of rain make life at sea in the Bay then a burden almost too grievous to be borne. The ropes swell so much that they can hardly be hauled through the blocks without any weight attached to them, and the sails become like boards for stiffness. But we had a steady northerly wind, nights of perfect beauty, and days of unclouded sunshine; so that but for the harassing want of good food, which attacked us as soon as we were clear of the land, our lot was as pleasant as any sailor can ever expect. Very little work of any kind was done beyond the necessary handling of the sails, for no doubt the officers felt that it would be unwise to attempt too much under the strained conditions of things.

And now in the long night-watches, when over a quiet sea, flooded with moonlight, the sturdy old vessel glided silent as a disembodied spirit, not a flap of a sail or creak of a rope breaking the solemn stillness, I spent many, many hours alone communing with my own soul. The old boy-life was fast slipping away from me, and the ugly sordidness of much that I had endured for the past seven years was already beginning to be mellowed by the softening haze of time. I felt deep, hungry longings for better things—often flushing hotly in the darkness as I remembered how I had wasted my opportunities in Australia, and again thinking wearily how utterly friendless and alone I was in the world. I felt that if I only had some one to work for, some one to whom my well-being was a matter in which they took a lively interest, that I was capable even now—in spite of my ignorance—of doing something in the world; and I built whole cities full of castles in the air upon the most filmy foundations. And then all my hopes and dreams would die in thickest darkness of despair. What gleam of bright prospect *could* there be for me, a mere bit of driftweed upon the awful ocean of humanity, with no destination, except that which I shared with all mankind? So I would lay musing, looking upward into the infinite blue overhead where the never-ceasing glory of the stars kept me most comfortable company. These nights were a grand counterpoise to the petty discomforts and miseries of the day, when the discontent of their lot made the men of my watch so humpy and disagreeable that I could hardly keep out of hot water with them. I had no books but a Bible, for which I am now most grateful, because I read that grand old book—a literature in itself—through and through from end to end

I know not how many times. And although I know I had not the smallest devotional intent, I am sure that the very fact of saturating myself from such a well of English undefiled was of the very greatest service to me. Religion, indeed, was a byword among us. We knew that the owners of the ship were considered a highly religious firm, and that Captain Bunker was believed by them to be a holy man. Illogically, we transferred some of our hatred of his hypocrisy to his employers, who were probably not in the least to blame for our sufferings. Therefore, in the many discussions which took place in the forecastle on things in general, the conversation usually turned upon the general worthlessness and scoundrelism of religious people in general, and our captain and owners in particular. There were no arguments, for we were all of one way of thinking, and there was no one to show us any light upon the subject. As far as I was concerned my early piety had all gone, with the exception of an awful fear of death, in what I felt was my unprepared (!) condition, and an utter inability to accustom my tongue to the continual blasphemy of sailor-talk. In other directions my language was as foul as anybody's, so that I had nothing to brag about if I had thought of doing so. As we drew down towards the African land, the question of food became very serious again. The flour which had been bought in Rangoon was already almost uneatable—full of vermin of various kinds, and of a dirty grey colour. Our cargo was not available, being unhusked rice, or "paddy," and the meat was the worst I had ever seen, with the exception of that in my first ship. A portion of it boiled, and left for a few hours, became white and hard as a piece of marble, with the exuding salt. There was an increasing monotone of grumbling, which nothing but the lovely weather and easy times prevented from breaking into open revolt. At last we made the land somewhere about East London, and it began to be whispered about among us that the old man meant going into Algoa Bay for supplies. What foundation there was for the rumour I don't know, but it had a marked effect upon every one's spirits, so that she was quite a different ship. Port Elizabeth had been the *Harrowby's* first port at the beginning of her long voyage, and probably that had some weight in making the skipper determine to call there again. Some of his old cronies would doubtless welcome him, for he had not then begun to practise leaving without settling his accounts. Whatever the cause, the confirmation of the rumour that we were going to put in re-invigorated us, and we all showed the utmost willingness at every task.

The weather now began to play tricks upon us: baffling winds, fogs, and cold, raw rain replacing the idyllic climate we had so long been enjoying. And, as we gradually crept south, more than one gale gave us a severe drubbing—sometimes blowing us so far off the land that we began to fear he would give up the idea of going in, after all. But when one morning the order came to get the anchor over the bows, and bend on the cables, all doubts and fears were silenced, and a general air of expectancy took their place. The next night the wind veered to the eastward, and blew hard; but under a heavy press of sail we stood in for the land, heading, as we believed, straight for our port. All through the night a keen look-out was kept, but nothing was seen. When the grey, cheerless dawn broke we were still plunging shoreward through the ugly cross-sea, making wretched weather of it, not a dry corner to be found forrard or aft. A dense mist prevented us from seeing many ships' lengths ahead, but that gave none of us forrard any uneasiness, as we believed that with all his faults the old man was a fairly good navigator. Two of us were on the look-out, peering through the grey veil, when suddenly on the starboard bow, not more than a mile away, appeared the tall spectre of a lighthouse, the red and white bands upon it just visible. A chill of horror ran through us all, added to the next moment by the appalling cry of "Breakers right ahead!" The helm was instantly put up and the yards squared, but oh! how lazily she answered her helm. Then the haze lifted, and, as she slowly paid off, we saw all along our starboard beam, and apparently not a cable's length off, the mighty foaming range of breakers that seemed hungry for us, flinging their tops high into the air and bellowing like a thousand savage bulls. Just as if there was some almost irresistible attraction drawing us broadside on to that tumult of death, we crawled along, burying the lee-rail under water with the tremendous press of sail we were carrying, and expecting each moment to hear a crack overhead, and see some of our spars go, sealing our death-warrant. But our end was not yet. Presently the most despondent among us could see that we were gaining ground, and gradually we clawed off that frightful reef out to the friendly sea again. A good offing having been made, we stood to the westward once more, for the lighthouse we had seen was Cape Recife, and our objective was but a short distance to the northward of it. We had just struck the wrong side of it, that was all. Still, with all our efforts, it was as much as we could do to get into Algoa Bay before dark, and anchor well to seaward of all the other vessels, in readiness to leave again.

CHAPTER XXVII.

DEEP-WATER COASTING.

Landing that night was quite out of the question, for all the surf-boats had been secured, and even had we possessed a good boat of our own (which we did not) we could not have landed in this tumultuous bay as ever was. So the anchor-watch was set, and everybody else turned in to sleep the curious, uneasy sleep of the sailor just in port, after a long series of watches at sea four hours on and off. But the earliest surf-boat out in the morning came alongside, and took Captain Bunker ashore. His last words to the mate were to "heave short" at noon, for he would then be off with the stores, and we should weigh immediately. That was all very well for him, but by ten o'clock a howling black south-easter was blowing, and we had a full taste of the delights of Algoa Bay. The gale blew right into the open harbour, and by noon the scene was one of the most savage grandeur. Every vessel there was plunging and straining at her moorings as if she must tear herself to pieces or uproot the steadfast anchors, while great sheets of spray often hid the labouring craft from view. Our position was dangerous in the extreme. Vessels anchored in Algoa Bay for any length of time always have a huge hawser bent to the cables, which, of course, has more elasticity than chain, and to this they ride, even in the worst weather, with comparative comfort. But we had no such device. In the first place we had no hawser fit for it, in the next we had made no preparations for such an emergency. So all that we could do was just to give her all the chain we had got on a single anchor, and stand-by to let go the other one in case of the first one carrying away. For hours we watched that tortured windlass, and listened to the horrible grind of the massive links around the iron-shod barrel thereof, wondering each moment whether the next would be the last or not. Again we were spared, although better-prepared vessels than ours came to grief, piling their poor remains up among the many other relics scattered about that ravenous shore. By nightfall the wind had taken off greatly, although the old sea still kept her leaping and curtseying like a lunatic, and made our sleep a mere pretence.

And we all felt sure that our reverend skipper was snugly ensconced in some red-curtained bar ashore, with a jorum of grog and a churchwarden aglow; and would be rather relieved than otherwise to know that his ship had come to grief, and thus prevented the catastrophe that was surely awaiting him on his return home. Along about noon, however, he hove in sight. When he came alongside the cargo he had brought with him set all our mouths watering. There was a side of fresh beef, two carcases of mutton, and a small cartload of potatoes, cauliflowers, and onions. But of sea-stock there was hardly any. Three packages comprised the whole—one of peas, one of flour, and one of lime juice. Yet with an obtuseness that is even now a mystery to me, no one raised any objection. The things were just hoisted on board, the boat left, and, when the order was given to man the windlass, there was not a dissentient murmur. Of course remarks were bandied about as freely as usual upon the never-failing subject of the old man's delinquencies; but that was because he stood upon the house aft, his knobbly face glowing like a port sidelight, his hands upon his hips, and his whole bearing that of a man whom a skinfull of whisky had put upon the best of terms with himself. Up and down went the windlass-brakes cheerily, while Bill and I hauled back the chain; but presently she gave a dive, and, when she sprang upward again, there was a sudden grind of the cable, and out flew several fathoms of it, tearing the chain-hooks from our hands, and treating us to an extremely narrow escape of following them. Then there was a chorus of language from the men on the forecastle. All sorts of epithets were hurled at our unfortunate heads for our failure to hold on. But while they yet spake, she gave another curtsey, and out went some more. That was sufficient to indicate the kind of a picnic we were in for, and no time was lost in rigging a big fourfold or "luff"-tackle, which was stretched right along the deck from a stout ringbolt near the mainmast, and the forrard end hooked on to the chain. The fall was then taken to the after-capstan, and we two ordinary seamen, aided by the skipper and the two boys, hove at it continually as the chain came slowly in. As long as there was any scope of cable out, things went on all right, but as soon as we were hove short, it looked as if some damage was bound to ensue. Sail was loosed, ready to get way upon her as soon as the anchor was off the ground, she all the time straining and jumping at her cable like some infuriated wild beast. At last she dipped her bows right to the level of an incoming swell, which, as it passed under her forefoot, flung her high in air. There was a rending crash, a shower of sparks, and she was free. "Anchor's gone, sir!" shouted the mate, springing off the forecastle amid a chorus of "—— good job, too," from all hands. As hard as we could pelt we got the sail on her, and in a few minutes were outside the Bay, the loose end of the parted cable hanging at the bows. So closed our expensive visit to Port Elizabeth, and before nightfall we were under all canvas, slipping down towards the Cape with the favouring current and wind at a great rate, our starboard anchor still hanging over the bows. All minor discomforts were forgotten, however, in the glorious feed provided for us by the cook. While we were revelling in the good fresh mutton and vegetables, that worthy came into the forecastle, and received our congratulations with the self-satisfied air of one who feels that he has deserved well of his fellows. Presently he informed us confidentially that he had received no orders as to the disposal of the provisions, and that it was therefore his fixed determination to serve them out to all hands, both forrard and aft, impartially, as long as they lasted. He kept his word right manfully. For a week, during which we hugged the land right round the Cape with the anchor still outboard, we lived as we had never done since we left Sydney. Our gaunt faces filled up their sombre hollows, our shrunken muscles developed, and we grew skittish as young colts. Then, without warning, our luxuries all ceased, and the same grim state of privation set in as before.

As I have so often experienced since, we took a steady southerly wind right off the pitch of the Cape, before which we hurried homewards under every rag of sail we could muster—every hour bringing us nearer home. According to all the established rules on board ship, we should now have begun that general "redding-up" to which every homeward-bounder is subjected as soon as she gets into the south-east trades. Thanks, however, to our skipper's peculiar notions of how to deal with his owners' property, we had no new ratline stuff on board wherewith to "rattle down"—as the process of fitting new rungs to the rope-ladders leading aloft is termed. We could not reeve new running-gear for the same reason, or fit new footropes, or repair the "service" where chafed out aloft. We had hardly any paint, or varnish, or tar, yet the apprentices declared that when she left home she was fully provided with such stores for a three years' voyage—as the owners were large ship-chandlers and never let their own ships go to sea meanly supplied. She had been out barely two years—very little of anything had been used—so that she was quite poverty-stricken aloft, and yet there was nothing left to make her look respectable coming home. We all had easy times, it is true; but that was not altogether a blessing, since sailorizing is generally liked by seamen, who would growl like tigers at the petty half-and-half scavenging often done on board such ships as the *Harrowby* under a pretence of smartening ship. So restless and irritable did the men become that it was easy to see trouble at hand. Only a spark was needed to kindle a big explosion. This was supplied by the unhappy cook, who burnt most scandalously the only meal we could really eat with any heartiness—our pea-soup. Poor wretch!—in answer to the ferocious inquiries of the men for something to stay their gnawing stomachs with, he could only bleat feebly that he "hadn't got nothing; nothing at all to give 'em." They knew very well that this was true; but our latest recruit, Sam, the ex-cook, swore he would have something to eat or he'd know the reason why. So, snatching up the steaming kid of soup, he rushed aft with it, and, in a voice broken with rage and excitement, demanded the skipper of the grinning boy at the cabin door. "Tell him I'm engaged—can't see him now!" shouted the skipper from within. That was enough. In bounced Sam, pale with fury, and, shoving the reeking tub of soup under the skipper's nose as he sat at the table, hissed, "W'at kinder stuff djer think *thet* is fer men t' eat?" Leaning back as far as possible from the foul mess the skipper panted, "Git out o' my cabin, yew impident scoundrel! What jer mean by darin' ter come in 'ere like thet?" Splash! and over went the kid of soup on top of the skipper's head, which rose from out of that smoking yellow flood like a totally new kind of Venus. The liberal anointing ran down the old man's beard and back, even unto the confines of his trouser-legs, while he spluttered, choked, and scooped at his eyes in utter bewilderment. As for Sam, he stood like a statue of wrath, in full enjoyment of his revenge, until the outraged skipper recovered his voice, and screamed for help. Down tumbled the mate through the after-companion, but the sight which greeted his astonished eyes fairly paralyzed him. "Seize him! put him in irons!" yelled the skipper, "He's scalded me! th' infernal vagbon's scalded me!" But Mr. Messenger was disinclined to undertake the job single-handed—knowing, too, how likely it was that any such attempt would almost certainly bring all hands on the scene ripe for a row. Therefore, Sam, after unpacking his heart of a few hearty curses upon skipper and ship, made good his retreat forward to the fo'lk'sle, where his version of the encounter was received with delirious merriment. The delight shown at this summary assault upon the old man actually took the place of dinner, and, although no substitute for the spoiled soup was forthcoming, nothing more was said on the subject. When the cabin-boy came forrard that evening with his nightly budget of stories about the common enemy, he convulsed us all by his graphic details of the skipper's struggles to free himself from the clinging mess congealed about him. But there was not heard one word of pity—no, not even when Harry told us that his bald head was as red as a beetroot. This affair kept all hands in quite a good humour for some days, until one evening, Chips, who rarely left his lonely den, came mysteriously into the fo'lk'sle and said oracularly, "Boys, we ort ter be gittin' pretty cluss ter Sant Elener. I don't blieve th' ole man means ter sight it at all; but if he don't we shall all be starved ter death afore we cross the line. *I* think we ort ter go aft in a body 'n tell him 'at we ain't er-goin' ter do another hand's turn less he goes in 'n gits some grub ter carry us home." All agreed at once, and the time for our ultimatum was fixed for the next day at noon. But I happened to be doing some trivial job on the main-royal yard next morning, and, before coming down, took, as I usually did, a long look all round the horizon. And I saw far aft on the port quarter the massive outlines of the island of St. Helena, fully thirty or forty miles away. This so excited me that I could not wait to descend in the usual leisurely fashion, but, gripping the royal backstay, came sliding to the deck like a monkey. Without losing a minute I rushed forrard and told my news. There was no longer delay. Headed by the carpenter, all hands came aft and demanded an interview with the skipper. As soon as he appeared the option was given him of either going in to St. Helena, or sailing the ship himself. He then informed us what was our exact position, and dwelt upon the length of time it would take to beat back against the strong trade blowing. Old Chips, however, was ready for him. He said at once, "Very well, sir, why not go into Ascension?" "Oh, they won't let us have any stores there: it's a Government dockyard, 'n they only supply men-o'-war." "That be hanged for a yarn," said Chips; "w'y, I've had stores there myself only two year 'n a half ago. Anyhow, cap'n, there it is: you k'n do wot yer like, but we ain't a-goin' ter starve 'n work the ship too." After a minute or two's cogitation, the old man replied wearily, "Oh, very well, I'll go and draw up the happlication, an' you'll all 'ave ter sign it." Artful old curmudgeon! Still, we didn't care as long as we got some grub; so, when he called us aft again and read out the string of fabrications he had concocted, carefully omitting all mention of our call at Algoa Bay, all hands signed it as cheerfully as if it had been their account of wages.

But the look-out that was kept from that day forth, and the careful calculations of course and distance every watch, I have never seen equalled in a ship's fo'lk'sle before or since. And when at last the rugged burnt-up heap of volcanic *débris* appeared above the horizon right ahead, our relief was immense. Our simple preparations for anchoring were soon made, and our one serviceable boat cleared for hoisting out, for, like the majority of that class of vessels, the boats were stowed and lumbered up with all sorts of incongruous rubbish, as if they were never likely to be needed; and the long-boat—upon which, in case of disaster to the ship, all our lives would depend—was so leaky and rotten, that she would not have kept afloat five minutes in a millpond. As we opened up the tiny bay, where the Government buildings are clustered, we saw, fluttering from the flagstaff at the summit of a conical hill, most prosaically like a huge "ballast"-heap, a set of flags silently demanding our business. Our set of signals being incomplete, we could only reply by hoisting our ensign and standing steadily in for the anchorage. But before we came within a mile of it, a trim cutter glided alongside, and a smart officer in naval uniform sprang on board. With just a touch of asperity in his tone, he inquired our business, and, upon being deferentially informed by the skipper, immediately ordered the main-yard to be laid aback while he went below to inspect the contents of our store-room. Apparently his scrutiny was satisfactory, for, returning on deck, he ordered the main-yard to be filled again, and conned the ship up to the anchorage. He then re-entered his boat and sped away shoreward, while we, as soon as ever the ship had swung to her anchor, just clewed up the sails, and then made all haste to get the boat into the water. As soon as this was done, four hands and the skipper got into her and pulled for the shore; the old man's last words being, "I 'spect I shall be back in an hour."

To while away the time, pending their return, I started fishing; but I never want to get among such fish as they were again. Lovely in their hues beyond belief, but with nothing else to recommend them, they tried my patience sorely. I have since learned that they were a sub-variety of *Chætodon*, having teeth almost like a human being, but so keen and powerful that they were able to sever copper-wire. After losing most of my hooks, I at last "snooded" with a few strands of silk not twisted together. By this means I succeeded in getting half a dozen of the gorgeous creatures on deck. But their amazing colours, fearful spikiness, and leathery skin effectually frightened us from eating them, as most of us were painfully aware of the penalty for eating strange fish. The swelled and burning head, lancinating pains, and general debility afterwards, consequent upon fish-poisoning, make sailors very careful to taste none but known kinds of deep-sea fish, and any queer shape or colour among reef-fish is sufficient to bar their use as food.

At the expiration of two hours and a half our boat returned, laden to the gunwale with bags and cases, showing plainly that here, at any rate, the old man had not been permitted to exercise his own judgment as to what his requirements were likely to be. In feverish haste we got the stores on board, the skipper appearing in a high state of nervous apprehension lest the keen-eyed watchers ashore should deem him slack in leaving. Indeed, the report of the boat's crew was to the effect that the skipper had been treated with very scant courtesy—not even being allowed to say how much of this, that, or the other, he would take; and, when he was leaving, being sternly admonished to lose no time in getting under way, or he would certainly find himself in trouble. Such was the haste displayed all through, that, within four hours from the time of the officer's boarding us, we were off again, our head once more pointing homeward.

From that time onward, until our arrival in Falmouth, we never had cause to complain of bad food. Everything supplied us from the Naval Stores was the best of its kind—as, of course, it should be. It filled us all with respect for the way in which men-o'-war's men are fed, even without the many opportunities allowed them for exchanging the service rations for shore provisions. In consequence of this welcome change everything on board went on greased wheels. The old man effaced himself, as usual, never interfering with anybody, and, for a month, we were as quiet a ship as you would find afloat. Slowly we edged our way across the belt of calms to the northward of the Line, inch by inch, our efforts almost entirely confined to working the ship and making sennit. By-and-bye we came into a calm streak, where sea and sky were so much alike that it was hard to tell where one left off and the other began: weather beautiful beyond description, but intensely aggravating to men tired of the ship and the voyage, and exceedingly trying to the temper of all hands. For a week this stagnant state of things prevailed; and then, one morning, we were all interested to find another barque within a couple of miles of us. In that mysterious way in which two vessels will draw near each other in a stark calm, we got closer and closer, until at last our skipper took a notion to visit her. So the boat was got out, and we pulled alongside of her. She was the *Stanley Sleath* of London, from 'Frisco to London, one hundred and sixty days out. She was an iron vessel, and never shall I forget the sight she presented as she rolled her lower strakes out of water. Great limpets, some three inches across, yard-long barnacles, and dank festoons of weeds, clothed her below the water-line from stem to stern, and how she ever made any progress at all was a mystery. She smelt just like a reef at low water; and it looked as if the fish took her for something of that nature, for she was accompanied by a perfect host of them, of all shapes and sizes, so that she rolled as if in some huge aquarium. She certainly presented a splendid field for the study of marine natural history. None of us went on board but the skipper; but some of the watch below leaned over the rail as we swung alongside and told us a pitiful story. Through somebody's negligence the lid of their only water-tank had been left off, with the result that some rats had got in and been drowned. This had tainted all the water so vilely that no one save a sailor burning with thirst could drink it, and nothing would disguise that rotting flavour. The captain had his young wife on board, and she had been made so ill that she was delirious, her one cry being for "a drink of water." And no one seemed to have had sufficient gumption to rig up a small condenser! It hardly seemed credible, had it not been that similar cases were well known to most of us. We had plenty of good water, and our skipper sent us back on board with orders to the mate to fill a two-hundred-gallon cask, bung it up tight, and lower it overboard. We were then to tow it back to the *Stanley Sleath*. As a cask or tank of fresh water floats easily in the sea, this was not a difficult task, nor were we long in executing it. It was the best deal made by our old man for many a long day, for he got in exchange a fat sow, weighing about fifteen stone, two gallons of rum, and a case of sugar. Followed by the fervent thanks of her anxious commander, we rowed away from the *Stanley Sleath*, our approach to our own vessel again being heralded by the frantic squeals of our prize, who lay under the thwarts, her feet securely bound but her voice in splendid working order. That evening a breeze sprang up, and, slow as we were, we soon left our late consort hull down. Thenceforward for nearly a fortnight we saw nothing of our teetotal skipper. The rum had been given us in lime-juice bottles, packed in the original case, so that nobody knew but what a case of lime-juice had come on board. And yet, as we had an abundance of lime-juice, we wondered why the skipper had not chosen something else in payment for the water. The cabin-boy, as usual, got the first inkling of the mystery. Somehow he was a prime favourite with the old man, who, I suppose, turned to Harry in his loneliness and made something of a pet of him, getting, in return, all his little weaknesses reported verbatim to the fellows forrard every evening. Going to call the captain to supper on the same evening we visited the other ship, the boy noticed an overpowering smell of rum, and, upon tapping at the state-room door, he heard a thick voice murmur, "'Mnor vry well shevenin'; shlay down bit." That was enough for Harry. Peeping in, he saw the skipper lolling on his chest, a big black bottle wedged securely down by his side, and a glass in his hand. From that spell of drink he did not emerge until the last of the bottles was emptied.

CHAPTER XXVIII.

WHICH BRINGS US TO PORT AT LAST.

Fortunately for us the condition of the skipper didn't count for anything, as we made our usual progress homeward indifferent to his pranks. The north-east trades hung far to the eastward, allowing us to make an excellent course northward; but, as we were very light, our gain from their favouring cant was slight. Just upon the northern verge of the tropic we lost them altogether, and lay lolling about in windless, stagnating ease for another week, exasperating all hands at this unlooked-for extension of our already lengthy passage. But even this enforced wait had its advantages. We spoke another barque—homeward bound from Brisbane—and again our adventurous commander would go ship-visiting. In fact, he allowed it to become known that, but for our determined attitude about calling at Ascension, he had intended to *beg* his way home—a peculiarly irritating practice much fancied by men of his stamp, who thus levy a sort of blackmail upon well-found ships. They pitch a pitiful yarn about bad weather and abnormal length of passage, with such embroidery as their imagination suggests, and generally succeed in getting quite a lot of things "on the cheap."

What sort of a yarn our mendacious skipper spun to this last vessel we had no means of knowing, as the boat's crew were not allowed to board her; but he succeeded in getting a couple of cases of preserved beef and some small stores. Much to his disgust, however, there was no liquor of any kind to be had. The only thing that the other ship wanted was a few coals for the galley fire; so, while our skipper stayed on board, the boat was sent back for them. Now it was Sunday afternoon, and when Bill and I were ordered to go down into the fore-peak and fill three sacks with coal, we felt much aggrieved. So, grumblingly, we dived into the black pit forrard, and began to fill the sacks. But, suddenly, a bright idea struck us. The only pretence at ship-smartening we were likely to make was "holystoning" the decks, and, to this end, several lumps of sandstone had been saved ever since we left Sydney. Now, I have before noted in what abhorrence holystoning is held by all who have to perform it, and here was a heaven-sent opportunity to make the job impossible. So we carefully interspersed the lumps of stone among the coal in the sacks, taking every precaution to leave not a fragment behind. Away it went to the other ship; it was hoisted on board, our boat returned, a breeze sprang up and we parted company, seeing each other no more. Two or three days after the order was given to get up the holystones for cleaning ship. Words could not express the wrath of the mate when it was reported to him that none were to be found. Every bit of coal in the fore-peak was dug over under his immediate supervision, he getting in a most parlous mess the while, but in vain. I never saw a man get so angry over a trifle. He swore that they had been thrown overboard by somebody, being certain that there had been an ample store. Singularly enough, he never dreamed of the real way of their going, and the actual perpetrators of the certainly immoral act were never even suspected. We had to do the best we could with ashes and brooms, but they made a poor substitute for the ponderous scouring of the stones. I regret to say that neither of us felt the slightest remorse for our deed, and, when we heard the delighted comments of the men were more puffed up, I am afraid, than we should have been by the consciousness of having acted ever so virtuously.

And now, as we were approaching the area of heavy weather, and our stun'sails were worn almost to muslin, we began to send down the stun'sail gear. The first thing that happened: the ex-cook, in sending down one of the top-gallant stun'sail-booms (a spar like a smooth scaffold-pole), made his "rolling-hitch" the wrong way. Perfectly satisfied that all was in order he sung out to us on deck to "hoist away." The moment we did so, and the boom swung out of the irons in which it had been lying, it assumed a vertical position and slid through the hitch like lightning, just missing the rail, and plunging end-on into the sea alongside. We were going about four knots at the time, and when it sprang upwards again it struck us under the counter with a bang that almost stove in the outer skin of the ship. And, instead of being at all chagrined at such a gross piece of bungling, the offender simply exhausted his copious vocabulary of abuse when the "old man" ventured to rebuke him. Oh, our discipline was grand! Hardly an hour afterwards, in taking in the fore-topmast stun'sail, the halliards carried away. The tack and sheet, rotten as cobwebs almost, followed suit, so we lost that too. The rest of the rags were saved for the old-rope merchant.

Still the fine weather persisted, and at last we crawled up under the lee of Terceira in the Azores, where we got becalmed within a couple of miles of Angra. That was on a Sunday afternoon—and if Captain Bunker didn't actually propose to go ashore and have a donkey-ride! He was perfectly sober, too. But this was too much for even our quiet mate's patience. He turned upon his commander at last. I was at the wheel, and heard him tell the skipper that if he carried out his proposal, and a breeze sprang up while he was ashore, he, the mate, would certainly make sail and leave him there. He was sick to death of the state of things, and he would have no more of it. This outburst frightened the old fellow terribly, and, with a feeble remark that he was "only joking," he disappeared below. The calm continued all through the night, some invisible influence setting the vessel so closely inshore that I began to fear we were going to lose her after all. Yet nothing whatever was done to prepare for such a contingency. The anchor was securely lashed in its sea-position on the forecastle, and, to all outward appearance, no notice was taken at all by the officers of our undoubtedly perilous proximity to the shore. Just before dawn, however, a little south-easterly breeze sprang up, to which we trimmed the yards, and soon glided away from all danger. Gradually the wind freshened and veered until at west-southwest it was blowing a strong steady breeze, and, with all square-sail set, the old *Harrowby* was bowling along at a good eight knots for the Channel. Faithful as usual, this well-beloved wind to the homeward-bounder never relaxed its strenuous push until the changing hue of the water, plain for all men to see, told us that we were once more on soundings. Oh, blessed sight, that never palls upon the deep-water sailor, the fading away of that deep fathomless blue which for so many, many weary watches has greeted the eye! Somehow or other, too, the green of the Channel of Old England has a different tint to any other sea-green. It is not a pretty colour, will not for a moment bear comparison with the blazing emerald of some tropical shore, but it looks welcome—it says home; and even the most homeless and hardened of shellbacks feels a deep complacency when it greets his usually unobservant eye. Contrary to my usual experience of the brave westerlies, this breeze of ours did not culminate in a gale; but as we neared the Scilly Isles it gradually took off, and the weather brightened, until one heavenly morning at daybreak we saw under a pale-blue sky, bathed in brilliant sunshine, those straggling outposts of dear old England like bits of fairyland—uncut jewels scattered over a silver sea. And here, to our intense delight, came a dandy: one of those staunch Falmouth boats with the funny little jigger perked up aft like the tail of a saucy cockerell. She made straight for us in a business-like fashion, rounded to alongside, and her commander climbed nimbly on board, while the other two men in her hove on board a splendid mess of fish. The enterprising boatman was the runner for a Falmouth tailor, who had come out thus far seeking customers. He was, of course, elated to find that we were bound into Falmouth, and that his diligence was likely to be rewarded. For few indeed are the homeward-bounders calling at Falmouth for orders, whose crews do not liberally patronize the Falmouth outfitters, getting good value for their money, and being able to choose their goods with clear heads, apart from the bestial distractions of sailor-town. And the captains of such vessels are never loth, *of course*, to allow their men to run up a bill with the tailor, and to forward the amount from the port of discharge, wherever it may be.

Favoured still by fortune we sped on toward the lovely harbour, and at four p.m. rounded the well-known old tower of Pendennis and entered the anchorage. Sail-furling and clearing up decks was got over as if by magic, and, by the time we were at leisure here was the prompt tailor-man with his leather-covered trunks full of boots and clothes, ready to reap the first-fruits of our labours.

Here we lay in serenest peace for a couple of days, the weather being more like late spring than November, so fine and balmy as to make us wonder whether we had not mistaken the time of year. Then orders came for us to proceed to London. We towed out of the harbour on a lovely afternoon, with the Channel looking like a glimpse of fairyland under the delicate blue of the cloudless sky. Under all sail we gently jogged along the coast, standing more to seaward as night came on, and noting, with comfortable compassion, the outward-bounders just beginning the long journey of which we were so near the end. I had the ten to midnight wheel, and, in consequence of the mild weather, was lightly clad in the usual tropical rig of shirt, trousers, and cap. Before half my "trick" was over there was a sudden change. The wind came out from the north-east, and piped up with a spiteful sting in it that pierced me through. My thin blood seemed to suck up the cold until I was benumbed and almost unable to move the wheel. But there was no chance to wrap up. All hands were as busy as bees shortening her down, for the wind rose faster than they could get the sail in, and at midnight it was blowing a gale, with squalls of sleet and driving banks of fog. One o'clock came before I was relieved, and then I had hardly enough vitality left to get forrard, my two garments being stiff upon my lead-coloured flesh. Somehow I got into the forecastle and changed my rig; then, rolling my one blanket round me, I crawled into my bunk. No sleep and no warmth could I get, nor did I feel more than half alive at eight bells. But I dragged myself on deck and suffered, till at five a.m. the cook shouted "Coffee!" as usual, and then the pannikin of boiling brown water did comfort my frozen vitals.

We were now just fore-reaching under two lower topsails, reefed foresail, and fore-topmast staysail—not even holding our own. Every little while the big flyers outward-bound would spring out of the fog-laden gloom, and glide past us under a pyramid of canvas like vast spirits of the storm. Or a panting, labouring tramp-steamer would plough her painful way up channel right in the wind's eye, digging her blunt snout into the angry brine, and lifting it aboard in a roaring flood that hid her for a minute entirely under a mantle of white foam. We had even some pity to spare for the poor devils in such evil case as that on those perishing iron decks, or being flung like a tennis-ball between bunker, bulkhead, and furnace-door in the Gehenna below, while the freezing floods came streaming down upon them through the grated "fidley" above. Fifteen days did that merciless north-easter thrash and wither us, until we felt that nothing mattered—we had reached such a dumb depth of misery. Still, we did make *some* progress, for on the sixteenth day we sighted Dungeness, the first clearly distinguishable land we had seen since leaving Falmouth. The arrival of the pilot cheered us up, as it always does. He seems to bring with him the assurance of safety, to be a hand stretched out from home able and anxious to draw you thither. And, as so often happens, too, the weather fined down almost immediately. Under his wise guidance we stole stealthily along the coast until, off Dover, a big tug-boat sallied out and made for us. None of us took any notice of him; we knew too well that we were not the sort of game he was after. A ship about five times our size was nearer his weight. Still, he came alongside and hailed us with, "'R ye takin' steam up, cap'n?" ironically, as we all felt. "Ah!" replied the old man, "yew're too big a swell f'r me." "Nev' mind 'bout that," promptly came back. "I'm a-goin' up, anyhow, 'n *you* won't make any diff'rance ter me. Come, wot'll yer gimme?" "Ten poun'," sniggered the old man. "Oh! Go on ahead!"—the interjection explosive, and the order snarled down the speaking-tube to his engineer. Before, however, the paddles had made one revolution he stopped them, and shouted back, "Looky 'ere, I ain't foolin'; I'll take ye up fur thutty poun'. Thet won't 'urt yer." "Can't do it," drawled the skipper. "Owners wouldn't pay it. 'Owever, ef yew mean bizness, I'm 'lowed to go ter twenty, n' not 'nother pice." Then the fun began. They argued and chaffed and swore until, finally, the tug got so close that her skipper stepped off the paddle-box on board of us, and, as he did so, we saw a bottle sticking out of his pea-jacket pocket. They both went below, and there was silence. When they reappeared our old man's face was glowing like burnished copper, and Oliver muttered, "I'm off'rin' big money thet bottle's empty, and the steam-boat man ain't a-hed much neither." But they hadn't settled the bargain. No; the next game was to toss one another—best two out of three—whether the tug should take us up for twenty pounds or twenty-five. Steam won; and the old man immediately signed to the mate to get the hawser up. Great Cæsar! how we did snake the hatches off before the order came, forgetting that we hadn't got a hawser fit for the job. That made no odds; the tug-boat man wasn't going to let a little thing like that stand in his way, especially as his coal supply was so low that every minute was precious. So he lent us his tow-line, and in less than five minutes the *Robert Bruce* was pelting away homeward as if nothing was behind her at all, and we were all admiring the first bit of speed the old *Harrowby* had put on since we had belonged to her. Night fell as we passed the Nore, but there was no delay. Onward we went, until, passing everything on the way, we anchored at Gravesend. Off went the tug with the last shovelful of coal in the furnaces, just in time. Then down came the fog, a regular November shroud, so thick that the mainmast was invisible from the poop. Somehow the "mud"-pilot found us, his boat taking away our deep-water man, in whom—such is the fickleness of mankind—we had now lost all interest. All the next day that thick darkness persisted; but about seven in the evening it lifted a little. The tug was alongside of us directly, so anxious was her skipper to get his cheap job over. We were mighty smart getting under way, being off up the river in less than half an hour from the first glimmer of clear. All went well till we entered Long Reach, when down came the curtain again thicker than ever. The tug turned round and headed down the river, just keeping the paddles moving as we dropped up with the young flood. It was a terribly anxious time. The river was full of craft, and every minute or two there was a tempest of howls as we bumped into some bewildered barge, or came close aboard of a huge ocean steamer. At last the pilot could stand it no longer, and, telling the carpenter to get his maul ready for knocking out the ring-stopper of the anchor, he shouted, "Stand clear the chain!" At that instant, as if by some pre-arranged signal, the fog rolled up, and in five minutes the sky was as clear as heart could wish. The tug swung round again, and, under a full head of steam, we rushed onwards, entering the Millwall Docks just at the stroke of midnight. The process of mooring in our berth was all a confused jumble of rattling chains, hoarse orders, and breathless, unreasoning activity, succeeded by that sweetest of all sounds to a homeward-bound sailor's ears, "That'll do, men."

Unearthly as the hour was, most of the fellows would go ashore, delivering themselves over to the ever-watchful boarding-house runners like a flock of sheep. But three of us—Oliver, Bill, and myself—rolled once more into our bunks, and, utterly wearied, soon fell fast asleep. When we awoke in the morning the new sensation of being our own masters, able to disregard the time, and lay in till noon if we chose, was delightful. But just because we could do as we liked we rose at daylight, had a leisurely wash, and, dressed in our best, climbed over the rail and sauntered along the gloomy, grimy quays towards the dock-gates. We had just two shillings and sixpence between us, sufficient to get a good meal only, but we knew where we could get more. And that is one of the first pitfalls that beset the path of the homeward-bounder. Many skippers have sufficient thoughtfulness to advance their crews a little money upon arriving in dock, and thereby save them from the dangerous necessity of borrowing from those harpies who abound and batten upon the sailor. Nothing of the kind could be expected from our skipper, of course, so we just had to take our chance. As I was at home and familiar with every corner, I became the guide, and led the way to a snug eating-house in the West India Dock Road, where I knew we could get a civilized breakfast. But Oliver hove-to at the first pub, and swore that what *he* needed was rum. I tried hard to dissuade him, assuring him that he wouldn't be able to eat any breakfast if he got drinking rum first. I might as well have tried to tie an elephant with a rope-yarn. He had his rum: a full quartern of the famous brand that used to be sold about sailor-town, whereof the bouquet was enough to make a horse sick. Then I hurried him off to the coffee-shop, where, with a lordly air, I ordered three haddocks, three hot rolls and butter, and three pints of coffee. Oh, the ecstatic delight of that meal!—that is, to us two youngsters. Oliver just pecked a little daintily, and then, turning to a burly carman sitting by his side who had just finished a mighty meal, he said coaxingly, "I say, shipmate, I ain't touched this grub hardly, can you help me out?" With a commiserating look the carman reached for the food, and concealed it like an expert conjurer.

CHAPTER XXIX.

CONCLUSION.

As I had no home, and cared little where I lodged, I was easily persuaded by Oliver to accompany him to the little beershop in the Highway, where he had put up before. I had my misgivings, for I knew that unsavoury neighbourhood well (it is somewhat different now); but it was necessary to find harbourage somewhere until the ship paid off, which was, as usual, likely to be three days longer. Bill departed unto his own place among the purlieus of Bermondsey, and we two trudged off to Oliver's hotel. After the glowing accounts of it I had received from Oliver, I was dumfounded to find it a regular den; the bar filled with loafers furtive of look and mangy of clothing, while the big taproom at the back was just a barn of a place open to all. The fat landlord seemed a decent fellow, but his fatter wife was a terror. She had vigour enough to command a regiment, and woe to the loafer who crossed her. Still I felt that it was now too late to draw back, and besides, I had little to lose; so I had my scanty kit brought up from the ship, and saw it shoved into a corner of the common room, where I reckoned it would be ransacked thoroughly as soon as darkness set in. The landlord lent me a sovereign readily enough, and, as soon as I received it, I bade good-day to Oliver, who was fast drinking himself idiotic, and, taking the train from Shadwell to Fenchurch Street, was whirled out of that detestable locality. All the rest of the day I roamed about the well-known streets, where the very buildings seemed to greet me with the air of old friends. I thoroughly enjoyed myself, and, with only a couple of shillings gone out of my sovereign, returned to my lodging shortly after ten. I found things worse than ever. The landlady was half inclined to abuse me because I hadn't been in to my meals, and every loafer in the place was sponging for a drink. Outside I knew was not healthy at this time of night for me, so I quietly asked permission to go to bed. Grumbling at such an unreasonable request, the landlady snarled, "You'll 'ave ter wite till yer bed's ready. 'Ow wos hi ter know as you'd wanter sleep all day?" I said nothing, seeing it was the wisest course; but perching myself in a corner under the big flaring kerosene-lamp, tried to read a book I had brought in with me. I had not been thus quietly engaged for more than five minutes, before an awfully repulsive-looking fellow came up to me, and, pushing down my book, said, "Got enny munny in yer close, young 'un?" I looked at him in silence for a minute, thinking hard how best to answer him. But growing impatient he growled, "Look 'ere, giv us the price of a drink, er I'll bash yer jor in." That settled it. Indignation overcame prudence, and I shouted at the pitch of my voice, "Mr. Bailey, do you allow this to go on in your house?" There was an uproar immediately, in the midst of which Mrs. Bailey cleared the room of the swarming loafers—my assailant escaping among them. Then, turning indignantly to me, she abused me roundly for making a disturbance, treating my statement as a "pack er lies." I got to bed safely, though, and really the bed was better than I had expected, although the room was just a bare box of a place with damp-begrimed walls, that might have been a coal-cellar.

Rising early in the morning I went down and had an interview with Bailey, in which I asked him to have my dunnage put away, as I was going on a visit and should not return that night. He was pleasant enough about it, and offered me a rum-and-milk at his expense, being greatly amazed at my refusal. Then I escaped and took up my abode at a lodging-house in Newman Street, Oxford Street. The time dragged rather heavily until pay-day, as I dared not do anything costing money; but at last I found myself once more at Green's Home, with my account of wages in my hand, telling me that after all claims were satisfied, I was entitled to sixteen pounds. It was a curious paying-off. Every man, as he got his money, gave the skipper a piece of his mind; and but that a stout grating protected the old man from his crew, I am afraid there would have been assault and battery. I came last, with the exception of Bill, and when I held out my account of wages to the clerk, the old rascal said, "I've a good mind to stop yer wages as I promised yer." What I said doesn't matter, but I never felt the poverty of language more. And when I saw that he had given me on my certificate of discharge an excellent character for conduct (which I didn't deserve) and a bad character for ability (which was utterly unjust), I felt that his malignity would pursue me long after I had seen the last of him. For such a discharge is a millstone round a young man's neck. Captains don't take much notice of a character for conduct—whether it be good or bad—but they do want their men to be of some use at their work, and will return such a discharge as mine was contemptuously. Bill took his pay without looking at it, and, without a word passing between him and the old man, joined me outside. We strolled away together along the East India Dock Road, he bungling over his money all the time, till suddenly he cried, "Why, I've got a five-pound note too much! Here, come on, let's get out o' this, case he sends after us." And thus was I avenged. The morality of the thing never troubled me in the least, I only felt glad from my heart that mine enemy would have to refund all that money.

And now I have reached the limit of my book. At the outset I only proposed to deal with the vicissitudes of my life on board ship as a boy. And with the close of this voyage I felt that I was a boy no longer. I was getting more confident in my ability to hold my own in the struggle for life, and, although I saw nothing before me but a dreary round of the drudgery of the merchant seaman's career before the mast, the prospect did not trouble me. I had no plans, no ambitions, nobody to work for, no one to encourage me to thrive for better things. I lived only for the day's need, my only trouble the possible difficulty of getting a ship. Of the future, and what it had in store for me, I thought nothing, cared nothing. And yet I was not unhappy. If at times there was a dull sense of want—want of something besides food and clothing—I did not nurse it until it became a pain. Only I kept away from sailor-town. The museums, picture galleries, and theatres kept me fully amused, and, when I was tired, a good book was an unfailing resource against dulness. In fact I lived in a little world of my own, quite content with my own company and that of the creations of my fancy or the characters of the books I devoured.

This unsatisfactory life, thank God! was soon to be entirely changed; but that, of course, was hidden from me, nor does it come within the scope of this book. As I write these last few words I think curiously whether, if ever they see the light, those who read them will think contemptuously, "This fellow seems to imagine that the commonplace details in the life of a nobody are worth recording." Well, I have had my doubts about that all along, and my only excuse must be that I have been assured, upon very high authority, that a book like mine, telling just the naked, unadorned truth about an ordinary boy's ordinary life at sea, could not fail to be of interest as a human document. And, in spite of the manifest shortcomings, the obvious inability to discriminate wisely always between things that are worth the telling and things that are not, I do confidently assert that I have here set forth the truth impartially, as far as I have been able to do so. I feel strongly tempted to draw a few conclusions from my experience; but I must resist the temptation, and allow the readers to do that for themselves. In the hope that some good may be done, some little pleasure given, by this simple recital of a boy's experiences at sea, I now bid my readers, respectfully,

SO LONG!

CPSIA information can be obtained
at www.ICGtesting.com
Printed in the USA
FFOW02n0945070618
47091696-49517FF